Janet Tanner

Janet Tanner is a prolific and well-loved author and has twice been shortlisted for RNA awards. Many of her novels are multi-generational sagas, and some – in particular the Hillsbridge Quartet – are based on her own working class background in a Somerset mining community. More recently, she has been writing historical and well-received Gothic novels for Severn House – a reviewer for *Booklist*, a trade publication in the United States, calls her "a master of the Gothic genre".

Besides publication in the UK and US, Janet's books have also been translated into dozens of languages and published all over the world. Before turning to novels she was a prolific writer of short stories and serials, with hundreds of stories appearing in various magazines and publications worldwide.

Janet Tanner lives in Radstock, Somerset.

Janet Tanner

FOLLY'S CHILD

BELL

First published in 1991 by Century

This edition published 2014 by Bello
an imprint of Pan Macmillan, a division of Macmillan Publishers Limited
Pan Macmillan, 20 New Wharf Road, London N1 9RR
Basingstoke and Oxford
Associated companies throughout the world

www.panmacmillan.co.uk/bello

ISBN 978-1-4472-6644-0 EPUB
ISBN 978-1-4472-7046-1 HB
ISBN 978-1-4472-6643-3 PB

Copyright © Janet Tanner, 1991

Acknowledgements

My grateful thanks are due to Tom Winward, who advised me about insurance claims and investigations, and Julie Dammers of Dammers Models, Bristol, who was such a fount of knowledge on the fashion industry in the sixties since she was herself a Mattli couture model at that time. If I have made any slips in authenticity, neither of them are to blame!

Thanks also to my daughters – Terri, whose thesis for her BA (Hons) degree in Fashion Design gave me the original idea, and Suzanne, who helped me devise the plot. To Rosemary Cheetham, who can always inspire me and make me determined to work harder. And of course, most of all, to my husband, Terry, for playing second fiddle to a word processor with such cheerfulness for a whole year!

From the *Daily Mail*, July 1967:
YACHT TRAGEDY OFF ITALY – FINANCIER AND
FORMER MODEL DIE IN MYSTERY EXPLOSION

A prominent American financier and entrepreneur and a former top fashion model are missing feared dead after a luxury yacht was lost yesterday off the west coast of Italy. Greg Martin, well known for his backing of enterprising ventures, and Paula Varna, the beautiful former model and wife of top fashion designer Hugo Varna, were holidaying at Mr Martin's villa near Positano in the Gulf of Salerno. When they failed to return from a day's sailing worried staff at the villa alerted the authorities and their disappearance was connected with an explosion which had been reported by fishermen. A search of the area revealed debris including a lifebelt belonging to the yacht – the *Lorelei* – but there was no sign of any survivors. Mr Martin, 40, is a single man but Paula, 29, and said to be the inspiration for her husband Hugo Varna's success, is the mother of a four-year-old daughter, Harriet.

From the *Daily Mail*, January 1990:
RETURNED FROM THE DEAD!
FINANCIER FAKED HIS OWN DEATH, WOMAN ALLEGES

A prominent US financier who was thought to have died in an explosion on his luxury yacht off the coast of Italy has been fooling the world for more than twenty years, according to a woman who claims she has been living with him as his common law wife ever since his so-called 'death'. The loss of the boat – and the lives of its two occupants, Greg Martin and the beautiful former model Paula Varna, wife of Martin's business partner, world-famous fashion designer Hugo Varna, made headlines around the world at the time but though debris from the boat was washed up along the Italian coast their bodies were never found.

Now Maria Vincenti, daughter of a wealthy Italian fabric manufacturer, has told police in Sydney, Australia, that the man sharing her luxury home at Darling Point, and known by friends and business acquaintances as 'Michael Trafford' is in fact Martin. 'The explosion was a way of escaping the threatened collapse of his business empire in the States,' she told police. 'Everything had gone wrong and he wanted to be free to start a new life.'

In 1967 Martin left behind him a web of intrigue – debts and crooked dealing which would certainly have brought him before the courts had he not 'died'. Now police in two continents are searching for him in order to substantiate the claims of his one-time lover and bring him to justice, albeit twenty years late.

PART ONE

The Present

CHAPTER ONE

Tom O'Neill came through the revolving doors on a blast of icy air and stepped out on the other side into a blanket of almost oppressive warmth. Outside London might be shivering in the biting cold of a January morning, here in the foyer of the British and Cosmopolitan Insurance building centrally heated air oozed steadily from a series of concealed vents to waft summer warmth into every corner.

Tom unbuttoned his overcoat, fished in the pocket of the dark suit which he scathingly referred to as his 'city uniform' for his identity card and flashed it at the uniformed security man. He did not like wearing suits and he liked a collar and tie even less. He was far more at home in jeans and a sweater or the favourite scuffed old flying jacket he had inherited from his father, who had been a Spitfire pilot in the war and he wore them whenever he could. Occasionally his job as a private insurance investigator allowed him this privilege but there were occasions which called for him to dress more formally. Visiting the Head Office of one of the companies that used his services in response to an urgent summons was one of them.

Without waiting for his nod and wave Tom strode past the security man to the block of six lifts beyond him. One had just arrived at ground floor level; Tom followed two girl clerks into it and pressed the button for the fifteenth floor. He felt rather than saw the two girls glance at him appraisingly but took no notice. At just over six foot, with thick curling brown hair and eyes that owed their startling blueness to his Irish ancestry, Tom was used to being the object of female appreciation whilst being slightly puzzled by it. He had never thought the reflection which looked back at him each morning from the shaving mirror was particularly handsome. His nose was too large and a little crooked since taking a devastating straight left in the boxing ring when he was fifteen years old, his chin too irregular. But women certainly seemed to like it and that of course had its compensations. Tom had not reached the ripe old age of twenty-nine without discovering quite a few of them.

The lift halted at the twelfth floor for the girls to get out, then whispered on towards the fifteenth. When the doors opened again Tom emerged into a corridor, thickly carpeted in grey. Like the twelfth floor, glimpsed through the lift doors when the girls had got out, the walls were covered with a pale lemon wash, unlike the twelfth they were hung with pictures, not Old Masters but not Boots the chemists either – prints of hunting scenes and ships and a beautiful soft sunset over a bay that might have been St Ives – pictures deemed suitable for the Executive floor of a great international company.

Tom passed them by without a glance, heading for the door at the very end of the corridor. He knocked briskly and without waiting for a bidding went in.

The secretary seated behind the desk in the outer office looked up accusingly, then her features softened and a faint pink flush coloured her cheeks. 'Tom!'

'Morning, Lucy. I understand the Great White Chief wants to see me.'

'That's right, he does. I'll buzz him.' She depressed the button. 'Mr O'Neill is here, Mr Swansborough.' She glanced up at Tom, a little regretfully. 'He says to go straight in, Tom.'

Tom nodded. 'Thanks.'

Watching him disappear into the inner sanctum, Lucy sighed. Why was it the gorgeous ones passed through so fleetingly while others, like that paunchy, moist-palmed Vic Tatum from Marine Claims always managed to delay in her office, ogling, leering and making suggestive remarks that she could probably take to a Sexual Harrassment Tribunal if she had a mind to!

'Come in, Tom, come in!' Roger Swansborough half rose from his executive chair holding out his hand in greeting. He was a big bluff man with a receding hairline and aggressively triple chin which somehow managed to make him look powerful but not fat – like a back row rugby player, Tom thought. He had already removed his jacket in the cloying warmth of the office but his white shirt was immaculate and as he reached across the desk Tom caught the gleam of gold cufflinks against the stiff white cuffs.

'I had a message that you wanted to see me urgently,' Tom said.

'That's right. Take your coat off, Tom, do. This place gets hotter every day. I'd open a window but . . .' He gesticulated towards the expanse of glass that surrounded the office on two sides. Beyond it the sky was lowering grey, shrouding the roofs of the buildings and filtering cold dull half-light onto the streets and the distant river.

From up here on the fifteenth floor the view was a panoramic one – unfortunately this morning it was also infinitely depressing.

Tom did as he was bid, hanging his coat on the heavy carved stand behind the door.

'What's going on then, Roger? Who's trying to swindle you this time?' he asked smiling wryly – his job had made him cynical.

The older man grimaced.

'Not *trying* to swindle us, Tom. This time it's a *fait accompli* – a bloody great sting to make your eyes water. Take a look at that.' A copy of the morning paper was lying on his tooled leather desk top; he pushed it across to Tom, stabbing at the story with a manicured index finger. 'You remember the Martin business? No, you wouldn't, of course. It happened twenty years ago, when you were still in short trousers. A luxury cabin cruiser blew up off the coast of Italy. There were two people aboard – Greg Martin, the owner, a financier with a finger in more pies than you'd care to name, and a woman, Paula Varna, wife of Hugo Varna the fashion designer. The boat was blown to glory, nothing was ever found of it except for a few bits of debris, and to all intents and purposes both occupants were blown to glory with it.'

'British and Cosmpolitan were the insurers, I presume.'

'Too right. Not only the boat but the lives of both Martin and Paula Varna – not peanut policies either of them as you can imagine. She had been a top model – her legs alone were insured for a five figure sum and he had enough hanging on him to bankrupt a smaller company. No, 1970 was not a good year for British and Cosmopolitan what with one thing and the other. But that's our business, taking risks, and it works well enough – as long as everyone plays by the rules.'

'And this time someone didn't?' Tom asked. He was trying to read the newspaper upside down without much success.

Roger Swansborough's hand balled into a fist and he brought it slamming down onto the desk top so that loose paperclips jumped in the big crystal ashtray.

'Too right they didn't. We paid out on the life of Greg Martin – and it seems the bastard wasn't dead at all but living a life of luxury in Australia.'

Tom whistled softly.

'For twenty years? Are you sure it's him?'

'It's him all right. He's been living in Sydney under an assumed name – Michael Trafford – with an Italian heiress named Maria Vincenti. He was part Italian himself, of course – I understand his name was Martino originally until he decided to drop the 'o' and Americanise it to Martin. But he was an American citizen, born in the States as far as I can make out.'

'So why was he insured with the British and Cosmopolitan?' Tom asked.

Swansborough shrugged. 'You tell me. I dare say the slippery bastard had a good reason. He left a fair old mess behind him, by the way, when he disappeared. He'd been sailing close to the wind for years and everything was just about to blow up in his face.'

Tom reached for the newspaper, turning it towards him. He scanned the print, seeing that it echoed more or less exactly the story Swansborough had just told him, then turned his attention to the photograph alongside – three people, obviously dressed for leisure. A thin-faced man, balding, in a shirt open at the neck to reveal gold chains, a woman, obviously beautiful in spite of the quality of the photograph, with her hair tied under a scarf Princess Grace style, and another man with a look of the Mediterranean about him whose face was partially obscured by sunglasses.

'That's Greg Martin?' Tom asked, pointing to the third figure.

'Yes. With Hugo Varna and Paula – on another trip which presumably did not end in disaster,' Swansborough said drily. 'They were quite a part of the international scene in those days from what I can make out. Since he's made his fortune Varna has become something of a recluse, of course. In fact there are those who claim he never got over his wife's death, in spite of the fact that he married again – Paula's younger sister, Sally, as a matter of fact.'

'Hmm.' Tom studied the photograph. 'Well, quite obviously Mrs Varna was a real stunner. And she was alone on the boat with Martin when the accident happened. Something going on there, was there?'

'Varna insisted not at the time. Said his wife had been in need of a holiday and he had been unable to get away. Martin was a close friend of the family as well as his business partner and Varna had been happy for her to go with him. But you can draw your own conclusions. She was English, by the way, which could explain why they chose to insure with us.'

'A doubtful honour, the way things turned out,' Tom said drily. 'So – British and Cosmopolitan was taken for a small fortune – and taken for fools too by the seem of it. How the hell did it happen? The accident was investigated at the time, you say?'

'Of course it was – and damned thoroughly too as you can see.' Swansborough tapped the file in front of him and Tom saw the thick wad of papers which protruded from it. 'But there was nothing we could get our teeth into. The boat had gone, not a doubt of it. Fishermen reported hearing the explosion and bits of debris were washed up for months afterwards. There appeared to be no survivors and there were plenty of witnesses to swear both Greg Martin and Paula Varna were on board when the yacht sailed – Martin was well known at the marina where he kept her and Paula was a highly visible character.' He smiled thinly. 'The papers treated it all as a great tragedy as you'll see when you look at them. *Financier and former model die in mystery explosion* was the headline at the time – and the emphasis of course was on the 'former model'. Beautiful woman, internationally known, wife of talented fashion designer – it was heaven-sent copy, especially for the more sensational press. And she was a mother too – she and Varna had a child – a little girl who was about four at the time. You can imagine the story it made.'

Tom nodded. 'I certainly can. So it wouldn't have just been insurance investigators ferreting about – it would have been the world's press as well. But in spite of the way it looked Martin had faked his own death – and done it damned successfully. And what about the woman – Paula Varna? Did British and Cosmopolitan also fork out a small fortune to her family to which they were not entitled? Her family were the beneficiaries, I suppose. Did she die – or is she, too, still living somewhere under an assumed name?'

Swansborough closed the file with a snap and pushed it across the desk.

'That, Tom is what I want you to find out.'

In a corner of the Salon Imperial of the Hotel Intercontinental, Paris, Harriet Varna braced her back against a statuesque pillar and looked steadily into the viewfinder of her camera, concentrating on her subjects so fiercely that she was almost oblivious to the electric atmosphere that surrounded her, bouncing off the Viennese décor and the sumptuous rococo ceiling along with the heat and the light as the models of the House of Saint Laurent moved gracefully along the hundred yards of catwalk to display the new season's couture collection.

Only the constant clicking of the camera shutters of the army of photographers and the intermittent bursts of rapturous applause broke the expectant hush that January afternoon, for Yves Saint Laurent is one of the few important couturiers to show in the old manner, with no mood-setting background music. In the late sixties he had declared 'Couture is dead!' and concentrated instead on off-the-peg designer wear, but twenty years later his revival had been both stunning and nostalgic and the long-term wealthy and the nouveau riche had come flocking, craving the glamour and excitement, and seeking the prestige that comes from owning a couture gown, specially, individually theirs after hours of masochistic fittings.

Now they sat eagerly on the rows of brittle gilt chairs with red velvet seats, their exquisitely made-up faces carefully devoid of expression as they made brief notes on their programmes, pretending not to notice that sometimes the clicking cameras were directed not at the catwalk models, all of whom had already done a photo-call session for the photographers the previous day, but at them – the society women of America and the international circuit, the bored charity conscious wives of big businessmen, the famed actresses of stage and screen, even the occasional European princess. The actresses, of course, were frequently loaned gowns by the house free of charge for the publicity that would be gained when they were pictured wearing them, and there were those among the society women who considered themselves above coming to the couture, ordering instead from the videos that nowadays replaced the weeks of shows of the old days – and staying away all the more determinedly as the great Paris houses vied with one another to tempt them to lend their presence to the occasion. But there were plenty of beautiful and recognisable faces to be seen amongst the anonymous, but none-the-less powerful, fashion editors, still enough buying power in this room alone to rock empires, even if no house made a profit from the couture but rather used it for a loss-leading advertisement and a mark of prestige.

It was at none of these that Harriet's camera was trained, however. Instead her zoom lens was pointed at the rear of the salon where the apprentices and publicity girls stood in small, highly-strung huddles, watching the gowns they had worked on and publicised pass by on the catwalk and leading the explosions of rapturous applause.

There was one girl in particular who interested Harriet, a small girl with hair cut gamin short, whose face was so expressive that it seemed to reflect every one of the emotions that they were all feeling, these midinettes who had basted hemlines and stitched hooks and eyes into place, positioned trimmings and sewed them into place with such tiny stitches that they were all but invisible to the naked eye. Harriet hardly dared blink as she watched her through the viewfinder, terrified she might miss the moment she was waiting for. Then, as a daring but romantic gown of navy blue silk crepe made its appearance, the moment came. The girl's face came alive, eyes sparkling, hands raised to her parted lips in an expression halfway between exultation and tears of joy, before she began to clap furiously. Swiftly Harriet depressed the button again and again. Perfect – perfect! *That* was what she had been waiting for, that unguarded, unforced, totally natural reaction of a lowly apprentice who sees her work unfold like a fairytale. In a world where so much was staged artificially it was like a breath of fresh air and Harriet experienced her very own glow of excitement and triumph.

For a minute or two longer she panned the camera, too much the professional to allow her pleasure to make her risk missing another good shot. But instinctively she knew she had what she wanted – the frames that would lend just the breadth and depth she needed to complete her picture story of the couture shows, and she let her camera fall back on its strap around her neck, rubbing her aching eyes and running her fingers up under the thick fringe of dark blonde hair that barely skimmed them.

Still the mannequins were appearing, their elongated clothes-horse frames moving with a grace which belied their tight-drawn nerves, still the bursts of applause rang out to drown the persistent clicking of the cameras, but Harriet leaned back against her pillar almost oblivious to them.

The clothes, beautiful as they were, interested her not at all. She had grown up amongst beautiful clothes, been dressed from childhood in designer fashion, been made to stand still for fittings for her graduation dress and her first ball gown, and hated every moment of it. Clothes were all very well, they were her father's life and she knew that all the privileges she enjoyed were hers because of clothes and the stupendous success they had brought him, but she couldn't care about them. Except when they made wonderful pictures. Pictures were what mattered. And in her camera was a reel of beauties.

Harriet glanced around, wondering if she could slip out unnoticed. It was heresy, of course, but the show was likely to last another hour at least – Saint Laurent was famous for the length of his shows – and afterwards there was bound to be the most fearful crush. Harriet hesitated, then her natural impatience won the day and she slipped quietly towards the exit. All eyes were on the catwalk and no one appeared to notice her, apart from a tall, grey-haired woman in the uniform of an atelier who moved towards her accusingly.

Instantly Harriet pressed her hand across her mouth in a theatrical gesture.

'I'm not feeling well', she whispered in somewhat imperfect French, and the woman moved hastily out of her way. Photographers – *cochons!* she was thinking in disgust. The girl had probably had too much wine to drink with her lunch.

As she emerged into the Rue Castiglione the cold hit Harriet like a slap in the face and she lifted her camera, easing the zipper of her sky-blue ski jacket right up under her chin and turning the collar up around her ears. Some of her hair caught inside it and she flicked it out, a careless fall of dark blonde that framed her even-featured face. 'You should go to a good stylist once in a while and have that mane tamed!' Sally, her father's wife, had advised her on more than one occasion, but Harriet had as little time for stylists as she had for clothes – and besides, she rather liked her hair just as it was. This way she could simply wash it each morning and let it dry naturally – start trying for *styles* and valuable minutes had to be wasted keeping them the way they were meant to be.

I must find a telephone, Harriet thought, as she hurried, head bent against the biting wind, along the Paris street. I can't wait to tell Nick I've got his job in the bag. Then I'll decide whether to post him the last reels of film in a Jiffy bag or fly back to London with them myself.

The thought gave her another fillip of excitement – her first job for *Focus Now*, the new picture magazine Nick was editing – and it was a corker, she knew it in her bones. Already she could visualise the lay-out – 'The Other Side of Fashion' she'd entitled it in her mind's eye when she'd discussed it with Nick. And as he had said, no-one was in a better position to do a photo story like that than she was.

'All the fashion magazines and the women's pages of the newspapers do straight fashion stories,' he'd said, tugging thoughtfully at the little gingery beard that sprouted from his angular chin. 'I want something different. And let's face it, *Focus Now* is going to be different.'

She'd nodded. She'd known Nick for years, meeting him when she'd come to London to visit her cousin Mark Bristow, Sally's son. She had just started out on her career as a free-lance photographer, with nothing but a little talent, a lot of determination and the best camera money could buy to help her make it. He had been a sub-editor in those days, working for a huge magazine corporation, and they had struck up an instant rapport, and when he was made first assistant editor and then editor, always moving from magazine to magazine, he had pushed work her way whenever he could. They had even had an on-off affair and Harriet suspected he was in love with her. But she couldn't take him seriously. She couldn't take any man seriously – or at least not one she'd yet met.

'I think you use me, Harriet,' he had said once, mock-serious.

'Well of course I do!' she had teased. 'Isn't that what friends are for?'

'Friends!' he'd echoed, his soft Scottish burr making it sound almost mournful, and Harriet had experienced a moment's sharp guilt.

But whatever his shortcomings as a prospective lover, Nick was good at his job – very good – and his talent and hard work had been rewarded when Paul Leeman, the publishing tycoon, had decided to launch the new magazine, *Focus Now*. Nick had landed the job of editor and when he had told Harriet about it his enthusiasm had been infectious.

'You remember *Picture Post*, Harriet? No, probably you don't.

You're too young. You weren't even born when it folded – and besides it was an English magazine.'

'But I know about it of course,' she'd protested. 'My mother was English, remember, and it was a classic, wasn't it? What photographer hasn't heard of *Picture Post* – though I suppose the American in me would argue that all those magazines were imitators of *Life*.'

'Right. Well, Paul believes the time is right to launch a new mag on the same lines. Stories told in pictures – less copy than the Sunday supplements, more slanted to letting the photographs tell the story. And perhaps with a social angle, too. But whatever, it's got to be *different*, a totally fresh way of looking at things. That's where you come in.'

'It sounds exciting. But more like photo journalism than just taking pictures. You think I could handle it?' In spite of her apparent self-confidence, in spite of her twenty-five years, in spite of having had the best that money could buy since she was a little girl, there was an ingenuousness about Harriet which sprung from a yearning need to prove herself – to her father, to her contemporaries, to the whole wide world. Sometimes being born with every apparent advantage in life spawns the deepest need to create something just by oneself, to say: 'This wasn't handed to me on a plate, but I did it just the same!'

'I know you can do it', Nick had said. 'You're a bloody good photographer and the work you've been doing for the last five years proves it. All you need is the opportunity to really express yourself – and *Focus Now* can give you that. I'm sure you'll come up with all kinds of ideas of your own, but for starters why don't you do something you know really well – the world of fashion.'

'Fashion!' Her tone had been scathing. 'Rich women with closets full of clothes they'll never get around to wearing. Fashion – one silly brainless bitch trying to outdo the others because she's bored out of her tiny mind and isn't interested in anything other than the way she looks.'

'Don't knock it,' Nick said seriously. 'You know as well as I do it's a damned great industry – and there are plenty of facets to it that never see the light of day. Find some of them, Harriet, mix them in with the glamour – and see what you get. More than enough for just one feature, I'll be bound. Enough for a whole series, probably. But start with Paris. After all, to most people Paris is still the centre, the sun around which all the other satellites revolve.'

'Well I sure as hell would hate to do Seventh Avenue,' she said with feeling.

'So – don't – or at least, not at first. What about the sweatshops of Korea, or the rich Kuwaiti women who buy merely for their own pleasure and hide their couture gowns under their abayas because they are not allowed to display themselves ... it's a far cry from the fashion world as it is usually depicted, it could make fascinating copy. Get out there and find it for me!'

And so she had. She'd done the photo session of couture gowns as well, of course, clicking away dutifully with those other photographers who were being dictated to by their fashion editors. But it was the unexpected shots that would provide the spice to the story – like the ones she had just made of the little midinette enthusing as she saw the dress she'd sweated blood for, if not created, come down the catwalk to the roar of applause.

Harriet pushed back the cuff of her ski jacket and glanced at her watch – the clear faced leather-strapped Patek Philippe man's watch that she always wore in preference to the elegant Cartier her father had given her, unless of course circumstances forced her into an evening gown. Perhaps, she decided, she would go back to her hotel and phone Nick from there. Then she'd call the airport, enquire about flights and take the pictures to London herself. She'd like to be on hand the moment they came out of the dark room. And it would be nice to see Nick again too. She raised her hand to hail a cab but the Paris traffic was zooming by at its usual break-neck pace. Then she spotted a public telephone and decided she could not wait another minute to call Nick and tell him the job was completed. She dived towards it, anxious some other would-be caller should not beat her to it and begin on one of those endless conversations the French seemed to have, searching through her pockets for change and trying to recall the International dialing code and the number of the line which connected direct with Nick's office, bypassing the busy switchboard, all at the same time.

'You have never got out of the childish habit of trying to do several things at once,' Sally had said to her once; Sally, so cool, so contained, so efficient she sometimes made Harriet feel as if she were still a child, though of course she would never admit it.

At the second attempt she made the connection and heard the telephone begin to ring at the other end. Then Nick's voice, that soft unmistakable Scottish burr.

'Hello? Nick Holmes.'

'Nick – it's me, Harriet. I've finished the job and I've got the most stupendous pictures. I'm just on my way back to the hotel and with luck I'll be able to get a flight tonight. I can be with you first thing in the morning – maybe even this evening, if you like.'

There was a slight awkward pause and in the tiny fraction of time that it lasted Harriet experienced a stab of pique. Nick was usually so keen to see her she had to fend him off. Now, just when she was bursting to talk to him about the job, he was going to be less than forthcoming.

'Unless you've already got something lined up, of course,' she said hastily.

'No. And I'm very glad you've finished the job.' What *was* that odd note in Nick's voice? It didn't sound in the least like him.

'Me too. You were right – knowing the background to the industry was a tremendous help. Anyway . . .'

'Harriet – have you seen a newspaper today?' he interrupted her.

She laughed shortly. 'You must be joking! I've been up to my eyes in mannequins and *haute couture*.'

'Well – I think you should.'

She frowned, feeling his discomfort with her pores as well as hearing it in his voice.

'Why? Someone else hasn't done my story have they? Or, oh no! Paul hasn't decided to fold *Focus Now* before it's even off the ground, has he?'

'No – no – nothing like that.'

'Then what? Nick – my money is running out . . .' She fumbled in her pocket for more change but before she could get in it into the coin slot she heard the click. 'Nick?' she said urgently but it was too late. The line was dead. She swore, banged down the receiver and stood staring at it. What the hell had he meant? Should she try and get him back again or buy a newspaper first and try to find out what in the world he had been talking about? A cloud of Gaulois smoke wafted past her ear and she became aware of a man standing behind her, stamping his feet as he waited with barely concealed impatience for the telephone. His presence made up her mind for her and she turned, brushing past him and heading towards a newspaper vendor who sat shivering behind his stall at the nearby entrance to a Metro station.

All the newspapers on the front of the stall were French and Harriet cursed herself for not being a better linguist. She had had every opportunity to be, for heaven's sake, but she'd never worked hard enough at it and now she did not feel like struggling with a foreign language to search for an item when she did not even know what she was looking for. But tucked away at the back of the stall were some English and American newspapers. Yesterday's? No, praise be, today's – the English ones, anyway. She pointed to one and pulled out her remaining change to pay for it. Then she retreated into the entrance to the Metro out of the biting wind and opened it.

She saw the story at once. The photograph seemed to leap off the page to hit her. Daddy. Mom. And . . . that man . . . Unexpectedly Harriet began to tremble.

'RETURNED FROM THE DEAD! FINANCIER FAKED HIS OWN DEATH, WOMAN ALLEGES.'

She inched back against the wall, part of her wanting to find some private place, yet knowing she would not – could not – move from this spot until she had read what the paper had to say.

As she finished her breathing was ragged, her eyes darting from the newsprint to stare unseeingly at the people pushing past her into the Metro and back to the newsprint again. In the street the traffic still roared past, a ceaseless thunder interspersed with the honking of horns, but she was no longer aware of it. Even the precious spools of film in the camera slung around her neck and tucked into the pockets of her jacket were forgotten. They might have belonged, all of them, to another world, another life.

Greg Martin, her father's former partner, was alive.

She hardly remembered him, of course. He was a shadowy figure from the past whose name was scarcely ever mentioned except on those rare occasions when they spoke of the accident, that terrible accident that had claimed the lives of him and her mother when Harriet was only four years old. As for the financial crisis they had gone through, of which she suspected Greg was the root cause, that was never spoken of at all. The whole episode had been so horrendous, so traumatic, that her father had chosen to wipe the board clean of it – on a superficial level, at least.

Harriet pressed a hand to her mouth and closed her eyes. The street seemed to be full of perfume now, wafting around her in the biting wind – the perfume that was the most evocative memory she had of her mother, a haunting perfume, light and teasing and sweet, a perfume that smelled a little like a summer garden at dusk, a perfume, the memory of which had possessed the power to bring tears to her eyes long, long after she had forgotten how to conjure up the image of her mother's face.

Mom – oh, Mom – why did you go away? She had cried it into her pillow at night, sobbing with the vain child's hope that tears would somehow magically make it all come right, that in the morning her mother would be there.

But of course she never was. Her mother had died in an explosion on a luxury yacht, they had explained to her. Gradually she had come to terms with it, accepted it as a fact of life, though the grief had been longer in going and the sadness was still sometimes there, an echo in the night.

But now . . .

If Greg Martin was alive then was it possible . . . was there the chance that it was in any way possible that her mother was alive too?

The enormity of it rocked her. For long minutes she stood there, her thoughts not so much running circles as buffeting chaotically. It made no sense – none – yet here in black and white was proof that nothing was the way it had seemed. For the first time in years Harriet was overwhelmed by a wave of homesickness, and not now for New York, but for the haven of her London flat, the bolt-hole she had made her very own. She folded the newspaper roughly, thrust it into her bag and walked zombie-like into the Metro. Get home as quickly as possible. Suddenly it was all that mattered. Get home. Then perhaps she could think things through and decide what to do.

Sally Varna stepped out of her bath, reluctant to leave the froth of delicately scented bubbles, reached for one of the enormous pink towels the maid had laid out ready for her and wrapped herself in it. Then she padded across to a low stool and sat down, surveying herself in the mirror that lined her bathroom walls on two sides.

The face that looked back at her was smooth, slightly flushed from the warmth of her bath, certainly not a face that looked its forty-six years. Even when made up with the finest cosmetics money could buy it would never be beautiful, but still . . . not bad for an ugly duckling, Sally thought, smiling wryly. She lifted one hand and pushed aside the fair, highlighted hair which skimmed her ears. Yes, the tiny tucks had almost gone now, just as the surgeon had promised they would. No-one need ever know she had had the facelift if she chose not to tell them. That was why it was so sensible to have it done early, before the little lines and pouches became obvious. And Sally had always prided herself on being sensible, if nothing else.

Sensible Sally. Sally 'the sensible one'. That was how she had been known as a child when people had contrasted her with her sister Paula. 'Sally is very clever. She has such a good head on her shoulders,' they had said, when what they really meant was that whilst Paula was a beauty, she was really very plain but they had to find something good to say about her. They had meant it kindly, she knew, but it had hurt all the same. She hadn't wanted to be sensible or clever. She had wanted to be beautiful like Paula, would have traded everything to be just a little like the sister whose stunning good looks had the power to attract and mesmerise wherever she went. But where Paula's hair had shone and bounced as if it had caught some of the morning's sunlight her own was straight and mouse coloured, where Paula's eyes were the clearest, sharpest green hers were muddied to a very ordinary shade of hazel. Her features were similar yet somehow blunted, her body stockier – not fat yet somehow altogether larger so that beside Paula she always felt clumsy in spite of being a full four inches shorter and almost two years the younger.

'Mummy, why don't I look like Paula?' she had asked, staring wretchedly at her five-year-old reflection in the mirror, but her mother, herself slightly bemused by the young beauty she had produced, had been unable to give her any satisfactory answer.

As the girls had grown older things had not improved. No matter how hard she tried to make the most of herself Sally had always been aware that she could not hope to rival Paula and the knowledge had damaged her self-confidence so that she always lived with the feeling that people on meeting her for the first time would exclaim behind her back: 'Paula's sister? That plain little thing? Goodness me, she was in the back row when looks were handed out wasn't she!' The fact that very few other girls she knew could hold a candle to Paula did not help much either. They didn't have to live with this goddess, they didn't have to compete with the legend.

In spite of this, Sally had adored Paula. When other girls, jealous of her looks and the doors they opened for her, jealous especially of the way the boys flocked after her, made spiteful remarks, Sally had always been her fiercest champion. No one had wanted to believe that Paula's beauty went right through her more than Sally did for she was a shining golden idol as well as a sister and it had been a shock to Sally when she had at last been forced to concede, in private at least, that the other girls might have been right in the accusations they made.

Sally stood up, letting the towel drop and shrugging on a silk wrap. It clung slightly to her still-damp skin and again she surveyed her image in the mirror, this time full-length. Years of dieting and exercise had banished that slight stodginess for ever; now her body looked lithe and firm, yet still blessed with more curves than Paula's had ever been, as much a denial of her years as her face. In some ways those days when she had lived in Paula's shadow seemed a very long time ago, in others they might have been just yesterday. She had never been able to equal her sister's matchless beauty, she knew, but at least she presented the world with a fair imitation of it. And she had everything she had ever dreamed of – more. This house on Central Park South, a ranch in Colorado, a home in Montego Bay, a private jet at her disposal, the wherewithal to buy anything which took her fancy. Not bad for a girl who had grown up on a council estate.

Most important of all, she was married to the man who had been Paula's husband. It was the final proof that perhaps, after all, she had not been as inferior to her sister as she had imagined.

Only one shadow lay over Sally's life, a secret shadow that none of the luxuries she enjoyed could quite banish. For a moment it hovered over her thoughts then, with an ease born of long practice, she pushed it away and went into her dressing room. Tonight she and Hugo were dining with an important senator who generally included show business personalities among his guests and she had not yet decided what to wear. She crossed to one of the racks which lined the watered silk walls, her feet sinking into the deep cream carpet, and took out a black gown, holding it against her. The neck was high and round, the sleeves decorously straight to the wrists. But at the back the bodice was slit from collar to midriff and the skirt was daringly short. Worn with her Van Cleef diamond earbobs and bracelet it would look quite stunning. Yes, she thought she would wear the black – or perhaps the strawberry crushed velvet . . .

The sound of someone entering her bedroom, which lay beyond the dressing room, made Sally turn, still holding the dress against her and frowning with annoyance. She had instructed the maids not to disturb her for she valued her privacy and having staff constantly on hand was one of the things she had found most difficult to become accustomed to. Very nice to be able to step out of used underwear and know it would be laundered and returned to its drawer pressed and scented, even better never to have to worry about clearing a table or washing up, but nevertheless there was something vaguely disconcerting about maids who went silently, sneakily about their duties under her very nose.

'Who is it?' she called a little sharply.

The door to the dressing room opened and to her surprise she saw that it was Hugo. Her eyebrows, which she darkened artificially so that they no longer merged into her skin, lifted slightly. She had not expected him home for at least another hour. At this time of day he was usually still at his office in the 550 building on Seventh Avenue.

'Hugo!' she exclaimed. 'What are you doing home so early?'

He came into the dressing room and closed the door, a middle-aged man of medium height wearing a grey suit with a white rollneck shirt. Then as he turned towards her the overhead lights that she had switched on to look through her dresses shone directly onto his face and she noticed how pale and drawn he looked, lines that were usually unnoticeable etched between nose and mouth, eyes almost feverishly bright.

'Are you all right?' she asked. 'You're not ill?'

He did not answer, just stood there looking at her as if trying to make up his mind how to begin.

'Hugo!' She took an anxious step towards him.

'Greg Martin is alive,' he said.

His words stopped her in her tracks. 'What did you say?'

'Greg Martin is alive. He's been living in Australia. He didn't die on the *Lorelei*. The whole damned thing must have been a fake.'

'Oh my God,' Sally said.

'I know. I couldn't believe it either. But I've had the story checked out, Sally. There is no doubt it's true. I had to come home and tell you immediately. Because you realise what it means, don't you? If Greg is alive then the chances are Paula is alive too.'

'Oh my God,' she said again.

The room seemed to have gone dark, as if someone had turned

off the lights, and she wondered if she might be going to faint. She stood frozen, still clutching the black dress against herself, looking at her husband and seeing only her world crumbling around her.

She had always known this moment would come one day. Now it had arrived and still Sally knew she was no more prepared for it than she had ever been.

It had begun to snow in London. The first great white flakes had melted on the pavements, now it was falling thicker and faster, building up on the window ledges and in the cricks and crannies, turning to slush on the roads as the traffic churned through it.

In her small workroom on the top floor of a crumbling old warehouse in Whitechapel Theresa Arnold shivered and turned on another bar of her portable gas fire. She couldn't really afford it and when she needed a new cylinder it had to be humped up three flights of stairs, always a nuisance for which she had to enlist the help of one of her boyfriends, but when she got cold Theresa's fingers turned numb, white, bloodless lumps that no longer seemed to belong to her hands. Then she could not work properly and it was imperative she worked or her new collection would never be ready on time.

Theresa rubbed her hands together to bring some life back into them and bent over the sheets of paper laid out on her work table, trying to forget the cold and concentrate on her designs. They had to be good – not just good but sensational – or she would let everyone down, all those who believed in her – her small workforce of pattern cutters and outworkers, the friends from art school who dropped in to lend their help and support, and most of all her mother, who had put her house up as collateral for the bank loan that had set her up and enabled her to get started.

Theresa sighed, the cold depressing her and quenching her usual defiant optimism. How easy it had all seemed then – how exciting! When she had graduated from the School of Fashion she had sold her entire degree collection to Lady Jane, a small but exclusive West End boutique, who had greeted her designs with such enthusiasm that she had believed the world was her oyster and everything was about to *happen* for her. Riding on a high she had decided to set herself up as an independent designer. But it was all so much more difficult than she had ever imagined it would be. Perhaps, she thought it was because Mark had been there at the planning stage – Mark Bristow, the dynamic young advertising executive she had met and fallen in love with when she had been chasing jobs in the heart of Somerset; Mark who, in spite of being English, had lived long enough in the States to absorb – and give off – some of the typically American blend of enthusiasm and energy. He had encouraged and praised her, bullied her a little when she needed bullying, and given her the love and support that had made her feel, even in the darkest moments of self-doubt, that she could rise above all the problems and emerge triumphant. It was Mark who had persuaded her to approach the bank for a loan, Mark who had suggested her old friend Linda George, who had graduated in business studies at the same time that Theresa had finished her fashion degree, should join forces with her to organise the commercial side, Mark who had given her enough confidence in herself for her to allow her mother to put up her house as security – something Theresa had fought against even whilst realising there was no other way to secure the loan she needed. And above all it was Mark who had made her feel loved and special. 'I am very proud of you, lady', he had said and she had glowed with happiness and a secret bubbling excitement that came from believing she could conquer the world with her talent.

But now Mark was no longer around. He had gone out of her life suddenly and without explanation and try as she might Theresa simply could not get over losing him. Why – why – why? she had asked herself over and over again, why did it end that way? We were so close – weren't we? We were in love – weren't we? How could I have imagined something like that? But the answers never made sense and the fact remained, whatever she had chosen to believe Mark had simply walked out on her and not bothered to come back. She had begun to accept it now, but there was still a yearning deep inside her, his absence a constant nagging ache in her heart, and her business enterprise seemed to have been affected too, for it was as though some of her confidence had drained away, running down her cheeks with her tears.

With Mark anything had seemed possible. Without him some of the magic had gone from her life and the dullness encroached into her work, no matter how she tried to compartmentalise it. Now the problems were paramount. A number of shops and boutiques had shown an interest in her clothes but she still had to produce them, innovative yet saleable, not too expensive for the market but of a good quality. In many ways it was a vicious circle – everything cost so much more if one couldn't produce in bulk, but to produce in bulk one needed capital – and plenty of outlets. And always she was haunted by the knowledge that if she failed her mother would lose her home.

What she needed desperately, of course, was a backer – someone to put up enough money to make her financially secure while she created. But as yet no genie had materialised, no matter how hard she metaphorically rubbed the magic lamp. Linda was working on that one too. Let's hope she comes up with something pretty soon; Theresa thought. If she doesn't I don't know how much longer I can carry on.

The sound of footsteps on the rickety staircase leading to her workroom made Theresa look up from her drawings, a small ray of hope that refused to be extinguished flickering to life. Somehow she could never hear disembodied footsteps on the stairs without wondering fleetingly if it might be Mark returning as unexpectedly as he had left. Then, a moment later the hope died as tall young man dressed in an aged reefer coat and brown leather cap appeared in the doorway.

'Weasel! Hi!' she said, smiling a greeting which she hoped concealed her disappointment. 'What are you doing here?'

It was not a question requiring an answer – Weasel was a good friend from art school days and often dropped in unannounced.

'Shit, it's cold in here, Terri,' he said now, stamping is feet in their Doc Martens. His breath puffed out like white smoke.

'You don't have to tell me that!' she snorted. 'Put the kettle on if you want a coffee.'

'Oh, I want a coffee, all right, and so do you – but not here. Come on, I'm taking you to that little café down the road – what's it called now?'

'Mario's – I think. It's always changing its name. But I can't stop to go out for coffee. I've got far too much to do. We can't all be gentlemen of leisure like you, living off the social.'

'Less cheek if you don't mind! One day someone will appreciate my sculptures, you'll see. In the meantime I intend to stay healthy enough to enjoy success when it comes and you'd be wise to do the same.'

'But I have to get these done.'

'You never will if you catch pneumonia. Come on, get your coat – or are you already wearing it? You're coming with me and I'm not taking no for an answer.'

'All right, stop bullying.' Theresa reached for her thick knitted shawl and knotted it around her shoulders – as Weasel had observed, she was already wearing her jacket in an effort to keep warm. She turned off the gas fire – must save the Calor gas! – and the lights and followed him out onto the landing, locking the door behind her.

'Things no better, I assume,' Weasel said as they tramped down th stairs, deftly avoiding those treads which had rotted.

'Fraid not.'

'Mind this patch, it's slippery,' Weasel warned as he traversed a landing where snow had drifted in through a broken skylight.

'I know, I know. I just wish they hadn't boarded up the windows. It makes the staircase so dark.'

Weasel reached the bottom and pushed open the door to street level.

'What you need, Miss Top Designer 1991, is a decent place to work from.'

She grimaced. 'What I need is a miracle.'

In the gutter a copy of the morning's newspaper lay discarded, snow and slush turning it to pulp and partially obscuring the headline FINANCIER RETURNS FROM THE DEAD.

As he passed, Weasel gave the newspaper a kick with the toe of his Doc Martens. Theresa did not even see it.

CHAPTER TWO

As the taxi swept along the Kensington street, its headlights tunnelling into the murky darkness, Harriet leaned forward and spoke through the half-open glass partition.

'Just here, please.'

The taxi squealed to a stop. Harriet, who had been watching the meter, pulled a note out of her bag and passed it to the driver.

'Thanks. Keep the change.' She swung herself out onto the snow-wet pavement, hauling her bags after her. Home! Thank God!

She almost ran up the path. Hers was the ground floor hat of a tall old house which had seen better days and the communal front door was reached by means of three stone steps. Harriet had climbed them and had her key in the lock when she heard footsteps on the path behind her and a male voice called: 'Excuse me!'

She swung round, surprised and a little wary. 'Yes?'

'Miss Varna?' There was a hint of authority but no menace in the gravelly voice and his overcoat, collar turned up against the cold, looked perfectly respectable, but for some reason Harriet's sense of unease only increased.

'Who wants her?' she asked shortly.

'I'm Tom O'Neill, acting for British and Cosmopolitan Assurance. I called on you earlier but there was no reply and I could see the place was in darkness. I was just leaving when your taxi arrived.'

'Thank you but I'm not in need of any assurance.' Harriet pushed the door ajar and removed the keys from the lock. 'If you'll excuse me . . .'

'I'm not selling insurance. I want to talk to you about quite a different matter. It concerns Paula Varna. Your mother, I believe.'

Harriet stiffened, totally taken by surprise and annoyed with herself for not realising the moment he mentioned insurance the reason why he was here. But it simply hadn't occurred to her. Of course when one thought about it rationally it was obvious there was bound to be an investigation of some kind, but throughout the long flight she had been too concerned with the purely personal implications of the news item to give a thought to those who might have a financial interest in the story.

'Paula Varna was my mother, yes,' she said, oddly defensive. 'But I'd really rather not talk to you or anyone tonight. I have only just flown in from Paris and I am very tired.'

'It won't take long,' he persisted without so much as a hint of apology, 'Just a few questions and I'll leave you in peace.'

'Mr O'Neill . . .'

'It might be easier if we talked inside.' Again, that suggestion of authority. Harriet bristled.

'I'm not in the habit of letting strangers into my flat – especially at this hour. How do I know you are who you say you are?'

'My card.' He passed it to her and she examined it briefly. Somehow she had no real doubts as to whether Mr Tom O'Neill was genuine. She almost wished he was not.

'You'd better come in then.'

She led the way into the communal hall which she personally had taken upon herself to brighten up with a vase of dried flowers and a couple of good, but ancient, rugs which she had picked up for a song at an auction sale. In the full light she was surprised to see he was much younger than his bulky, overcoat-clad figure had led her to believe – and a great deal better looking. Not handsome exactly. That was not a word one would apply to Tom O'Neill. But certainly hunky, with strong, irregular features, a full, jutting lower lip and very blue eyes. She turned her back on him, unlocking the inner door, and as the warmth from the storage heaters wafted out to greet them she thanked God that she had had the foresight to leave them on – she didn't think she had been properly warm since reading the newspaper this afternoon – no, not even on the plane. She was longing for a drink – some of her emergency ration of scotch – but she did not see how she could have one herself without also offering one to her visitor, something she had no intention of doing.

She switched on the fights, dumped her bag on the table and turned to him abruptly.

'Well, what can I do for you?'

'As I said, I'd like to talk to you about your mother.' He was regarding her closely, his very-blue eyes disconcertingly direct. 'As a representative of the company who insured both her life and that of Mr Martin, not to mention the boat, I am anxious to discover the truth of what happened.'

'I'm afraid there is nothing I can tell you. I was four years old when my mother died.'

Something unspoken hung in the air between them. She felt it with her pores, saw it in the slight lift of his eyebrow and the way one corner of his mouth tucked. Then he asked suddenly:

'When did you last see your mother, Miss Varna?'

'I told you – when I was four years old. It was the night before she left for her trip. She came to my room to say goodnight to me . . .' She broke off as another memory stirred . . . that same evening, but later, raised voices coming from her mother's room, her child's feet pattering along the landing, peeping through a crack in the door . . . Her eyes darkened as she relived it and his sharp investigator's eye noticed it.

'And?' he prompted her. 'After that?'

'I tell you I didn't see her again after that night.'

'But something happened.'

'Nothing happened. For God's sake . . .'

'What did she say to you, then, when she looked in to say goodnight? Did she seem her usual self?'

'I don't know. I don't remember. Mom was always . . . Mom. And I can't see that what she said to me is any of your business.'

'I'm afraid a quarter of a million pounds sterling paid out on your mother's life makes it my business.' He crossed to a small occasional table, picking up a silver-framed studio portrait. 'When was this taken?'

Suddenly Harriet had had enough.

'Put that down!' she snapped.

'It is your mother, isn't it?'

'Yes it is. It was taken before I was born, as a matter of fact, when she was still modelling – she was a top model, you know. But you have no right to come in here meddling with my things. Even a policeman wouldn't dare poke about without a search warrant – and you're not a policeman. You are a private investigator. I don't have to talk to you.'

He looked up from the photograph, totally unruffled.

'I usually find that the people who lose their tempers when I start asking questions are the ones with something to hide,' he said easily.

'What the hell do you mean by that?'

'I'm sure you can work it out for yourself, Miss Varna.'

'No, I can't. Spell it out for me, please. You're accusing me of complicity in fraud, is that it?'

'A four-year-old child? Heaven forbid! However, it would seem that Greg Martin, your mother's companion when the yacht was lost, has been fooling us these past twenty years. He has turned up in Australia, hasn't he?'

'I'm sure you know a great deal more about it than I do. I only know what I read in the papers.'

His eyebrow lifted again, an expression of polite disbelief.

'Really? Then this must all be very distressing to you.'

She ignored the somewhat patronising platitude.

'As far as I can make out no one has yet said conclusively that this man *is* Greg Martin', she argued.

'True. That is something that has to be established. However, assuming it is, then we must look very carefully at what happened to your mother. After all, she too might have survived the explosion.'

His words jarred Harriet and she swallowed at the ball of nerves that suddenly seemed to be constricting her throat. In a way he was only echoing her own thoughts but to hear them spoken aloud and by this unsympathetic stranger was oddly disturbing.

'And if she isn't dead then where the hell is she?' she demanded.

'That is what I am being paid to find out. I had hoped you would be able to help me but since you say you can't I shall have to pursue other avenues. It may take me a little longer but . . .' he smiled, and his confidence made her dislike him more than ever, 'I promise you I shall get there in the end.'

'Then in that case I suggest you make a start right away,' Harriet said. She crossed to the door and threw it open. 'Goodnight, Mr O'Neill.'

'Goodnight Miss Varna. Thank you for your time.'

She did not reply, simply stood holding the door until he had gone. Then she leaned against it, realising that in spite of the fact that she was still wearing her ski jacket in the warm flat, she was shivering again. She levered herself away from the door, crossed to the heavy old sideboard and took out the bottle of whisky and a glass. Taken neat the spirit burned her throat and she held the glass cupped between her hands, staring into space.

Was it possible Paula was still alive – and did she even want her to be? Of course the immediate answer was 'Yes! Oh yes!' but in truth it was not that simple. What sort of woman would willingly choose to leave her husband and child without a qualm, allow them to grieve for her and believe her dead? Certainly not the dream mother a bereaved child had created for herself. With a sense of shock Harriet realised that in the last hours Paula had become more of a stranger to her than she had ever been during the twenty years she had believed her dead. A beautiful face in a photograph, a few misty memories, a haunting perfume tugging at her senses, and Paula had been whatever Harriet wanted her to be. Now for the first time she was face to face with fragmented suggestions of reality, distorted perhaps, like the sun glancing on water, but hinting at something very different from the fairy tale princess the child Harriet had claimed as her own.

Could you have done such a thing, Mom? Harriet asked silently and was as far as ever from an answer. The image was all she had. She knew nothing of the real woman behind it.

The long hours of the night stretched ahead of her and the prospect opened a well of loneliness within her. Despising herself for her weakness she reached for the telephone, dialling Nick's number. For a long while the bell rang and Harriet felt the sense of loneliness deepen. He wasn't there. Then just as she was about to replace the receiver she heard his voice, that soft familiar Scottish burr.

'Nick', she said, choky suddenly.

'Harriet – is that you? You're back then.'

'Yes. Just. I was beginning to think you weren't there.'

'I'm listening to some music. I had it turned up a bit too loud. I didn't hear the phone at first.'

In the background she could hear The Anvil Chorus from Il Trovatore.

'Nick – do you think . . .?' she began hesitantly.

'You want me to come over?' he asked, reading her mind.

'Would you? I know it's late but . .'

'I'll be with you in . . . twenty minutes.'

'Oh Nick – thanks!'

'My pleasure,' he said drily. 'You ask me, Harriet, all too seldom.'

'And for goodness sake,' she said, looking at the almost-empty Scotch bottle, 'bring something good and strong to drink with you.'

In the time it took Nick to arrive Harriet forced herself to wash and change into a clean sweatshirt, though the most mundane of everyday actions seemed a huge effort. By the time she heard his car squeezing into a parking space outside she was calmer, at least outwardly, opening the door to him with what she hoped gave the appearance of nonchalance.

'Hi! Sorry to drag you out on a night like this.'

'Don't even think of it.' He kissed her briefly on the lips and came into the flat, a slightly-built sandy-haired man in his mid-thirties wearing a heavy black overcoat over a sweater and cords. From one of the voluminous pockets he produced a bottle of Scotch and put it down on the table. 'Drinks – as ordered. I take it you are in need.'

'Too true! What a day! Oh, bless you Nick.' She fetched her

glass. 'Pour me one, will you, when you've taken your coat off. And what about you? Are you drinking too?'

'I'll keep you company. But better make it a small one – if I'm driving.' There was just the hint of a question in his tone. She ignored it, habit making her play it coolly even now, in her moment of need.

'I got the pictures, Nick. Some beauties, I think.' She was annoyed to hear the slight tremble in her voice.

'Great.' He had tossed his coat over the back of a chair and was pouring whiskies. He handed one to her, looking at her directly. 'You didn't ask me over here to discuss the pictures though, Harriet – admit it. It's . . . the other business, isn't it? I take it you did as I suggested and got hold of a paper.'

'Yes.' She gulped at the whisky, then thought better of it. 'I'll get some ice.'

When she returned from the kitchen he had made himself comfortable on the sofa. She went over and perched herself on the ottoman at his feet.

'I've had the insurance investigators here,' she said.

He raised an eyebrow. 'Already? They don't waste time.'

'No. I suppose, as the man said, with at least a quarter of a million at stake they can't afford to, but all the same, it wasn't very pleasant. Especially since I'd only just arrived back from Paris.'

She proceeded to relate the interview, keeping nothing back apart from the effect it had had on her, but Nick knew her too well to be fooled.

'It must have been pretty gruesome,' he said.

'Yes – well – it's such a damned cheek! First suggesting I was involved in some insurance fraud and then as good as saying Mom walked out on us! I realise from his point of view his company would be a quarter of a million better off if they could prove it should never have been paid in the first place, but . . . it is my mother he was talking about dammit!'

'Oh Harri, darling Harri . . .' He reached for her, pulling her up onto the sofa beside him and putting his arm around her. 'And what do *you* think?'

35

'What do I think? Well, she's dead of course. She'd never do that to us . . .' She broke off. 'No, to be truthful, that's what I told him, but deep down I don't know. I honestly don't know.' She gulped her drink.

'Does it matter?' he asked.

She shook herself free of his arm.

'Well of course it bloody well matters!'

'Why? You've lived the last twenty years without her, whatever.'

'That's not the point.'

'Do you really want to know the truth? It might be a pretty upsetting business.'

'I'm upset already,' she admitted. 'In any case – I'm going to have to face it sooner or later. That O'Neill man isn't going to let up now he's got his teeth into it. He's going to dig and dig. God what a job! Imagine doing a shitty job like that!'

'Not unlike a journalist really,' Nick observed drily. 'Well, Harri, you can either sit back and let him do the digging or you can do a little investigation yourself.'

'I don't know. I don't know whether I want to.'

'I was rather hoping you'd do a nice follow-up photo session for me', he said slyly.

'On what?'

'That's up to you. But you didn't cover Kuwait in this lot, did you? Or the sweatshops of Korea, or the rip-off merchants in Hong Kong? A trip East may be just what you need.

'Yes.' But she sounded less than convinced.

They sat in silence for a while, then he looked meaningfully at the whisky bottle.

'Shall I have another drink? Or am I going to be driving?'

She laughed shortly but it came out as a half-sob.

'Oh Nick, what would I do without you?'

'That is the first time I've heard you admit it,' he said ruefully. 'You generally seem to manage by yourself very well.'

She did not answer.

'Well?' he pressed her. 'Do I have that other drink or not?'

She reached for the bottle and half filled his tumbler.

'Have the bloody drink, Nick. And please . . . I would like you to stay.'

At first she slept, heavy, exhausted, whisky-induced sleep. Then suddenly she was wide awake, nerves jangling again, thoughts chaotic.

She eased herself out of Nick's embrace and he did not stir. How she hated sleeping in his arms! Making love was all very well, pleasant and soporific if not exactly ecstatic, but afterwards . . . she needed her space.

I'm a bitch, she thought sometimes. I use Nick shamelessly and I don't like myself for it. But he's got no one to blame but himself. He allows me to do it. If I were a man I'd tell me to get lost – and fast!

Tonight, however, she had no room for such introspection. There were other things on her mind.

She eased herself out from under the duvet, reaching for her heavy wool man's dressing gown and tying it firmly around her, crossed to the window. It had stopped snowing now and the sky was clear and black with a few stars. Beneath her window she could see the white humps of the pot in her backyard – pots that in summer she filled with geraniums and petunias in an effort to bring some colour to the uniform greyness, beyond them the wall that bordered the yard was also white-crusted. A familiar scene, yet one that had changed subtly since yesterday – just as everything else had been changed by that newspaper item, the whole of her life being undermined making her feel that nothing was quite as it had seemed.

In one way, of course, Nick had been quite right when he had said that whatever the truth it made no difference. There was no going back now, no way to rewrite the years as she had known them. And they had been good years. With a child's resilience she had quickly adjusted to the loss of her mother, who had never been more than a glamorous appendage on the periphery of her world, and Sally had stepped in to fill the breach more than adequately.

Now, looking back with the wisdom of adulthood, she could appreciate what she had taken for granted at the time. The moment the news had broken Sally had been there, comforting her, buffering her, cuddling her when she cried. There was a warmth about Sally that superceded all her amusing little vanities and softened the acid remarks she was prone to making – which were in reality a defence mechanism. Sally had a great capacity for love and a down-to-earth quality that Harriet presumed was a throw-back to her early upbringing and which had been honed and tested in the fire when she had given birth to – and kept – an illegitimate son in the days when illegitimacy was still a scandal. To Harriet Sally had become a surrogate mother and after she had married Hugo that position had been strengthened so that Harriet had felt secure and loved, never questioning her importance to the people who were important to her. Although the glamorous world of fashion and wealth spread wide around her, Harriet's own family circle was tight – her father, Sally, and Sally's illegitimate son, Mark Bristow.

Mark had been educated in England and later decided to live there, and it had been because of him that Harriet had first decided to come to London, though nowadays she saw little of him. He was in advertising; he and his partner, Toby Rogers, had their own agency, and paradoxically Mark had spent most of the last year back in the States. He was there now, setting up some important job or other. Had he not been she might have telephoned him instead of Nick, when she had been desperate for company. But then again, she might not. In a way Mark was too close to home, too much a part of the world whose foundations had just been rocked, yet somehow on the outside. No matter what the truth might turn out to be it would not affect Mark. The foundations upon which his life were built were intact. Winds of change might blow around him but his basics were not under threat.

Beneath the duvet Nick stirred, flinging his arms across the empty space where Harriet should have been. She stood stock still, hoping he would drift off to sleep once more without realising she was not there. But after a moment he turned over again, mumbling thickly: 'Harri? Where are you?'

'I'm here,' she hissed. 'Go back to sleep.'

'What are you doing out of bed? You'll catch your death.'

'No I won't.' His concern irritated her. Wasn't that what she had wanted, though? Someone to be here, to care about her? So why now did the very fact that he was awake and talking to her seem like an invasion of her privacy?

'Come back to bed, love.'

'I'm all right.'

'No, you're bloody not!' He got out of bed, exclaiming as the cold air enveloped his warm sleepy frame. 'Christ, this place is like an icebox! Hasn't your heater come on?'

'I don't have one in the bedroom, Nick. It's healthier not to.'

'Healthier! To catch bloody pneumonia!' He caught her, steering her back to the bed, bundling her in, dressing gown and all. She allowed him to do it though her irritation mounted. She couldn't ask him to stay then yell at him for caring for her. She lay stiffly as he huddled close, sharing the warmth.

'I was thinking,' she said into his shoulder.

'Not now,' he protested. 'There will be plenty of time for that tomorrow.'

'No, there won't,' she said. 'I've made up my mind, Nick. I have to try and learn the truth. If Mom is still alive I have to find her. If she's not, well . . .'

He did not answer.

'I'm going home,' she said. 'On the first available flight. I'm sorry.'

'Don't be sorry. I suppose you'll do what you have to do.'

'Yes.'

'Only one thing – be sure you take your camera with you.'

She laughed softly. 'Oh Nick, always first and foremost the editor!'

'Always that.' There was regret in his sleepy voice.

She was growing warmer now and drowsier. With the decision made she felt a kind of temporary peace.

'All right, Nick,' she murmured. 'I'll take my camera with me.'

'Promise?'

'I promise.'

She had no way of knowing that he was thinking not so much of the next photo story she would submit to him as the necessary therapy it might provide. A journey into the past, with skeletons rattling in cupboards at every dark turning, was almost bound to be upsetting. Nick, with his unfailing journalist's instinct, felt in his bones that this one would be more traumatic than most.

CHAPTER THREE

In his office high up in the twenty-five storey building that is 550 Fashion Avenue, mecca of the New York fashion industry, Hugo Varna sat at his desk and fiddled with the executive toy Sally had bought for him last Christinas. It was a stupid thing, he thought, three gold baubles on springs that set up a continual motion, banging one against the other, and he kept it on his desk only to please her. But today with his mind too preoccupied to work he seemed quite unable to keep his hands off it. It clicked irritatingly and Hugo pushed it aside, swivelling his chair around to face the window and the panoramic view of Manhattan.

Hugo Varna's showrooms occupied an entire floor of the 550 building and from the moment a potential client stepped out of the brass elevator she was treated to an ambience of unashamed luxury. The vast foyer was carpeted in the softest green imaginable, the walls were even paler, so that at first glance they might have been taken for white, and the Venetian blinds were a perfectly blended shade of moss. The minimum of furniture emphasised the impressive size of the foyer – only small modern tables bearing huge smoked glass ash trays, two or three low chairs and a huge arrangement of dried ferns and foliage in shades of brown and gold graced the enormous expanse. From cunningly concealed speakers piped music wafted, but music played so softly that it was almost inaudible to the human ear, a faint teasing melody that soothed the soul and created a restful atmosphere almost without one being aware of it.

This soft green womb formed an oasis of peace in the chaotic tumble that was Fashion Avenue. Outside in the street the traffic might roar, here there was hush broken only by that soft subliminal music, outside the air might be heavy with the mingled smells of petrol fumes and donuts, Macdonalds' burgers, trash cans, and sweat, here there was just the faintest perfume of a pine pot-pourri, subtle as the music.

Even the bustling atmosphere of the 550 building itself seemed not to have invaded the Hugo Varna floor. Here the sales staff glided about with languid grace more reminiscent of Paris than New York, the house models managed to look like elegant advertisements for Varna even after a long session of standing stock still while a toile was pinned and draped and adjusted around them, and even when a rail of sample clothes had to be wheeled across the hallowed expanse of green, carefully hidden inside grey and black sample bags to make sure they were safe from the photographic eye of a fashion spy, it was managed with what Hugo referred to as 'panache'

'The simplest of jobs can be done with panache', he would instruct whenever one of his staff fell short of his standards of perfection – the standards that endeared him to his 'Shiny Set' customers and staff alike.

Hugo himself was lithe, elegant and charming with a slight edge of fascinating middle-European foreignness that came from his Bulgarian father. But it was his own formidable talent that set him apart.

Mostly nowadays Hugo took for granted all the assets that talent had brought him. Twenty years at the pinnacle of his profession had paid him handsomely and he accepted the accolades and the financial rewards as no more than his due. But on occasions he stopped in his tracks to wonder just what he was doing here, amidst all this elegance and opulence, numbering the rich and famous and powerful amongst his clients – and his friends.

Not bad for the son of a penniless illegal immigrant, he thought then, not bad for a boy raised on the wrong side of town.

'Where exactly do you hail from, Hugo?' Margie Llewellyn, the chat-show queen, had asked him once when she had interviewed him, and he had mesmerised her millions of viewers with the story

42

he had told. His father, a seaman, had jumped ship to seek a better life when Bulgaria had been on the brink of civil war in the 1920s. He had taken the name of Varna from the name of the port from which he had sailed but he had lived his life in terror of deportation, a fear that had haunted him long after it had ceased to be a real threat, so that he had never been able to enjoy his son's success, seeing it only as something which drew unwelcome attention to the Varna family.

Hugo had been perfectly happy to talk at length on the Margie Llewellyn Show about the days when he had played on the streets of the Bronx, and how in this unlikely setting a talent for sketching had developed into an interest in designing clothes. Apart from his father, Hugo's family had consisted entirely of women – his mother, his three sisters, his maternal grandmother and various assorted aunts and cousins all of whom (his mother excepted) had striven to dress with what Hugo would later call 'panache' on a pittance. He had taken far more interest in their efforts than his father had thought was right and proper for a boy and when Leonie, his eldest sister, had been apprenticed to a dressmaker his fascination had grown. From sketching the outfits she made to inventing designs of his own was but a short step and by the time he left High School he knew exactly what he wanted to do. His sisters, all working by this time, supported him through a course at the New York Fashion Institute of Technology. They were inordinately proud of him, if slightly puzzled by their unusually talented brother.

When he graduated Hugo took a succession of low-paid jobs in 7th Avenue and the optimism with which he had set out began to be dimmed by the sheer sick-making banality of what he had to do – cutting samples in the disgusting fabrics with which the greedy cutthroat manufacturers he worked for made their living. But all the while he was learning and soon the time had come when he was no longer satisfied to design for others. He began cutting his own samples on his mother's kitchen table and getting them made up by his sister and her friends at the dressmaker's where she worked.

The situation could not last, of course. One day Leonie's employer had got wind of what was going on, sacked Leonie and placed a telephone call to Victor Nicholson, the ignorant, ill-tempered manufacturer Hugo was contracted to at the time. A distraught Leonie tried unsuccessfully to contact Hugo to warn him and the first he knew of the débâcle was when he was summoned to Nicholson's cramped stale-tobacco smelling office. The moment he walked in at the door he knew something was very wrong. Nicholson, who could often be found reading cartoon comics at this time of day, was pacing the untidy office like a caged lion, his face and his thick neck suffused ugly puce above the none-too-white collar of his shirt.

As Hugo entered the office he whirled round, blundering into his flimsy chair and almost overturning it.

'What the hell is going on, eh, you little runt? You trying to ruin me, is that it?'

Totally taken by surprise Hugo could only stare. Nicholson reached across the desk, grabbing Hugo by the lapels and pulling him towards him.

'Don't stand there looking like Shirley Bloody Temple. You know what I'm talking about. You've been cheating me, you stinking ass hole, letting me pay you for second-rate designs while you market the best ideas yourself.'

Hugo understood then. He began to shake, not because he was physically afraid of Nicholson, though the man was twice his size, but because he could suddenly see his world falling apart around him. He'd taken a chance and he'd been found out.

'I suppose this means you want me to leave,' he said with what dignity he could, half-sprawled across the desk with his chin six inches above the remains of a take-away pizza and a cardboard cup of coffee dregs.

'Too right it does. And that's not all.' Nicholson released him, pushing him back so hard he almost fell. 'Now hear this and hear it good. I'm suing you, Varna, for every cent you've made from your dirty little deals – and for the designs. They belong to me – you're under contract, don't forget.'

Hugo snorted derisively. Although the very thought of court

action had brought him out in a cold sweat, the same grittiness which had enabled his father to jump ship and seek a new life now came to his rescue.

'Waste your money on lawyers if that's the way you want it,' he retorted. 'You'll make a fool of yourself though. Those designs are mine, done in my own time and made up by my own outworkers. You'd never use them anyway. They have too much class for the women who buy the rubbish you produce.'

Nicholson had turned such a deep shade of purple Hugo thought he was about to suffer a stroke.

'Get out of here!' he yelled. 'I don't want to see your ass around here again – understand? Get out!'

Hugo had got out. He had left the squalid little office that afternoon never to return. It was the most important thing he had ever done in his life, he had told Margie Llewellyn, and across a nation the rich and famous, the elegant and the glittering society women who were his clients wholeheartedly echoed the sentiment.

Nicholson had never carried out his threat to sue, though Hugo had endured some worrying weeks waiting to see if papers would be served on him, and the experience had made him determined never to work for the likes of Nicholson again.

His early ventures into freelance design had been reasonably successful; with Leonie's encouragement he worked long hours as a restaurant porter to earn enough money to buy a couple of ancient industrial machines which he set up at one end of the living room of his mother's house. Soon the place was alive with their busy whirr as Leonie and one of her friends stitched samples; to their accompaniment Hugo worked on new designs.

The story of this far from illustrious beginning was one Hugo never tired of telling, for the fact that he had started with nothing but raw talent and stubborn determination was something of which he was justifiably proud but he was less forthcoming about what had happened next. When Margie had mentioned his association with Greg Martin, the financier who had made him the loan which had set him up in a small showroom and enabled him to move the sewing machines out of the living room and into a work room, Hugo became not so much evasive as totally silent.

Without a doubt it had been Greg's backing which had propelled him into the big league; without him, for all his talent, Hugo might have been trapped in small-time design and manufacture for ever. But the very mention of Greg Martin's name was painful to Hugo. He had skilfully evaded Margie's questions, moving on to talk instead about Kurt Eklund, the financial genius he had hired after Greg's death to help him avoid what had seemed at the time almost certain ruin. It had been Kurt who had set up the dozens of licensing deals for menswear and toiletries, bedlinen and beachwear, soft furnishings and costume jewellery, all bearing the name of Hugo Varna, which had not only saved him from bankruptcy but also made him his first million. In the process Kurt had graduated from business adviser to trusted friend; Hugo had rewarded him with a fifteen per cent share of the business and never regretted it.

Margie had not pressed Hugo to talk about Greg Martin though her professional instincts had nagged at her that if she could probe a little into the association it would produce some riveting television. But she also sensed how deep Hugo's hurt ran and since his first wife's death was also connected with the man she told herself it would be tasteless to dwell on it.

The truth was, of course, that hard-nosed journalist though she was, Margie was as attracted to Hugo as was almost every other woman who met him and she actually wanted him to *like* her.

The momentary weakness had bothered her for weeks afterwards as she worried as to whether she had lost her professionalism along with the opportunity to grill Hugo Varna over the truth about his relationship – and Paula's – with the man who had died as he lived in a blaze of publicity. But whether she had been right or wrong, Hugo had been allowed off the hook. He did not talk about Greg Martin. He did not even think about Greg Martin if he could help it. As he left the studio after the interview his well-programmed defence mechanism had come into operation, and he had pushed the painful memories into a corner of his brain where his conscious mind could not reach them.

Now, however, to his intense discomfort, Hugo found there was no way he could prevent himself from thinking about Greg Martin. From the moment the news had broken that he was not dead at all but very much alive in Australia he had been unable to think of anything else. None of the usual tricks for shutting off memory would work now; whatever he did, whichever way he diverted his attention it would only come wandering back, like a man in a maze who continually finds himself back in the same spot. It was insufferable – awful. He was beginning to think he was going mad. His nerves jangled in time with the balls on the executive toy on his desk and his brain felt as thick and muzzy as the grey January sky above the skyscrapers of Manhattan.

A slight commotion in the outer office attracted his attention.

His secretary's voice, raised in agitation: 'I'm sorry – Mr Varna is not to be disturbed. You can't go in there!'

And another voice, one he instantly recognised: 'Like hell I can't!'

The door flew open and Harriet burst in. Behind her the secretary floundered helplessly.

'I'm sorry, Mr Varna, I couldn't stop her.'

'It's all right, Nancy. This is my daughter.'

'Oh, Mr Varna, I'm so sorry . . .' she stuttered, even more horrified by her gaffe than she had been about letting a strange woman push her way into the holy of holies. Nancy Ball had only been with Hugo for a few months and it was much longer than that since Harriet had visited him at the office. It had simply never occurred to her that the young woman in a ski jacket with faded jeans tucked into her boots might actually be Hugo Varna's daughter!

'Don't worry about it, Nancy,' he said comfortingly. 'You weren't to know.'

She retreated, casting one last flustered glance at Harriet. Sally, Hugo's wife, was always so beautifully turned out, while this girl was . . . well, frankly almost scruffy! Women simply *never* turned up at the showrooms of one of America's top designers dressed like that, and with practically no make-up. Hugo's daughter! Well! well!

'Dad – I had to come,' Harriet said as the door closed after the secretary. 'You've heard the news, of course.'

'Yes.' Even without the simple affirmation his face would have given her the answer; he looked pale and drawn, as if he had slept even less than she had. 'I tried to call you but there was no reply from your flat.'

'I was in Paris on a job. I saw a newspaper there. I rushed back to London, packed a few fresh things and came straight here.'

'Harriet . . . I'm so sorry.'

'Why should you be sorry?'

'It must have been a terrible shock for you . . .'

'And for you!' she said hotly. 'After all this time – it's almost unbelievable. Do you suppose there's any truth in it?'

He spread his hands helplessly. 'I wish I knew. But I can't see why anyone should invent a story like that.'

'Maybe she's some kind of nut.'

'Maybe. But as you said, Harri, it's such a long time ago. Most people have forgotten all about Greg Martin. I can't imagine what would prompt this woman to dredge it all up if there wasn't some truth in it. I can think of a dozen men of much more recent notoriety if she was simply inventing it for some cranky reason of her own. Besides . . .' He broke off, staring for a moment at the glinting gold balls, then raising his eyes to meet Harriet's directly, 'if you look at the past, it's quite feasible that she knew Greg. There was a connection.'

'You knew her?' Harriet asked, surprised.

'No, but I know of her family.'

'Who is she then? The paper said she was Italian, didn't it?'

'That's right. Her family were fabric manufacturers with mills and factories around Lake Como. Greg was working on some kind of deal in Italy not long before he . . . before the accident. It's quite conceivable they were involved in it and he met Maria as a result. He swept her off her feet, I shouldn't wonder.' His lip curled in a bitter smile. 'He was very attractive to women, was Greg.'

Harriet ignored the implication.

'But Dad – twenty years! If it's true and he is alive where has he been all this time? And why the hell should he have pretended to be dead if he wasn't?'

'Because I guess it suited him.' Hugo ran a finger under the roll collar of his shirt. It felt tight and hot in spite of being made of the softest combed cotton. 'He left one hell of a mess behind him, Harriet.'

'Financial difficulties, you mean?'

'And some! Oh yes, he'd overstretched himself, all right. And there was the suggestion of fraud, too. It took months – and the best financial brains in New York – to unravel his dealings and what they found was a web of debt – and worse. What a time that was!' His eyes darkened at the memory. 'For a while I thought we'd go down because of it. If it hadn't been for Kurt I would have done. He rescued me, not a doubt of it, and thank God he did. But as for Greg . . . I suppose you could say I was all kinds of a fool to trust him, but I'm a designer, not an accountant. And I wasn't the only one taken in by him – far from it. There were plenty of others with more experience in these matters than I who were deceived. Oh yes, if Greg had been around when the storm broke he'd have faced ruin – and probably gone to gaol into the bargain. No doubt about it, he made a very timely exit one way or the other.'

Harriet was silent for a moment, chewing on her thumbnail. So . . . Greg had been little better than a crook on the business front – and he had very nearly dragged her father – and his stupendous talent – down with him. She had suspected as much, though it had never occurred to her that Greg's death had been anything but an accident. But important as all this might once have been it did not concern her now. Hugo had weathered that particular storm with Kurt's help and backing. No one had charged him with anything more serious than naivity and now he was one of the most successful fashion designers in New York. Besides, business dealings never figured very largely in Harriet's reckoning. There were other, far more important aspects to life – and death.

'Greg is only half the story though isn't he, Dad?' she said quietly.

His eyes narrowed, emphasising the small lines and creases around them. 'What do you mean by that?'

'Oh Dad!' she remonstrated. 'You know very well what I mean. What about Mom?'

He looked away. 'What about her?'

'Dad – come out from that clam shell of yours. I know how good you are at hiding away inside it when you don't want to face up to the real world. But it's out here and it won't go away.'

'Your mother is dead', he said flatly.

'Is she though?' Harriet shook her head slowly. 'We don't really know that any more do we? We were always led to believe there were survivors when the *Lorelei* blew up. Now it seems that wasn't the case. If this Maria Vincenti is to be believed, Greg survived. So I repeat – what happened to Mom?'

'Harriet . . .' He leaned on his desk wearily, not looking at her. 'It's so long ago now.'

'What difference does that make? Twenty weeks – twenty months – twenty years – the questions are still the same and they have to be answered. If we don't ask them someone else will. The insurance people are already starting to probe. One of them came to see me last night when I got back from Paris. He wanted to know when I last saw Mom.'

He blanched visibly. 'Bastards! I was afraid of something like this. So they think . . . yes, I suppose they would. What did you tell him?'

'That I'd never seen her from that day to this, of course. But that's no longer enough, is it? For God's sake what happened when the *Lorelei* blew up? And what happened afterwards? Don't you want to know? Dad – stop fiddling with that damned desk toy and *listen to me!*'

He straightened, whirling round on her suddenly, much as he had turned on Victor Nicholson all those years ago. Gone was the vagueness, gone the composure. His eyes were bright now with suppressed passion and pain.

'No, Harriet, you listen to me. There are some things best left alone – some things it's better not to know.'

'But the explosion might not have been an accident,' she persisted. 'Have you thought of that? It would explain how Greg manages to be in one piece while the *Lorelei* is nothing but a few planks of driftwood. And if what you say about the state of his finances is true then he'd have every reason for faking his death to escape the music. But it doesn't answer my question. What happened to Mom?'

'Your mother is dead.'

'So you keep saying. It's almost as if you want to believe it.'

'Perhaps I do.' His voice was tired. 'Perhaps even that is preferable to thinking she could just disappear and let us think she was dead.'

'But Dad ...

'How would you feel if you discovered that was the case? That she could abandon you – her four-year-old child – and never see you again? Is that what you want to hear?'

'No, of course not!'

'There are things I hoped you'd never, find out, Harriet,' he said. 'But I see now there's no point in hiding them any longer. Besides, you are a grown woman now, and I dare say the truth will come out whether I tell you or not. Your mother was having an affair with Greg Martin. She was besotted by him. When she followed him to Italy I believe she had already made up her mind to leave us and go to him. That was why what happened on the boat makes very little difference to me. Whether she was killed or not is almost immaterial. As far as I am concerned, she was dead to me the moment she walked out the door.'

Harriet crossed to the window and looked out. The towers of Manhattan seemed almost to be touching the cold grey sky. Far below, in the street opposite the 550 building, stood the tall statue of the Garment Worker, strangely distorted from this angle, and around the plinth on which it stood ant-like figures of vagrants and layabouts sat, oblivious to the cold. For long minutes Harriet stared down, unseeing.

It was not her father's revelation of an affair that surprised her. The official story had always been that Greg was simply a close family friend, but a child could have seen through the pretence and she had not been a child for a very long time, perhaps not since that long-ago night when she was four years old and had stood, unseen, outside a bedroom door ... No, it was her father's attitude that had shocked her. 'She was dead to me,' he had said and she could see he meant it. She was used to his ostrich ways – his ability to bury his head in the sand and shut out the things that displeased or upset him. But all the same ... Harriet gave her head a small shake, hardly able to believe that even he could be quite so coldly dismissive.

'Could I have a drink?' she requested.

'Coffee? I'll buzz Nancy.'

'No – a proper drink. The alcoholic sort.' She broke off with a short laugh. 'Don't look at me like that, Dad. This may be the middle of the afternoon to you, to me it's evening – and the end of a very long day.'

'Whisky? Bourbon?' he asked, opening the elegant black-laquered cabinet.

'Whisky, please. Scotch if you've got it – or are you waving the emerald flag for the benefit of certain up-and-coming Irish politicians of the lineage of the closest thing we in the States have to a royal family?'

'I have Irish whiskey, of course – but also Scotch.' He poured her some and handed it to her. 'I won't pretend it pleases me to see you drinking it, Harriet. I know you're a grown woman but so are most of the others who lurch their way down the not-so-primrosy path to the Betty Ford Clinic.'

'Dad!' She rolled her eyes heavenward.

'I know. I sound like a nagging father. But I've seen a few of them on the slippery slope – the Shiny Set, the stars, the Washington widows ...'

'Inadequates.'

'Don't be so sure. It gets a hold of you, Harriet.'

'All right, Dad, you've made your point. I wish I hadn't asked for the damned drink now. But as I said, my body hasn't adjusted to the time-lag yet. When it does, I promise not a drop will pass my lips before dinner. Except of course ...' she broke off to toss back the rest of the whisky and set the tumbler down on Hugo's desk, 'except of course that I don't suppose I shall be here long enough to make the adjustment.'

He was unable to hide his disappointment. 'You're going back to London?'

'No. Not yet. I'm going to Australia.'

'Australia? . . . oh!'

She nodded. 'Yes. I'm going to try and find Greg Martin. I'm sorry, Dad, but I can't just let this thing pass – sit back and pretend it hasn't happened. It's very important to me – and, I should have thought, to you too. It's Mom we're talking about – not a stranger in a sensational newspaper item – and there are too many unanswered questions about her death – or her disappearance. If Greg Martin is alive then perhaps he is the only person in the world who can supply the answers.'

'But Harriet, it sounds as if he has gone into hiding again. If the police can't find him what makes you think you could? And if they have picked him up he'll in in custody. They'd never let you see him.'

Her mouth set in a stubborn line he knew so well.

'You may be right. But I have to try. Perhaps you don't want to know the truth – that's how it looks from where I'm standing. But I want to know. I want to find out what happened. Damn it – I'm *going* to find out!'

He shook his head. 'What good do you think will come from it, Harriet? If she is alive and you find her – do you think that would mean you'd have your Mom back? Of course it wouldn't. But I honestly believe she is dead. I have thought so for a very long time.'

'If that is so then it is all the more important to find out the truth,' she said quietly.

'Why? What difference can it make now?'

'Because it seems as though Greg arranged the accident in order to fake his own death. That's what the woman alleged and what you have said confirms it is quite likely. But when he sailed Mom was with him – no dispute about that is there? So if he survived and Mom died then – don't you see? He murdered her.'

'Harriet – for God's sake!'

'I'm sorry, Dad, but it's true. It has to be a possibility. And that is why I'll see Greg Martin if it's the last thing I do.'

His eyes were distant. He looked like an old man suddenly and she realised how he had aged since she had seen him last. Aged since yesterday, perhaps? Never a big man, overnight his frame seemed to have become almost frail and the sinews in his neck were raised and stringy above the cotton roll-neck. She put her arms around him.

'I don't want to upset you, Dad, but I have to do it. You must see that ...' She stopped speaking as the buzzer on his desk interrupted her. He broke away, depressing the button.

'Yes, Nancy? What is it?'

'I'm sorry to disturb you, Mr Varna, but I have a Mr O'Neill here who says he is from the British and Cosmopolitan Assurance Company. He insists on seeing you.'

'The man who more or less forced his way into my flat last night!' Harriet said grimly. 'What is he doing in New York?'

'Come to see me, obviously,' Hugo returned drily. But his smile was strained and Harriet was alarmed by how drawn and old he suddenly looked.

'Leave him to me, Dad. I'll deal with him.'

Tom O'Neill was in the outer office looking at one of the pictures that lines the walls – Rena, Hugo's favourite house model, wearing a loose cut trench coat over a tailored shirt and doe-skin pants.

'Mr O'Neill, I really would prefer it if you didn't bother my father just now. There is nothing he can tell you beyond what I already have – that as far as we are concerned my mother has been dead for more than twenty years.'

'Perhaps.' Today, in the half daylight, half white neon of the office, his eyes managed to look bluer and sharper than ever, like the ice-cold waters of a sunlit fiord. 'Nevertheless I am afraid I must insist on seeing him, Miss Varna.'

'Look – he's in no fit state ...' Harriet argued. 'Why don't you go to Australia and talk to the Vincenti woman before you start bothering us?'

'That is my next port of call,' he said easily. 'But right now I am here. So if you would kindly tell your father . . .'

'Mr O'Neill, I'm telling you . . .'

'Quit trying to protect me, Harriet.' Hugo was standing in the doorway of his office. 'I know you are only trying to help but the sooner we get this over with the better. I'll see Mr O'Neill now. I have nothing to hide.'

'Dad!'

'You go home, Harriet. I'll see you at dinner. And perhaps you'd warn Sally I might be a little late.'

'Dad!'

'Come this way, please, Mr O'Neill.'

The door closed after them and Harriet could do nothing but glare at it impotently. Dammit, he deserved to be reported to whatever professional body insurance investigators belonged to and if he upset her father she'd see to it that he was.

Still fuming at the insensitive arrogance of the man she turned and left the office.

CHAPTER FOUR

In her room at Hugo's Central Park triplex Harriet was dressed and ready for dinner. At home in London she rarely bothered with such irrelevances; here she knew it was expected of her and accordingly she had showered, dumped her travel-weary jeans into the laundry basket from which they would be rescued by a maid, washed, ironed and returned to her next day, and dressed herself in a loose silk jersey jacket and pants suit, simple and easy enough to please her yet enough of a transformation to satisfy her father and Sally.

She was tired out now, her eyes ached from lack of sleep and jetlag, and she glanced longingly at the king-sized bed with its lace-trimmed peach silk sheets. Oh to be able to fall into it and sink into oblivion! But it would be several more hours yet before she could do that.

Was her father home yet? she wondered. She was anxious to see him the moment he arrived, and make sure he was all right after the trauma of the interview with the insurance investigator. But when she went to the head of the stairs and looked down she could see that his study door was ajar and the house was quiet and she returned to her room. He had said he might be late, after all, and she decided to snatch a few more moments of privacy to recharge her batteries in the one place in the whole luxurious house where she was able to relax and feel she was her own person.

What was it about unashamed luxury, Harriet sometimes asked herself, which made her feel so uncomfortable? Most people would be only to happy to be able to enjoy such surroundings. A top line interior decorator had been given a free hand when Hugo had bought the triplex two years ago and no expense had been spared – the walls were hung with some of Hugo's collection of Old Masters, glowing against the background of watered silk, the shelves were lined with leather bound first editions which neither Hugo nor Sally would ever open, much less read, every nook and cranny was filled with treasures and *objets d'art* displayed on dainty pedestals. The sofas and chairs were deep and soft enough to fall asleep in, a fireplace was topped by an Adam mantel which Hugo had had flown out from England and everywhere there were fresh flowers – long stemmed hothouse roses, orchids flown in from Singapore, daffodils and narcissi and heavy perfumed hyacinths.

But to Harriet the grandeur and studied comfort were somehow artificial, the atmosphere more reminiscent of a luxury hotel than a home. Perhaps, she thought, it was because she had never lived in this house. There was nothing to arouse childhood memories.

Only in the room Sally had chosen especially for her was Harriet amongst familiar echoes of the past and she never entered it without feeling a wave of gratitude towards her aunt. Here, at Sally's instigation, were many of the things Harriet remembered and loved from her childhood and growing-up years – the rosettes she had won with her pony, her graduation dress, her old collection of Osmond and Jackson records, her early attempts at photography, proudly framed, a pressed flower that reminded her of her first proper date. Small things, but important, the little touches that were typical of Sally and which made it possible to feel charity – and love – for her when she was fussy or critical or just plain annoying as she had been when Harriet had arrived without warning this afternoon.

'Why didn't you let us know you were coming?' Sally had chided when the taxi had dropped Harriet off and she had bundled unceremoniously into the house. 'You should have called, darling, and warned us. I might have been out or anything.'

'There wasn't time,' Harriet had said, kissing her. 'And anyway, you weren't out.'

'No, but I will be tomorrow. I have a charity luncheon to attend and . . .'

'I probably won't be here tomorrow either. It's a flying visit only.'

'Oh if only I'd known! I'd have asked Mark to dinner. He's in New York, you know, though he insists on staying with a friend in that dreadful apartment over on the West side. He'd have loved to see you.'

'And I'd have loved to see him. But that's not why I'm here, Sally.'

'Why then? Oh no, don't tell me.' Sally held up a manicured hand. 'I don't think I want to know. Your father and I talked about nothing else last night. Harriet, I'm sorry, but I don't think I could stand to begin going all over that again – not just now. And I think I just might try to get hold of Mark. It might not be too late to invite him to dinner, if he's got nothing else planned. I'll warn Jane we shall be at least one, possibly two, extra . . .'

'Sally, hang on a minute.' Harriet managed to interrupt her flow. 'I can understand your reluctance to talk about what's happened but you can't just push it to one side. That's Dad's trick, but it's not like you.'

'It's just that I don't like wasting my energy worrying about things I can do nothing about,' Sally said matter-of-factly. 'Please, Harriet. I have had it up to here!' She drew an imaginary line across the base of her throat, brushing her double-strand pearl choker. 'Can't we just leave it?'

Harriet sighed. 'No, I don't think we can. I called in to see Dad before coming here and while I was there an insurance investigator called Tom O'Neill came to see him. The same man was at my flat last night asking questions and for all I know his next visit will be here, to see you, so . . .' She broke off. Sally's hand was clutching at her pearls now and she had turned very pale beneath her makeup. 'Sally, are you all right?' she asked swiftly.

'An insurance investigator, you say?' Sally repeated in a shocked voice.

'That's right. There was a big pay-out on Mom's life, wasn't there? Well, the insurance company seem to have got it into their heads that if Greg Martin is alive Mom might be too. They're more or less accusing us of some kind of fraud.'

'My God,' Sally said.

'It's not the end of the world,' Harriet exclaimed, irritated by Sally's uncharacteristic behaviour. 'As Dad said, we have nothing to hide and hopefully he'll soon realise that and go away. But it's pretty unpleasant, especially for Dad, to have all this raked up. He's under a terrible strain.'

'Aren't we all?' Sally said faintly.

'Perhaps, but it's different for us,' Harriet said, mindful of what her father had told her. 'She was his wife, after all.'

'And your mother. And my sister.'

'Yes, I know that. But all the same . . . I think we should do all we can to support him. Sally, are you listening to what I'm saying?'

Sally was staring into space, still plucking at her pearl choker in agitation. A tiny muscle was working near her mouth, making her lip tremble.

'I knew something like this would happen,' she whispered. 'It's what I've been afraid of.'

Harriet stared at her.

'I suppose it's inevitable,' she conceded. 'But there's no point getting so worked up about it. I just wanted to warn you, that's all. And to ask you to support Dad.'

'Yes.' Sally collected herself. 'I expect you'd like to bath and change, Harriet. You must be exhausted. And I was going to try to get hold of Mark. I'll ask Danny to bring up your things.'

'It's all right, I can manage them. Don't bother Danny.' Danny was the chauffeur. Harriet picked up her hold-all and escaped. She was puzzled by Sally's reaction. Anger, yes, she'd expected that. But Sally had seemed really upset, not at all her usual contained self. She was getting quite neurotic, Harriet reflected, and the same thought occurred to her now as she checked her image in the full length mirror, tucking her camisole top more neatly in at the waist of her pants and straightening the ornamental clasp of the loose belt she had fastened around her hips. She only hoped Sally was able to get hold of Mark. It would be nice to see him and his presence would lighten things. Mark always managed to be deliciously irreverent, no matter how heavy things got. It was the

English in him, she supposed, that laid-back refusal to take himself – or anyone else – seriously.

Somewhere in the house a telephone was ringing. Harriet took no notice of it but a minute or two later there was a tap at her door and a maid stood there with one of the portable receivers – there was no extension in Harriet's room.

'For me?' she asked, surprised. The maid nodded. Harriet waited until the door had closed after her and flicked the button, feeling oddly apprehensive. The last thirty-six hours had held too many unpleasant shocks for comfort. 'Hello?'

'Harriet – it's me.'

'Nick!'

'Hi. I'm just about to go to bed and I thought I'd ring and see how things are with you.'

'Oh, I'm fine.'

'You arrived safely then?' He sounded so close he might almost have been in the next room instead of the other side of the Atlantic ocean.

'Yes. I've seen Dad and we shall soon be having dinner.'

'Good. Tired, I expect?'

'Exhausted.'

'But otherwise all right?'

'Yes.' There was a silence. There was really nothing else to say.

'I won't keep you then. I just thought I'd let you know I was thinking of you.'

'Thanks, Nick, it was sweet of you.'

'OK. Take care then, Harriet. And keep in touch.'

The slight sense of claustrophobia he could always arouse in her stirred. 'Yes. Goodnight, Nick. Thanks again for ringing.'

Then he was gone and she held the receiver for a moment feeling unexpectedly bereft. He was so good to her. So caring. Why couldn't she let him in to that private part of herself that sometimes cried out for – what? But she couldn't. Nick was there for her and she was grateful, but that was all. The moment she knew it she didn't want him any more, simple as that. What the hell is the matter with me? Harriet wondered briefly.

She glanced at her watch. Half an hour or so to dinner. She might as well go down, have a pre-dinner drink with Sally and see if her father was home yet.

Halfway down the stairs she heard voices and through the partly-open drawing-room door caught a glimpse of Sally in peacock-blue cashmere and the tall figure of a young man, fair hair above a chestnut brown suede jacket. Her heart leaped and she ran the rest of the way like a child in her delight.

'Mark! Oh, it's so good to see you!'

'Hey, steady!' He set down his glass and hugged her. 'Fancy you being in New York too. What a turn-up for the books!'

'I know. But I had to come. You've heard the news, of course.'

'Yes. I talked to Sally on the telephone last night. It must have come as one hell of a shock for you, Skeeter.' It was his nickname for her; he had started calling her that when she was small and it had stuck even though she was now a respectable five-feet-seven.

'For all of us.' She glanced at Sally, but her aunt seemed to have regained her composure. 'Is Dad home yet?'

'No. I hope he's not going, to be much longer.'

'I left him with an insurance investigator,' Harriet explained to Mark.

'Mark – get Harriet a drink,' Sally said. 'I'm going to ask Jane to hold dinner back a bit.' She hurried out, but not before Harriet had seen the haunted look was back in her eyes.

'What will you have, Skeeter?' Mark asked.

'Oh – better make it Martini. I've already had one telling-off from Dad today for drinking Scotch. If he finds me at it again he'll be convinced I'm on the slippery slope.'

'Right.' He poured it for her and watched with one eyebrow raised as she gulped at it. 'It's all been a bit bloody, I gather.'

'Yep.' She brought him up to date with what had happened. 'Your mother seems to have taken it pretty badly', she concluded.

'Yes, she does look a bit grey for her doesn't she? Of course she was very close to Paula, I understand. Anyway, let's talk about something quite different. What have you been up to?'

She told him about Paris and her new assignment for *Focus Now*.

'And what about you?' she asked. 'How is the advertising business?'

'Booming. I think I've just sewn up a deal on a new account.'

'Good for you!' She looked at him over the top of her glass. 'You're spending a good deal of time in New York now, Mark. I thought you were in love with London.'

'I'm in love with wherever the business is. And at the moment it's in New York.'

'Are you sure that's the real reason? It's not that you're deliberately staying away from London by any chance is it?'

He tossed back his drink. 'Now why should I do that?'

'Oh I could think of several reasons.' She eyed him shrewdly. 'But I think the most likely is that it has something to do with a girl.'

The moment she said it she knew she had hit the nail on the head. It was there in his expression though he feigned bored impatience.

'Now why the hell should you think that?'

'Feminine intuition. Who was it, Mark? What went wrong? You must have cared an awful lot about her to deliberately stay away from London because of her. Now wait a minute – it wouldn't be that young fashion designer, would it? The one with the place over in Whitechapel?'

He set his glass down sharply. 'What do you know about her?'

'Nothing really. Just that someone told me you'd been seeing her. It is her, isn't it? Oh come on, Mark, you can tell me!'

'Hasn't it occurred to you, Skeeter, that I might not want to? Being my step-sister doesn't give you a God-given right to know all my business.' His tone was still laconic but she heard the undertones and was warned. Mark could bite if upset – and of course he was quite right, she shouldn't pry into what was none of her business.

'Sorry,' she said.

'It's all right.' But he still looked a little spiky. The girl must have given him the elbow, Harriet decided. Most unusual – where Mark was concerned it was usually the other way round.

'Shall we have another drink?' he suggested.

She hesitated, then pushed her glass towards him.

'Why not? If Dad is going to brand me an alcoholic I might as well have the game as well as the name!'

When Hugo returned home dinner was served as soon as he had had time to change. It was a sombre meal in spite of Mark's presence. Hugo looked even more tired and strained than he had earlier, Harriet thought, and Sally was edgy and preoccupied though she seemed greatly relieved when Hugo told her that the insurance investigator, Tom O'Neill, had seemed satisfied with what he had been able to tell him and had not expressed any desire for a further interview or the need to come to the house to speak to Sally.

'He tells me he is going straight on to Australia to see Greg,' Hugo said. 'Let's hope the whole thing ends there. Though somehow I doubt it.'

'Why? Why should you doubt it?' Sally demanded. Harriet noticed her hands were shaking.

'Because the son of a bitch won't let up while he thinks there is the slightest chance of getting back his quarter of a million,' Hugo said.

'Then why don't you just give it to him?' Sally suggested. 'It would be worth it, Hugo, to get him off our backs.'

'If that were the case he could have it and welcome. But it would simply look like an admission of guilt and I'm damned if I'm going to do that when I've nothing to hide.'

'Sydney, New South Wales,' Harriet said irrelevantly. They all looked at her questioningly and she explained: 'I was just thinking aloud'.

'You're not still entertaining this foolish idea of going to Australia to try to see Greg Martin yourself, I hope,' Hugo said sharply.

'Yes', Harriet said. 'I am. I'm sorry, Dad, but I can't see it the way you do. I'm not prepared to simply brush it under the carpet and try to pretend it hasn't happened. I want to find out the truth.'

'For goodness' sake, Harriet, don't do anything so foolish . . .' Sally had turned pale again. 'You don't want to see Greg!'

'It'll be a wasted journey. If he's in police custody as he may well be by now they'll never let her see him,' Hugo said.

'I intend to try.'

'All I can say is I hope you weren't too rude to that insurance investigator then,' Mark put in drily. 'If you want to see Greg then he's got to be your best chance. You should persuade him to let you pose as his secretary or something.'

'Oh for heaven's sake, Mark, do you have to make everything into a joke?' Harriet demanded.

'I'm not joking – I'm perfectly serious. He'll be given access to Martin, I should think. He is a professional investigator, after all.'

'I wouldn't ask him for help if I were on a sinking ship and he was the only one with a lifebelt!' Harriet said decisively.

At that moment Sally knocked over her glass of wine. It ran in a red river across the polished table top and cascaded onto her peacock-blue cashmere skirt. She leaped up, dabbing at it with a napkin.

'Oh no! It'll be ruined! I must take it off at once and give it to Donna so that she can rinse it . . .' She hurried from the room.

'Sally is in one hell of a state,' Mark said easily. 'This business has made her really jumpy. She's not herself at all.'

'Is it surprising?' Hugo snapped. 'I should have thought anyone with a grain of sensitivity would realise how painful it is for all of us to have this all raked up again. As if it wasn't bad enough for us to live through it once . . .'

Harriet stood up. 'I'll go and see if she's all right. I don't want any more dinner. I am honestly not hungry.'

'Neither I think are any of us,' Hugo observed.

In her room Sally eventually managed to get out of her dress though her hands were trembling so much she had great difficulty with the zipper. Then she kicked it away and sank onto the bed covering her face with her hands.

God in heaven, where was this nightmare going to end? Was it really only the day before yesterday when everything had been so pleasant and normal? When she had been able to plan her charity lunches and her dinner parties, go shopping, gossip with friends, look at her life and know that at last she had achieved all she had ever wanted, even if sometimes it was a little lonely, a little empty? Now in every corner, wherever she looked, the ghosts of the past seemed to be congregating to mock her until she felt sure she must be going mad.

A tap at the door and without waiting for her answer it opened a fraction. 'Sally?' It was Harriet's voice, Harriet's anxious face peeping round. 'Are you all right?'

'Yes.' Somehow she got a hold of herself and went to pick up her dress. 'How could I be so clumsy?'

'You're upset. Let me take the dress to Donna while you find something else to put on.'

Sally let her take it. Then before she could stop herself she asked: 'You're not really going to Australia are you, Harriet?'

'Yes, I am.'

Sally caught at her arm. 'Don't go, darling, please. You never know, you might find out something you'd rather not know.'

Harriet's brows came together in a puzzled little line.

'Dad said something similar. You're afraid, both of you, that I might discover Mom isn't dead at all, aren't you?' Sally said nothing, and Harriet went on: 'You don't really think she could do something like that, do you? Disappear and let us all think she was dead if she wasn't?'

For a moment Sally did not answer.

'Your mom was a very determined lady when she wanted something,' she said, avoiding Harriet's eyes. 'She usually got it one way or another.'

'You mean you *do* think . . . Sally, she was your sister, dammit!'

'Yes', Sally said softly. 'She was my sister all right.'

She crossed to one of her closets, sliding hangers along the rail.

'Go back to the others, Harriet. I'm all right. I'll be down in a minute.'

For a moment longer Harriet hesitated, then she nodded.

'If you're sure you're all right.'

'Yes, really. Go along with you.'

The door closed after Harriet, and Sally rifled through her wardrobe looking for a dress of mauve-sprigged white seersucker, slightly yellowed now, and quite out of place amongst the designer gowns. She should have thrown it out years ago but somehow she'd never had the heart. She'd loved that dress, felt so grown up in it! She slipped it off its hanger and held it against herself and it was almost as if the face looking back at her from the mirror across it was fourteen years old again. As she stood there holding it the memories came flooding back – and not all of them pleasant. For she had been wearing this dress the night she had first glimpsed the truth about her sister, a truth that was as unpalatable now as it had been then.

'Oh Paula!' she whispered and suddenly tears were running down her cheeks, making rivulets in her carefully-applied make-up. 'What happened to you? And dear God, what happened to me?'

She stood quite still, holding the dress with arms folded around her waist, and remembered.

PART TWO

The Past

CHAPTER FIVE

As she climbed the stairs Sally could hear the low voices and the giggles coming from the bedroom she shared with her sister and knew what it meant. Paula had brought her friend Louise home with her and they would be sharing the sort of older-girl talk that always made Sally feel like an intruder – and a very gauche, childish intruder at that. She hesitated, torn between the unaccountable shyness she always felt in Louise's presence and the overwhelming desire to be in on whatever it was they were giggling about, even if she was only a barely tolerated spectator. Fascination with the older girls won just as it always did and she crossed the landing, an expanse of lino dotted with what her mother referred to as 'slip mats', pushed open the door and went in.

Two pairs of accusing eyes focused on her. Paula, wearing tight pedal pushers and a cotton off-the-shoulder jersey, was sprawled on her elbows on the tiled fire-surround, smoking and puffing the smoke up the chimney whilst Louise, stripped to her sexy black lace underwear, was lying on the bed pounding at her thighs with some kind of massager which appeared to consist of a collection of rubber pimples on a brush head.

'Sally! What are you doing here?' Paula demanded.

'It's my room too,' Sally said defensively. 'I can come in if I like.'

'Oh you're such a nuisance! Go and listen to the radio or something.'

'There's nothing on the radio. I want to get a book.'

'Well hurry up and leave us alone.'

'Oh, *chérie*, don't be so hard on her!' Louise said, still pounding away at what she considered to be her fat legs. Louise was French and luscious, as every male in the district between the ages of fourteen and eighty-four would testify – most from wishful thinking but quite a number from experience. Louise was what was known as an 'exchange student'; at home in Nîmes she was training to be an English teacher and she was doing a year's exchange as part of her course, teaching French conversation at the local grammar school. She and Paula, who was in the sixth form, had struck up a close relationship; when Louise was not occupied in tantalising and inflaming some poor young man she and Paula were always together, drinking endless cups of espresso coffee to the accompaniment of Elvis and Cliff and Tommy Steele on the juke-box in the Black Cat Coffee Bar, haring about on Louise's smart little Lambretta scooter, or simply spending an evening painting one another's toenails, plucking one another's eyebrows and generally trying to make themselves even more fatally attractive to the opposite sex, which, without doubt, they already were.

'You are not kind to your little seester!' Louise said reprovingly. 'Don't stand in the doorway, Sally, come in. Come in quickly or the smell of smoke will go downstairs, will it not?'

'Oh no!' Paula wailed. 'If Mum finds out I've been smoking she'll kill me. Don't you dare tell her either, Sally, or *I'll* kill *you*!'

'Of course I won't tell. But she's bound to smell the smoke anyway.'

'She won't. It's going up the chimney. And if you stay you're not to tell her what we're talking about either. Go on. Louise, you were telling me about Roger Clarke. Is he a fast worker? Everybody says he is.'

Louise giggled, ''ee theenks 'ee is. But I could teach 'im a thing or two. All he wants to do is to get his hand inside my blouse or up my skirt, but if I gave him the chance to do anything more he'd be so scared he'd wet his pants.'

'You wouldn't let him though, would you?'

'I might. And then again I might not.' Louise gave her thigh one more enthusiastic pummel, then sat up. 'There – that ees better. Do you want a go with this theeng, Paula?'

'No, it's made your legs go all red.'

'That will soon go. And it's better than being fat. But then, you are not fat, are you, Paula?' She gazed enviously at Paula's long legs, slim and shapely in the skin-tight pedal pushers. 'What about you, Sally? Do you want to try?'

'Don't encourage her,' Paula warned.

'Why not? Why shouldn't Sally look nice too?' She turned to Sally, who was kneeling in the corner beside her bookcase, trying to make herself unobtrusive. 'Come on, Sally, let me look at you. You 'ave fat legs like me. We big girls must stick together.'

Sally was unsure whether to be pleased that Louise was including her or annoyed that she had called her fat. She wasn't fat, but then neither was Louise, so perhaps it was all right.

She slipped out of her cotton skirt and the enormously full paper nylon petticoat she wore beneath it. It lay like a great wounded butterfly on the rug. Then she sat on the bed, trying not to wince as Louise rubbed cream into her thighs and pounded at them enthusiastically.

'What are you wearing to the youth club dance on Saturday night, Louise?' Paula asked, stubbing out her cigarette and concealing the end in an empty lozenge tin she used as an ashtray.

'Oh, I don't know . . .'

The older girls drifted off into one of their exclusive conversations and Sally bit her lip against the rasp of Louise's massager and wished desperately that she could go to the youth club dance too. Not only would it make her feel almost as grown up as Paula and Louise, but Pete Jackson, with whom Sally was hopelessly in love, was certain to be there.

Pete was in her form at school and whenever she looked at him little quivers she could not identify started deep inside her. Sometimes she thought from the way he seemed to watch her that he might like her too but he had never said anything and Sally was beginning to be afraid he never would. But if they were to meet away from school, out of uniform, no longer under the watchful eye of the masters and mistresses in their chalk-marked black gowns, then maybe it would be different.

'Do you think Mum would let me come too?' she asked.

'I shouldn't think so,' Paula said quickly.

'There is someone you *fancy*?' Louise asked perceptively, and when Sally blushed she turned to Paula. 'Oh, we could tell your mother we will look after her. Then she would let her go, no?'

'No!' Paula protested. Most of her life, it seemed to her, she had been hampered by having to look after Sally and she had no intention of having her Saturday evening's fun spoiled. There was a boy she fancied herself – Jeff Freeman – and she was busy laying plans to entice him away from his steady girlfriend. The presence of her kid sister would inhibit her horribly. 'She hasn't got anything to wear anyway', she continued scathingly.

'Then I shall lend her something of mine. We are about the same size, no? I shall make her so beautiful no boy will be able to resist.' She ran the massager up the inside of Sally's thigh again but suddenly it did not hurt any more. As the rim brushed her groin Sally felt a sharp sweet pleasure which seemed to shoot up inside her on silken cords to that deep core where the trickles of excitement played every time-she thought of Pete. As Louise moved away she experienced a powerful urge to grab the massager and tug it close to her secret places again but she did not dare. She just lay thinking how wonderful it would be if she could actually make Pete notice her. It had always seemed such an impossible dream, but with Louise talking about it so matter-of-factly it seemed almost a *fait accompli*.

Much to Paula's annoyance Louise persuaded Gwen Bristow to allow Sally to go to the dance. Sally was triumphant, but by the time Saturday came she was almost sick with excitement and apprehension.

Oh, if only she looked more like Paula! she thought longingly. If only she could lose her puppy fat and get her hair done at a proper salon instead of having it cut by Ivy Tucker who lived down the road and who did hairdressing for pin money. But it wasn't easy to lose puppy fat when Mum fed her on stodgy good home cooking – stews with dumplings and meat pies with pastry crusts and steamed sponge puddings, and there was no money to spare for proper hairdressing salons. Sally knew her mother had trouble making ends meet on the nine pounds ten shillings a week that her father brought home from his job as an electrician's mate and she didn't have the heart to plead for luxuries she knew they could not afford as Paula did. Too often she had seen her mother frowning with anxiety as she divided the contents of her father's wage packet up between the jars labelled 'Rent' and 'Electric' and 'Coal Money', too often at the end of the week she had watched her count out the pennies for a pound of sausages only to be able to buy just a half-pound, two for her father, one each for Paula and Sally, and only the scrapings of the pan to go with her own potatoes.

'When I grow up I'll make sure I've always got enough money for a whole pound of sausages and eggs to go with them,' Sally thought, but she never said anything. She did not want to add to her mother's troubles.

At four o'clock Louise arrived on her scooter and parked it outside the Bristow's council house. The house was semi-detached, which put them on a higher social level than the people who lived in the long uniform ranks, a pleasant, gravel-faced house which had been built after the war and which had a good sized garden back and front, three bedrooms, a bathroom – and an outside toilet, coal house and glory hole. Sally loved the house. Before moving into it the family had lived with Sally's grandparents and it had been very cramped. Their grandparents had made the lounge into a bedroom so that Grandad didn't have to do the stairs with his bad legs and a bedroom had been turned into a sitting room and furnished with a table, chairs and sideboard that her parents had acquired when they got married though they had no house to put it in. When Paula and Sally played records on the wind-up gramophone in the sitting room Grandad banged on the ceiling with his stick to warn them to be quieter.

After this the council house seemed the height of luxury to Sally. She kept rabbits in a hutch in the back garden behind the rows of cabbages and the clump of rhubarb and did not mind at all that in winter she had to wash at night in a bowl set on a sheet of brown paper in front of the living room fire because there was no heater in the bathroom.

Louise was carrying a large bag which she had managed to balance on the handlebars of her scooter. Paula and Sally took her straight up to their bedroom.

'Thees is the dress I bring for you,' she announced, pulling it out of its tissue paper and spreading it, slightly creased, on the bed. 'You like it?'

'Oh yes!' Sally gasped. It was a beautiful dress, white seersucker dotted with small mauve flowers. It had a deep 'sweetheart' neckline, little puffed sleeves and a full skirt gathered into three tiers.

Next out of the bag came a paper nylon petticoat with many more layers of frothy rainbow-coloured net than the one Sally carefully washed in sugar water after each wearing, and then, to Sally's delight, a saucy little white basque, boned and trimmed with lace.

'She can't possibly wear that!' Paula exclaimed, scandalised. 'She's much too young – and it will never fit her, anyway.'

'Of course it will. It fits me. And with this dress she needs a tiny waist. Why can't she wear it?'

'You could have lent it to me,' Paula said, peeved.

'No, it is for Sally. Please try it on, Sally.'

Sally held her breath as Louise fastened the multitude of little hooks and eyes and tried not to notice the little roll of fat that squeezed out above and below it.

'Now the petticoat.' It rustled satisfyingly. 'And the dress . . . well, what do you think, Sally?'

Sally tipped the dressing table mirror to get a view first of her top half, then her lower.

'It's lovely – but what about shoes? Mine are clumsy and awful.'

Louise dived into her carrier bag again. 'Voila!' she said, producing a pair of strappy white sandals.

Sally squeezed her feet into them and surveyed her image again. Unbelievable! Just wait until Pete saw her! He was certain to ask her to dance when she looked like this!

'Now – your hair,' Louise said matter-of-factly. 'We will make it wet and put it in rags. It will be dry by the time we leave for the dance.'

Sure enough, it was. When the rags came out the mass of frizz made Sally screech with horror but when Louise had teased it a hide with her Mason Pearson brush and a long tail comb Sally saw that the usually severe schoolgirlish cut had been transformed into a mop of pretty curls.

Paula and Louise were looking lovely too – Paula in a little white top with a boat shaped neck and a bright turquoise circular skirt, Louise in a figure hugging number which left none of her curves to the imagination – but for the first time in her life Sally felt she could compete with them on equal terms.

'Be sure to come straight home after the dance. And make sure you stay together,' Grace warned.

Paula pursed her lips and tossed her head, looking annoyed. But Sally scarcely noticed.

By nine-thirty the dance was in full swing. As it was a special fund-raising dance instead of the regularly fortnightly hop, a three-piece band had been brought in to replace the usual stack of gramophone records and there was 'real food' – fishpaste sandwiches, sausage rolls and cheese and pineapple on sticks – which the 'committee' had spent the entire afternoon preparing.

Paula and Louise had been nominated to sell the raffle tickets and did a round of the hall, flirting outrageously and telling all the boys the tickets were 'sixpence each or two shillings a strip'. Naturally most of the boys opted for 'the strip' and each time the innuendo was made the girls pretended it was terribly witty and original, if a little naughty, just as they did when they were asked for the twentieth time if perhaps *they* might be the prize.

Selling the tickets gave Paula an opportunity to make her play for Jeff Freeman. She waited for Jean, his girlfriend, to go to the Ladies, and then pounced, flirting madly and manoeuvring him into bartering with her that he would buy two whole strips if she would have a dance with him. Then without the slightest compunction she thrust her basin of money and book of tickets into Sally's lap and let him drag her, protesting theatrically, onto the dance floor. When Jean returned from the Ladies there was no sign of either of them, for at the end of the dance they had slipped unnoticed out of one of the wide-open fire exits and around the back of the hall where only courting couples went.

Half an hour later they were still missing. When she finished selling the remaining tickets Sally looked around for them, realised what had happened and went back to sit on one of the hard upright chairs which lined the hall. She was feeling wretched. For her, the evening had not turned out at all as she had hoped. Several boys had asked her to dance but she had refused them all, afraid she might miss her chance with Pete, but he seemed not to have noticed her at all in spite of Louise's dress. Once she had thought he was corning in her direction and her heart had begun to pump with excitement but he had walked straight past, heading for the bar that was selling soft drinks only (with a crate of beer hidden under the counter for the benefit of the band). Tears pricked her eyes and she stared hard at the floor.

'Wanna dance?' a voice enquired and Sally, looked up to see a boy in a velvet-collared jacket, drainpipes and crepe-soled shoes standing in front of her, a lick of greasy hair falling across a face shiny with perspiration.

'No thank you,' she started to say, then caught sight of Pete – dancing with someone else. Her heart dropped like a stone and somehow she got to her feet. The boy grabbed her hand with his sweaty one. She danced in a haze of misery, scarcely noticing when the music changed from vibrant rock-and-roll to 'the creep' and when the lights were lowered and he pulled her close she couldn't be bothered to protest though she was revolted by the smell of beer on his breath (where had he got it?) mingling with strong body odours. The teddy-boy seemed to take her listlessness for acquiescence. His hands strayed down to a spot just below the first frill on her skirt and he pushed his hips against hers so that she could clearly feel the bulge between his legs.

Suddenly it was all to much for Sally. She grabbed his hands and removed them from her bottom. Then she turned and fled from the dance floor, pushing her way between the smooching couples and heading for the Ladies, a box of a room with pegs lining two walls, a flyblown mirror over a grubby cracked china sink and two cubicles. Ignoring the girls who were primping in front of the mirror she ran to the cubicles and dived inside one, slamming the door after her and leaning against it. What a disaster! If only she could just go home, hide away and never have to see anyone again – but she had promised to stick with Paula and there would be all kinds of awkward questions and recriminations if she arrived home alone.

High heels pattered across the cloakroom floor and someone pushed at the toilet door.

'Damn,' said a voice outside. 'They're both occupied.'

'Never mind, they won't be long.'

'I haven't got long. If I don't get back and find Jeff soon it'll be time for my last bus and I can't go without seeing him. He is supposed to be my boyfriend, after all.'

'Supposed to be. Some boyfriend if you ask me!'

Sally stood motionless. She had recognised the voices – Jean, Jeff's girl and her friend, Peggy.

'I wouldn't stand for it if I were you,' Peggy was saying indignantly. 'I wouldn't let him treat *me* like that.'

'It's not his fault. It's that Paula Bristow – Lady Muck herself. Who does she think she is?' Jean's voice was rising; she sounded tearful.

'Don't upset yourself, Jean. He's not worth it. Nor is she. She's a fast cat. She'll let the boys do what they like. That's why they flock round her. You ask my brother. The things he could tell you about her would make your hair curl. She's got no pride. She just doesn't care.'

Sally began to quiver with anger. Forgetting her own misery and embarrassment she threw open the door. 'That's my sister you're talking about!'

For a moment the two girls stared at her, shocked, then Peggy recovered herself. 'It's true, anyway,' she said defiantly. 'And you're as bad as she is! You'll let any boy paw you too. I saw you just now with Gary. His hands were all over you!'

'You're just jealous!' Sally cried, her face scarlet. She pushed past the girls and marched over the the wastepaper bin beneath the sink. It was full of used cloakroom tickets, torn paper towel, bits of face-powdery cotton wool and the shavings of eyebrow pencils. She picked it up, went back to the two girls and dumped it unceremoniously over Peggy's head. Then she ran from the cloakroom, down the narrow dark passage and out into the night.

The sound of merriment emanating from the hall jangled her nerves, the sight of the courting couples pressed against the wall was enough to bring her to the edge of tears again. What an evening! Bad enough that Pete didn't want her. But to overhear Jean and Peggy saying those things about Paula was somehow almost worse, for in her heart Sally knew they were not far removed from the truth.

For the first time in her life she felt as if the veil had been stripped from her idol and she was looking at the real person who hid away inside a beautiful body, seeing her through the eyes of others who had no family love for her to colour what they saw. Paula was a flirt. She did think she was a little bit better than everyone else. And she was prepared to go to any lengths to get what she wanted – and almost always succeeded.

'Oh sugar!' Sally said. And therein the darkness, with half an hour to wait before she could even start looking for Paula with a view to going home, she began to cry.

CHAPTER SIX

After three weeks of misery Sally woke up one morning and realised she was no longer in love with Pete. The fact that her stomach no longer turned over when he looked at her came as a surprise and disappointment – even unrequited love was better than no love at all. A fortnight after she had made this earth-shattering discovery she was amazed when he stuttered out an invitation to the cinema. Hoping to rekindle the fire Sally accepted, but it was no use. Close to, she discovered, Pete smelled of carbolic scop, a dreadful turn-off, and when he kissed her in the dark it was so wet and sloppy she longed only to search for her handkerchief and wipe her mouth dry.

During the next year Sally fell in and out of love a half dozen times and each time it proved to be just as disastrous. A few boys asked her out but never the right ones, never the ones she wanted to ask her, and Sally began to wonder how two people ever came to be in love with one another at the same time. It was a miracle that so many people managed it – and for long enough to get engaged and married. But perhaps they were luckier than she was, or just plain less fussy.

Paula certainly never seemed to encounter such problems. She had a string of boyfriends and no matter how badly she treated them there were always others lined up and waiting. But then of course Paula was so lovely she had only to look at a boy to have him crazy about her, Sally thought wretchedly.

Then, in the spring when she was sixteen, the miracle happened. His name was Edward Blake and he was nineteen years old – really grown up! Besides this he was stunningly handsome.

It was the beginning of the tennis season. As a member of the school team Sally was expected to stay behind after school to practise. One afternoon after an especially long session she was forced to catch a much later bus home than usual. She sprinted across the playground, hampered by her satchel and tennis racket, just as the bus was about to pull away, and leaped aboard. The bus was full and the conductor grumpy. 'Hold on tight now!' he called, ringing the bell. Sally staggered down the aisle, trying not to bang the other passengers with her tennis racket.

'Let me take that,' said a male voice and turning she found herself looking into a pair of startlingly blue eyes. 'There's a seat here,' he went on, moving to let her in.

She sat down, settling her satchel on her lap and stealing another glance at him. Thick fair hair, a wonderful complexion – not a sign of a spot! – and those blue eyes! Sally felt a little flush of excitement creeping up her cheeks and she was acutely conscious of her gingham uniform dress and the beret which school rules said must be worn at all times when outside the school grounds. Failure to do so was punished by being forced to wear the hated beret for a whole day in school – for lessons, lunch, *everything*, a badge of shame Sally had so far managed to avoid. But just now she thought she would willingly endure any punishment if only she dared take her hat off without making it perfectly obvious she was making a pass at him.

'You aren't usually on this bus,' he said and Sally felt her cheeks grow hotter.

Oh please don't let me blush now! she prayed.

'No, I'm late. I've been playing tennis.'

'That explains it.' He shifted the racket between his knees. 'Do you play a lot?'

'When I can.'

'Are you good?'

'Not bad, considering the shaky start I had. When I was a first year I was put in as ballboy and I didn't know the rules. I kept throwing the ball back to the wrong player. Every time I thought I'd got the hang of it the service changed. And then I was sent to retrieve the balls from the headmaster's garden. I was terrified of knocking on the door of the house to ask permission but I was even more terrified of going back and making a fool of myself because of my ignorance on court so I spent the rest of the afternoon skulking behind the sweet peas.'

He laughed. He had a nice laugh, she thought. They chattered until Sally realised the bus was pulling up at her stop.

She scrambled to her feet. 'I get off here.'

He handed her her racket. 'When can I see you again?'

'Oh!' She knew her cheeks were flaming now. 'I don't know . . .'

'Are you getting off or not?' the conductor yelled, his finger on the bell.

'Can you get to Bath? I'll see you on Saturday – half past seven at the bus stop,' the boy said.

'Yes, all right . . .' She staggered down the gangway, shell-shocked, and walked home feeling as if she was floating on air but as Saturday approached the nervousness began. She could get a bus to Bath, but how would she get home again? Where would he take her? What should she wear? She didn't even know his name but she did know that this time she was IN LOVE!

The question of what to wear was easily settled. Louise had gone back to Nîmes now but she had left Sally the white dress as a parting gift and even without the waspie-waisted basque it was by far the nicest thing Sally owned. She wore it with a pair of new white sandals and a lacy white cardigan her mother had knitted for her.

At a quarter past seven she got off the bus in Bath worrying that he might stand her up. But he was there waiting and looked more handsome than ever in a grey suit with a white shirt.

'Would you like to go to the dance at the Regency?' he asked.

'Oh yes – only I've got to catch the last bus home and it leaves at a quarter to eleven . . .'

'Don't worry, I'll have you on it,' he promised.

The Regency had once been a Palace of Varieties. There was a bar selling alcoholic drinks and two milk bars, one at floor level, one in what had once been the balcony, and a huge multi-faceted glass ball which hung over the dance floor. A narrow gallery ran around the other three sides of the hall from which it was possible to watch the dancers or enjoy the band – a real band, at least a dozen musicians, all in uniform blazers and bow ties. Sometimes the big name bands came to the Regency – Kenny Ball and Ted Heath, Acker Bilk and The Temperance Seven, but tonight it was the resident band. The whole place seemed to be throbbing with the music they made.

Sally left her bag in the cloakroom and met Edward in the balcony milk bar where he had a strawberry milk shake waiting for her. She sipped it through a straw looking around with interest. The place hadn't filled up yet but she noticed that the boys were congregating at the end of the hall beneath the balcony and on the left hand side while the girls were spread between the tables and chairs on the opposite wall, chatting and giggling and trying to pretend they were not waiting to be asked to dance. A few girls were dancing together as they did at the youth club hops and the dancing was of the proper 'ballroom variety' – waltzes, quicksteps and foxtrots. When Edward suggested they dance Sally was grateful for the lessons she had endured in the school gymnasium with Miss Smart the games teacher yelling 'slow, slow, quick quick, slow' in time to the music.

Edward danced well, guiding her with confidence, and soon he was holding her very close. Unlike Pete he smelled nice – Sally thought it was Old Spice – and when he pressed his hips against hers she was excited by the sensations it aroused, not revolted as she had been with the Teddy Boy at the youth club dance. Over his shoulder she glanced at the clock over the door – the hands seemed to be moving very fast and she was reluctant to say it was time she was going.

At last she could postpone it no longer – she had just ten minutes to get to her bus! She collected her bag and hand in hand they ran all the way – just in time to see the bus disappearing along the road.

'Whatever will I do? Mum will kill me!' Sally wailed.

'Don't worry, I'll get you a taxi,' he promised.

He'd never ask her out again now, Sally thought gloomily. But as they walked to the taxi rank he said: 'Could you get into Bath in the week? We could go to the pictures,' and she agreed happily.

Edward paid the taxi driver in advance and all the way home she sat in a happy daze. The curtains twitched as the taxi pulled up outside her house and her mother was in the doorway.

'What on earth are you doing coming home in a taxi?'

'Edward got it for me.'

'Edward is it? Well all I can say is he must have money to burn!'

'He just wanted to make sure I got home safely,' Sally said smugly. For the first time in her life she felt she had outdone Paula, who had never, ever, arrived home in a taxi.

That summer was the most exciting Sally had ever known. Twice weekly she went to Bath to meet Edward, though ever afterwards he made sure she was on the last bus home. Sometimes they went to the cinema, sometimes they sat in coffee bars holding hands across the table, sometimes they walked in the park, and on Saturdays they almost always went to the dance.

Sally lived in a happy whirl marred only by worrying about *how far she should go.* After the first few dates when he had kissed and cuddled her and only touched her breasts through her blouse, he had started slipping his hand inside. Although she felt a little guilty about letting him do it Sally found she quite liked the feel of his fingers stroking her flesh and teasing her nipples but when he tried to put his hand up her skirt beneath her scratchy petticoats she tried to stop him.

'Don't, please,' she begged, grabbing his hand.

'Why?' he asked, creeping up further.

'Because.'

But he refused to take no for an answer and after a few unseemly tussles Sally decided it was easier to give in and let him explore inside the leg of her panties. At first it wasn't too bad but soon his finger was prodding right inside her and that hurt, a sharp, squeaky sort of pain like someone drawing a fingernail across a sheet of plastic. As he prodded around all the dreamy romantic feelings she. experienced when he kissed her disappeared and all she could think of was when would he stop, and couldn't he please just hold her again, very close, with the firm bulge of his body against her, far more erotic through several layers of clothes than his scratching, poking finger.

The next thing was that he wanted her to hold the bulge. The first time was in the cinema. In the darkness, under cover of which they had been kissing cuddling so much (with his hand inside her blouse) that she had not the first idea what the film was about, he took her hand and guided it down to his lap. Sally almost jumped as she encountered the rigid roll. She took her hand away, but Edward only replaced it.

What was she supposed to do? Taking a deep breath she gripped the roll and held onto it, not moving. She simply couldn't bring herself to stroke or rub it. But Edward seemed satisfied. He kissed her fervently and they stayed that way until the lights went up and the usherettes began moving down the aisles with their trays of icecream.

Sally sat with her hands folded in her lap, squinting down to make sure her blouse was done up properly and embarrassed to meet Edward's eyes. Presumably everybody else in the world did it she thought. But remembering still made her blush all over.

One thing she was quite certain of – she was in love with Edward and that meant she would have to continue to *let him* – or he would find someone else who would. Boys were like that – the girls at school said so. The trouble was that if you permitted intimacy you would be thought of as 'cheap' and perhaps be talked about as the girls at the dance had talked about Paula, only by the boys, which was worse, but if you didn't no boy would be prepared to bother with you for long. The dilemma threatened to spoil Sally's happiness but one thing she was certain of – whatever it took she would do it because she couldn't bear to lose him.

'Sally, I want you to do something for me,' Paula said. Her voice had that familiar note that was halfway between wheedling and autocracy and Sally's heart sank. When Paula used that tone it usually meant trouble.

'What?' she asked, rather aggressively.

'Sally!' Paula gave her a hurt glare. 'I don't very often ask you to do anything for me – and I *did* lend you my ear-rings when you went out with that Edward last week.'

'All right – what is it you want?'

'Help me get out of going to Gran's on Sunday.'

Once a fortnight on a Sunday afternoon the girls went to tea with Gran Bristow in the little house that had once been their home. Sally quite enjoyed the visits but Paula had no patience for making conversation with Gran, who tended to have very old-fashioned, dyed-in-the-wool ideas and was easily shocked, and she hated having to eat her way through the ham salad and bread and butter, Victoria sponge and tinned fruit and cream which. Gran not only laid on but also piled high on her plate because she thought Paula much too thin.

'Oh Paula!' Sally scolded. 'You know how Gran looks forward to seeing us. And Mum and Dad are going off on holiday on Saturday, so they won't be popping in to visit for a couple of weeks.'

'Exactly. That's why you can tell Gran a white lie and she won't know any different.'

'What sort of a white lie?'

Paula's face took on a vixenish wickedness. 'I did think you could say I had a cold because you know how frightened Gran is of catching colds. But it's a bit boring and it is the middle of summer. So tell her I broke the heel on my shoe as we were walking over.'

'Won't she expect you to come over once you've been home and changed your shoes?' Sally asked reasonably.

'You can say I twisted my ankle when the heel broke,' Paula improvised.

'But why don't you want to go to Gran's?' Sally asked.

'It's a drag. All my friends will be at the coffee bar.'

'I'm not telling lies for you just because you want to go to the coffee bar,' Sally objected. 'In fact I don't like telling lies for you full stop. If you don't want to go you'll just have to say so.'

'Well, if you're going to be like that . . .' Paula said slyly, 'I might just tell Mum what you and Edward get up to in the pictures.'

'What do you mean?' Sally demanded, but a scarlet flush was creeping up her neck at an alarming rate and flooding her cheeks.

Paula smiled, enjoying her sister's discomfort – and the feeling of power it gave her.

'As if you didn't know! But if you really want me to go into details Valerie Mitchell was sitting not far from you last week. And she was pretty shocked, I can tell you.'

Valerie Mitchell lived in the next road and travelled to work on the same bus as Paula. What she had actually said was: 'Your little sister has grown up, hasn't she? Well, enough to have a good time in the back row at the pictures anyway,' and she had certainly not elaborated. But Sally was not to know that and she was mortified.

Oh God, if *Valerie* had been shocked perhaps she *was* going too far! And if Paula should tell her mother she thought she would die of shame!

'I shouldn't think Mum would let you go out with Edward again if she knew what you get up to,' Paula said carelessly. 'But of course if you tell Gran about my broken shoe on Sunday there really won't be any need for her to know.'

'Sometimes I hate you, Paula,' Sally said. 'Sometimes I wish you weren't my sister. You really aren't very nice at all.'

Paula shrugged, looking very smug.

'Who cares about being nice?' she asked. 'Getting what you want is much more important. And I *am* going to get what I want, aren't I?'

Sally nodded. 'Yes,' she said in a small, ashamed voice. 'Yes, I suppose you are. You always do.'

In spite of all the worrying about it the next stage with Edward still took Sally by surprise when it actually happened. They were in a dark corner behind the bandstand in the park and had quickly gone through all the other stages, including the one Sally liked best, kissing and pressing the lower half of their bodies close together as if they were dancing. Tonight her skirt was rucked up almost to her waist and she found this was even better than usual because the bulge fitted neatly between her thighs and touched even deeper chords of excitement. So ecstatic was she that she did not notice Edward fumbling with his clothes until she became aware of moist clingy flesh, thrusting and rubbing. Her heart came into her mouth with a great choking leap.

'Edward – stop it!' she gasped.

He did not seem to hear her. He was rocking and moaning, his breathing heavy and catchy.

'Edward!' she protested, wriggling. She could feel the tip probing up the leg of her panties and she knew it should not be there. This was not just embarrassing, it was downright dangerous.

She put her hand down to push him away and he grabbed it, squeezing it around the erect penis and forcing her to rub it up and down. As she felt the muscular ridges pulsing and throbbing she almost sobbed aloud from a mixture of fear, curiosity and excitement, but at least the thing was no longer between her legs. Then she felt it jerk violently and Edward shuddered and bit her neck as warm sticky fluid spurted into her hand. She stood quite still not knowing what to do and after a moment he pulled away, reached into his pocket for a handkerchief and wiped himself, his hand and hers. Then he threw his handkerchief into a bush.

'Can't take that home,' he said with a shaky laugh.

Sally felt shaky too. She wriggled her skirt down over her thighs and when she risked a look she was relieved to discover Edward had done his trousers up again. Suddenly she longed to have him kiss her again and hold her close. That would somehow make everything all right. But he no longer seemed interested.

'It's time for your bus,' he said.

Inexplicably Sally felt like crying. He held her hand as they walked through the streets but Sally could not feel any of the warmth she so desperately needed. It was a clear night and there was an enormous moon which was reflected in the dark waters of the river Avon – it should be so romantic, Sally thought, but somehow it wasn't. She felt sadder than ever.

'I'll see you on Saturday, same time, same place,' Edward said giving her a quick peck and pushing her up the steps of the bus.

On the way home Sally could feel people looking at her and wondered why. It was only when she got home and looked in the hall mirror that she saw the enormous dark red love bite on her neck. Quickly she covered the bruise with her collar. Heaven knew how she would conceal it at school tomorrow, especially as she had games. Perhaps face powder or foundation?

Sally felt even more like crying. She loved Edward. But why did it all have to be so messy and complicated? Why did it have to make her feel so horrid and ashamed?

She was still looking in the mirror making sure there were no other tell-tale signs of the evening's activities when the living-room door was thrown open and her mother, looking very stern, appeared.

'Sally – come in here this minute!' she ordered.

Sally quaked inwardly. Oh God, she must have been found out! But who could have seen her in the park and reported back this quickly? Nervously smoothing her skirt and praying there were no stains she had missed, she went along the hall and into the living room.

She knew at once it was serious because her father was still up. Having to get up very early in the mornings he tended to be in bed by the time she arrived home on the last bus from Bath. But here he was, still sitting in his chair (and looking as though he wished he weren't) whilst her mother stood on the hearth-rug, arms folded and wearing a furious expression. Sally began to tremble in earnest.

'Well, madam!' her mother demanded. 'What I would like to know is why you saw fit to tell barefaced lies to your grandmother while your Dad and I were on holiday.'

Sally was so surprised she could only stare.

'And what a stupid lie too!' Grace went on furiously. 'Saying she'd broken the heel on her shoe! The minute your gran told me about it I knew it wasn't true – and so did she, or suspected as much, anyway. Why did you do it, Sally? You know I won't have you telling lies.'

'I . . . well, Paula told me to,' Sally said miserably.

'Oh yes, made up a story like that that she'd have known her gran would see through . . . I can believe that.'

'She did. She told me to say it.'

'I've already talked to Paula about this,' Grace said sternly. 'She tells me she wasn't feeling well. That was what you were supposed to tell your gran.'

'No.'

'Don't he again, Sally. I suppose you thought you'd paint Paula in a bad light and make it seem as though she couldn't be bothered to go. Well, I'm ashamed of you, I am really. No!' she wagged a finger to silence Sally's protest, 'I don't want to hear any more. But I promise you this, my girl, if you tell lies again, particularly spiteful ones, then I shall find some way of punishing you that you won't forget in a hurry. Go on to bed now.'

Sally went, relieved at not having had her love bite spotted but filled with indignation at having been blamed so unjustly for the Gran Bristow episode.

Paula was already in bed, reading a paper novelette.

'I've just caught it hot and holy for telling Gran lies,' Sally yelled at her. 'You've got to tell Mum I only said what you told me to.'

Paula did not even look up from her book.

'No. Why should I?'

'Because it's not fair! They think I did it to get you into trouble or something. You've got to tell them the truth!'

'I'm not saying anything. I'd only end up in the doghouse myself wouldn't I? Just leave it, Sal.'

'But why should I get the blame?' Sally cried.

'Because you're the twit.'

'And you're a horrible, selfish cow and I hate you! Oh, how I hate you!'

There was a loud bang on the door and Grace's angry voice

called: 'And you can stop that quarrelling, the pair of you. You're like a pair of tom cats!'

'I hate you! I hate you!' Sally hissed under her breath.

'Keep quiet, Sally, you heard what Mum said.'

'And I'll never forgive you. Never!'

But even as she seethed she knew it was not true. By this time tomorrow the whole thing would be forgotten and she would have forgiven Paula.

Paula could not help herself. It was just the way she was. Others might say they hated her and mean it. Sally never would. Whatever Paula did, however mean and underhand, however selfish, in the end Sally would find an excuse for her. Wasn't that what sisters were for?

CHAPTER SEVEN

Ever since she had left school Paula had worked in one of the big department stores in Bristol and she loved it, although the lengthy journey made for very long days and the bus fares ate holes in her meagre salary. But to Paula Ladies' Fashions was a veritable Aladdin's cave of delights.

She loved the rails of beautiful clothes – the tailored suits and the beaded evening dresses, the taffetta and lace and wool baratheas and most of all the furs, and when she could she would slip into one of the changing rooms and try things on. Because she was so tall and slim all the clothes looked marvellous on her and the other girls would groan their envy. It simply was not fair that anyone could look so good in absolutely everything!

Paula disagreed. The greatest unfairness, she thought, was that the women who could afford to buy the beautiful clothes simply did not do them justice, while she, who showed them off so well, had to save for weeks, even given her staff discount, for the most modestly priced item. All too often she had to watch the garment she had set her heart on disappear out of the store inside one of the giant shiny carrier bags with rope handles. One day, she promised herself, she would be rich enough to buy whatever she wanted – not only clothes but jewellery and perfume, real leather shoes and the very best cosmetics – no more Miners and Outdoor Girl from Woolworths!

Jenkinsons, the department store, occupied a grand old building in the heart of Bristol and a good third of the top floor was taken up by a restaurant – The Palm Court. Genteel and restful with lace cloths on the little tables, parlour palms in pots around what might almost have been a dais for a three-piece orchestra, and table service by waitresses in neat black dresses and white lace caps and aprons, the Palm Court was invariably at its busiest with morning coffees and afternoon teas when shoppers were tempted with an array of dainty cakes and pastries and hot toasted teacakes in silver dishes complete with lids. The clientele made a perfect captive audience and in the early autumn of Paula's second year at the store the management decided to bring in models to show the new season's fashions at the times when the restaurant was most likely to be full of ladies who had accounts with Jenkinsons and cheque books in their capacious handbags.

A local model agency provided the girls for the twice-weekly shows and Paula was detailed to help 'backstage'. When the three girls arrived she was surprised to find that in spite of their sophistication they were not much older than she was and as she watched them glide out in the first selection of fashions she felt a small prickle of excitement. If they could do it – why shouldn't she? She was as tall as they were, she wore the clothes just as well and she was just as pretty, if not prettier. Whilst dressing the models she tried to chat to them and ask how they had come by their jobs but they were not very forthcoming. It was as if they considered themselves above socialising with a mere shop assistant. Paula was annoyed but not subdued. Her own self-confidence made her impervious to the intended snubs.

One morning as she was rushing back to the changing rooms one of the models slipped and twisted her ankle. As she hobbled and hopped in agony Mrs Freer, the Fashion Buyer, fumed.

'We haven't shown the cornflower blue yet and I particularly wanted it to have an airing. At the price it is, the sooner I can find a buyer for it the happier I'll be.'

Paula, who was zipping one of the other models into a cocktail dress, felt her skin begin to prick with excitement.

'Let me wear it, Mrs Freer!' she suggested. 'It fits me. And I could model, I know I could!'

The other girls looked at her with dislike but Paula ignored them.

'Very well,' Airs Freer said after a moment's consideration. 'Try it on. Hmm. It does look good on you. But you'll need a little more eye shadow – blue to bring out the colour of the suit. And will the hat sit right on your hair?'

On the shop floor Paula wore her hair in a French pleat. Now she let it down and tied it at the nape of her neck with a scarf. Above it, the hat sat perfectly. A touch more eyeshadow and mascara and she twirled for Mrs Freer. 'Will I do?'

'Yes. Now take your time, won't you? Don't rush. Give the customers plenty of opportunity to see you from all angles and let them feel the cloth if they want to. And don't, for heaven's sake, bump into a table or one of the waitresses . . .'

'I know,' Paula said impatiently. Hadn't she been watching the models for weeks and dying for a chance to imitate them? As she walked onto the floor her heart was beating fast with excitement but her face was a smiling serene mask. She moved with natural grace, gliding between the tables, approaching customers who showed an interest to give them an extra twirl, unbuttoning the little figure-hugging jacket and posing with her hand on her waist, rucking up the jacket slightly to display the blouse underneath as she had seen the professional models do. She was enjoying herself so much that she stayed on the door longer than she should have done and it was only when she saw Mrs Freer making furious faces at her from the doorway that she turned and glided back. She felt as if she were floating on air.

'Over exposure won't help one bit!' Mrs Freer hissed as she passed her and in the dressing room the other models pointedly turned their backs on her, annoyed that an untrained shop girl should have been allowed to trespass in their territory. But to Paula's triumphant delight the suit was snapped up the moment it went back onto its hanger – a solictor's wife who had stopped for a coffee had fallen in love with it, even if the skirt did have to be taken up four full inches to make it fit her less-than-willowy tall frame.

'You did quite well,' Mrs Freer admitted grudgingly, then spoiled it by adding: 'Don't let it go to your head.'

The remark was lost on Paula. She knew now without a moment's doubt exactly what she was going to do.

On her very next day off Paula made herself up carefully, put on her smartest suit – a cheap version of the one she had shown in the restaurant – and caught a bus to Bristol. The model agency office was in a tall old house in Clifton and Paula splashed out some of her savings on a taxi so that she could at least arrive in style. Her stomach was turning nervous somersaults as she rang the bell but she was determined no one should realise it.

Arlene Frampton-Cox, who ran the agency, had once been a model herself – and it showed. She was tall and beautifully groomed with iron-grey hair, a smooth, high-cheekboned face and a most intimidating manner. When Paula was shown into her office Arlene looked up from a sheaf of photographs which were spread on her desk with just a hint of impatience.

'Yes?'

'I want to be a model,' Paula said directly. 'Could you take me onto your books?'

Arlene looked her up and down with a practised eye. Although she gave no hint of it, she liked what she saw.

'What training have you had?' she enquired.

'I haven't,' Paula admitted. 'But I did stand in for one of your girls at Jenkinsons last week – and I sold the suit I showed.'

Arlene's scarlet lips tightened a shade. She did not approve of amateurs, especially amateurs who thought they could step into the shoes of professional models.

'I'm sorry but I'm afraid there is no way I could take an untrained girl onto my books. Though it may look easy there is a right way to walk, to sit, to turn, to remove a coat.'

Paula's heart sank. She had thought she knew how to do these things but this imposing woman was making her feel very gauche, very uncomfortable.

Arlene's mouth twitched slightly but Paula did not notice it.

'Of course, if you wish to learn I do run classes in the art of modelling,' she continued smoothly. 'Twelve lessons is normal, though if a girl is particularly adept eight might be sufficient. I use a room at the Grand Hotel twice weekly, on a Tuesday and Thursday evening and do all the teaching myself. That way I can be certain my pupils are properly trained.'

'And if I took the classes then you would take me onto your books?' Paula asked.

'If you do well enough I would consider it.' The steely-grey eyes ran over Paula again. 'How tall are you?'

'Five nine and a half.'

'And what are your measurements?'

'33 – 21 – 32.'

'Too big in the bust,' Arlene said shortly. 'But I dare say we could get around that. A good strong binder instead of a brassiere – it's been done before.'

Paula shuddered. She had spent most of her life wishing she had 'more up top'. To be told she would have to get rid of some of the little she had was not what she had expected – or wanted to hear. But she was too determined to be put off now.

'When can I start?' she asked.

For the first time during the interview Arlene smiled faintly.

'Come along next Tuesday and I'll see you are enrolled,' she said.

'Modelling?' Grace repeated in horror when Paula told her of her plans. 'I've never heard of such a thing! Whatever put an idea like that in your head?'

'Why shouldn't I?' Paula argued. 'I'm the right shape – Mrs Frampton-Cox said so. And I want to do it! It's a wonderful job!'

'You have a good job.'

'No I haven't. I've got a crummy ordinary dogsbody job. I want to do something special.'

'But modelling! Whatever will people say? I've always been so proud of you, Paula. I'd never be able to hold up my head again!'

'Oh really!' Paula retorted. 'I shall be modelling clothes, not doing a strip-tease.'

'One thing leads to another,' Grace said darkly. 'It's the *life*,

Paula. It's not right for a young girl. Is it, Reg?' she appealed to Paula's father, who was reading the *Daily Mirror* and enjoying a Woodbine after his well-earned tea.

'I don't suppose she'll come to much harm, Grace,' he replied mildly.

Grace sighed with exasperation. Couldn't Reg ever take anything seriously? Couldn't he see, as she could, the moral dangers of getting into that sort of fickle world?

'I don't care what you say, I'm going to do it,' Paula said and Grace shook her head resignedly. Paula might look as if butter wouldn't melt in her mouth but when her mind was made up to something it took a stronger woman than Grace to talk her out of it. It had always been the same, ever since she was a little girl.

'Well I hope you'll look out for yourself and remember how we've brought you up', Grace warned.

Paula smiled, all sunshine now she had her own way, and treated her mother to a hug that was enthusiastic yet somehow oddly impersonal.

'I will. And when I'm famous you'll be proud of me,' she promised.

After only eight lessons Arlene asked Paula to wait at the end of class.

'If you're interested I have a job for you,' she said shortly.

'Really?' Paula's heart leaped. 'You mean you think I'm good enough?' she asked tentatively. She had enjoyed the classes but the first thing they had taught her was how much she did not know, denting her confidence somewhat, and she was still terrified of the daunting Mrs Frampton-Cox.

'You've done quite well,' Arlene conceded, keeping to herself the growing excitement with which she had been watching Paula over the past weeks. The girl had something – quite apart from her natural grace and outstanding good looks, quite apart from the lithe, leggy body that was simply *made* for modelling, there was a quality about her that made her stand out from all the others girls in the class, which drew the eye and held it, so that even someone as cynical as Arlene looked and wanted to go on looking.

Sometimes, in fact, she had felt she was in danger of neglecting the rest of her pupils for though her voice continued to drone on, snapping out an instruction here, a correction there, she was in reality watching Paula out of the corner of her eye, and experiencing the same excitement of discovery that she had felt on the day when Paula had first walked into her office.

The girl could be a top model, not a doubt of it. She needed a little experience here in the provinces first, of course, just enough to give her finesse and confidence, not too much so that she became jaded, and then . . .

I can get her work in London – I know it! Arlene thought, barely able to conceal her jubilation. Anyone would be delighted to have her, maybe even the top couture houses. The thought was a heady one. Though she had been quite a successful model herself Arlene had never reached those giddy heights – the thought that now a pupil and protégé of hers might achieve it made her prickle with excitement.

She glanced at the girl standing eagerly in front of her.

'It's a fashion show for charity,' she explained. 'Two of the big stores in town are getting together to put it on. There will be two rehearsals, one on the previous Saturday, one on the afternoon of the show. I shall expect you to be there promptly, with a selection of shoes. The stores will provide the jewellery and accessories. The show is on the Thursday evening, by the way. Can you do it?'

'Oh yes!' Paula breathed. Already her mind was busy with the practical problems – did she have the right shoes and if not how could she afford to buy them. And Thursday was not one of her days off – how could she be free in the afternoon? But somehow she would manage it. She'd beg, borrow or steal the money for the shoes, and if she was given notice at the store when she insisted on having the afternoon off, well, so be it. Modelling was going to be her career from now on. And she was going to make sure that nothing stood in her way!

CHAPTER EIGHT

Edward had a car – an ancient but still magnificent-looking Ford Zephyr. When Sally got off the bus he was waiting for her, leaning against the bonnet, smoking a cigarette and looking more than ever the dashing young man-about-town.

'Well, what do you think?' he asked her.

'It's beautiful!' she gasped, much impressed.

'I thought we'd go for a drive and put her through her paces,' he suggested.

Sally agreed readily. To go for a drive in a boyfriend's car seemed the height of sophistication. She only wished there was someone who knew her to see her climbing in.

The car had a bench seat in the front and smelled of warm leather and old cigarette smoke. Edward took her on a tour of Bath – perhaps he was also hoping to be seen by someone who knew him! – and then headed out into the country. It was a fine warm autumn evening and although the fight was already dying out of the sky the trees still looked magnificent, shades of gold and red blending with some still-green foliage. As they bowled along the country roads Sally sat erect on the bench-seat feeling like a queen.

After about an hour's driving Edward pulled onto the forecourt of a country pub.

'This is supposed to be a nice place,' he said. 'All the best pubs are out of town.'

The pub was picturesque and cosy with beams laden with gleaming horse-brasses, farm implements on the walls and a huge inglenook fireplace. They found a wooden bench seat in a corner and squeezed into it with their drinks – Edward had a pint of bitter and Sally a Babycham in a pretty glass decorated with a dancing fawn in a blue neck-bow.

Edward put his arm around Sally and little prickles of excitement started deep inside her. She sat quite still enjoying them. Why didn't they last when Edward tried to go further, she wondered? When she *thought* about the things he did they became even sharper, so that it felt as if an electric shock was passing right through the centre of her body. But the reality was different. All the lovely prickles and twists stopped and she was left with nothing but a feeling of panic, able to think of nothing but how could she stop him without making him angry. And afterwards there was just a feeling of let-down, of wanting him to hold her and kiss her and pet her like a little girl. No – *pet* was the wrong word. Petting meant doing *that* so no, she certainly did not want to be petted and much less to pet Edward. Perhaps there was something wrong with her, Sally thought glumly.

'This is the life?' Edward said, squeezing her gently. 'What a day!'

'We had some excitement at home yesterday,' Sally offered. 'My sister is going to model in a charity show. I told you she was taking classes, didn't I?'

'Yes, you said.' Naturally Sally talked about Paula. For one thing she was very proud of her, for another when she talked about her lovely sister and her exciting life she felt as if some of the glamour rubbed off onto her. But Edward had never met Paula.

'Sounds as if she's doing well,' Edward said.

'I know. She's only done half the course, and already she has been picked out for this job. I think she's going to go a long way – which she deserves to.' Sally speared the cherry which was floating in her Babycham and popped it into her mouth.

'Where is the show?' Edward asked.

'Bristol. Why?'

'Don't you think we ought to go along and support her?'

Sally was so surprised she almost choked on her cherry. She did not think men were interested in fashion.

'Now that I've got the car we can do things like that,' Edward went on. 'We could take your sister home afterwards – if she wants a lift, that is.'

'So we could,' Sally said, pleased. The thought that she was the one with a boyfriend with a car made her feel very important – one up on Paula for a change!

They finished their drinks and left. It was completely dark by now, a black velvety night sprinkled with stars. Sally sat close to Edward on the bench seat and he drove with one arm around her, somehow managing to change gear with his right hand.

When they were almost home Edward pulled into a farm gateway and turned off the engine. He pulled Sally close, kissing her, and she wound her arms round his neck, enjoying the first little prickles of yearning. All too soon however his hands began their usual wandering, slipping inside her blouse to unclip her bra hooks, pushing her skin well up her thighs and trying to slip her panties off. Sally sat down hard on them, forcing her legs together, but as usual in the end he won and she retrieved the panties from the floor, pushing them behind her on the seat before they were trampled underfoot.

'Let's get in the back. It would be much more comfortable,' Edward suggested.

'No!' Sally said, realising the dangers of the back seat. 'We ought to be getting home. Mum will be expecting me to be on the bus, remember.'

Edward ignored her protest, somehow contorting himself so that he could kiss her breasts, bare now, since her bra was around her waist, and still keep his hand between her legs beneath the rucked-up skirt.

Something about the feel of his lips tugging at her nipples began to excite Sally and though she still felt nothing but discomfort from his probing finger she relaxed a little, leaning her head back into the corner provided by the bench seat and the window. It really was a rather pleasant sensation. Edward contorted again, biting first at her throat and then kissing her full on the mouth, forcing her lips apart with his tongue. Sally could taste the cigarettes and beer and found that that too was exciting. Then somehow she was spreadeagled along the seat and he was half-kneeling, half-lying on top of her and suddenly she did not think that what was between her legs was his finger. It was less sharp, bigger, hotter and instead of scratching painfully it felt good. Carefully Sally moved against it and felt a sort of yearning begin in the sensitised area between her thighs. She moved again experimentally. It was nice – oooh, really nice. Edward was still kissing her, his tongue circling inside her mouth, but all she could think about was this new sensation between her legs, a little like the way she felt when they danced, but even better.

'Oh, Sally!' he whispered, his breath ragged. Then suddenly he lunged and the pleasant sensation was gone, replaced not by pain but by a strange, *full* feeling and Sally began to feel frightened again. She wanted him to stop yet at the same time wanted him to go on in the hope that the lovely sensations would begin again. She was also dimly aware that they had passed the point of no return – now she had allowed him inside her it seemed wrong to yell at him to stop or begin fighting him

After a few thrusting minutes Edward gave a strangled cry that seemed to come from deep in his throat and jerked out of her. He sprawled back behind the steering wheel, eyes closed, breathing heavily and clutching a handkerchief to himself. Sally lay without moving, looking at him in the light of the moon. She felt stunned, as if what he had done to her had somehow paralysed not only her limbs but her senses too, leaving her tense. There was no satisfaction, no pleasure, just a kind of aching emptiness. Then suddenly she became aware of how inelegant she must look, sprawled there with her skirt up around her hips and her bra dangling out of her open blouse. She sat up, straightening her clothes just as Edward opened the steamed-up window of the car and dumped the handkerchief out into the hedge.

'You won't have any hankies left as this rate,' she said, then giggled with embarrassment. What a stupid thing to have said!

'Who cares?' Edward asked grandly.

He reached for her to kiss her again and Sally clung to him

hoping that somehow the contact would make everything come right. But after a minute he put her away and started the engine.

'I'd better get you home,' he said.

Sally felt like crying again. There must be something wrong with her. They'd gone all the way and still she didn't feel any of the things one was supposed to feel – elated, contented, *together*. Now that it was over Edward seemed to have gone a very long way away from her, as if she was no more than a stranger to whom he was giving a lift.

For the remainder of the journey she fiddled with her clothes, trying to make sure she would look respectable when she arrived home and arranging the neck of her blouse to cover her throat where she was sure she must have another love bite.

'See you on Saturday – same place?' Edward said as he stopped the car outside her house.

Sally nodded, the feeling of let-down growing. She had hoped he might arrange to come and collect her now that he had the car – and now that things were, well, *serious* between them. But she didn't like to suggest it.

As she slammed the car door she saw curtains at lighted windows twitching up and down the road. Well, at least he'd brought her home. At least the neighbours would know she had a boyfriend with a car.

Walking up the path to the front door on legs that felt slightly wobbly Sally realised she would have to be satisfied with that.

Sally and Edward sat in the very front row of the audience at the Fashion Show on canvas hospital-style chairs. Two feet in front of them was the catwalk, a bare narrow wooden platform angling away from a curtained entrance. Sally stared at the curtains wondering what was going on behind them. Chaos, probably. Paula had told her there were twelve models in the show and each of them had to wear at least ten outfits. One hundred and twenty outfits, not to mention all the shoes and hats and gloves. How on earth did they keep track of them all? When she was dressing to go out Sally was invariably unable to find the belt she wanted, one shoe had gone missing or one stocking developed a ladder. But one hundred and twenty outfits – what a nightmare!

She glanced around at the audience who were appearing in twos and threes. Mostly they were very smart women in suits and soft draped dresses. Sally had agonised over what to wear – she was so afraid of letting Paula down – but eventually she had settled on a neat shirt-waister blouse and pencil skirt and Paula had loaned her a poplin duster coat in duck-egg blue with a thick soft grey Lucca Lamb collar. Sally felt good in it – the fur was gorgeously soft when she buried her chin in it and she thought that at least she could hold her own in the midst of all this elegance.

The background music stopped and was replaced by an expectant hum, then that too ceased as the curtains parted and a man in a dinner jacket and black bow tie stepped out onto the catwalk.

'Ladies and gentlemen – welcome!' he boomed. His microphone whistled a little and Sally winced in embarrassment.

The first model appeared on the catwalk, looking so glamorous, so unbelievably chic, that Sally could scarcely believe that her very own sister could be a part of this glittering performance. But a few moments later there she was – tall and beautiful in a little green boucle dress with matching jacket.

'It's her – it's Paula!' Sally hissed, almost falling off her chair in excitement.

'That is?' Edward whispered back, stunned.

'Yes, doesn't she look marvellous?'

Someone behind them coughed pointedly and they went quiet but Sally was wishing she could shout to the whole room: 'That's my sister!' She was so proud she thought she would burst. And so happy and excited that it did not occur to her to worry about the devastating effect Paula was having on Edward.

Behind the scenes Paula slipped out of one outfit, letting it fall to the floor, and reached for the next, hanging in the correct order on her clothes rail. The girl who was dressing her pulled up the zipper while Paula kicked off a pair of black suede shoes and eased her feet into crocodile ones. A quick flick of a comb through her hair – there was no hat to accessorise this dress – she reached for the crocodile clutch bag and moved towards the doorway for Arlene to give her a quick check before she stepped out onto the catwalk again.

She felt alive as never before, and her eyes were glittering with excitement. Her initial nerves had all gone now although it still felt strange to be on a catwalk rather than the carpeted floor of the room at the Grand Hotel. Arlene gave her a small push to indicate it was time and she moved out. She couldn't wait to be back under the lights again with all eyes on her.

As she sashayed down the catwalk she caught sight of Sally and Edward. The first time out she had seen nothing but a sea of faces, so hard had she been concentrating on what she was doing. Now she let her eyes dwell on them for a moment – Sally glowing with pride, Edward with a slightly dazed expression on his handsome face.

Not bad! Paula thought. Not bad at all. You have quite a catch there, little sister.

She did not dare look at them for too long for fear of missing her footing or forgetting a move but the look on Edward's face added another notch to her enjoyment. She twirled slowly, feeling his eyes on her so that it was as though she was receiving an injection of adrenalin, Oh how she was enjoying herself! She wanted it to go on for ever and ever! She was back at the curtains again. Time to turn, hold one last pose, then move out. But there were still eight outfits to go. Paula intended to make the most of every one of them.

'Well, did you enjoy it?'

'Oh yes! Paula, you were wonderful!'

The show was over, the audience had drifted away to a reception room where they would be further wooed with a glass of champagne and a selection of canapes and nibbles and Paula, dressed now in one of her own suits, smart black barathea, had emerged from the dressing rooms to meet the waiting Sally and Edward. She was still on a 'high', the potent adrenalin pumping through her veins, eyes sparkling, cheeks glowing with a becoming flush that owed nothing to the skilfully applied make-up.

'Did you see anything you'd like to buy?'

'Oh yes – everything! But you know very well I can't. And anyway, it was you we came to see.'

'You weren't supposed to be looking at me. You were supposed to be looking at the clothes,' Paula said artlessly. She was watching Edward out of the corner of her eye. Yes, he was every bit as good looking as she had thought he was when she had glimpsed him from the catwalk. And he owned a car! Not bad at all. He was only an office worker, of course, a clerk of sorts, Sally had said, not quite in the class that Paula intended to aim at, but very presentable for all that. And to think he was going out with Sally! The fact was somehow offensive to Paula's ego. In that moment she made up her mind. She didn't really want him, of course but she simply had to prove to herself that he would prefer her to Sally, given the choice.

She smiled at him and felt his quickening interest. It was so easy, so incredibly easy. What was the expression? 'Taking candy from a baby.' It summed up the situation perfectly.

'Did Sally say you might be able to squeeze me into your car?' she asked, fluttering her eyelashes.

'Hardly *squeeze*,' Sally began, embarrassed, then broke off. Edward was not listening. Neither of them were. Edward was staring at Paula and Sally did not like the expression on his face. She felt the pit of her stomach fall away. 'It's a big car,' she finished lamely.

'Are you sure I'm not making a nuisance of myself?' Paula gushed.

'Of course not. I have to drive Sally home anyway.' The way he said it made Sally feel like a parcel for delivery.

'I won't be long. I'll just get my things . . .' Paula disappeared through the swing doors. Edward gazed after her. There was a glow about him that all men had when they were around Paula. Sally felt sick.

'What are we going to do on Saturday?' she asked, catching at his arm, desperate for reassurance.

'Hmm? Oh . . . I don't know. Where does your sister go? Perhaps we could make up a party. That would be fun.'

For you, maybe, not for me! Sally thought.

Paula reappeared, carrying the little modelling case she had had to buy and equip with cosmetics, shoes and spare tights.

'I was just saying to Sally, why don't you come out with us on Saturday?' Edward suggested. 'We could go as a crowd.'

'Oh what a shame! I've already made arrangements for this week.' But her eyes were flashing – nice try, Edward. Ask again sometime. Who knows?

'Are you ready?' Sally asked. All the shine had gone out of the evening. Suddenly all she wanted to do was get home and bury her head under her pillow.

On Saturday Edward was late. Sally was frantic. He had never let her down before. Suppose something had happened to him?

She waited and waited, the feeling of living a nightmare that had been with her ever since Thursday intensifying. At last just as she was contemplating getting the next bus home he arrived. She ran to meet him, weak with relief, but he was very vague as to why he was late and there was a remoteness about him that she could not penetrate. Something was wrong she knew though she could not have said what it was and she was not in the least surprised when he made some excuse about being a bit busy next week and unable to see her. When he stopped the car on the way home Sally threw herself at him. Tonight she would have been quite willing to let him do anything he wanted just as long as things would go back to being the way they had been. But Edward just didn't seem interested.

'When will I see you again?' she asked desperately.

'I'll be in touch,' he said vaguely and though it was a long time before she would admit it to herself Sally knew it was all over.

That night she cried herself to sleep wondering where she had gone wrong and thinking she could not bear it if she never saw Edward again. It was probably because she was always so reluctant to let him make love to her, she decided. Everyone knew it was what boys wanted. If only she had been a bit more accommodating, a bit more enthusiastic. As it was he had obviously grown tired of the regular struggles and gone off to find someone who gave in more readily. But in spite of what had happened at the fashion show she did not think Paula had any hand in it until next day at breakfast. Paula, nibbling an Energen roll spread with reduced-calorie marmalade, said airily: 'Oh, who do you think came into the store yesterday? Your friend Edward! And I think you should know he wanted me to go out with him.'

Sally began to tremble. 'What did you say?' she asked.

'That I couldn't possibly two-time you, of course,' Paula said, watching Sally slyly. 'I told him that whilst he was dating my own sister it was quite out of the question. He argued, of course – said that there was nothing serious between the two of you and you knew that. But I was adamant all the same.' Her eyes narrowed. 'You are still going out with him, aren't you?'

'I don't know,' Sally said miserably.

'Well the rat!' Paula said, but she looked pleased.

'You . . . you wouldn't go out with him, would you, Paula?' Sally asked, hating herself for still wanting him.

'Oh Sally, what do you think I am?'

Sally did not answer. She did not think Paula would have liked what she had to say.

Edward never did get in touch with Sally again. She was sick with wretchedness, convinced she had only herself to blame – and of course the devastating effect Paula had on men – but still puzzled that it could have ended so suddenly without a word of explanation on his part. Besides being heart-broken she felt foolish and a failure. But she never did find out if he was successful in persuading Paula to go out with him now that he was free. She did not want to know.

Once, months later, when she went to the Regency on a Saturday night with some girlfriends she practically bumped into him on the stairs. But he merely looked embarrassed and said: 'Oh – hi!' as he passed as if she was just a casual acquaintance. During the evening she caught sight of him a few times, always dancing, holding his partners very close, and managing to avoid her eyes.

After that night Sally never saw him again.

CHAPTER NINE

'I have a very important assignment for you, Paula,' Arlene Frampton-Cox said. She inserted a Du Maurier cigarette into her long tortoiseshell holder and sat back, looking at Paula, who was seated in the visitor's chair on the other side of the desk, long legs crossed elegantly.

Paula looked every inch a model these days, Arlene thought with a touch of proprietorial pride. Her long hair, shining gold, was swept back and caught at the nape of her neck with a bow, make-up, expertly applied, accentuated the classically beautiful lines of her face, and she wore her well-cut suit with all the panache that was expected of her. A good suit was a working model's uniform – Paula now bought two each season and wore them with perfectly matching accessories, hat, bag and shoes. This one was in soft light green with a boxy shaped jacket and narrow skirt and the same green-and-white check material of the little sleeveless blouse had been used to line the jacket and face the wide reveres. Paula's bag and shoes were patent black leather, her gloves white, and she carried a long walking umbrella neatly furled in its fur-trimmed case. Perfectly groomed from head to toe and with all that assurance, she was ready to take on the world, Arlene thought with satisfaction, for she looked on Paula as her very own creation. The raw materials might have been there before – indeed, hadn't it been she, Arlene, who had spotted them? But the transformation of a leggy young filly into a sleekly beautiful racehorse had been her doing.

'What assignment is that?' Paula's voice was well-modulated now – eighteen months on the model circuit had eliminated all trace of her former Somerset accent. She had listened to Arlene's own voice and set about imitating it for she held her mentor in the highest esteem whilst still being a little afraid of her.

'The House of Mattli is expanding from couture into ready-to-wear and one of the big Bristol stores, Taylors, are putting on a show to publicise the fact that they will be stocking the new *prêt-à-porter*', Arlene explained. 'I have been asked to supply the models and I would like you to be one of them.'

'Mattli!' Paula repeated, impressed. The House of Mattli was a husband and wife team who were numbered amongst the top ten names in the Incorporated Society of London Fashion Designers. Furthermore Madame Mattli was a Frenchwoman, an accident of birth which added to her glamour, for was not Paris the fashion capital of the world?

'Madame Mattli will be coming to Bristol herself,' Arlene continued. 'Taylors have a certain amount of stock but she will be bringing extra samples from London especially for the show. I only want the best of my girls on this job. Madame Mattli, remember, is used to the best. We can't afford any sloppiness. I can count on you, Paula, I feel sure.'

'Oh yes,' Paula said, brimming with suppressed excitement. 'You can count on me!'

Madame Mattli was almost exactly as Paula had imagined she would be, a petite perfectly turned out woman with an air of chic that was unmistakably French. Her dark, grey-streaked hair, which she wore in a long bob, had been cut by Vidal Sassoon and she wore a beautifully tailored black suit relieved only by a little white flounce at the neckline.

In the fitting rooms at Taylors she fussed and fretted over her creations like a mother hen and though Paula was overawed by the great designer she also liked her on sight. Madame Mattli might be a stickler for detail, with a generous helping of the artistic temperament which kept her tight-coiled as a spring and which would explode into frenzy if the smallest detail was not as it should be, but she also had a kind face and deep perceptive eyes.

Halfway through the day's programme of shows, while the dressers went off to grab a sandwich and the model girls, who would not dare to eat while they were showing, revived themselves with cups of black coffee, Madame Mattli took Paula to one side.

'Little one, I would like to speak with you.'

Paula's stomach turned a somersault. Had she done something wrong?

'I have been watching you work,' Madame Mattli said directly. Her accent reminded Paula of Louise – perhaps that was why she warmed to her in spite of the fact that she was so awe-inspiring. 'You are exactly right for a couture model. You have all the physical attributes.'

'Thank you,' Paula said faintly.

Madame Mattli waved a dismissive hand. 'Do not thank me. I am not saying this to make your head swell. On the contrary. The fact is that I have a vacancy arising for a couture model. I believe you are exactly what I am looking for. I would like you to come to London to work for me.'

Over Madame Mattli's shoulder Paula could see Arlene watching her, a tiny smile lifting one corner of her scarlet mouth, and Paula knew her well enough by now to know exactly what she was thinking. She did not want to lose Paula, who was one of her best models, but already she was enjoying the reflected glory that came from having personally trained a house model for one of the great London couture houses. She had known about the vacancy at Mattli and hoped that the job might be offered to Paula. It was the seal of approval for her own judgement.

'Well?' Madame Mattli demanded.

'Can I have a little time to think it over?' Paula asked boldly.

'A little. But please do not delay too long. My present house model leaves at the end of the month and there are plenty of girls who would jump at the chance.'

'I'm sure. But all the same I couldn't make such a move without giving it some thought,' Paula said grandly.

But inside she was bubbling with excitement. Time to think? She didn't need a single second. The moment Madame Mattli had offered her the job she had made up her mind. She was going to take it – of course!

A month later Paula, smartly dressed in a new tweed suit with the obligatory matching bag and shoes, and lugging both her modelling case and a brand new cream leather suitcase, took the train to London to begin her new career.

She had booked herself a bed at a YWCA hostel for the time being. It was not quite what she envisaged for herself but it had the advantage of being cheap and it went some way towards satisfying Grace, who was convinced that London was a den of iniquity waiting to swallow up her unsuspecting daughter.

From the hostel it was only a short tube ride to South Audley Street where Madame Mattli had her showrooms – yet another advantage, Paula thought, trying to weigh up the points in favour of the hostel, which she hated on sight. Sharing a small spartan room with two other girls – Northerners whose accent Paula found almost incomprehensible and with whom she had nothing in common, making breakfast in the communal kitchen, queuing for the bath, adhering to a strict curfew after which time the doors were locked and bolted – none of these were restrictions Paula had the slightest intention of enduring for long. But for now it would have to do. And at least she was in London, centre of the British fashion industry.

As for the House of Mattli, it might have been in a different world to the hostel, with its air of being a cross between a workhouse and a boarding school. The first time she rang the bell and went in through the front doors of the elegant old house where the showrooms were situated (Mattli had no rear entrance) Paula felt she was stepping into the place of her dreams.

Deep carpet covered the floors and the stairs swept up to the showrooms and the warren of workrooms beyond, and though the window drapes and furnishings were ever-so-slightly faded, as if they had seen better days, they were of the finest silks and velvets and every corner was swept, polished and cleaned daily so that no single speck of dust, let alone a cobweb, dared show itself. The showroom was neither large nor small, decorated in muted shades of aubergine which would not detract from the clothes. There was a low table and three or four dainty chairs with aubergine velvet seats and gilded spindle legs. The crystal chandelier was for effect only – lighting that would show off the clothes to their best advantage was brilliant yet discreet, and along one wall were racks holding some of the ready-to-wear garments.

In contrast to this elegant frontage the workrooms beyond were a hive of frenzied activity. Pattern cutters, fitters, sewing hands and their assistants all worked at an incredible speed.

This, Paula soon discovered, was the way of the fashion world – a constant frantic rush against the clock, to have collections ready on time or to complete individual couture garments for customers who always considered their order more urgent, more important, than that of anyone else.

Paula was amazed by the security arrangements that were necessary to ensure that the new season's collections remained exclusive – the windows at the rear of the premises were heavily barred and practically the first thing she had to do on commencing her employment was to sign a contract promising that she would not breathe a word about the designs she saw.

On her second day Madame Mattli took her to Vidal Sassoon's salon in Grosvenor House so that her hair could be cut in an up-to-the-minute style. Unlike some couturiers Madame did not mind if her model girls did not have the same colour hair but she did insist on identical styles. By the time Vidal Sassoon had finished with her Paula's long fair locks had been shorn to a sharp geometric shape and she scarcely recognised the reflection that looked back at her from the mirror. Among the rich and famous who had come to the salon to have their hair cut, tinted and set, Paula recognised Dusty Springfield, the pop singer, her eyes big and sooty, her lips pearly pink, and was unable to suppress the thrill of excitement which ran through her. This was her very first taste of only the best being good enough – and she liked it!

It was Paula's job to show samples, parading slowly up and down in front of the clients as they sat on the elegant spindle-leg chairs taking in every detail of the garments with a critical and practised eye. Sometimes they came alone, sometimes with a man in tow – to foot the bill! Paula guessed. The appearance of a famous face in the show rooms always caused a stir amongst the girls, who all longed to hook a wealthy husband – and if he had a title, like the Aly Khan, or was a film star like Omar Shariff, then so much the better!

Not everything that Paula had to do was quite so glamorous, however. In the long hours when there were no customers to show she was expected to lend a hand with some of the unskilled tasks – running errands and making tea, unpicking a seam or a hem, even sewing on a button or a hook and eye when she had been taught the proper way to do it. Paula was not very clever with her needle but she soon learned to be careful so as not to incur the wrath of the seamstress.

There were new tricks of modelling to be learned too – how to remove a coat, sliding it carefully off her shoulders with the sleeves hanging in perfect balance, never for one moment allowing the inside to be on view, for samples were often unlined. This trick took hours of practice, up and down the landing at the hostel while the other girls looked at her as if she had taken leave of her senses.

Although she enjoyed her job Paula was lonely. Even the most popular of girls soon discovered that in this highly competitive world where models vied with one another for the most glamorous jobs and the wealthiest and best-looking men there was far more bitchiness than in the provinces – and Paula was far from popular. The other girls disliked her for her outstanding looks and her haughty ways and made no attempt to be friendly on anything but the most superficial level and the pattern cutters and sewing hands hurried home to their families and boyfriends the moment they finished their long day's work. Paula spent most of her free time alone, window shopping, visiting News Theatres, where she sometimes watched the programme of cartoons twice round, and drinking endless cups of Espresso coffee in cafes and coffee houses. Her favourite was the coffee shop in Fenwicks in Bond Street for this was the haunt and the meeting place of all those from the world of fashion.

One lunchtime when she had been at the House of Mattli for a few months Paula went there for her usual coffee and the cottage cheese salad that was her staple diet now that it was so important that she did not add a single half-inch to her wand-slim figure. She took her tray to the pay desk, opened her bag and felt for her purse. It was not there. Frantically she rooted round, then checked her pockets without success.

'I'm sorry. I seem to have lost my purse . . .' she explained.

The girl behind the till stared at her stonily. Paula was going hot and cold by now. Had it been stolen? No, she remembered her bag tipping over in the cloakroom at Mattli – it must have fallen out then. But without it she could not pay for her coffee and salad.

'Having trouble?' a voice beside her asked. 'Don't worry. Let me.'

Paula turned gratefully, then gasped with surprise as she recognised the slight figure in black roll-neck sweater and skin tight pants.

'I don't believe it! Gary Oliver! What are you doing here?'

'The same as you I expect, Paula – getting my strength up to face the rest of the day. Let me pay and then we'll have lunch together and do some catching up – unless you're meeting someone, of course.'

'No – no, I'm not.' Paula picked up her tray and moved aside, waiting for him, flushed with pleasure at seeing a familiar face. Gary Oliver was a designer, young and very talented. She had met him back home in the west country when he had come to supervise a show put on by one of the big ready-to-wear labels, Carnega, for whom he worked as a junior member of the design team. For a whole week they had worked closely together, sharing flasks of coffee and packets of cigarettes and Paula had grown to like the pixieish little man who by his very nature offered her no challenge – and no threat. Gary should have been a girl, she had thought, for he was half a head smaller than she was with fair curling hair, baby-blue eyes and long thick lashes that were the envy of every woman who met him.

'Shall we sit over there in the corner?' Gary suggested. He led the way, his slim hips in the tight fitting pants snaking gracefully between the tables.

They unloaded their trays on to a table.

'What are you doing in London then, Paula? Apart from mislaying your purse, I mean.' He grinned at her impishly. She told him.

'And what about you? Aren't you with Carnega any more?'

He shook his head. Dimples played in his cheeks.

'No – now I'm with the House of Oliver.'

'The House of Oliver . . .? Oh!' she squealed as light dawned. 'Your *own* house? You've set up as a designer in your own right, Gary?'

'Yep. In a small way at the moment, of course, but things are happening. I came into a bit of money when my grandmother died and I decided to put it to good use.'

'Isn't it a bit of a risk?' Paula asked.

He shrugged his narrow shoulders.

'Perhaps. But I wanted to work for myself. Designing clothes for Carnega was all very well and I made a good living at it I won't deny but I wanted to be free to do my own thing – and to have my own name on the labels. I have quite a few contacts – people who knew me when I was designing for Carnega – and they have been very encouraging. So I have decided to move to London and open a showroom. In fact I have just been looking at a place in South Audley Street, not far from Mattli. If it works out we shall practically be neighbours, Paula.'

'What a small world! I had no idea,' Paula said, surprised she had not already heard the news. Usually the slightest whisper travelled like jungle drums through the world of fashion. Until now Gary had been an out-of-town designer, of course. But if he was moving to London his new fashion house would soon be a talking point.

'We must keep in touch,' Gary said as he finished his cheese roll. 'Promise you'll look in and say hello when you have time.'

'I will. Apart from anything else I owe you a coffee.'

'True. I don't suppose I could persuade you to work for me in return? I'm looking for a couple of good models. Though I don't suppose I could afford to pay you as well as Mattli does – yet. Maybe one day . . .'

Paula laughed. 'I don't earn that much! By the time I've paid for my room at the YWCA and bought all the make-up and clothes I need there never seems to be anything left over. I'm looking for a rich husband to take me away from it all.'

'And I'm sure one day you'll find him. In the meantime, don't forget your friends, eh Paula?'

'I won't,' she promised, glancing at her watch. 'Oh hell, I shall have to go.'

'Me too. But it was great to see you again, Paula.'

They walked back to South Audley Street together, weaving their way through the lunchtime crowds on the pavements, the tall, striking girl and the young man whose pixieish looks belied his twenty-six years.

Outside the front entrance of the House of Mattli Paula turned to give him a quick impulsive hug.

'Thanks for the lunch, Gary. And good luck with your new venture!' She held up her fingers, tightly crossed for him.

He grinned. 'I'll need it. Don't forget to come and see me, will you? I shall be expecting you.'

'I won't forget. 'Bye for now!' she called, and ran in through the imposing front door.

Madame Mattli was furious. In all the time she had been with her Paula had never seen her so angry.

'I hear you have been seen going into the House of Oliver,' she said, her immaculately painted lips tight with fury.

Beside her Monsieur Mattli, a small Greek-looking man, some ten years her senior, was also quivering with indignation.

'Not once but several times,' he added. It was so unusual for him to contribute anything to the conversation that Paula glanced at him in surprise. Though he was always in evidence it was invariably Madame who did all the talking, giving orders, fussing around clients, so that Paula was never quite certain what his role was.

'Gary Oliver is a friend,' she said defensively.

Madame Mattli snorted angrily. 'I do not pay you to have friends in rival fashion houses.'

'He's not a rival . . .' Paula broke off. It seemed ridiculous that a newcomer like Gary could be any threat to a well-established house like Mattli. But in the cut-throat world of fashion up and coming designers were to be feared – and already Gary's reputation was growing.

'You know that we insist on complete loyalty.' Madame Mattli continued. 'The security of our designs is paramount. Oh Paula, how could you!'

'But I would never mention anything I have seen here!' Paula protested.

Madame snorted again. 'How can I be sure of that? Even if you do not intend to be disloyal there is always the risk that you might be careless. Pillow talk is the most dangerous.'

'Pillow talk!' Paula repeated, stunned. Close though her friendship with Gary had become she had never once breathed a word to him about the new collections she saw taking shape at Mattli – and as for 'pillow talk' the notion was absurd. There was nothing like that between them and never would be. Gary was not interested in girls. Surely that must be obvious to everyone who met him.

'You must stop visiting him,' Madame said firmly. 'Either I have your word on it or I am afraid you can no longer remain in my employ. I want you to promise me here and now that you will not see Gary Oliver again.'

Paula was trembling. Her job with the House of Mattli was her life. But to allow herself to be dictated to in this way when she knew she had done nothing wrong was tantamount to admitting guilt. And she couldn't bear the thought of being sucked back into the ebb tide of loneliness again either. With Gary she enjoyed a relationship she had never experienced with anyone else – the easy-going friendship of a male who made no demands whatever on her – and it meant more to her than she had realised.

'I have never betrayed any confidence and I never will. But you can't expect me to cut myself off from my friends,' she said.

'I am afraid I do expect it, Paula, in this case.'

'I can't promise not to see Gary again.'

'Very well,' There was a hint of sadness now in Madame's eyes but her mouth was set and determined. 'I shall be sorry to lose you, Paula. You are a good model and you suited me very well. But you leave me no choice. Please do not bother to come in again. I shall contact the agency for a replacement immediately. And I warn you, if any of my designs or anything like them turn up in the showroom at the House of Oliver I shall sue – and win the sort of damages that will put your little friend out of business for good. Do I make myself clear?'

Paula was still afraid of Madame Mattli – and she was also close to tears. But she was determined Madame should not be aware of either.

'Yes, Madame. I'm sorry to leave you, but I assure you you need not worry on that score.'

The showrooms of the House of Oliver were smaller and less grand than those at the House of Mattli but the décor was newer and fresher, pale grey drapes, ultra modern black furniture and a great deal of gleaming stainless steel.

Gary was in the workroom when Paula arrived, pinning a length of vibrant pink chiffon sarong-style around one of his models. His mouth was full of pins. 'What are you doing here?' he asked without moving his lips.

Paula perched herself against the cutting table trying to look nonchalant. 'I've left Mattli,' she said.

Gary stared at her for a moment, pins spewing from his mouth and catching on the front of his black jersey. Then he unpinned the length of chiffon and let it fall to the floor. The model stood motionless, clad in nothing but her bra and stockings, waiting for his instructions.

'We'll leave this for now, Claudia', he said. 'See if you can rustle up a cup of tea for Paula and me, please.'

The girl pulled on her wrap and moved to the door looking back over her shoulder as she went and Paula was aware of the hostility in her gaze. Why was it all women hated her so, even when they didn't know her? She shrugged. Oh well, she should be used to it by now . . .

Gary got up, took Paula by the arm and led her over to the low sofa.

'What's all this about, lovey? You can't have left Mattli.'

'I have.' Paula related what had happened and saw Gary turn pale.

'Oh Lord! You mean she thinks you've been spying for me! If she sues I'll be ruined. Even worse, someone of her stature could make a hell of a lot of trouble for me, even if she doesn't.'

'But Gary – I haven't been spying for you! I haven't even mentioned a single detail of the Mattli collection.'

'You know that and so do I. But suppose I've done something similar? It happens every season – by sheer chance and law of averages some of the ideas are bound to come up. There are always accusations of piracy and copy-catting, though they can't usually be substantiated. But if she can prove that you and I . . .'

That's nonsense! We haven't done anything wrong.'

Gary ran a distracted hand through his mop of fair hair. 'You're going to have to describe the Mattli collection to me. Every detail.'

'Gary!' she objected, shocked. 'You're an original. You can't steal their ideas!'

'No, idiot – not so that I can steal them. So that I can go through my designs and make quite certain that there is not one collar, not one cuff detail, not the slightest influence that they could accuse me of copying from them. Oh Jesus Christ! – suppose there's something major? My peg top evening gown – my beautiful cerise lace – I could end up having to rethink the whole collection!'

'For goodness sake stop panicking!' Paula said, though she could feel the seeds of panic herself. 'I'm sure there's nothing to worry about.'

'I only hope you're right!' he said in anguished tones.

The model came in with the cups of tea, still glowering darkly at Paula from beneath her fringe of false eyelashes. It was clear she was blaming Paula bitterly for the interrupted afternoon and her boss's drastic change of mood.

'That girl is a dog!' Paula said when they were alone again. 'I'm sure she can't do justice to your designs. And with a miserable face like hers I'm surprised you ever get any work done at all.'

Gary looked crestfallen. 'She's the best I could get . . .'

'Oh what rubbish!' Paula said roundly. 'Anyway, you've got me now so you can get rid of her.'

'What do you mean?' Gary asked. He looked like a worried small boy.

'I told you – I've left Mattli. I'll come and work for you.'

'Oh Paula!' Gary's expression became even more anxious. 'You know I'd give my right arm to have someone as good as you to model for me! But I told you before – I couldn't afford to pay you what you're worth. Well, not for ages, anyway. It's going to be a long struggle getting established and until I am I don't see how . . .'

Paula smiled. For the first time she felt the stirrings of something like power. It was not unlike the feeling she experienced when men looked at her and wanted her though she knew it could not be that for there was nothing sexual between her and Gary and never would be. But it was just as exciting, nevertheless. It made her feel strong, invincible almost, and just a tiny bit as if she had drunk too much wine. Her smile spread.

'Pay me what you can, Gary,' she said. 'You're going to make it big one day, I know you are, and when you do I shall claim my dues. Until then . . . well, I'll help you out. After all, isn't that what friends are for?'

He looked at her with something close to adoration in his eyes and the feeling of power swelled again. Oh yes, it would be pleasant to have a top designer owing her his undying gratitude – and that was what he would be one day, she was certain of it.

'We'll do great things together, you and I,' she said smugly.

'If we don't get sued . . .'

'We won't.' From the feeling of power had come confidence. 'Now, are you going to get rid of that girl? You might as well do it straight away. Strike while the iron is hot.'

His sweet face took on a look of anguish. Paula sighed and shook her head.

'Well if you don't want to I suppose I shall have to do it for you,' she said, pretending reluctance.

'Would you really?' he said gratefully and Paula almost laughed aloud in delight. Oh, how she would enjoy telling that snooty cow she wasn't required to work here any more!

There and then Paula made up her mind. From now on Gary would run things her way. And she was going to love every minute of it!

CHAPTER TEN

'Gary Oliver, I think it's high time you hired a secretary,' Paula said, gazing at the mound of unfiled paper spilling out of the wire trays onto the black laquered top of his stylish desk. 'Look at this lot!'

Gary pulled a wry face. 'I know. But there's nothing there that matters. Everything that needs dealing with is there' – he indicated another wire tray and a tall metal spike – 'and I just about manage to keep my books in order with Bobby's help'. Bobby was a friend of Gary's – and perhaps a little more than a friend, Paula suspected – who came in for a few hours a week to help sort the accounts, pay the bills and make the relevant entries in the ledgers.

'You can't rely on Bobby for ever,' Paula scolded. 'It was all very well in the beginning but now you're too successful for such an amateurish approach. You need professional help and you need it fast before you go bankrupt, get arrested for tax evasion, or drown in a sea of paperwork.'

'I'll think about it,' Gary promised, poring over his sketch pad, intent on capturing a new idea which had come to him.

'Don't think – act,' she said, coming up behind him to peep at the design – a short evening gown with a beaded bodice and frothy net skirt. 'The fact is I know just the person for the job.'

Gary added a few final strokes to his design and looked up at her, grinning impishly.

'Oh, yes, I might have known this was more than just a lecture about the state of my desk. All right – who is it?'

'My sister – Sally. She has just finished a year's course at Secretarial College and she's dying to come to London. She has all the right qualifications – shorthand, book-keeping, economics – and first class honours in typewriting. She is also very practical. She'd have you organised in to time.'

'Practical? *Your* sister?'

'We're not much alike,' Paula admitted.

'No, it doesn't sound like it,' Gary teased. 'Book-keeping, typing . . . you must be opposite sides of the coin, lovey.'

'Well?' Paula pressed him. 'What do you say? You'll have to make up your mind pretty quickly or she'll be press-ganged by Mum into working for the Admiralty or something. Shall I get her to come up so that you can meet her?'

'Why not?' Gary said grandly. He had been told by his bank manager that morning that a large new loan had been approved to help him expand his ready-to-wear operation – probably spending some of it on administrative help would be an investment. 'No, don't bother with the preliminaries, lovey. If she's as good as you say she is, just get her. I don't want to waste time on unnecessary interviews.' He got up, going to a shelf and pulling out a bolt of beige chiffon and another of coffee-and-cream lace. 'Now come over here, there's an angel, and let me drape this on you. I want to see if it looks as good together as I think it will . . .'

Smiling as she always did when she got her own way. Paula did as he asked.

From the first moment when she stepped off the train into the smoke-blackened glass dome of Paddington station Sally knew she was in love with London.

Perhaps it was because she had wanted to come here for so long, she thought, as she ducked to avoid a kamikaze pigeon. Her mother and father had tried to dissuade her – it was bad enough to have lost one daughter to the city they regarded as a den of vice – to lose two was unthinkable. But Sally had been determined. To her London was synonymous with glamour and excitement – to follow Paula there would be to have a little of the gloss rub off onto her in much the same way she had expected to attract some of Louise's

Frenchness when she had borrowed her dress for the youth club dance all those years ago.

She had dreamed about it whilst struggling with the unintelligible squiggles of Pitman shorthand and breaking her nails on the metal-circled keys of the ancient Imperial typewriter that was cunningly concealed in her classroom desk and the dream had spurred her on, making her determined to conquer both the squiggles and the stubborn keys. Now it all proved worthwhile. She stood on the platform, excited and nervous, and feeling a little as if she were about to launch herself from a very high precipice into a new and unknown world far below.

Paula was at Paddington to meet her and she took Sally by taxi to the flat in South Kensington where she now lived and which Sally was to share with her. Though she realised the taxi was an extravagance typical of Paula, Sally was slightly disappointed. She had been looking forward to going by tube. But there would be plenty of opportunity for that, she reminded herself. Paula might be able to afford taxis – she certainly would not be able to.

The flat was tiny – no more than a bed-sitter – one large faded room furnished with a lumpy sofa bed, table and chairs and an ancient cooker. Paula also had the use of a kitchen and a bathroom, the key for which had to be collected from the landlord who lived in the basement. The flat was not at all what Sally had expected – there was certainly no glamour here, not in the sofa bed, which was still made up with sheets and blankets from the previous night, not in the grease-caked oven or the rings onto which milk had boiled over, not in the heavy old furniture and faded furnishings.

Oddly Paula, always so immaculately turned out, seemed not to mind or even notice her seedy surroundings. She had been glad to get the place, she told Sally, and it was very convenient because Gary had a larger flat downstairs where she spent a great deal of her time.

As soon as they arrived she took Sally down to meet him and they shared a supper of fish and chips which Gary fetched from a nearby take-away while Paula picked at a few lettuce leaves and a pot of cottage cheese.

'Is he really the other way?' Sally asked Paula when they went back upstairs again. She had never met a homosexual before.

'Yes.'

'And he never even bothers you or tries to get you into bed?'

'Of course not.'

'Does he have boyfriends?'

'I suppose so. Honestly, Sally, I don't really think of Gary that way at all. He's just a friend. What he does for sex is none of my business – or yours.'

Sally said nothing but her mind was boggling as she tried to picture neat, slight, effeminate Gary with another boy doing whatever it was they did. But soon there were more pressing problems to occupy her – what she could do with all her belongings, for instance. Paula had cleared a couple of drawers and a tiny space on the curtained rail where her suits and dresses hung, but it was nowhere near enough, even for Sally's meagre wardrobe.

'I'm sure Gary will let you put some of your stuff in his flat,' Paula said. 'He has plenty of room.'

Gary was approached and agreed, just as he always did to Paula's suggestions – bulky items like coats and jackets could be kept in his cupboard.

Sally was not too happy with the arrangement – though she liked Gary she still felt curiously ill at ease with him. He was pleasant to work for, so grateful to be relieved of the headache of the paperwork that he left her to her own devices, and apart from occasional outbursts about the demands some client was making on him he was easy going. But Sally was puzzled by the close relationship he and Paula shared, closer in many ways than existed between the two sisters, and more often than not she felt shut out by it. Besides this she was still fascinated – and slightly repelled – by the fact that he was 'different'.

I must be old fashioned, she thought, Paula is relaxed with him – I've never seen her so relaxed with anyone before, boy or girl. Why can't I be? But the uneasiness persisted.

At first Paula enjoyed showing Sally around the capital, doing the tourist sites as well as her own favourite haunts. It made her feel very worldly wise. But it was less fun – and a good deal more expensive – than being squired by one of her string of boyfriends and when Sally had been in London for about six weeks Paula decided it was time to do something about it.

'How would you like to go to a club for dinner and dance?' she asked Sally one evening. 'I've talked to Graham about it and he says he'll bring along a friend for you.' Graham was ten years older than she was and had a used car business in Clapham – not quite Paula's ideal, but he was good looking in a rather smooth way, generous, liked the high life and owing to his business drove a succession of impressive motor cars.

'I haven't anything to wear,' Sally said feebly, experiencing an attack of nerves, although she had been dying to see something of the London scene nightlife.

'Rubbish! How can you say that – and when you're Girl Friday to a designer too!'

Gary was prevailed upon and he agreed to let Sally have one of the season's samples which had not sold well but which Sally adored – a simple sheath of sea-green satin. On Sally, who was a whole size larger than the models, it was sexily tight and revealing even though it was let out to the limits of the seam allowances and it had to be shortened by several inches.

'Why am I so short and fat?' Sally wailed.

'You're not short or fat,' Gary comforted her. 'It's just that models are such beanpoles.'

He said it as if he actually preferred Sally's shape, professional considerations aside, and she felt herself warming to him. It *was* nice to be paid compliments by a man when one knew he was not saying it in order to try and talk one into bed!

By Saturday evening Sally was having second thoughts. She had never liked blind dates – someone was bound to be disappointed and anyhow how could you possibly talk normally to a man knowing you had been forced upon him and had an obligation to be entertaining? But it was too late to back down now.

When the men arrived Sally was favourably surprised. Tony, her date, was tall and rangy with thickly waving dark hair and in his black dinner jacket and frilly shirt he looked almost aggressively handsome. She cast sidelong looks at him as she sat beside, him in the back of Graham's car – a powder-blue Jaguar. Not bad – not bad at all! As for Tony, if he was disappointed in her he certainly did not show it. In fact he was eyeing her curves, clearly obvious beneath the satin sheath, with frank approval and even before they were out of London he had reached for her hand and was holding it on his black-trousered leg.

In spite of being flattered Sally was glad she was not alone with him. He was so much older than any of the boys she had been out with.

The club, some way out of town, was another new experience for Sally. The tables looked out on the floodlit river and behind them the orchestra played for dancing on a floor almost as large as the Regency ballroom. Everyone wore evening dress and for once Sally did not feel envious of Paula, for Tony was extremely courteous and attentive to her. They drank champagne and Sally began to feel a little light-headed. When they danced Tony held her very close and she laid her face against his shoulder, further intoxicated by the smell of his aftershave and the faint aroma of cigars.

When it was time to leave Tony helped her on with her stole and left his arm around her shoulders. She teetered along beside him on her high heels, the fresh air making her faintly dizzy. In the back seat of the Jaguar he began to kiss her and she tried to wriggle away, casting embarrassed glances at Paula and Graham. But Paula was snuggled into Graham's shoulder as he drove fast and expertly and the swaying of the car threw Sally back into Tony's arms. He kissed her again, differently, more deeply than she had ever been kissed before. There was something erotic but also a little threatening about the way his mouth took hers and when he drove his tongue inside she could scarcely breathe. His hand was inside her dress, fondling her breasts with a pumping motion that was in no way hesitant and she did not know how to stop him without attracting Paula's attention. She was beginning to feel trapped and frightened, wondering just what was expected of her, and the glamour of the evening was fast fading into something almost sordid.

She was greatly relieved to find herself back in Kensington but her relief was short lived for it quickly became apparent that the others considered the night to be still young.

'Coffee?' Paula suggested, waving her keys teasingly under Graham's nose, and they all bundled out and climbed the stairs.

Paula disappeared into the little kitchen, Graham following, and Sally was left alone with Tony. Without any preamble he dragged her down on the sofa bed thrusting his hand up inside her narrow satin skirt. Sally resisted, almost more afraid that he would tear it than she was of his probing fingers.

'Come on, baby, what's the matter with you?' he whispered.

'The others will be back in a minute!' she whispered back.

He laughed. 'No they won't. Not for half an hour at least.'

'I'm going to help Paula with the coffee.' She wriggled free and went out onto the landing. The kitchen door was almost closed. She pushed it open and froze. Paula was backed up against the sink, skirt rucked up to her hips, long legs splayed. Graham was hunched over her, his face buried in her tiny breasts. Although his back was towards her Sally knew that his trousers were open.

She gasped and backed out of the kitchen, colour flooding her cheeks. Ridiculously she was shocked. She knew Paula was – well, free with her favours, had known for years, but to actually find her like that in the kitchen, shamelessly doing it up against the sink . . .

Tony had followed her onto the landing. As she turned there he was leering at her. Suddenly he didn't look handsome at all, merely lecherous. Sally was overcome with panic and could think of only one route of escape.

'I have to go downstairs for a minute,' she blustered.

As she ran down the stairs she saw the crick of light around Gary's door and was overcome with longing for his undemanding company. This was what Paula liked about him, she realised. He was a man to be at ease with, who could be trusted not to try to force himself upon you – not to think of it even.

She knocked on Gary's door and tried the handle. The door was locked. 'Gary?' she called. 'Are you there?'

The sounds of movement within the room gave an affirmative answer though it seemed a very long time before the door opened a few inches on its safety chain and Gary peered round. He was wearing a dressing gown, she noticed, and he did not look very pleased to see her.

'Gary please . . . can I come in?' she asked.

Gary coloured. He no longer looked only unwelcoming, but also flustered and almost shifty. 'It's not really a very good . . .'

'Gary! Who is it?' a man's petulant voice called from within the flat.

'It's Sally from upstairs,' Gary called back.

'Well get rid of her, can't you, for Christ's sake?'

Gary's flush deepened. 'I'm sorry,' he said helplessly. 'I've got company and . . .'

'It's all right,' Sally muttered. 'I'm sorry – for interrupting.'

She turned away, ridiculously embarrassed. She had known about Gary, of course, but it was still a shock to practically catch him in the act, just as it had been to walk in on Paula and Graham.

She went into the little lavatory, locked the door and sat down on the wonky seat, feeling rather sick and extremely sorry for herself. What was the matter with everybody? All any of them wanted was sex – sex – sex! All except her. Perhaps it wasn't the rest of the world that was out of step. Perhaps it was her. What the hell was the matter with her? She must be frigid. She would never be normal. But if this was normal then she didn't want to be. It was awful. She felt so terribly mixed up . . .

Some time later she heard footsteps, tapping on the door, and Paula calling in a low anxious voice: 'Sally, are you in there? Are you all right?'

'Yes, I'm all right,' she called back.

'Well come out for goodness' sake.'

She was trembling. 'I don't want to.'

'Don't be so stupid! What's the matter? Sally, open this door!'

Reluctantly she did so.

'What the hell are you doing in there?' Paula asked furiously.

'Everybody wants the loo. You're behaving like a child!' Her hair was mussed, her lipstick smudged. She didn't look glamorous any more, just *used*, Sally thought wretchedly.

'Where is Tony?' she asked.

'Gone home. He said you were a waste of time – a cock teaser. Sally, how could you?'

'How could *you*?' Sally threw at her through chattering teeth. 'I saw you, Paula, in the kitchen. You're disgusting.'

'At least I'm not a stupid little baby. Oh come out of there for goodness' sake. Nobody's going to rape you.'

Because there was nothing else to do Sally did as she was told. But halfway up the stairs the taste of stale champagne rose in her throat, bitter now like bile, and Sally dived into the kitchen where she was violently sick.

CHAPTER ELEVEN

One autumn morning Gary came bursting out of his workroom in a state of great excitement. Plans were underway for the annual private showing by the Incorporated Society of London Fashion Designers, a charity event for an invited audience which always included royalty, and this year the House of Oliver had been invited to take part.

'How do you like this, lovey?' Gary asked ecstatically, whhling Paula round the showroom in a wild dance that sent one of his tubular chairs flying. 'We've made it! Just imagine, you'll be showing to the Queen Mother!'

'I'd be showing to the Queen Mother if I'd stayed with Mattli,' Paula pointed out. 'In fact I'd probably have done it last year as well. The House of Mattli is always included.'

'Don't preen, lovey. I don't intend to let you spoil this for me. I've made it – and I'm going to steal the show!'

'I'm only teasing, Gary.' She kissed him. 'I'm really happy for you. When is it?'

'At the beginning of December. In the Crush Bar at Covent Garden. Oh hell, will I ever be ready?'

'Of course – if you stop dancing about and get down to some work!'

'Seven outfits! Seven glorious outfits! They have to be perfect.' He turned to Sally. 'Get Madame Fontaine on the telephone for me, will you? I must talk to her about this at once.' Madame Fontaine was the milliner who made the hats to compliment Gary's clothes. 'Then chase Courtaulds. The houndstooth suiting I ordered from them hasn't arrived. You did place the order, didn't you?

Jewellery. Let's think about jewellery. I think I'll approach Asprey or David Morris. Might as well start at the top . . .'

'And while you're about it you'd better order some sandwiches,' Paula added. 'If there isn't food at Gary's elbow he'll probably forget to eat!'

Sally nodded, making notes on the pad she carried around with her. She was growing used to the constant whirl now and she quite enjoyed it. She was good at her job, she knew, and realising how much Gary had come to depend on her gave her a new sense of her own worth. Maybe she would never be as glamorous as Paula, maybe she would never have her talent for attracting men, but she had found her own little niche at last and in her own way she almost felt herself Paula's equal.

The grey days of November raced by at breakneck pace. The Christmas lights had been switched on in Oxford Street but they were too busy even to notice. Gary was working around the clock and he expected his entire staff to do the same. But at least they went home to their beds every night, albeit late and exhausted. Gary often did not. He had taken to sleeping on the couch in the little office at the rear of the showroom, partly so that he could continue working until he was ready to drop, partly for security reasons.

'If anyone stole my collection now I'd top myself,' he said to Paula – and she was inclined to believe he meant it. His nerves were tight as a drawn spring and he veered wildly between elation, panic and depression when he agonised over his recurring nightmare that his designs would be greeted not with enthusiasm but by silence or perhaps only the most restrained patter of polite applause. Thin as he was he still managed to lose half a stone in weight and he was liable to scream hysterical indignation or even burst into tears if anyone said a wrong word.

The first time this happened Sally was embarrassed, the second irritated and the third seriously worried. What on earth would they do if Gary cracked up? But somehow after a cup of black coffee, a comforting hug from Paula and one of the chocolate biscuits from the tin they kept in the office he always bucked up, reverting to the enthusiasm that verged on desperation.

When the great day arrived they had to be at Covent Garden by six in the morning for rehearsals. Preparations had reached fever pitch. Assistant stage managers rushed around with sheafs of notes, florists put the finishing touches to huge impressive displays and the air was occasionally split by loud winnings and explosions of music as Strand Electrics tested and corrected the sound equipment.

In the theatre the Royal Ballet were rehearsing but to Paula's chagrin the girls had all been forbidden to watch.

'Do you think we might be able to creep in during our lunch break?' she suggested to Sally.

Sally looked doubtful. 'We'd be murdered if we were caught.'

'It would be worth it though. Let's try.'

Partly because she was so used to following Paula's lead and partly because she felt oddly responsible and thought she might be able to urge caution on her headstrong sister Sally gave in. The two girls crept upstairs to one of the boxes, opened the door a crack, terrified someone might glance up and see the sliver of light, and crawled into the box on hands and knees. Then with the door safely closed again they cautiously raised themselves so that they could peep over the edge at the magic scene below.

When rehearsals recommenced it seemed some order was at last emerging from the chaos.

'I wonder if the Queen Mum knows what we go through to put this on?' one model groaned to Paula, massaging her aching feet after yet another trip down the glorious sweeping staircase to the catwalk.

'She probably goes through much the same herself,' replied Paula, who had always thought that smiling and waving and shaking endless rows of hands must be even more wearing than modelling. 'In any case this time tomorrow it will all be over. Make the most of it while you can!'

Amongst the audience who headed for the Crush Bar that evening was a young American designer who had created a great stir on the New York fashion scene.

Already Hugo Varna was a name to reckon with. He had a showroom on Seventh Avenue, appeared regularly in *Vogue* and *Womens Wear Daily,* and had been hailed as one of the most exciting designers in years, along with Bill Blass, who had transformed the 'fat lady' image of Rentner's into something more youthful and glamorous, and was now a vice-president of that company; Oscar de la Renta, Elizabeth Arden's stylish new designer; and Geoffrey Beene. At thirty-three years of age Hugo exuded an aura of success which somehow made those who met him forget that he was not a handsome man. Without it his unimposing height (five-feet-six in his stockinged feet, five-feet-eight in the high-heeled cowboy boots he liked to wear), his prematurely receding hairline and the slight flatness of features which he had inherited from his father might have made him appear ordinary. But he was also the possessor of a towering personality and energy powerful as a surge of electrical current and no one, not even his enemies, of which there were certainly a few, thought of Hugo as ordinary.

Although he spent his life surrounded by beautiful women Hugo had never married, and occasionally it was whispered that, like so many male designers, he might be AC/DC. But the simple truth was that he had never had time to form a relationship. To Hugo work came first, last and in between; he ate, drank, slept and lived fashion. Apart from the socialising which was a necessary part of building up a clientele, every waking hour was spent in the studio which he had found with the help of Greg Martin, his friend and financial adviser, and after the dinner parties and balls, which were more an exercise in public relations than a pleasure, he returned to his apartment and fell into bed alone.

Twice a year Hugo went to Paris to take a look at the best of the new seasons' designs, but otherwise he hardly ever left the United States, taking a rare holiday, when he felt the need for one, in the sunshine of Florida or the peace of the cottage he had bought as a hideaway in New England. But when the invitation to the

Royal Showing had arrived in his morning mail he was sorely tempted.

Like all Americans Hugo was fascinated by the British heritage and the idea of spending an evening in the company of Her Majesty Queen Elizabeth the Queen Mother and a princess of the royal blood, even though he was unlikely to see them except at a distance, appealed to his romantic nature. Perhaps he should accept, and have a look at what the British designers were doing, he thought, inventing excuses so as not to admit, even to himself, that he was starstruck. And besides, the House of Oliver was amongst those showing this year. Hugo had met Gary Oliver when he had visited New York as a Student of the Royal College and the two had become friends. It would be interesting to see how he had turned out.

Hugo accepted the invitation and flew into Heathrow on the morning of 1st December. The skies through which his plane descended were grey and lowering and when he emerged from the airport buildings a cold wind whipped swirls of dust into his face. He must have been mad to come, Hugo thought, pulling his neat dark overcoat around his thin frame. He would have been better advised to go to Florida and soak up some sun to set him up for the biting winter expected in New York. But it was too late now to duck out and he might as well make the most of it.

Hugo took a taxi to the London Hilton where he had booked a room. Tomorrow he would do a little sightseeing and then get a flight back to the States. Perhaps he would still be able to manage a few days in Florida before returning to the grindstone.

He watched the dull grey London streets unfold outside the windows of his taxi and little knew that by the time he left London everything in his ordered world would have turned on its head and nothing would ever be the same again.

Paula sailed down the sweeping staircase into the Crush Bar wearing the first of Gary's outfits – a beautiful After Dark Suit in midnight blue lurex brocade entitled Premiere – to a burst of applause. Behind the scenes all was still organised chaos but not a hint of this had been allowed to intrude into the Crash Bar where the guests, all in evening dress, were assembled and not a trace of the nerves that had her strung taut as a greyhound were allowed to be apparent either. This was the most important show she had ever done and she must carry it off perfectly for Gary's sake as well as her own.

Sally had slipped in at the back. She held her breath as Paula appeared, as excited by her sister's glamour as she had been the very first time she had watched her work, but nervous now too, for the build-up to the great occasion had got to her and she was also terrifyingly aware of all the things that could go wrong.

In his seat in the fifth row Hugo had also stopped breathing and he knew it was not the shimmering beauty of the suit that caught his attention. All the clothes that had preceded it had been striking, each of them designed with a certain social event in mind – and each stunning in its own way. But not one of them had made him feel as he felt now – as if his chest had constricted beneath the weight of a stone slab.

No, it was not the suit that had affected him so – it was the girl modelling it. Hugo watched, unable to take his eyes off her until she was lost to view, then began to leaf through his programme. The models were listed, all forty of them, but there was no indication as to which was which. Several of the names he was familiar with but the others . . . Renatta, Julie, Diana, Christine, Virginia – two Virginias – she could have been any of them. He closed his programme, willing himself to concentrate on the next outfit – a cloque evening dress by Norman Hartnell entitled Crush Bar – but he could think of nothing but when would the girl appear again, see nothing but her lovely, clear-featured face and shining cap of golden hair.

You have taken leave of your senses! he told himself. You are thirty-three years old and you are behaving like a school boy! But it made no difference. The palms of his hands were damp and the blood was pounding at his temples. He couldn't remember feeling this way about a woman ever – unless it had been the little Italian girl – what was her name? Maria something? – back home in the

Bronx when he had been twelve years old. Hell fire, he had forgotten all about her until now, when a wave of emotion unexperienced for more than twenty years brought it all rushing back.

The models entered, paraded, posed in an ever-changing kaleidoscope pattern of colour and glamour but Hugo found himself existing only for the reappearance of his mystery girl. Here she was now in a tomato red wool coat which flattered that lovely gold hair so that she reminded him a little – though he had no idea why – of a rainbow, and now in a sharp green cocktail dress, topped by a coat of ranch mink. With a falling away of his stomach Hugo realised he would not see her again – or not on the catwalk anyway. She had done her job. In a trance he watched the final spectacular 'The Big Top', when models dressed as everything from clowns to circus palaminos paraded, each sponsored by an Associate Member of the Incorporated Society of London Fashion Designers – the milliners, the furriers, Berlei foundations and Aristoc stockings – and barely noticed one of them. He could think of nothing but the girl – and thank his lucky stars that she worked for Gary. Because he knew him an introduction would be that much easier but whoever she worked for Hugo's mind was made up – nothing would stop him setting out to win her. For the first time in his adult life Hugo was in love. It was a strange and somewhat disturbing experience.

'Paula, there is someone who is dying to meet you, lovey,' Gary said. He was flushed with success – and with the free-flowing champagne.

'Oh – who?' Paula sipped her own champagne, unsurprised by the statement. There was always someone who wanted to meet the models after a show.

'Hugo Varna. He's over here from the States.'

'Oh, right.' Paula had heard of Hugo. Who in the world of fashion had not?

'Just be careful,' Gary warned. 'He seems very smitten. I don't want to lose you, lovey, and I think he may try to poach you and whisk you off to model for him in New York.'

'Wrong,' said a voice at Paula's elbow. 'I don't want to poach her, Gary. I want to marry her.'

'This is getting beyond a joke, Paula,' Sally said severely as she staggered into the tiny bedsit with yet another armful of red roses. '*More* flowers! We ran out of vases the day before yesterday and anyway there's not a square inch left to put them. Even the delivery boy has had enough. He says he's fed up with climbing all these stairs three times a day and will you *please* put the poor man out of his misery and agree to go out with him.'

'Why should I? He's obviously crazy,' Paula said coolly.

'Crazy about you. Paula, you'll have to see him if only to tell him to stop it! This place is like Chelsea Flower Show gone mad.'

'It's hardly my fault,' Paula said crossly. 'I can't be held responsible for every nut case in London.'

'No – but what a nut case!' Sally took the latest consignment into the kitchen, dumped them in the sink and turned on the tap. Deep down she knew that part of her irritation stemmed from envy – no one had ever sent her flowers, not so much as a single carnation – and here was Paula practically drowning in the most exotic blooms imaginable, Singapore orchids, delicately perfumed white freesias and armfuls of long-stemmed red roses – in December! 'Aren't you even going to read the card?' she asked.

'No.'

The doorbell shrilled.

'Oh my God!' Paula whirled round in exasperation. 'That's the front door now. You'll have to go, Sally.'

'Why? It's bound to be for you.'

'I can't go down like this.' Paula was wearing her old checked woollen dressing gown and she had not yet put on any make-up. 'Get it, Sally, there's an angel. And if it's more flowers, tell them to take them round to the hospital or something.'

Sally sighed. 'What did your last servant die of?'

But she ran down the stairs anyway. Minutes later she was back.

'Not more flowers?' Paula asked.

'No. Special delivery. But for you – of course.' She handed Paula a small square package, gift wrapped. Paula glanced at the card.

'It's him again. What this time?' She tore off the paper, opened the box and gasped. 'Oh my God!'

Inside the box a pair of diamond ear studs lay on a bed of midnight blue velvet, each perfectly cut facet catching and reflecting the light from the overhead lamp.

'I don't believe it,' Sally said, stunned. 'He really is crazy!'

'And obviously very determined.' There was a strange new light in Paula's eyes; it seemed almost to reflect the glitter of the diamonds. 'I suppose you're right. I really will have to see him now. If only to tell him I can't possibly accept his extravagant presents.'

'I guess you won't believe me if I tell you I don't make a habit of this sort of thing,' Hugo said. They were having dinner at the Savoy – the box containing the diamond earrings lay on the table between them.

Paula smiled. 'Actually I do believe you. Not even a millionaire can afford to go around throwing presents like this at every strange woman he meets. Well, maybe a multi-millionaire could . . .' she added looking at him speculatively over the rim of her champagne glass.

'I'm certainly not that,' Hugo said firmly. 'One day maybe, but not yet. But the flowers didn't seem to be working so I thought – well, time for something a little more personal.' His mouth quirked and she caught some of the force of his personality.

'Of course I can't possibly keep them,' she said, steeling herself not to weaken.

'Why not?'

'Why not? Because . . .' She broke off, unable to think of a single good reason.

'Beautiful women have accepted presents from their admirers throughout the ages. Enjoy it.'

'I can't be bought,' Paula said firmly.

'I never thought you could. Heaven forbid I should insult you by trying.'

'Then what . . .?'

'I wanted you to have them.'

'But why?'

'This may sound damned stupid but it suddenly occurred to me there's not much fun in making a lot of dough if you haven't got anyone to spend it on. You're a beautiful girl, Paula. You should have beautiful things. Now admit it, I don't suppose Gary pays you enough for you to be able to buy this kind of thing for yourself. So – let me buy them for you. Where's the harm in that?'

'Well . . .' Paula hesitated, pretending reluctance.

'Let me put them on for you.' He leaned across the table, reaching out to unclip one of the paste sapphires she was wearing and replacing it with the diamond. His fingers were cool and steady. 'Now doesn't that feel good, knowing you're wearing the real thing?'

A tiny smile played about Paula's mouth. It certainly did feel good – even better than the feeling of power that came from working for Gary for a pittance. And there was something intoxicating about being pursued with such lavish determination too.

'I'm afraid I can't reach to do the other one,' he said. 'You'll have to put that in yourself.'

Her smile broadened. It was a game, all a game, with the diamonds taking the place of chess pieces. If she picked the earring up now and put it on she would be signifying her willingness to play.

Slowly, almost languidly, her eyes never leaving his, she slipped off the other paste sapphire and laid it on the table beside her plate. Then with the same deliberation she clipped on the diamond.

For a long moment they sat motionless, their eyes still locked, and Paula was aware of a quiver of excitement deep within. The diamonds, the champagne, a man to cosset, spoil and care for her – they were all there now within her reach – everything she had ever wanted.

On the table Hugo's hand covered hers and she did not attempt to draw it away. His eyes still burned into hers.

'Clever girl.' The slightly ironic note was tempered by wry humour.

'You won't regret it, Paula, I'll see to that.' He paused, looking for the first time at the menu. 'Now perhaps we should order. I think the smoked salmon and the steak – rare. Yes?'

'Yes,' she said.

Gary had the wide-eyed bemused look of someone who had just felt the ground slip away from under his feet.

'You can't be serious, Paula! You're not really going to the States? I warned you about Hugo, didn't I? What the hell will I do without you?'

'Don't you mean where the hell are you going to find someone else to work for you for as little as I do?' She raised one eyebrow, enjoying as she always did the feeling of supremacy that came from reminding him of it.

'Oh Paula . . .' His face became anxious. 'I know I've never yet been able to repay you, but I will . . .'

'Oh, just forget it, Gary!' she said, impatient suddenly. That game was almost over now – she'd had her fun from it, now it was time to move on to a new game – one that she thought would be even better. But even so she could not resist adding: 'If ever I need anything, though, I shall know where to come. I don't suppose I shall want for money – Hugo is wonderfully rich – but sometimes it's nice to be able to call in favours from a friend.'

'You know you can count on me, Paula. But oh, I shall miss you! Are you sure you won't change your mind and marry me instead of Hugo?'

She laughed. It seemed she had laughed more in these last days than in the whole of the rest of her life. Not that Hugo made her laugh – he didn't. He was powerful and exciting and vital, but not amusing. No, the laughter must stem from the deep well of happiness within her, the feeling that she was standing on the brink of the wonderful world of all her tomorrows.

'Marry *you*? Oh Gary, I don't think so.'

'Why not?'

'You know damned well why not. I need a man – and so do you. We'll always be friends but marriage – oh no, definitely not.'

'No, I suppose not.' He looked almost regretful. 'Pity. It would be so nice, so uncomplicated. I could make you beautiful clothes and you could cook me cheese on toast and . . .'

'There's a little more to marriage than that.'

'Yes. It's strange, I never really thought that Hugo . . .' He broke off, turning away. 'He's really swept you off your feet, hasn't he?'

'Yes.'

'So when is the great day?'

'Two weeks' time, at Caxton Hall.'

'Am I invited?'

'What do you think? If Hugo doesn't ask you to be his best man then you must give me away.'

'Give you away, lovey? Oh, that's a joke. You were never mine to give.'

The world's press was there as they emerged onto the steps of Caxton Hall, the famous American fashion designer and the beautiful model. Flash bulbs exploded around them like confetti and crowds who had never heard of Hugo Varna or Paula Bristow gathered to catch a glimpse of the celebrities and speculate on their identity.

'Is it Adam Faith?' someone asked.

'No – isn't he married already?'

'Don't know – they all get hitched and divorced so much you can't keep up with it.'

'I think it's that film star – what's 'er name? You know – the one in the Alfred Hitchcock film.'

'Don't talk daft! How could it be her?'

But whoever it was, they all agreed, she made a radiant bride. Too good, really, for that nondescript looking man. She stood there for a moment, beautiful and glowing in her dress and coat of ivory silk with an enormous ivory picture hat, holding on to her new husband's arm. Then she turned, tossing her bouquet of cream orchids straight into the waiting hands of a girl in a kingfisher blue coat and tiny netted pillbox hat.

Sally caught it – and with the bouquet she felt, as she had so many times before, as if she could catch a little of Paula's glamour.

She buried her face in the flowers, closed her eyes and made a wish.

She wished that one day some of the gifts which Paula attracted so effortlessly would be hers too. That she would be beautiful and feted and happy and these things would be hers as of right instead of reflected like sunlight on a mirror from her sister. Sally wished that one day she would be able to step out of Paula's shadow. But in making the wish she had no idea what it would cost her to gain these things for her own.

CHAPTER TWELVE

Sally missed Paula dreadfully. All too soon the first novelty of having the bedsitter to herself began to wear off and she realised how much she had depended on her sister for company. All very well to have extra space to hang her clothes, lovely to have the whole of the sofa bed to herself instead of sometimes waking up clinging to the edge or half covered, wonderful not to be faced with a stack of dirty coffee cups and overflowing ashtrays which had to be collected from all around the room before they could be washed up. But there was something very bleak about the ordered tidiness and Sally began to feel restless. At least her job kept her occupied for up to twelve hours a day, but even that was not the same as it had been now that Paula was no longer there.

Though Sally was ready to be friendly with Gary's other employees she found that being Paula's sister had 'tarred her with the same brush' as her mother would have put it. The other model girls, who were even more jealous now that Paula had married Hugo Varna, mistrusted Sally, and the women in the workroom considered her a snob. Added to this she had never learned to be totally at ease with Gary.

Perhaps she should look for a new job, Sally thought, one which offered her the chance of a totally fresh start and the chance to make new friends. The world of fashion was so rarified – it would be nice to get out and breathe some fresh air. And there seemed to be endless opportunities in London for a secretary with her qualifications.

When Sally handed in her notice to Gary he expressed regret

but did not try to persuade her to change her mind. Perhaps he was as ill at ease with her as she was with him, she thought.

A temping agency welcomed her with open arms, but Sally soon discovered she did not much care for this life either. Highly qualified though she was, Sally was a creature of habit. She liked to use a typewriter with which she was familiar and hated having to accustom herself to different filing systems, office methods and boss's foibles. Some might sing the praises of variety – to Sally it was like the trauma of starting a new job every week or so with none of the benefits. And although she was continually meeting new people she was never in one place long enough to make real friends.

One Saturday morning towards the end of the summer Sally had just returned from her weekly expedition to buy groceries and visit the launderette when there was a knock at her door. Sally propped her carrier bags against a chair and went to answer it.

The girl who stood there looked vaguely familiar though for the moment Sally could not place her.

'Hi – I'm Laura-Jo. I've just moved into the flat downstairs,' she said breezily and Sally's brain clicked into gear.

Gary had moved out of his flat a few months ago and into something more in keeping with his new successful image. Since then Sally had seen a young couple going in and out but now she realised the tenant must have changed again. She had probably seen this girl on the stairs – that was the reason she looked familiar,

'Look, I'm having a housewarming party tonight,' the girl rushed on, 'and if you'd like to come down you're very welcome. I thought it would be easier to invite everybody in the block rather than have them complain about the noise.' An American accent was apparent now – that explained her exuberant friendliness, Sally thought.

'You're a long way from home,' she said.

'Yeah. I'm supposed to be taking a year out of college to do Europe but it's been two years and here I still am!' She laughed.

'Why not come in and have a coffee?' Sally offered, liking her and reluctant to let the opportunity pass by.

The girl checked her watch, then pulled a face.

'Why not? The others can wait!'

'My sister is married to an American,' Sally said when they were seated at the heat-scarred table with mugs of coffee.

'Really? Where's he from?'

'New York. She lives there with him now.'

'Small world! What's he do?'

Sally hesitated. She did not want to foul up this promising meeting by what might sound like boasting.

'He's in business,' she hedged 'I'm Sally, by the way. Sally Bristow.'

'And I'm Laura-Jo Bayne. But I told you that, didn't I?'

They chatted on. By the time Laura-Jo left an hour later Sally had accepted the party invitation – and made a new friend. Perhaps things were looking up a little at last, she thought.

By nine-thirty the party was in full swing and Sally was enjoying herself. Laura-Jo's friends were an uninhibited crowd, many of them Americans themselves, and they treated Sally like an old friend. The only awkwardness arose because Laura-Jo insisted on telling them that Sally's sister was married to a New Yorker and hiding the truth about his identity stretched Sally's ingenuity to the full. As she struggled to evade the questions of one particularly persistent soul a voice in her ear whispered: 'You might be able to fool them, you know, but you can't fool me!' and she turned to see a young man smiling at her over the rim of his beer glass.

Her first impression was that he was very like Edward – so much so that her stomach fell away. Then she registered the differences. His face was thinner, his hairline receding slightly to accentuate, a high forehead and his nose was more prominent – classical Greek, or was it Roman? Sally wondered. His eyes were a lighter shade of blue and deeper set and there was a trace of a Northern accent in his voice. No, definitely not Edward, but enough like him to stir all kinds of old memories – and to make her warm to him, forgetting how Edward had hurt her and remembering only the good times.

'Can't fool you?' she repeated, smiling. 'Now what do you mean by that?'

'Oh come on, it's not so easy to hide celebrities' lights under bushels. You realise most of the guys here would flip if they knew who your sister is – and most of the girls would go bananas if they knew your brother-in-law is Hugo Varna.'

'Shh!' Sally hissed, covering his mouth with her hand. 'Please – don't say anything. I'm sick to death of being Paula's sister. I want to be me.'

He took her hand with his own, his light blue eyes teasing, 'All right, I'll keep quiet. But there is a price.'

'What is that?'

'You don't try and run away from me. You're the best-looking girl here tonight, did you know that?'

'Oh yes? Compliments slip off your tongue very easily, don't they?' she said, trying to sound cynical, but secretly she was flattered.

'It's no more than the truth. Oh come on, don't look like that. You've been told so before.'

'No, I haven't.'

'I don't believe you. Hey – your glass is empty. Can I get you another? What are you drinking – uh, what was it they called you?'

'Sally. But I thought you knew everything about me.'

'I do – all I need to know at least. You are very beautiful, Sally, and very modest, and I am going to see you home tonight.'

She laughed aloud. 'You won't have very far to go. I'm from upstairs.

'Well, well.' There was a twinkle in his eye. 'So what do you say I get us both a drink and we take them up to your flat, where it's quieter.'

'How dare you!' But it was impossible to be angry with him, so irrepressible, so wicked . . . and so like Edward.

They had another drink and another. His name was Stuart, he told her, and he was a representative for a paper firm – he toured offices selling stationery and taking orders for individually printed advertising calendars. The flat was very crowded now and very noisy and the air was a blue haze of cigarette smoke. Squashed in a corner of the kitchen they were still chatting but Stuart's arm had crept around her waist and his mouth closer and closer to her ear and she had not objected. More than that – she was enjoying it!

Ironic, really, she thought – or perhaps a stroke of incredible good fortune. During the long and lonely nights Sally had made up her mind to stop objecting the next time a man who was halfway decent came along. Objecting was not the best way of making friends and influencing people. On the contrary it seemed a sure-fire way of driving them away. Sally had sat wrapped in Paula's old woollen dressing gown filing her nails and thinking of all the relationships she had ruined by being too much of a prude. There had once been a time when she had thought that men didn't respect girls 'who did'. Bitter experience had changed her mind. It was girls 'who didn't' they despised because there was no station along the line that was acceptable as a stopping point. All very well for actresses like Grace Kelly to look glacial and regal on screen – a normal-looking girl behaving with similar frostiness would be written off, not relentlessly pursued. But after that first show of warmth then any girl who failed to deliver was labelled a cock teaser. Though she had not been a virgin for a very long time Sally had continued to behave in a way that parodied the virginal. Now, she had decided, it was time to let go a little and see if that produced any better results.

It was one thing, of course, to plan a retreat from innocence, quite another to carry it out. She had worried about it a good deal – and worried because she was worrying. Paula had never had such doubts, or if she had she had never showed them and since school age Sally had been ashamed to discuss her worries about her own sexuality with any of her friends. To admit to them seemed the very essence of failure.

Now, however, with Stuart's hand moving up to surreptitiously fondle her breast she began to experience the tingly heady waves of desire. Perhaps this time it would be all right. Perhaps this time she could forget she was a small-town good girl and actually enjoy being wicked.

'Shall we go now?' he whispered. His breath was hot on her ear. Small shivers ran down her neck.

She nodded without speaking. She felt shameless, abandoned – and it was wonderful! He guided her through the smoky kitchen and bodies parted to let them pass. Sally felt quite floaty and intoxicated though she did not think she had had very much to drink.

'I ought to thank Laura-Jo,' she said when they reached the door.

'Thank her another time.' He nibbled her ear and her knees went weak. 'She's busy. She'll understand.'

They went out onto the landing which was lit by one garish bulb. He pushed her against the wall, cupping his hands under her buttocks and squeezing her close against him so that she could feel his body, hard and eager.

'You are beautiful.' He kissed her, his mouth running a line of kisses down her throat and back to her mouth. 'You are very beautiful, Sally.' His words were like wine to her. His hands followed the curve of her body and the warmth of them seemed to burn through the thin silk of her dress. She groaned, desperate with wanting him.

'Let's go upstairs.'

It was what he had been waiting for. Arms around one another they staggered up the stairs, then outside her door he pressed her against the wall again, lifting her skirt high enough to enable him to run his fingers up her soft inner thighs above the tops of her stockings. She groaned, parting them a little, and he eased his fingers under the filmy silk. Thank God she was wearing a suspender belt, not one of these terrible roll-on girdles, or even pantie girdles, that some girls wore! Gently, probing, he rotated his finger and felt her squirm. He kissed her again, parting her lips with his tongue and flicking it in and out in time with the movement of his finger. Her body had begun to move now in unconscious rhythm and he stopped, sensing she was already on the point of climaxing.

As the movement ceased Sally opened her eyes, puzzled. She had been on another plane – she simply wanted it to go on and on. 'Let's go inside,' he whispered urgently.

'Oh yes . . .' she was pliant, acquiescent. She fumbled in her bag for her key and opened the door. They stumbled inside and he began fondling her again before she had time to change her mind.

The sofa bed was already pulled out – Sally had thought it would be nice to fall straight into it after the party. They collapsed onto it and as he pulled down her panties she wriggled free of the constricting silk. She felt the hot hardness of him against her thigh and then he was inside her. No pain, no discomfort, she had been moist and ready for him. He moved with eager thrusts and she clung to him enjoying the experience for the first time in her life. Then suddenly he withdrew, spurting wetness across her stomach. Her sense of let down was enormous, she writhed trying to recapture the aching ecstasy. He slipped his hand between her legs and she moved against it aware of nothing but her mounting excitement. It couldn't go on getting better and better . . . could it? Her lips parted in a silent scream and wave upon wave of tremors shook her. Beautiful . . . beautiful! Oh beautiful! Then she was coming down again from that high plateau, floating down, down . . . and reality was intruding.

'Oh heck, what have we done?' Sally asked in sudden panic.

'It's all right.'

'Are you sure?'

'Of course I'm sure. There's your proof.' He took her hand and pressed it to her stomach. She withdrew it quickly, oddly embarrassed and a little frightened now by the speed of what had happened and how easy it had been.

'Do you want a coffee?' she asked. It seemed an incongruous thing to say yet she could think of no other way to restore normality.

'Yes, why not?'

She got up, surreptitiously wiping herself dry with her petticoat and avoiding looking at him. She set the kettle to boil and when she came back into the room he was sitting there like any other visitor flipping idly through a magazine that had been lying on the table beside the sofa bed.

'Well, Sally Bristow, and when am I going to see you again?' he asked.

Happiness scared. Somehow with that one simple question he had made everything all right.

'Well I'm a bit busy,' she lied, intent on maintaining her new image. 'Shall we say the day after tomorrow?'

'I should watch out for that Stuart Harris,' Laura-Jo said 'He has a reputation for being a womaniser, you know.'

She and Sally were drinking coffee in the kitchen – what luxury to have a kitchen of one's own Sally thought.

'I don't know him that well,' Laura-Jo went on. 'He's a friend of a friend really, but they do say . . .'

'I'm sure he's all right,' Sally said smugly. 'I've been out with him two or three times and he seems very nice.'

'Oh well, as long as you know what you're doing.' Laura-Jo shrugged. Just as long as she'd warned her. Sally was a big girl. It wasn't for Laura-Jo to interfere. And when a person had that look on her face that Sally was wearing now, Laura-Jo had the feeling that she would take no notice at all.

'Here – have one of my brownies,' she said, pushing a plate of chocolate cakes towards Sally. 'They are almost – though not quite – as good as Mom used to make.'

Sally took one. She had completely given up worrying about calorie counting and watching her weight this last few weeks. She had too many other things on her mind. Like being in love.

She was seeing Stuart almost every night now and making love almost as often and it was almost always just as wonderful as that first time – better, because she had stopped being embarrassed or worrying about it. Stuart was careful – he 'took precautions' as he put it – and she wondered why she had been so terrified of something that could be so wonderful. Even better he had started talking about getting engaged and married, clear proof, if one were needed, that the old advice about men not marrying girls 'who did' was nothing but hokum. The first time he had mentioned it had been in a little pub in Kensington where Flamenco dancers performed and Sally thought there could have been no more romantic

152

background to a proposal than the wonderful wild music and the rhythmic click of high heels and castanets.

Sally stretched, deliciously happy. Already she had begun to plan the wedding. It would be at home, she decided, in the local church, not at Caxton Hall like Paula's, and she would wear a dreamily romantic dress with a fall skirt and a veil. Perhaps Hugo would design it for her. Paula could be a matron-of-honour and perhaps she would ask Laura-Jo to be a bridesmaid too since it was through her that they had met. They might even go to America for their honeymoon. It was like a dream, a lovely exciting fairytale. Sally hoped fervently she would never wake up.

Sally was worried. She sat hunched up on the sofa bed, her diary on her knee, doing quick calculations. Had she made a mistake? No, her period was definitely three weeks overdue. And last month she had been very late too and when at last to her immense relief she had found the tell-tale stains on her pants on one of her frequent hopeful visits to the bathroom the 'period' had been strangely short and light – a few hours of extreme stomach cramp, a couple of lightly soiled Tampax and nothing more. What was even more ominous was that not only did her breasts feel swollen and tender but also she had felt definitely queasy the last two mornings and this afternoon at work she had almost fainted. She had laid her head down on her typewriter and taken deep breaths until the room had stopped spinning, but the queasiness had not gone away. She could feel it now, a leaden weight deep inside her, and the misgivings seem to rise and whirl from it.

I can't be pregnant! she thought. Stuart is always so careful! But despite all the arguments she put to herself deep down she knew that she was.

For another week she continued to pray that she might be mistaken, waking each morning with fresh hope only to feel it slipping away with the onslaught of nausea. At last she could bear the suspense no longer. She paid a visit to her doctor and was upset but not surprised when he confirmed her suspicions.

'Oh yes, you're going to have a baby all right,' he said,

straightening up from examining her. 'In about six months, I should say.'

Sally lay very still on the couch. She had known it, yes, but hearing him put it into words was still a shock.

'There's no doubt?' she asked shakily.

'None. I'll run a test if you like but I'm sure it will be positive.' He was a Scotsman; his soft accent seemed to wash over her like a mountain stream. He turned his back to wash his hands and she slipped down from the couch, standing in her bare feet on the cold surgery floor.

'You're not married are you?' he asked, casting a shrewd glance over his shoulder.

'No,' she said a trifle defiantly. 'But I am going to be.'

'Good – good. Telephone my receptionist in three days or so for the test. And make an appointment to see me again in a month.'

Sally nodded. She felt a little as if she might be drowning in a sea of unreality.

When she left the surgery she walked for a long time. The keen November wind was cutting along the street, blowing the leaves that had fallen from the trees into sad huddles and the traffic swept past in an endless stream. Sally thrust her hands into her pockets and walked unseeing, her head bent.

Pregnant. No big white wedding, no lovely carefree honeymoon in the States. Her parents would be shocked and disappointed. She dreaded telling them and facing their disapproval. Even more, for some reason she could net explain to herself, she dreaded telling Stuart. So far she had not mentioned her fears to him. She had kept them to herself because to put them into words was to give substance to the shadow and inexplicably she was afraid of his reaction. But now there could be no more shilly-shallying and self-deception. Plans had to be made and quickly. If they acted immediately perhaps the white wedding at least could be saved. She wouldn't be the first bride to walk down the aisle in a froth of lace that concealed a spreading waistline. And if there were a few whispers behind cupped hands – well, so what? She and Stuart had intended to be married anyway and if everything was happening a little faster than they had meant it to, well, they would just have to adapt their plans accordingly.

Through the pockets of her coat Sally surreptitiously ran her hands across her stomach. It was still quite flat though she had noticed the waistband of her skirts were tighter recently. A baby. Deep inside her a new life was beginning – and already begun. A baby. A real live bundle of tiny arms and legs, perfect little fingers and toes. Was it a boy or a girl? Would it be like her or like Stuart? Not that it mattered. She thought of the only baby she had ever known, born to the family who had lived next door to their council house home, remembering the powdery smell of him, the silken cap of hair, the way his blue eyes had gazed up at her, unwinking, trusting, and the wave of tenderness she had felt for him. And that had been someone else's baby. This one would be hers – hers and Stuart's. Perhaps being pregnant wasn't so bad after all. Merely a bit inconvenient.

Sally lifted her chin, looking around. Where on earth was she? She must have walked for miles. A taxi was cruising along the street and she raised her hand to hail it. Unreal. All so unreal.

You'd better start getting a hold of yourself, my girl, she said to herself.

'Where to?' the taxi driver asked. He was looking at her curiously.

'South Kensington,' she said. 'And please hurry.'

'Pregnant?' Stuart said. '*Pregnant?* You've got to be joking.'

They were in their favourite Indian restaurant; they had ordered but the food had not yet come. Stuart's expression was frankly disbelieving and his voice was loud enough to carry to the nearby tables. Sally began to wish she had waited until they were at home to tell him but now that she knew for certain she had been unable to keep it to herself for a moment longer.

'Shh!' she cautioned him. 'The whole restaurant will hear you.'

He scowled. 'What do you expect?' But his tone was lower. 'What kind of thing is that to say to me? Pregnant!'

'It's true,' she said. 'The doctor ran some tests and I got the result today. I'm three months pregnant, Stuart.'

'Bloody hell'

The waiter arrived with their curries. Sally stared down at her hands, knotted in her lap, as he deftly set out the plates and the dish of chips Stuart had ordered.

'Have you everything you require?' he asked carefully. He was grinning. Sally wondered if he too had overheard Stuart. But even if he had his English was probably not good enough to understand. There was a quick turnover of waiters at the Rajah, all young men fresh from India – cousins, perhaps, or nephews or some other distant relatives of the proprietor, all using the restaurant as a stepping-stone to a new life.

'We have everything,' Stuart said impatiently and added as the waiter moved away: 'Let's eat and get out of here. For Christ's sake, Sally, did you have to spoil a good meal?'

'I'm sorry . . .' She lifted her fork, played with the rice and knew she would not be able to swallow a single mouthful. 'I had to tell you. I couldn't keep it to myself any longer.'

He tipped his dish of chips onto the mound of curry and rice, without replying. His face was like stone.

'Stuart – say something please!' she begged.

He glared at her resentfully. 'What do you want me to say?'

'I don't know . . .' she said helplessly. 'I never expected you'd be like this . . .'

'Oh – you thought I'd jump for joy, I suppose. Sorry to disappoint you. But I don't know why you're telling me anyway. It's not mine, is it?'

'Stuart!' She stopped forking rice, staring at him in horror. 'What are you talking about? Of course it's yours!'

He snorted, a sound conveying disgust and disbelief. 'For goodness sake eat. Everyone is looking at you.'

Her face burned, embarrassment compounding her misery.

She tried to eat, but could not. Her stomach simply refused to accept food. She glanced at Stuart. He was like an angry stranger. She knew now why she had been afraid to tell him. She had known deep down he would take it like this. She had caught glimpses of the cold, unrelenting persona beneath the jovial charming exterior.

Strangely it had formed part of the attraction, knowing there was a deeper side to him, and if it was also a little dark then perhaps that made it all the more exciting. She loved him. She could handle it – or so she had thought. Now suddenly she was not so sure.

He finished his meal in silence while Sally forced down a few mouthfuls.

'Aren't you going to eat that?' was all he said.

Sally shook her head. He rolled his eyes, waved to the waiter and settled the bill. Then he propelled Sally along the street to where his car was parked. She hunched into the passenger seat. Stuart sat staring straight ahead. In the amber glow of the street lamps his profile looked hard, arrogant and uncompromising.

'Stuart – please . . .' she begged.

He half-turned. 'You'll get rid of it, of course.'

Her stomach fell away. 'No!' she said, shocked.

'Well what are you going to do then?'

'What am going to do? Surely this should be a joint decision.' He stared stonily. 'Stuart – you don't really believe what you said in there do you? That the baby isn't yours? How could you even suggest such a thing?'

'I know I was careful.'

Suddenly she was angry. 'Obviously not careful enough. How dare you accuse me of letting someone else . . .'

'Well, how do I know you haven't?'

'How? Surely you know me better than that. I love you. We're going to be married. This will just mean bringing it forward a bit. I know it's not how we planned it but we would have had a family eventually wouldn't we? It'll just be sooner than we intended.'

'Like hell.'

'What do you mean?'

'Christ, Sally, I don't intend to start off like this. Saddled with a kid.'

'But we haven't any choice now. You must see that.'

'We've every choice. Get rid of it. Have an abortion.'

'What are you saying? I couldn't do that! Kill my own child – our child? Anyway I wouldn't know how to go about it. It's illegal.'

'There are ways.'

'No I couldn't!'

'Well if you're squeamish, get it adopted then.'

'No!' This was a nightmare, it had to be. In a minute she'd wake up. 'Please, Stuart, stop this. Let's get married. We'll manage. Other people do.'

'I'm not other people. If you think I'm going to tie myself down with a wife and an unwanted kid you've got the wrong bloke. There are too many things I want to do first.' He started the car. 'If you're stupid enough to get yourself pregnant, Sally, that's your problem. Leave me out of it.'

She couldn't answer. She was trembling so much no words would come. He pulled the car into the kerb outside her flat but did not switch off the engine.

'Aren't you coming in?' she asked, hating herself for sounding so meek, so pleading, but unable to help it. In all her life she could never before remember feeling as lonely and panic-stricken as she did now, and illogically she clung to the belief that if only they could sit down and talk about it then everything could still come right.

'Please . . . just for a little while . . .' she begged. But Stuart only revved the engine impatiently by way of reply.

'Not tonight. I think I'm going to get drunk. I'll make some enquiries about abortions and I'll phone you.'

'Well thanks, Stuart. Thanks a lot!' She slammed out of the car, her eyes burning with angry tears. Even now she was desperately still hoping he would change his mind and follow her. He did not. The car roared away and she was left alone on windswept pavement.

'Honey, maybe it would be wise for you to have that abortion,' Laura-Jo said. She brought a cup of coffee across to the table where Sally was sitting, her head in her hands. Her pleasant face was anxious. Since Sally had confided in her a week ago she had been able to think of little else. Men! They really could be the most unbelievable swine. She felt responsible too. After all it had been at her party that Sally had met him.

'I won't have an abortion,' Sally said stubbornly. 'I don't want to be messed up by some back street quack.'

'There are other places. It would cost you, but wouldn't your sister lend you the money? Nobody need ever know. A few days in a clinic and they'll call it appendicitis or something.'

Sally shook her head. 'It's not just that. I've discovered morals I didn't know I had. I can't murder my own baby.'

'It's not a baby yet.'

'To me it is. It's alive. I can feel it – here.' She pressed her hands to her midriff. 'I know it's only a flutter yet but I can feel it. I couldn't live with myself, knowing I'd killed it.'

'Oh honey!' Laura-Jo pulled out a chair and sat down beside Sally. 'What are you going to do then?'

'I don't know. I keep hoping Stuart will change his mind.'

'You'd still have him – after this?' Laura-Jo asked.

Sally nodded. Tears squeezed out of the corners of her eyes.

'I still love him. Oh, call me crazy if you like but he's not really like this.'

'You could have fooled me.'

'He's just shocked. Maybe when he gets used to the idea . . .' Laura-Jo sighed. She didn't want to tell Sally that she had spoken to Stuart herself, trying to make him shoulder his responsibilities, and had been told in no uncertain terms to mind her own business. Stuart wasn't about to change his mind, she was sure. She glanced at Sally, at her white drawn face and the huge dark circles under her eyes. She looked as though she was going through hell.

'Well if you won't have the abortion while there's still time then you'd better start looking after yourself, otherwise goodness knows what will happen to you – and the baby. I guess we'd better get some advice for you, Sally. You are going to need all the help you can get.'

The months dragged by, each as nightmarish and unreal as the one before. Sally continued to work as long as she was able, hiding her growing girth beneath flowing cotton dresses although she was well into her sixth month before she had a recognisable bulge. She managed to avoid going home. Her mother and father did not know as yet and she didn't want them to. Laura-Jo arranged for Sally to see a social worker and reluctantly she agreed – after all she had to be practical. Hiding away and pretending nothing was happening would not make it go away.

The social worker was bland, middle-aged and matter-of-fact with untidy greying hair.

'Is there no possibility of you marrying the man?' she asked;

'None,' Sally said. No one had heard of Stuart for weeks. Sally had seen him a few times after that first dreadful evening when she had broken the news to him but he had been just as unhelpful. He had supplied Sally with an address where she might get an abortion and become abusive when she had refused, point blank. Now word was that he had gone abroad and Sally had come to realise that whatever there had been between them, it was all over. She was on her own.

'So – do you intend to keep the baby or have it adopted?'

'I don't know.'

'Well, let's discuss it. Either way there will be problems. Bringing up a child on your own won't be easy – I'm sure you know that. But adoption is no easy answer either. There are plenty of couples only too anxious to take an illegitimate child and give it a good home and it might be the best solution for your baby's sake. But don't imagine for a moment giving it up would be easy. Maternal ties are very strong.'

'I don't think I have any choice, do I?' Sally said.

'Wouldn't your family support you?'

'I don't want to go home.' Sally did not tell her that her parents were in blissful ignorance of her situation.

'In that case I think the best solution will be to book you into a Mother and Baby Home. You can stay there with your child for at least the first six weeks. You will be with other girls in the same situation as yourself and it will give you the chance to see how you feel when Baby is actually here. It's best not to make any firm decision until then.'

Six weeks with the baby! I'll never be able to give it up if I have to spend six weeks with it, Sally thought and realised that without being aware of it, she must have already made up her mind.

'I don't want to do that either,' she said. 'A Mother and Baby Home sounds like an institution. I'd rather just decide now. Can't it be adopted at birth without me ever seeing it?'

'We are not in agreement with that practice,' the social worker said sternly. 'That way lies certain trouble. You would be burdened with guilt at denying your child the most basic love – I've seen too many girls in and out of mental hospitals for years as a result of it. Whatever you decide I feel the only course is for you to mother your child for at least two weeks.'

Sally nodded numbly. 'Very well. But I'd like it to be adopted as soon as possible.'

The social worker looked disapproving. Don't say I haven't warned you, her expression seemed to say.

'I'll take some details and pass them on to an adoption agency. Do you have any preference as to religion?' Sally looked blank and she went on impatiently: 'What religion would you like your baby to be brought up to? What is your persuasion?'

'Church of England', said Sally, who had not been inside a place of worship for at least ten years.

'Very well. I'll put you in touch with the Church of England Adoption Society,' the social worker said. 'They will point out the pitfalls just as I have.'

She pushed her empty coffee cup back across her cluttered desk and smiled impersonally. Sally realised the interview was at an end.

The baby was born in May and the moment Sally saw him she knew that whatever the difficulties she could simply never part with him.

She lay in her hospital bed, exhausted by the long hours of labour, sore beyond belief from her stitches and with breasts already throbbing and taut although she had been given an injection to stop the milk coming in, and ached for the nurses to bring him to her again. He was so sweet with his moist little head dented from pressure during the birth, wide blue eyes and a button nose. Who ever had said babies were red, wrinkled and ugly? Sally wondered. Mark certainly wasn't. He was perfect and she adored him.

Mark. In spite of deciding on adoption she had chosen names because not to give a baby a name seemed like depriving it of individuality – Mark for a boy, Sarah for a girl. She had felt a moment's dismay when they told her she had a boy for the adoption society had a couple lined up and waiting for her if the baby had been a girl. Then the relief had come rushing in. There would be no pressure. She would have borne a girl for that unknown couple. A boy was hers and hers alone. Lying strung up like a chicken with her legs in stirrups while the doctor worked to 'tidy her up' as they called the stitching process, she had experienced a moment's triumph and for the first time she was actually glad that Stuart had left her. She didn't want to share her baby with anyone, not even him. Certainly not him!'

Next day Laura-Jo came to visit her laden with flowers, chocolates and grapes. She had peeped in to the nursery on her way to the ward and seen Mark.

'He's gorgeous!' she enthused.

'I know,' Sally said smugly. 'Don't you think he's the most beautiful baby in the nursery? And they say he's very good. Even when the others bawl he refuses to join in.'

'You're never going to part with him,' Laura-Jo said.

'No,' Sally agreed. 'I know. In fact I can't imagine how I ever came to consider it.'

Laura-Jo grinned. She too had fallen in love with Mark.

'In that case we're all going to have to rally round and help you, aren't we?' she said.

It wouldn't be easy, Sally knew. The first euphoria quickly wore off and the problems came crowding in. Her parents had to be told – presenting them with a *fait accompli* was much worse than preparing them, but when they emerged from the first stages of shell-shock they begged Sally to come home so that they could help Sally bring him up. Sally refused. Now more than ever she needed to be independent. She persuaded the landlord to let her keep on the bedsit for the time being at any rate until Mark needed space to run around, and arranged for a baby minder. Laura-Jo and her friends took on the roles of honorary aunts and spoiled Mark dreadfully but Sally, exhausted from broken nights and long working days, knew that the ultimate responsibility was hers and hers alone. She would have no real social life, no time to herself, no money to spare for years and years. There would probably be no boyfriends – except the ones who thought an unmarried mother must be an easy target. Perhaps there would never be anyone willing to take her on with someone else's baby. She faced that thought and shrugged her shoulders. So be it. She did not care. Men had brought her nothing but misery. They were a sorry selfish bunch of bastards. Now she had Mark and he was all she wanted. She was going to be a very, very good mother to him.

Sometimes when Sally thought she was on the very point of exhaustion a small triumphant thought came to cheer her.

At least I beat you to something, Paula! At least I beat you to something!

PART THREE

The Present

CHAPTER THIRTEEN

Tom O'Neill arrived at the police headquarters exactly two minutes early for his appointment. He was shown into a sunny office where the light streamed in bars through the Venetian blinds and the police chief rose from behind his paper-strewn desk, holding out his hand.

'Good day, Mr O'Neill. Robert Gascoyne. What can I do for you?'

Tom shook the outstretched hand.

'I'm grateful to you for sparing me your time. As I told you on the telephone I am working for the British and Cosmopolitan Insurance Company. They paid out on the lives of both Greg Martin and his companion, Paula Varna, when his yacht blew up in 1967 and naturally they are anxious to ascertain whether in fact they were the victims of fraud. According to what we read in the newspapers this may well have been the case. A woman has made a report to you, I understand, to the effect that Greg Martin, at any rate, is very much alive. A Maria Vincenti from Darling Point as far as I remember.'

'Maria Vincenti. Yes. Won't you sit down, Mr O'Neill?'

The police chief, Robert Gascoyne, was big, bronzed and with an indifferent manner. He had been born and raised in the flat farmland around Echuka, Victoria, but he had lived in and around Sydney for the past thirty years and the laid-back attitude of the Sydneysiders had rubbed off onto his naturally taciturn manner just as the year-round sunshine had tanned his skin. Besides this a career in the New South Wales police service had made him cynical; now, approaching retirement, he longed only to be free to spend more time on his boat, fishing, with nothing but the seabirds and a few cans of Fosters or Castelmaine XXXX for company. People – you could keep them. He'd had enough dealings with the shits of this world in the last thirty years to last him a lifetime. Bums, hoodlums, petty crooks and murderers, he'd dealt with them all. He knew a loser when he saw one – and the Italian woman who had come to him with a far-fetched story about the supposedly re-incarnated Greg Martin was a loser, even if she did live in luxury and was supposed to be the heiress to a family textile fortune back home in Italy. Worse, she was a lush. Gasgoyne had no respect at all for people who couldn't hold their drink.

'I understand she claims to have been living with Greg Martin for the last twenty years,' Tom said, settling his file on the desk.

'So she says', the police chief agreed non-committally.

Tom's eyes sharpened. 'You don't believe her?'

'If I believed every story I'd been told in my career I wouldn't be sitting where I am today,' the police chief returned, unsmiling. 'Look at it this way. There is always a certain amount of glamour attachéd to a story like this and there will always be crooks and cranks searching for some kind of notoriety. How many times, for instance, has someone come up with a sighting of Lord Lucan? As for Mrs Vincenti, or Trafford, as she has been calling herself, she is hardly the most reliable of witnesses. You haven't met her, I take it?' Tom shook his head. 'Well, when you do you'll see what I mean. She has money, yes, and plenty of it. She's been used to attention all her life, one way and another, and now she isn't getting it. She drinks like a fish. Besides all that she is clearly a woman with a grudge – against Michael Trafford, her common law husband. Have you any idea the lengths a woman scorned will go to, Mr O'Neill? Believe you me she would not be the first lady to try to land a man in one hell of a lot of hot water for the sake of revenge.'

'So you are not following up her claim?' Tom persisted.

'I didn't say that.' The police chief ran a hand through his thinning hair. 'Look, I'll be straight with you, and save both your time and mine. There is more to this business than meets the eye – a few details the press haven't managed to get their mucky paws on yet.

The story Mrs Trafford came to us with wasn't a straight forward accusation as to the identity of her common-law husband. That was only part of it. The rest was a charge we do have a duty to investigate, whether we believe there's any substance to it or not. But before I tell you about it I must have your assurance that you will treat what I am going to say as confidential – I won't expect to read the gory details in my morning newspaper.'

'That goes without saying,' Tom said stiffly. 'I don't like the gutter press any more than you do.'

Gascoyne nodded. 'Very well. According to her story, Mrs Vincenti's reason for coming to us was because she believed herself to be in danger. She alleged an attempt had been made on her life and that her common-law husband had taken out a contract on her.'

Tom whistled. 'A contract for murder? Why the hell should he do that?'

The chief sat back rolling a pencil between his fingers. 'As I mentioned earlier, Mrs Vincenti is a very wealthy woman. I would imagine it is her money that set them up in their mansion on Darling Point and has kept them in style all these years. Oh, they were well established as a couple, and known to be big spenders. Michael Trafford dabbled in real estate and the world of finance and probably made more in a year than I make in ten but the real shekels came from her. Now it seems Trafford has set his sights on a younger woman and wants to set up home with her. Tough on poor old Maria, but to tell the truth, having seen her I can't say I blame him. But of course she is the one with the purse strings. Leaving her would cut him off from the main source of his income. Besides which her will is in his favour. So, according to Maria, he decided the best way to get his freedom *and* the wealth he had come to enjoy would be to have something happen to her.'

Tom nodded thoughtfully. 'Dramatic stuff. What aroused her suspicions?'

'A few weeks ago she narrowly escaped being run down by a car. At the time she was shaken, but thought nothing of it, though she alleges Trafford "reacted strangely" – her words. Then she began to suspect she was being followed and she saw what she took to be an intruder lurking in the garden late at night when Trafford was out with a business associate and it was the maid's day off. The doorbell was rung but she refused to answer it and rang for police assistance. One of my men went out to the house but found nothing suspicious, though there was no doubt Mrs Trafford was terrified out of her wits. According to her story Trafford returned home some time after midnight bringing his business acquaintance with him – so that he would have a witness to the discovery of the body, according to Maria. She alleges that he appeared shocked at finding her alive. After the colleague left there was one hell of a row. Trafford threw some belongings into a suitcase and walked out. She hasn't seen him since.'

'And what does Trafford have to say about all this?' Tom asked.

'Sweet FA. We haven't been able to interview him yet. Maria doesn't know where he went that night and his office don't know either or if they do they aren't saying.'

'But you are looking for him?'

'Enquiries are in progress. But I wouldn't hold your breath. He could be anywhere. Australia is a big place, Mr O'Neill.'

'So I've noticed,' Tom said drily. 'As a matter of interest, what is your gut feeling? Do you think she's telling the truth?'

Gascoyne shrugged. 'Stranger things have happened. But I'm a cynic. An illegal immigrant with a profile as high as Martin's living under our noses for twenty years? It takes a bit of swallowing. And off the record the woman is a hysteric with a drink problem. As I said earlier, we have a duty to investigate allegations of attempted murder. But it's my guess we'll find nothing more sinister than a domestic situation. The guy has walked out on her, simple as that. But she can't – or won't – accept it.'

'How did the newspapers get hold of the story?' Tom asked.

'She told them. She was put out, I think, that her report to us didn't get us running around like headless chickens.'

'But she didn't tell them about the attempts on her life.'

'No. Apparently not.'

'That's strange, don't you think?'

'Not really. There's no explaining how a woman as unstable as Maria will behave. She got cold feet no doubt. Anyway, her story has attracted enough attention just as it stands. Half the newspaper hacks in Australia are camped out at Darling Point. We've had to station an officer out there to stop them bothering her – after bringing the whole shebang down on her own head she had the gall to complain they were trespassing on her property.'

'So she got what she wanted,' Tom said thoughtfully. 'Police protection.'

'A pretty ham-fisted way of going about it.'

'But successful. Not even the most brazen hit-man would try anything with half the world's press and a copper on the doorstep.' He stood up. 'Thank you for your time, sir. And thank you for being so frank with me.'

'Will you be pursuing your investigation?' Gascoyne asked.

Tom nodded. 'I have a few more lines of enquiry to follow up, yes, if it's not treading on your toes. I have to be quite sure that the whole thing is a figment of Maria's imagination before I close the file. You see unlike you I have some very good reasons for hoping to prove Greg Martin and Micheal Trafford are one and the same – given all the component parts, a million good reasons, you might say.'

Gascoyne held out his hand. 'Well, good luck to you. I only hope that if you unearth anything you think we should know about you will be as straight with me as I have tried to be with you.'

'Naturally.' Tom shook the outstretched hand. 'I'll be in touch. And thanks once again for all your help.'

He left the office and Gascoyne stared after him, deep in thought. Was it possible he was wrong about Maria Vincenti? Could it be there was a substance to her allegations? Well if there was O'Neill would get to the bottom of it, he was confident. And if not . . .

Gascoyne stared at the mound of reports on his desk and sighed. For a moment he wished he was young and keen again like Tom O'Neill instead of jaded and bogged down by the morass of paperwork which seemed to have very little to do with real police work. But it was a fleeting desire only. In his time he'd done it all.

Now he wanted nothing more than to be free to close his office door on the lot of it for the last time, take out his boat and get on with some serious fishing.

The taxi descended the hill to Double Bay, swung around and began to climb again towards the luxury homes that stood like jewels in a crown on exclusive Darling Point. The sun beat down mercilessly, shafts of bright burnished gold in the clear Australian air. The sky was aggressively blue, almost close enough to touch; far below the sea was precisely the same shade of blue but freckled with silver.

In the front passenger seat of the taxi Harriet sat hugging her bag on her knees. Sydney – city of silver and blue. The almost hurtful brightness of it had been her first impression as the 747 came in to land – the bay, the Harbour Bridge, the many faceted roof of the Opera House, all catching the brilliant sunshine and reflecting it in a mesmeric kaleidoscope of light. In spite of her preoccupation she had been impressed – who could fail to be? But already after a night at the Sydney Hilton the spectacle had faded, relegated to the back burners of her conscious mind. If she had come as a tourist she might have dwelled on it, savoured it. If she had come to work her photographer's eye would have been busy looking for new angles to capture it on film. But she had come as neither. Sydney was merely the place where she might at last, after twenty years, learn of the fate of her mother.

Harriet shifted slightly in her seat. Her stomach had tied itself into knots of tension and her silk shirt, moist from perspiration, clung both to her neck and to the vinyl seat. The houses they were passing were large and impressive, architect-designed, red brick or slabs of shining white like an elaborately iced wedding cake, each with its own verandah, and in front of them the gardens were vivid with marigolds and roses. This was to be expected, of course. The Greg Martin who had juggled millions of dollars – albeit sometimes illegally – would never have settled for anything but the best and Maria Vincenti or Trafford or whatever she called herself was an heiress in her own right. Money would be no object to her. Perhaps it was the reason why they had been able to live undisturbed here for almost a quarter of a century. Riches bought respect, whatever the cynics might say.

Far below the sparkling blue bay was busy with yachts from the marina at Rushcutters and glancing down at it Harriet felt her stomach tighten another notch. Did one of them belong to Greg Martin – once a sailor always a sailor? Or did he feel after the explosion that he never wanted to set foot aboard one again? No – impossible. If he had been haunted by the experience he would never have chosen to settle here within sight of the marina however prestigious the homes. Further proof, if any were needed, that what had happened off the coast of Italy had been no accident.

Harriet averted her eyes sharply then forced herself to look again. Before this was over she might well have to face something a good deal more painful than the sight of a few luxury yachts. If she was not prepared for that she might as well abandon her quest and go home here and now, bury her head in the sand as Sally and her father were doing. And she had no intention of doing that.

Behind her sun-glasses Harriet's eyes narrowed slightly. She was puzzled by their attitude, their anxiety that the carefully constructed veils of twenty years would be stripped away and the past, and whatever had happened in it, come to light. It was a response she would have expected from her father – he had always played the ostrich where unpleasant facts were concerned, and she could understand that he had no wish to re-open old wounds. The pain he still felt was evident – perhaps it stifled any curiosity he might otherwise have felt. But Sally ... Harriet could not understand Sally's attitude at all. Surely she must want to know what happened to Mom just as I do, Harriet thought – to know for sure if she is alive or dead. If she is alive, to see her again, if she is dead to make sure justice is done to the man responsible for her death. But Sally seemed even more reluctant to face the ghosts of the past than Hugo was, and right up until Harriet's departure she had continued to beg her niece not to go, to leave well alone.

'There's no point raking it all up, Harriet,' she had said. 'She's dead – for God's sake let her rest in peace.'

Her face beneath her carefully applied make-up had been deathly pale and the dark circles beneath her eyes were evidence of a sleepless night.

'I'm sorry, Sally,' Harriet had told her. 'I can't just go back to London and pretend none of this has happened. Anyway, that damned insurance investigator won't let her rest in peace, as you put it, until he's dug out every bit of the truth and I don't want to hear it second hand even if you do. She was my mom – I want to be right there when – if – he finds her.'

'What will you do?' Sally had asked, knotting her hands together to keep them from trembling.

'First I shall go to Sydney and talk to this Maria Vincenti. If it's true that she has lived with Greg Martin for twenty years then she must know something.'

'How do you know she'll see you?'

'She'll see me,' Harriet had said, her lips setting in a determined line.

Once in Australia, however, she had been less sure. In her hotel room at the Sydney Hilton she had lifted the telephone to call the woman, then replaced it again. Perhaps Maria Vincenti *would* refuse to see her. Perhaps she was already regretting the hornet's nest she had stirred up. In any case she might not wish to talk to the daughter of a woman who had once been involved with her lover. She was after all Italian – and Italian passions and jealousies run high. Perhaps it would be better to arrive unannounced, Harriet had decided – use the same shock tactics Tom O'Neill had used on her, even if it did not make for a very pleasant first meeting.

'Photographer, are you?' the taxi driver asked. Harriet came back as from a long way off to see him nodding at the camera that was peeping out of her bag. 'Which paper are you with? The *Sun? News of the World?*' Or is it one of the Yankee papers?'

'I'm not here to take photographs,' Harriet said.

The taxi driver laughed. 'Well, you could have fooled me. Though most of 'em don't exactly try to hide it.'

'Most of them?'

'The paparazzi. Jeez, lady, you're a cool one. Well, good luck to you, I say. And with the crowd that's already there I reckon you'll need it. Here we are now – you'll see what I mean.'

They rounded a bend and suddenly Harriet understood. Since they had left the bustle of Sydney's centre the streets had been quiet but here quite a crowd had gathered on the road outside and opposite a large white stuccoed house. Some stood in groups, smoking, others sat on the kerb in the shade of the trees, cameras resting on their knees. The paparazzi – the world's press – all here waiting for a glimpse of the woman who had blown the whistle on Greg Martin after twenty years.

'Shit,' Harriet said softly.

The taxi driver laughed again. 'What did you expect, lady – an exclusive? I don't know what the guy did – I was too busy bumming around and getting on with my own life twenty years ago to bother much with newspapers. But whatever it was it must sure as hell have been worth doing.' He stopped the cab, leaving the engine running. 'Reckon that's as far as we go.'

Harriet looked at the crowd in dismay. What a fair! There was even a policeman stationed at the gate. She had not a cat in hell's chance of getting past him. He would assume that she was another enterprising newspaper hack, just as the taxi driver had.

'Where is the nearest telephone?' she asked.

'Dunno. You want me to look for one?'

'Yes . . . no.' She didn't want to make such a delicate phone call from a public booth with the danger of the money running out just as she was trying to explain herself. 'Take me back to the Hilton.'

He looked at her as if she were mad, then shrugged. 'Suit yourself.'

As he began to turn the car Harriet's brain clicked into gear. Chicken! Any excuse not to face Maria Vincenti. Any excuse to put off the moment of learning the truth. Is that what she had come halfway round the world for – to give up at the first hurdle?

'Stop!' she said sharply.

He pulled up, shaking his head. If he had had any doubts before, now they were confirmed – she *was* mad. But then so were all the paparazzi – and no wonder. What a way to make a living!

Harriet rifled through her bag to find pen and paper. The paper came from the pad she used to list details of photographs she took – it was printed with the logo of the film processing company. No good. That really did mark her out as a photographer and unless Maria Vincenti had heard of her and knew what she did she would be bound to be suspicious. Harriet pushed the pad back into her bag and tore a page from her diary. Not perfect, but it would have to do. For a moment she thought about what she should say, then scribbled hastily. Another search through her bag revealed just what she was looking for – an old envelope bearing her name and the address of her London home. Surely that should identify her? She placed the note inside.

'Please wait,' she said to the taxi-driver. 'I may need you if this doesn't work.'

He rolled his eyes. 'Pay me now for what's on the clock if you don't mind.'

'Oh right . . .' She paid him, left the cab and walked back along the street. The paparazzi came to life like a bunch of magic toys at the stroke of midnight, craning, pushing, eliciting. Harriet ignored them. One enterprising hack broke away from the bunch and made for the taxi – to see what the driver would be prepared to tell him about her, presumably. Well, too bad. They'd be able to trace her back to the Hilton if the taxi driver broke confidence – and a couple of hundred dollar bills would soon persuade him to do that – but he didn't know her name. If there was any hint of trouble she would simply check out and move on.

As she went through the gate onto the broad gravelled drive the policeman intercepted her.

'Sorry, but you are trespassing. You'll have to wait outside with the others – for all the good it will do you.'

'I'm not a reporter.' Harriet held out the envelope. 'Will you please give this to Mrs Trafford?'

He looked doubtful.

'This is a personal matter. I am quite sure Mrs Trafford will see me,' Harriet said in her most authoritative tone and to her relief after a moment's hesitation he took the envelope.

'All right – but you'll have to wait outside the gate until you have permission to come any further.'

'I refuse to be treated like a criminal,' Harriet said.

On the point of insisting the policeman changed his mind. There was something about the girl: he couldn't put his finger on it but he supposed it could be summed up in one word – class. She had class. Unlike most of those bums who would use any trick in the book to get inside the house for their story.

'Wait here – but don't try anything,' he warned.

Harriet waited, looking at the house. Very grand, very colonial with its balustrades and elaborate verandah. But the shutters at the windows were half-closed; like sightless eyes they gave nothing away. Was Maria Vincenti looking at her from one of them now? Possibly. The thought was unnerving. Harriet dug her hands into the pockets of her slacks, deliberately casual, and willed herself to stand quite still, not pacing or wandering.

After what seemed an eternity the policeman emerged. Harriet's heart came into her mouth. What would she do if Maria Vincenti refused to see her? Her exit would be ignominious to say the least. Worse, she would have come all this way for nothing.

The policeman's face gave nothing away.

'Well?' she demanded.

'She'll see you. You can go in.'

'Thank you.' But suddenly she was afraid, just as she had been in the taxi. Did she really want to know the truth? Might it not be far more comfortable to remain in ignorance? Unpleasant facts, once known could never be buried again. She would have to live with them for the rest of her life.

Harriet tossed her head. Her hair, tied in a long bunch at the nape of her neck, bounced defiantly. Who the hell was Maria Vincenti anyway? Harriet walked past the policeman and into the house.

'Holy Mother of God,' Maria Vincenti said softly.

She drained her tumbler of vodka and tomato juice and crossed the room to the drinks cabinet to refill it, a short overblown woman with the ample bosom and hips of a typical middle-aged Italian.

Maria had never been beautiful, but in her youth her big thrusting breasts, her full mouth and dark flashing eyes had caused men to think of her as voluptuous. Now another word was sometimes used to describe her and the word was blowzy, for she had lived life too fully to have retained that glorious fleeting Mediterranean bloom – too much passion, too much pasta and lately far too much alcohol had hastened the deterioration of her face into paunchiness and her body to fat.

She drank again, gulping greedily as if her life depended on it, then looked again at the note scribbled on a page torn from a diary. Holy Mother of God, why had she started any of this? She didn't think the police believed the story she had told them but the newspapers had latched onto it like vultures. Then there had been the insurance investigator – what was his name, Tom O'Neill? – with his probing questions. And now this girl ... already Maria was regretting having agreed to see her. But it was too late to change her mind now. She would already be on her way in. Maria crumpled the note viciously and dropped it in the wastepaper basket. Her hand was shaking.

Paula's daughter. Paula Varna. Now there was a name from the past! Maria had tried not to think of Paula for years; now in her mind's eye she could see her all too clearly, tall, beautiful, glowing, all the things she, Maria, could never be. But what a cow! Maria thought bitterly. A husband of her own and still not satisfied. Cuckolding him, encouraging Greg – not that Greg had required much encouragement! – a strange mixture of spoiled little girl and *femme fatale*. Maria's insides seemed to tighten as if squeezed by a relentless hand and she gripped her glass until her knuckles turned white.

Paula Varna, I hope you rot in hell. If it hadn't been for you Greg and I might have been happy. Bitch! Silly, spoiled, persistent little bitch!

As the wave of hatred passed Maria's heavy dark brows knitted together in perplexity. Bitterness she could understand. The shadow of Paula had hung over her for more than twenty years. But why should she feel jealousy? Hadn't Greg left Paula for her, Maria? Hadn't the two of them planned it all together? Then why . . .?

Because you know in your heart the choice wasn't made for love, she thought. It was made for money. Yes, money – the great god at whose altar Greg has always worshipped. If Paula had had access to the sort of money that she, Maria, had had, and if she had been free to lavish it on him then perhaps he would have chosen differently. Throughout the years Maria had known which of her assets it was that had attracted Greg to her. In the beginning she hadn't cared. She would have done anything to have him near her; God alone – and the parish priest who had heard her confession – knew that. But as time went by the bitterness had begun to creep in. Gradually Greg's greed and callousness had eaten away at the obsession she felt for him until it had turned to hatred and despair. And now it had come close to destroying her.

Maria gulped again at her vodka, taken neat this time, with only the melting ice in the glass to dilute it. The alcohol burned her throat and stomach and sent small fiery flickers through her veins.

A tap at the door made her turn. The maid had opened the door and the girl who stood there might have been a young Paula. Not as tall, but that glorious dark blonde hair, those clear features, figure slender yet shapely in her cream silk shin and tawny linen slacks. Maria's heart seemed to stop beating and any thoughts that she might have had that this could be a trick vanished.

This was Paula's daughter, without a shadow of a doubt.

'Miss Varna,' she said and the edge to her voice said it all. 'What a surprise. Do come in.'

'Thank you for seeing me,' Harriet said.

After the bright sunshine outside it was dim inside the room behind the half-closed shutters but as Harriet's eyes adjusted she took in the cane and rattan furniture, the abundance of cushions in different shades of cornflower and delft blue, the floor tiled. Mediterranean style and strewn with rugs and dhurries. As the exterior of the house had suggested it would every detail spoke of money, but old money. If she had expected the brash Stateside gloss that might have been the trademark of a self-made American financier, it was certainly not here.

She held out her hand. 'You must be . . . I'm sorry, should I call you Mrs Trafford?'

Maria ignored the outstretched hand. 'I think I would rather drop that name. It has too many unpleasant connections. There's no point any more in not using my real name, Vincenti. What can I do for you, Miss Varna?'

'Harriet, please. I know this is an imposition, but I had to come. As you probably know, my mother was a friend of Greg Martin's back in the States. She was with him on his yacht when it blew up.'

'So they said.'

Harriet looked at her sharply. 'What do you mean?'

'Nothing. Please go on.'

'Well, I have always believed she died with him. Now I understand you are claiming Greg is alive and . . .'

'He is.' Maria laughed shortly. 'At least, he was the last time I saw him, a week ago.' She lifted her glass; half-melted ice clinked as she drained it. 'Very much alive and just the same old Greg as he always was. He may have changed his name and his appearance but underneath it all he is just the same. A cheat, a liar, a womaniser – maybe a murderer.' She crossed to the drinks cabinet to refill her glass. 'You want a drink, Miss Varna?'

Harriet shook her head. If anything could bring home the truth of her father's warning as to over-indulgence it was the sight of this woman, soaked with vodka like a piece of old blotting paper.

'Too early for you, huh? What about coffee? That's what you Americans drink all the time isn't it – coffee?' She rang a bell and the maid reappeared.

'Coffee for Miss Varna'. She crossed to the window, looked out and gesticulated impatiently towards the road. 'Those damned reporters! I almost thought you might be one, you know, trying to trick your way in. They never give up. You'd think they had something better to do. They have even pushed notes through the door offering me money for my story. Money! To me! I could buy and sell their stupid newspapers several times over.'

'I don't trick my way in anywhere. I'm not a tricky person.'

Maria's lip curled. 'Hah! Not much like your mother, then?'

'I wouldn't know,' Harriet said. 'I was only four years old, remember, when whatever happened to her . . . happened.'

Maria's eyes fell away, a shaft of something almost like guilt piercing the alcohol-induced haze. Of course the girl had been just a bambino then. Maria remembered the photographs of her in the newspapers, chubby-cheeked, golden-curled, dressed in a frilly frock, very short, with long white knee socks. Harriet Varna, poor little rich girl, four years old and motherless. Ah well, Paula should have thought of that before she started playing about, dabbling in her dangerous games.

'So you never saw her again,' she said flatly.

'No, of course I didn't. I would hardly be here now, asking questions, if I had.' Harriet's tone was sharp; hearing her own voice she glanced quickly at Maria, afraid she might have offended her. But Maria seemed not to have noticed. 'The thing is, I thought that if Greg Martin did not die in the explosion then perhaps neither did my mother. I don't know what happened that day. I don't understand any of it – yet. But you must see I have to try to find out. And I thought you might be able to help me.'

Maria turned the glass in her hands. How much *did* the girl know? She must suspect at least that her mother had been Greg's lover – that much was obvious, surely. Why else should she have followed him to Italy? Why the hell *did* she? Maria wondered savagely. If she had not perhaps things would have been different. It wouldn't nave changed the way Greg had treated her, of course. Nothing short of a miracle could have kept him faithful to her, louse that he was. But at least she might have had some peace of mind instead of the terrible doubts that had assailed her all these years.

'I know nothing,' she said shortly. 'Greg never told me what happened to your mother and I never asked. Perhaps I didn't want to know.'

The maid brought the coffee, poured it and left. As the door closed after her Harriet tried again.

'If Greg is alive, as you say he is, then he must have escaped when the boat blew up. Surely you haven't lived with him all these years without knowing how he managed it?'

Maria turned sharply. 'Oh, I know how he managed it, all right.' There was a note of bitter amusement in her voice. 'He managed it because I helped him.'

'You . . .!' The jerk of surprise shook Harriet's whole body; coffee slopped from the cup into the saucer.

'Yes, me, fool that I was. Haven't you ever been in love, Miss Varna? Don't you know what it's like to lose you head over a man? No, I don't believe you do. You are like your mother, cold. It is different for me. I have Latin blood and when I love – I love. Well, I hope you never find out what it can be like. I tell you it is the worst pain in the world to sell your soul for a man and then find out he is an utter bastard.'

Harriet set her cup down on a low table. She could not trust herself to hold it any longer.

'What did you do?' she asked.

For a long moment Maria was silent. All these years she had told no one. Not when Greg had deceived her with other women, or when he had humiliated her, not when he had finally embroiled himself with his newest love, a former beauty queen, and Maria had known he was using her money to buy expensive presents for the hussy. Beneath it all she had suffered – God alone knew how she had suffered – but she had kept his secret. Even when she had suspected he intended to have her killed so as to have unlimited access to the money which would all become his under her will, and to be free to go off with his paramour into the bargain, and she had been sufficiently frightened to denounce him, she had still kept silent about her own part in what had happened. If she had told the whole story perhaps the police would have believed her but she had not been able to bring herself to do it. Now, suddenly, she was overcome with an unstoppable urge to talk about what she had done. It was time, she thought, that someone knew just what lengths she had been prepared to go to for him – and who better than the daughter of the woman who had caused her so much anguish?

She took another deep slurp of vodka; her eyes flashed in her sallow face.

'All right, I'll tell you, Harriet Varna,' she said. 'I'll tell you all I know, for what it's worth. I hope you'll keep it to yourself, but if you don't, well, I don't care much any more. I've opened my mouth so far and I might as well tell the full story. You were too young to remember Greg, I suppose?'

Harriet nodded. She could barely trust herself to speak. She didn't remember Greg, except as a vague shadowy figure. Until a few days ago she hadn't even known what he looked like. Every photograph in which he figured had been removed from the family albums – and understandably so. Hugo had wanted no reminder of the man who had cost him his beloved wife.

'Well, he was a charmer, not a doubt of it. He took me in, and plenty of others besides. His whole rocky empire was built on charm. He talked big – and people believed him. He had a finger in plenty of pies but he wanted a stake in the fashion industry – that was why he put up the money to get your father started. But he wanted to do it Italian style. Did you know he was of Italian descent? His name was Martino until he changed it to Martin. Anyway, in Italy the fashion business is run almost on the same lines as the Mafia. It's a cartel, with the fabric supplier, the factory owner and the designer all getting together to market a label as a successful business enterprise. They have the magazines in their pockets too, so they get just the coverage they want. In those days, of course, it was only just beginning. But Greg wanted to be in on it. My father is the president of our family fabric firm – we have factories at Lake Como. Greg started wooing him. That was when I met him.'

She paused, cradling her glass between her hands. Harriet remained silent, afraid that any word from her might interrupt the flow. Yet at the same time she sensed that Maria was talking now from the bottom of her fiery Latin heart, her tongue loosened by drink, spilling out things that has festered too long within her.

After a moment Maria continued. She was not looking at Harriet; she might almost have been talking to herself.

'Holy Mother, how I loved him! I was a young fool, I know that now, but I have been an old fool for him too. Why do we women always love the bastards? My father warned me about him. He was a clever businessman and he could see right through Greg. "Have nothing to do with him, Maria," he told me. "He is trouble, that one." But did I listen? I thought my father was old and staid. He had been head of the family and of the business empire for so long and I thought he just wanted to be able to tell me what to do, as he had done when I was a child. Most of all I thought he had forgotten what it was like to be young and in love. I defied him. I met Greg whenever I could and the more I saw of him the more head over heels in love with him I was. Oh, how he wound me round his little finger! Even when he told me everything was about to blow up around his ears back in the States I still did not see that he was no good. I thought he had been unfortunate – and all I wanted was to be with him. When he told me what he was planning to do and asked me to help him I rushed in like the little idiot I was.'

She broke off again, and as the shadows chased fleetingly across her bloated face Harriet knew she was reliving the way it had been. Then she sighed heavily and shook her head.

'He planned it all so carefully,' she said. 'He got himself a false birth certificate and passport – he took the identity of some poor man who had died, I believe. Yes, there really was a Michael Trafford once – funny isn't it? Anyway, Greg decided the best way for him to disappear was to make people believe he had died in an explosion on his yacht. It was a beautiful boat – he kept it in a marina within easy reach of his holiday villa at Positano, in the Gulf of Salerno. I don't know how he could bear to destroy it – he must have been desperate to even think of such a thing. The plan was that he would take it out for a few days' sailing with plenty of witnesses to his departure, head south and land quietly on one of the deserted beaches near Pizzo. Then he would send it back out to sea on automatic with an explosive device rigged to go off a couple of hours later. I was to pick him up in Pizzo and drive him back to Roma. From there he would get a flight out of the country using his false passport. It worked like a charm. By the time the news broke that the yacht had blown up Greg was on his way to Australia. I waited nearly a year, until all the fuss had died down, and then I joined him there. And when I stayed on I told my parents it was because I had met a man called Michael Trafford.'

Her eyes glazed; she took another quick slurp of her vodka, found the glass empty, and refilled it. Harriet was staring at her, speechless, and Maria misinterpreted her look.

'You think I drink too much, huh?' she asked with a flash of something close to aggression. 'Perhaps you too would drink if you had lived with this all these years.'

'What about my mother?' Harriet asked. Her mouth was dry.

Maria turned away but not before Harriet had seen the shaft of pain behind the dark blood-shot eyes.

'I know nothing about what happened to your mother.'

'But she sailed with Greg. Everyone said so.'

'I know nothing I tell you,' Maria insisted. 'She was not part of the plan. He had told me everything was over between them. He wanted only me.'

'But when you saw in the newspapers that she was on the boat you must have asked him about it,' Harriet persisted. 'I can't believe you didn't.'

Maria's face crumpled fiercely. For a moment Harriet thought she was going to cry. Then it hardened again.

'I did ask him what the hell she was doing there, of course. He said she had turned up unexpectedly at his villa just before he left. He said he tried to reach me by telephone to warn me there was a hitch but he couldn't get hold of me. So he went ahead as planned. He couldn't let her ruin everything, he said. "I couldn't let her ruin everything" – those were his very words.'

'So he sailed with her aboard. But what happened to her?'

185

'I swear to God I don't know.' Maria's voice dropped to a whisper. 'I didn't press him. But if you want to know what I've suspected all these years – I'm very much afraid he killed her.'

Harriet could not speak. She was trembling. It was what she too had suspected but hearing it put into words was still a shock and so melodramatic as to be unreal.

'Why else has she never turned up?' Maria asked. 'She had no reason to disappear. I tried not to believe it. I told myself I was wicked to even think of such a thing. The man I loved . . . But I know now just how ruthless he is. He has tried to have me killed, you know, because he has no further use for me. And if Paula had lived she could have ruined everything for him. She wouldn't have kept his secret, not when he had walked out on her. No, I truly believe that under those circumstances Greg would have been capable of murder.'

Harriet pressed her hands to her mouth. Yes, if Maria was telling the truth – and Harriet believed she was – it all hung together too neatly. As Maria had said, Paula had no reason to disappear. Besides, a face as well known as hers . . .

'You say it was a year before you joined him in Australia,' she said, grasping at straws. 'Is it possible she was with him here during that time?'

'Possible, but I don't think so. I picked him up at Pizzo, remember, and he was alone.'

Harriet's hands balled into fists. 'Where is he now?'

Maria laughed bitterly. 'If I knew that, Miss Varna, the police would have him by now I hope. He's gone to ground with his new lady friend – the bitch. Well, at least they won't get a penny more out of me. I'm changing my will. He might get away with what he's done but at least he won't do it on my money.'

'He won't get away with it,' Harriet said. 'Not if I can help it.'

'I can see you don't know Greg Martin,' Maria said. Her voice was becoming slurred as if telling her story had held the effects of the chink at bay but now she had finished it was hitting her all at once. 'I can't tell you any more, Miss Varna, and I want to be alone. So if you don't mind . . .'

'Yes. Thank you.' Harriet held out her hand, again Maria refused it. She couldn't bear to touch Paula's daughter, not even now after all these years.

When Harriet had gone she walked unsteadily to the drinks cabinet and refilled her glass. The room might be rocking around her like a ship in a storm but no matter. She simply wanted to drink and drink herself into oblivion. After the passion and torments of her wasted life it was all that was left to her.

In London the snow had quickly melted on the pavements and no more had fallen, but the damp, bone-chilling cold was far more penetrating than the crispness had been.

In her small workroom at the top of the crumbling old house in Whitechapel Theresa Arnold was talking on the telephone to one of her fabric suppliers.

'Yes – yes, it's arrived. But it's the wrong design. No, I'm certain I quoted you the right sample number – I have it in front of me now. Z2034. Yes, it is black, but with a stripe woven in. The one I wanted has a random pattern. I think you've sent me Z2024. Look, I'm desperate for it. If I return this bolt to you today can you dispatch me the one I want by special delivery? You can? Thank you, I'd be most grateful.'

She replaced the receiver with hands slightly clumsy from the cold in spite of the woollen fingerless gloves she was wearing and shook her head despairingly at the young woman who was perched on a stool opposite her, warming herself at the portable gas heater.

'I should know better than to place my orders by telephone. All it takes is for some stupid office girl to press the wrong key on her computer, or whatever it is they use, and I get a whole consignment of useless fabric'

'Such is life.' Linda George, her business partner, said prosaically. 'I'm afraid it's not your day, Terri. I've got more bad news for you. That's why I'm here.'

Theresa groaned, coming around to join Linda by the fire.

'I don't think I want to know.'

'I'm sure you don't, but you'll have to, all the same. *Sister Susie's* have gone bust.'

Sister Susie was a chain of boutiques who had supported Theresa with sizeable orders.

'Gone bust? You mean . . .?'

'They've got the receivers in. I heard this morning.'

Theresa felt sick.

'But I thought they were doing well!' she wailed.

'A charade, obviously. You know it's been a hell of a couple of years for fashion retail. Even the big High Street stores have been feeling the pinch so it must nave been terrible for the smaller ones with tight profit margins. Anyway, I thought I ought to let you know straight away about *Sister Susie*. They don't owe us much, thank God, I chased them up over their account only a couple of weeks ago, so it could be worse.'

'But it will hit my new season's sales,' Theresa said anxiously. 'I need not have chased that silk manufacturer if I'd known – a good half of it was for blouses for *Sister Susie*. Where am I going to get rid of them now?'

'Leave it to me.' Linda squeezed her friend's arm. 'Stop worrying, Terri. You need to keep your head clear so you can do what you're good at – creating. I'll sort something out.'

'I hope so.' Theresa tried to keep her voice cheerful and failed. 'That's two good accounts we've lost in as many days. And my rent's due for review soon. If that goes up with a leap and a bound – and I have a horrible feeling it might, judging by some of them round here – that will be the last straw. I just don't know how much longer I can keep going.'

'Oh come on!' Linda was wearing a very full calf-length corduroy skirt and jodhpur boots; she aimed a kick at Theresa with one of them. 'Don't be such a defeatist.'

Theresa smiled ruefully. 'You're not the one who has to sit here all day freezing to death. Being cold all the time is so depressing!'

'But you're going to stick it out, aren't you?'

Theresa nodded. 'I've got to, haven't I? If I don't make a success of it Mum will lose her house. But – oh, sometimes I feel as though I'm running against the tide.'

'Chin up. You're a brilliant designer and one day the world will realise it. What you need is a princess to discover you and ask you to make her wedding dress. You'd be well away then. There's still Prince Edward to go – wonder who he'll marry and when? And Lady Sarah Armstrong-Jones – she'd look gorgeous in one of your designs.'

Theresa laughed. 'Pipe dreams. What I need is a backer. Someone to take all the financial worries off my shoulders.'

'Pity Mark Bristow isn't still around,' Linda said speculatively. 'He seemed to have an answer for everything.' Theresa said nothing. 'Oh Terri!' Linda scolded, seeing her expression. 'You're not still carrying a torch for him, are you? For heaven's sake forget him! He's not worth it.'

'You're right. He's not.' Theresa moved away from the fire. Her denim jeans smelled as if they might be burning but she was still cold. 'I've got to get on, Linda. Next thing Weasel will be up here trying to drag me out for a coffee and he won't take no for an answer.'

'Another of your admirers.'

'Don't be ridiculous,' Theresa said. Her sense of humour always deserted her when she was so cold.

'All right, I'll leave you in peace. And I'll spread the word that the brightest young talent in London is looking for a backer. Someone like Peder Bertelson or the mystery man who backed Rifar Ozbek. Not even Rifar himself can remember his name, if he's to be believed. All he'll admit to is that he is a Pakistani living in Geneva. But then he's probably shit-scared if he let on everyone else would try to jump on the bandwagon.'

She buttoned her jacket, bright red wool lined in black with a swinging hip length skirt that fell from a trenchcoat-style yoke – one of Theresa's samples from last season. Even with the cord skirt and boots it looked good – with a short black skirt and high heels it would have been stunning.

'See you, Terri. Tomorrow night? Perhaps we could grab a Chinese takeaway.'

Theresa shook her head. 'Cash flow problem, Linda. It'll have to be something made up of soya mince, I'm afraid. And that'll be a luxury after a week of baked beans and jacket potatoes.'

As Linda clattered down the stairs Theresa stood for a moment deep in thought. Surely some time things must take a turn for the better? If they didn't it would be the end of the road. The thought fired Theresa's determination and before the creeping disease of despair could attack again she went back to her bench and started work once more.

CHAPTER FOURTEEN

Tom O'Neill had been busy. His first visit to Maria Vincenti had been an almost total waste of time, for she had refused point blank to answer any of his questions, taking refuge in a pretence of not understanding. It was a stupid ploy, since it would have been obvious to anyone but an imbecile that no-one could live in an English-speaking country for twenty years without gaining at least a working knowledge of the language, but one he had found impossible to get around, though it had confirmed his suspicions that Maria knew a great deal more than she was telling. He had decided to leave her alone for a while and then make another attempt when perhaps he would catch her in a different mood. And in the meantime he had a number of other leads to follow up.

First Tom had tried to follow the tracks of 'Michael Trafford's' business interests. These were diverse and were connected only by a string of registered offices across the southern half of Australia. Tom called numbers in Canberra, Melbourne, Adelaide and Perth, but in each case he drew blanks. No, they could not help with the whereabouts of Mr Trafford. No, they had not seen him and had no forwarding address. And even if they had confidentiality would forbid . . . Tom understood. He had come up against this kind of blank wall before; he was, after all, an insurance investigator not a policeman. But he rather suspected the registered offices were telling the truth. Michael Trafford – or Greg Martin – was elusive and tricky. Tom suspected those young ladies who tried to sound so knowing and businesslike had probably never set eyes on him at all.

The next line of enquiry had proved more fruitful. Martin's new love was a former beauty queen named Vanessa McGuigan and during the early stages of their relationship she had talked a little too freely to friends about the man she was becoming involved with. Mention had been made of a firm of contractors and land developers in Darwin, Northern Territory, in which Vanessa had boasted her boyfriend had a controlling interest. This piece of information had appealed to Tom's investigator's instincts. Darwin was a transient place, where many of the population were drifters and misfits, men passing through – or lying low. Isolated at the Top End of the Territory it managed to retain something of the feel of the old frontier town in spite of having been almost completely rebuilt on modem lines after being virtually flattened by Cyclone Tracy in 1970. It was exactly the sort of place a man could happily disappear if the necessity arose. Perhaps Greg had known that he might one day have to beat a hasty retreat from Sydney and had prepared a bolt-hole for himself accordingly.

Tom did some checking on the construction company. There was no mention of a Greg Martin or a Michael Trafford among its directors – but there was a Rolf Michael. Again Tom's spine had tingled the way it did when his instincts were telling him he was on the right track. *Michael* Trafford – Rolf *Michael*. With almost no evidence to support his hunch, he felt quite certain they were one and the same.

It was at this point that Tom had decided to go back and see Maria Vincenti again. He had found her more morose than ever and almost too drunk to be coherent. But she had said one thing that surprised him.

'I've told her daughter all I know. If you want to know what happened, ask her. I can't go through it all again.'

Her daughter. Harriet. Here in Sydney. Tom's eyes had narrowed thoughtfully. He had been uncertain as to just how far he trusted the Varnas and Harriet in particular had been very defensive. Now, if Maria was to be believed, it seemed she was in possession of some additional information – and perhaps very potent information at that. Tom badly wanted to know what it was.

There were, of course, two entirely separate hurdles to overcome. The first was – where to find her. But on consideration that was hardly a problem at all. Someone with her money and background would almost certainly be staying in one of the best hotels in Sydney – the Regent, the Hilton or the Sheraton in all probability. An enquiry at their reception desks would quickly elicit which. No, it was the second problem that was the more ticklish – her aggressively unhelpful attitude towards him.

Tom rubbed his chin thoughtfully. Time to see Harriet again – and quite clearly time for a different approach. He was not unaware of the effect he had on women when he set his mind to it (and quite often when he did not) and he was not averse to making use of this asset when it suited him. Perhaps charm would work on Harriet where assertiveness had failed. And since Harriet was a very attractive woman herself the idea of trying it was not unappealing.

Tom smiled faintly and reached for the telephone.

Harriet was sitting at one of the tables in the open air café in the Botanical Gardens, nursing a glass of ice-cold orange juice and feeling exhaustion, both mental and physical, creep through her.

She had enjoyed walking through the gardens, for here, amongst the exotic palms and peach trees the heat seemed less oppressive. In the branches of a huge spreading yellow tulipwood a currawong squawked, ibis buried their long black bills in the mud at the lake side, and sparrows and budgerigars rose in untidy flocks at her approach and she had thought how strange it was that at home both London and New York were shivering, and only a few days ago she had been muffled up in ski jacket and boots, trying to escape from the biting wind in Paris. But the observation had only taken her thoughts full circle and now, sitting in the café, she recalled once more the story Maria had told her.

Was it the truth? And was Maria right to suspect that Greg had murdered Paula? Or was she simply an embittered old soak whose brain was so fuddled by alcohol that she could no longer distinguish between fact and fantasy? Perhaps – but there had to be a reason for her disintegration. Once she had been an heiress with the world at her feet, strong enough to defy her father and give up everything for the man she loved. Something had happened to change her. Perhaps it was just as she had claimed – that she had lived for twenty years with the conviction that that man was a murderer.

Harriet sipped her juice and forced herself to face the implications of it head on. Maria claimed that she had been unable to bring herself to ask the pertinent questions; Harriet knew she would never rest until she knew for certain what exactly had happened to her mother. She had been alive when the boat sailed, no question of that, and she had never been seen again. Had Greg abandoned her to die in the explosion – or was she already dead when he put ashore? The likelihood must be that she was – either that, or unconscious or tied up and helpless in the cabin. Harriet shuddered, imagining her mother's terror. It didn't bear thinking about, yet somehow the uncertainty, the pictures conjured up by an imagination left to run riot, was far worse than the prospect of learning the truth and facing up to it.

The problem was that if Maria was to be believed only one person in the world knew the answers to the questions – Greg Martin himself. And he had disappeared into the vastness that was Australia.

She finished her drink and walked back through the gardens, across the massive frontage of the State Library and into Macquarie Street. The old colonial buildings here were stately and impressive but she scarcely glanced at them, crossing Martin Place and walking down George Street on her way back to the Hilton. In spite of her fears no inquisitive journalist had followed her there but she still glanced around a trifle defensively as she entered.

'There was a telephone call for you, Miss Varna,' the receptionist informed her as she collected her key and her eyes narrowed warily.

'A call .. for me?'

The receptionist noted her reaction with a mixture of curiosity and professionalism. 'It was a gentleman. He didn't leave his name but he said he'd call again.'

Harriet felt herself relax slightly. Nick, she thought. It must be

Nick. Who else would call me here? Unless of course it was Mark
. . .

In her room she slipped out of her linen top and walking shorts and began running a bath. Over the gush of water from the taps she heard the telephone and hurried to pick it up.

'Hello? Harriet Varna.'

'Miss Varna, this is Tom O'Neill. I expect you will be surprised to hear from me again, but when I learned you were in Sydney I thought it might be a good idea if we compared notes.'

Tom O'Neill! Harriet experienced a quick rush of irritation. Did the damned man never give up?

'I really don't think we have anything more to say to one another', she said coolly.

Undeterred he continued smoothly: 'I understand you are here on much the same sort of quest as I am. The fact is I have been making progress with my investigations and I wondered how you were getting along with yours.'

Ahah! she thought smugly. He thinks I have something he has missed – and if Maria was as unforthcoming with him as she said she was then he is quite right. But if he thinks I am going to tell him what she told me then he has another think coming!

Aloud she said: 'I'm progressing too. But I don't want to talk about it at the moment.'

There was a slight pause, then he said: 'That's rather a pity. I thought if we got together over a spot of dinner perhaps we could pool our information and be of help to one another.'

There was something about the way he said it, a hint of that old confidence, perhaps, that made her curious. Was he bluffing or was there more to it than that?

'What do you know?' she asked.

At the other end of the line Tom O'Neill smiled. But he did not allow that smile to creep into his voice.

'Oh, I'm afraid you'll have to have dinner with me to find that out', he said tantalisingly. 'But I do think it's something you would find very interesting.'

'Mr O'Neill . . .'

'I have a table booked at Alexandra's Restaurant at Hunters Hill for eight. I was hoping you'd meet me there. But if you won't then I suppose I shall have to find some other pretty lady to share it with me.' His tone was light now, she could almost have believed he was trying to date her, not bleed her of whatever information she had managed to gather. 'Well, Miss Varna?' he pressed her.

Harriet made up her mind. She was still unsure as to what he was up to, but with no new leads of her own she could not afford to pass up the chance of learning something new. As for the rest ... Harriet thought she could handle the situation satisfactorily.

'Very well. I'll be there. Eight, did you say?'

Hunters Hill – 'The French Village' – is one of Sydney's most exclusive suburbs. Here on a peninsula of the harbour villas and cottages were built by the finest French stonemasons and Italian artisans from the sandstone beneath its own hills. Bougainvillaea and climbing roses cover the trellis work and balconies, age-old jacaranda and fig trees shade the pathways and pavements.

Harriet's taxi swung west from the city and over the harbour bridge. The setting sun had turned the shimmering blue waters to a pool of flame; seeing it Harriet wished she had her camera with her for the sight was the stuff a photographer dreams of. Then, even as she watched, the sun fell below the horizon and soft velvet blackness dropped like a veil over the harbour with the lights of the Opera House forming the centrepiece of a new and different spectacle – Sydney by night.

Alexandra's Restaurant, historic and beautifully restored, once the main general store for the area, is on the outskirts of Hunters Hill. Harriet paid off her taxi and went in.

Tom O'Neill, casually dressed in open-neck shirt and slacks, was enjoying a pre-dinner drink at the bar which was separated from the dining area by an exquisite stained glass partition.

As she went in – inexplicably nervous – he rose.

'Well hullo. I'm glad you came. I wasn't sure that you would. What will you have to drink?'

'Campari and soda,' Harriet said. 'With ice but no lemon.'

With the drink in her hand she felt some of her confidence returning.

'Well, Mr O'Neill, I was intrigued by your invitation,' she said. 'I only hope it's not intended for your benefit only.'

'Of course not. As I said on the telephone, I think we can both be of help to each other. But what do you say we drop the formalities? I'd much prefer it if you'd call me Tom.'

She nodded briefly. She thought she would have preferred to let the formalities stand, but could not find a way to say so without sounding foolish.

The waiter was hovering with menus; they were a little late for their reservation, Harriet guessed.

'Shall we order?' Tom suggested, setting his glass down on the hand-carved bar of solid oak which had been brought over from England, it was said.

Harriet was not in the least hungry but she perused the menu and selected the lightest items – oysters and chicken – whilst Tom opted for giant prawns in matafi pastry and pork fillets with a Dijonaise sauce. When the waiter had taken their order they remained in the bar long enough to finish their drinks before being shown through into the dining room with its baby grand piano, polished brass, and so many leafy green plants it gave the appearance of a luxurious conservatory.

When they were seated at a lace-covered table Harriet said:

'I must confess I was very surprised to get your call. How did you know where to find me?'

'Guesswork. Let's put it this way – I didn't think you'd be at the People's Palace.'

'I see.' Harriet, always touchy about her wealthy background, coloured slightly. Was she so obvious? She liked to think of herself as an ordinary working girl, facing the world in denim jeans with a camera slung around her neck, but when the chips were down she had automatically gone for the best. Suddenly she was acutely conscious of her dress, a deceptively simple Comme des Garcons which had cost half a month's salary. Without money behind her she would never have dared buy it – all very well to play at being like everyone else, truth to tell she wasn't. Harriet wished heartily she had not worn it this evening. It wasn't ostentatious, none of her clothes were, but she felt sure Tom O'Neill was quite capable of looking at it with that cool blue gaze and putting a very accurately assessed price tag on it.

'So, what is it you've learned that is going to be of interest to me?' she asked crisply to hide her discomfort.

Tom speared a prawn before answering.

'I know where Greg Martin might be found.'

His tone was casual, throwaway almost, but taken completely, by surprise Harriet's skin began to prickle as if every tiny nerve ending had suddenly become sensitised.

'You know where he is?'

'I have a very good idea.'

'Where?'

'Oh!' He shook his head. 'Not so fast. It's your turn now.'

'What do you mean – my turn?'

'You're going to tell me how you have been getting on.'

She shrugged. 'There's nothing really to tell.'

'Come on, Harriet. I thought we were going to work together. What did Maria tell you?'

She looked up sharply. 'What makes you think she told me anything?'

'She assured me she did. It's a fair trade, isn't it? You tell me what Maria Vincenti said – I'll tell you where I think Greg Martin might be found.'

Harriet hesitated. This was exactly what she had hoped to avoid. She didn't want to talk about what Maria had said. For practically the first time in her life she knew how her father felt when he buried his head in the sand. Talking about something gave it substance. Better to just press on to the next hurdle – finding Greg Martin. Then perhaps she would be more prepared to face whatever unpalatable truths had been hidden all these years . . .

'She's a very strange lady,' she hedged.

'Granted. But also a very frightened one. That means she knows a good deal about things it might be safer not to know. Did she tell you how it was done?' Harriet was silent. He put down his knife and fork. 'Look, we are going to have to start trusting one another some time.'

Harriet looked up, meeting his eyes. Tonight they looked less cold; in fact there was something about the very hardness, of his face that was almost comforting. 'We have to start trusting one another . . .' Perhaps he was right. She was getting nowhere on her own and wouldn't unless she traded some information. But how much?

'All right,' she said. 'Maria says Greg rigged the whole thing with her assistance. She claims she picked him up at Pizzo and helped him to get out of the country.'

'And your mother?' he asked steadily.

Her eyes fell away but not before he had seen the flash of pain. She crumbled a bread roll between her fingers, watching the crumbs fall in a steady stream onto her plate. He waited. When she spoke her voice was steady but the effort needed to control it was obvious.

'Maria believes Greg murdered my mother.'

'*Murdered?*'

'I know it sounds melodramatic' She gave a small apologetic laugh. 'But you have to admit it fits the facts.'

'I think it's a little early to be sure of that. This investigation has only just begun.'

Harriet dropped the remains of her bread roll onto her plate and looked up at him.

'Don't think I want to believe it,' she said passionately. 'It's my mother we are talking about, remember. All my life I believed she was dead. Then the news broke that Greg Martin was alive and for a little while I hoped . . . yes, I did. Stupid, wasn't it? To actually hope that my mother had walked out on me *by choice*, not been there any of the times I needed her, just so that she could be alive. I just wanted her to be alive! But I don't think she is. Maria suspects Greg murdered her and I believe her. But not because I want to. Accepting it is just like losing her all over again.'

Suddenly he thought how very vulnerable she looked. Her hands were clenched into fists on the lace-covered table, her eyes were deep and liquid. In that moment he could almost believe she was telling the truth and he felt a brief pang of guilt knowing he was using her. Then he brushed the moment of weakness aside. She was Paula Varna's daughter and there was a small fortune riding on the case. He, Tom O'Neill, had a job to do. He couldn't afford to go soft now.

'So,' she said, gathering herself together, 'I've told you what Maria told me. Now it's your turn. Where is Greg Martin?'

'Very well. Fair's fair. I think he may be in Darwin.'

'Darwin! That's right up in the north, isn't it? What makes you think he is in Darwin?'

'My investigations suggest that he might be. I'm flying up there first thing tomorrow to try and locate him.'

The waiter appeared at Harriet's elbow. They waited in silence whilst he cleared their plates and brought the main course. Tom began on his pork but Harriet sat, fingertips pressed to her chin.

'Aren't you going to eat?' he asked.

She folded her fingers into a basket, looking at him directly.

'Could I . . . do you think I could possibly come with you?'

'Come with me?'

'To Darwin. I'm every bit as anxious to see Greg Martin as you are.'

Tom's eyes narrowed thoughtfully. He still was not completely certain he trusted her, but if she was feeding him a line as to what Maria had told her then she was one hell of an actress. It wasn't impossible, of course. He'd met consummate actresses before – and some of them had never so much as set foot on a stage. Tom O'Neill always believed in travelling fight. But at least if he took her with him to Darwin he would be able to keep an eye on her.

And besides . . . he cast a glance at her across the table. Without a doubt she was a very attractive woman. Taking her along would not be an unpleasant exercise.

'My plane leaves early in the morning,' he said. 'I suggest you telephone the airline right away to see if there are any seats available.'

When he returned to his hotel room Tom put a call through to his London office and asked to speak to Karen Spooner, his assistant.

'Tom? Hi! How y'doing, boss? What's it like in Oz?' Her voice was breathless, with a slight affected American accent, and Tom smiled to himself. Karen watched too many detective movies and worked hard at styling herself on her archetypal heroine, hence the twang and the habit of addressing him as 'boss'. She also had spiky black hair, large sooty eyes and dressed in black leather jackets and skin-tight jeans with 'designer rips' in the knee and seat, but she was a good girl, bright and keen, and he knew he could trust her to do an efficient job.

'Fine. Look – I'm off to Darwin tomorrow, and I'm taking Harriet Varna with me.'

'Harriet Varna? The daughter?' Karen sounded peeved; like so many others she carried a torch for Tom, and though he had never given her the slightest encouragement he also knew better than to upset her.

'I don't entirely trust her,' he explained. 'I want to be where I can keep an eye on her. And I think she might be useful to me. Now listen, what I want you to do is check up on the movements of the Varna family around the time of the explosion. It won't be easy of course. In fact after all this time it may be nigh on impossible, but . . .'

'Leave it to me, boss,' Karen said. She liked nothing better than a challenge.

'Good girl. I'll let you have the number where I can be reached as soon as I'm installed and again when I move on. I want to know the minute you come up with anything, no matter when it is, so don't worry checking time differences. Right?'

'Right. Wilco.'

Tom replaced the receiver and went back to packing his bags.

'Hey, Terri, I think I just might have swung it for you!'

Linda came bouncing into Theresa's workroom, slightly out of breath from running up the stairs. Theresa looked up.

'Swung what?'

'A deal, a big beautiful deal.'

'What sort of deal?'

'Sit down and I'll tell you. No – don't sit down – keep working! If this comes off you won't have time to draw breath!'

'For heaven's sake, Linda, will you tell me what this is all about?'

'OK. I went out "on the knocker" as they say, looking for business for you and I happened to call on a boutique called *Gypsy* – very trendy, very exclusive and *very* expensive. I didn't think I was getting very far. The owner was a snooty bitch and she was saying she only sold established names – ones she could put the right price tag on presumably, without anyone batting an eyelid. Then she was called away to deal with a customer and I got chatting to her husband – or rather he got chatting to me. He'd popped in to see her and had been sitting in a corner listening to everything I'd been saying. It seems he's rolling in money – he bought the boutique for his wife to give her an interest, would you believe?'

'I believe. Some people have all the luck.'

'Well maybe now a little of it will rub off on you. I told him all about you and what you are trying to do and he was very, very interested. Not only will he make sure his wife takes some of your stuff for the boutique, but also he might be persuaded to come up with some backing. And we're meeting him next week to discuss it.'

'Meeting him where?'

'At a plush restaurant in the West End. So you'll get at least one square meal out of it if nothing else. Beats baked beans and jacket potato, doesn't it?'

'Yes – as long as . . .' Theresa broke off, biting her lip.

'As long as what?'

'I'm not sure. It just sounds too good to be true.'

'Believe in yourself, my dear! It's confidence you lack these days. This could be your big break.'

'Yes, I suppose it could,' Theresa said, and wondered why when she should be excited and enthusiastic she could feel nothing but a kind of creeping apprehension.

CHAPTER FIFTEEN

Darwin in the Wet.

Harriet had heard the expression without attaching much importance to it. Now the reality was inescapable and she wondered how anyone – even a fugitive – could live here from choice.

The moment the doors of the 727 had been opened the heat had rushed in to envelop her – damp, cloying heat not unlike a sauna. Rain was falling in a thick curtain from lowering grey skies and evaporating in clouds of steam the moment it touched the tarmac; any views of the town or the sea, the lush tropical vegetation or the sharp modern architect-designed buildings, were lost in it. Already her skin felt clammy and breathing was an effort. Harriet remembered hearing that shoes left in a cupboard could turn white with mildew after a couple of weeks in the Wet and now she believed it.

Steamy tropical Darwin – the back of beyond. From freezing in Paris, London and New York to sweltering in Sydney to practically *poaching* in Darwin, and all in the course of a few days! I must be mad, thought Harriet, irritable from lack of sleep and the long flight, wedged into the 727 beside Tom, who had taken the aisle seat to accommodate his long legs.

They had talked a little and dozed a little, picking at the food that came regularly with each leg of the journey – croissants, fresh and delicious, with orange juice and coffee between Sydney and Brisbane, more coffee and biscuits between Brisbane and Townsville, and a light lunch between Cairns and Darwin.

As the Boeing put down and took off again on each of the short hops Harriet tried to see something of the countryside but she could make little sense of it. Wide expanses of desecrated brown land that she imagined were lumber forests and saw mills, patches of lush green that might have been sugar cane, and the sea, deepest blue shading to green and brown like the land where it washed over the Great Barrier Reef. But from the air the perspectives were all wrong and the narrow aircraft windows and the grey jut of the wing restricted vision annoyingly and Harriet gave up the effort. Then they were descending into the misty greyness of Darwin, jostling through the small airport buildings and emerging into the steam bath outside. Everything was dripping though for the moment the rain had stopped, the buildings cascading rivulets onto the tarmac, the trees, their leaves hanging low with the weight of water, spraying down intermittent showers. Tom and Harriet took a taxi, Tom sitting beside the driver, Australian style, Harriet squashed into the back with her bag containing her camera balanced on her knees.

At Telford Top End they registered in a tiny reception office where they were given yet more coffee while they waited to be shown to their rooms – ground floor and motel style, very basic but bright and clean. Harriet dumped her things and crossed to look out of the French windows. They opened onto a swimming pool and she wondered if a dip might relax her and take some of the ache out of her limbs. But the rain had begun again, sheeting down onto the green water of the pool, and Harriet remembered that in any case she had no swimsuit with her.

She turned back to the room. The bed looked extremely inviting. Perhaps she would lie down for five or ten minutes before unpacking. She drew the curtains to shut out the greyness, turned back the yellow coverlet and threw herself face down on the pillows. Bliss! Until that moment Harriet had not realised how tired she was. Perhaps I should have taken off my dress, she thought. I'll scrunch it to glory and heaven knows if there is an iron in this place. But she simply could not be bothered to move.

Damn you, Greg Martin, I wonder if you know how close I am on your tail now? she thought.

And then without any warning, without any drifting or drowsing, she was asleep.

It was quite dark when she awoke. For a moment she lay frowning into the pillow wondering where she was and trying to fight her way through the clouds of cotton wool inside her head. As they cleared she sat up, jerking aside the curtains to let in some grey faded fight and looking at her watch. Seven thirty? No – it couldn't be! She couldn't have slept like that! But clearly she had, without moving an inch from the position she had fallen into. Her hair, damp with perspiration, was glued to the side of her face, which was furrowed by the creases of the pillow, and her dress, creased into a sunburst of irregular pleats, was also damp. What a mess! Angry with herself she set the jug kettle on the breakfast tray to boil and dunked a teabag in milk. Wake up – wake up! You're not here to waste time sleeping!

She dragged a comb through her damp hair and without bothering to change went out and knocked on the door of the neighbouring room. There was no reply. She knocked again, wondering if perhaps Tom O'Neill had fallen asleep too, but still there was no answering movement from inside the room. So – he must have gone out.

Harriet returned to her own room. The kettle was boiling. She poured water on to the teabag, started the shower running and peeled off her creased dress, checking the time again. She'd have a shower then ring Nick. He should be at the office by now and she ought to let someone know where she was in case there were any messages. The water felt good on her flushed skin and she washed her hair, taking longer about it than she intended. By the time she emerged wrapped in a lightweight cotton kimono her tea was cooling. She drank it whilst dialling direct international and Nick answered almost immediately.

'Nick? It's me – Harriet.'

'Harriet? Where are you?' There was a slight time lag between her speaking and his reply, otherwise he might have been in the next room instead of half a world away.

'Darwin.'

'Darwin? What the hell are you doing in Darwin?'

'Trying to find Greg Martin. Tom O'Neill – he's investigating on behalf of the insurance company – seems to think he might be hiding away here.'

'Tom O'Neill ... isn't he the fellow who came to see you in London?'

'Yes. We seem to be following the same leads but making progress in different directions so it seemed only sensible to pool resources and I persuaded him to let me tag along with him.'

'Tag along? That doesn't sound like you, Harriet.'

'Well there are places an official investigator can go that I'd have problems with.'

'Yes, I suppose so.' Nick sounded faintly disgruntled. 'But I thought you didn't like him. Arrogant and bullying, I thought you said.'

'I'm beginning to see there's a place for behaving like that,' Harriet said. 'And anyway because I'm making use of his pull doesn't mean I have to like him.' She was interrupted by a knock at the door. 'Hang on a sec,' she said to Nick.

She crossed to the door and opened it. Tom O'Neill – talk of the devil. 'Come in,' she said, suddenly overcome with an irrational fear that he might have overheard her. 'I'm on the telephone but I won't be a minute ...' She returned to pick up the receiver, brushing aside her wet hair to nestle it against her ear. 'I'd better not stay now, Nick, but I'm at the Telford Top End if anyone wants me. I'll ring again when I move on.'

'Before you go, Harriet, those pictures of yours are sensational,' Nick said. 'I'm running them in the May edition. I'd like to do a regular Harriet Varna feature, build you up with the readers, so don't waste too long scouting in the past. Or if you do, take your camera with you. I'll need the next set within the month if they are to go in the June issue.'

'Oh Nick, I don't know if I can ...'

'You'd better if you don't want to waste a golden opportunity. This could be the break you've been waiting for.'

She bit her lip. He was right, of course, but just at the moment it was impossible to believe it had ever been that important to her.

'I'll ring you, Nick.' She put the phone down and felt the familiar rush of guilt. She treated him badly, she knew. He had given her the chance she had wanted and she was throwing it back in his face just as she did with everything he offered her.

She turned to see Tom O'Neill looking at her and something in the depth of his gaze disconcerted her.

'I'm afraid I've been asleep,' she said. 'I suppose I've been through too many time zones in the past few days and I just crashed out.'

He smiled. It was rather a nice smile, she thought suddenly, and was surprised by her own admission.

'Can't say I blame you. I feel much the same myself,' he said.

'But you had more self-control.'

'I wanted to get on with the job.'

'So – where have you been?' she asked.

His eyes narrowed fractionally. How did you know I've been anywhere if you've been asleep? he was wondering. Aloud he said easily: 'I've been to the offices of the firm of land developers I believe Greg Martin might be associated with.'

'And what did you find out?'

'From them, not a great deal. To describe them as close as a clam would be to compliment the clam. They are much much closer. But it makes me all the more certain we are on the right track. And I have one or two other avenues to explore.'

'Such as?'

'The young lady receptionist was not quite as hostile as the partner I saw. In fact I have high hopes of her. I'm taking her out for a drink this evening.'

'Oh really.' She could not have explained the prickle of dismay but he heard it in her quick unguarded reply and smiled faintly.

'Don't worry, we'll grab a bite to eat first. I wouldn't like to leave you to eat alone.'

'There's no need for you to feel responsible for me,' Harriet said quickly. 'I'm quite used to looking after myself.'

'I expect you are,' he agreed. 'But Darwin is very much a man's town – not the most comfortable place for a woman alone. There's a bistro here, literally just around the corner – it's a part of the

hotel. We might as well eat there. I'll pick you up in, say, fifteen minutes.'

He turned away, letting himself out, and Harriet could do nothing but shake her head in disbelief. How did Nick say she had described him? Arrogant and bullying? Perhaps that was a bit strong – after all he had a job to do. But *bossy* certainly. Very, very used to telling others what to do. And also undeniably attractive . . .

For a moment Harriet stared after him, deep in thought. Then she sighed, slipped out of her kimono and began to get dressed for dinner.

The bistro reminded Harriet of a saloon from an old black and white B movie western. A mirrored bar stretched the length of the room and the tables, great chunks of unvarnished wood, unadorned by cloths, sported white ring stains from the bases of innumerable beer glasses and the occasional cigarette burn. Service was equally basic – after choosing from the limited menu Tom and Harriet filtered through a narrow galley kitchen where chefs sweated over the glowing griddles to collect their steaks, and pile a selection of salads onto their platters. But the food was delicious, wholesome and plentiful, and for the first time in days Harriet attacked it ravenously. *Haute cuisine* was all very well but there was nothing quite like a char-grilled steak and a jacket potato oozing butter to resurrect a nagging appetite.

Carrying her plate back to the table Harriet realised for the first time what Tom had meant when he said Darwin was a man's town.

The bistro was almost exclusively a male preserve – apart from two women sitting with their men and matching them pint for pint and the barmaid – a pretty blonde in a low cut top and skimpy miniskirt – Harriet was the only woman in the place. All eyes swivelled to her in frank appreciation of her freshly washed hair bouncing against the nape of her neck, trim figure and long shapely legs displayed to advantage in her lemon-and-grey checked walking shorts. But Harriet was more aware of the look the barmaid aimed at Tom when he bought their drinks, flirting with him unashamedly, her mascara-smudged eyes teasing from behind her thick bleached

blonde fringe. In a bar full of men it was no mean achievement to be so obviously favoured.

'What do you think – the barmaid is English,' Tom said when he brought the drinks back to their table. 'Now isn't that just the last thing you'd expect in a way-out all-Australian place like this?'

'So what is she doing here?' Harriet asked.

'Working her way round the world. She's been out here six months, starting with relatives in Tasmania, then bumming all over Australia. She aims to go down to Queensland when the weather lets up a bit.'

'Good for her.'

'Even stranger is the fact she comes from Bristol. Wasn't that your mother's home?' His tone was still easy, conversational, but some sixth sense made her look up sharply and she caught him watching her, eyes narrowed speculatively.

'Near there, yes,' she said, deliberately vague. 'Tell me, did she say why on earth she chose to come to Darwin? Especially in the Wet? I'd have thought anyone with a grain of sense would have avoided it.'

When they had eaten Tom glanced at his watch.

'I'd better be going if I'm not to keep my date waiting. I'll see you to your room.'

'There's no need. I'll stay here and have another drink.' She caught his look and laughed. 'If your English barmaid can survive here on her own, so can I. Besides . . . I've been thinking. I'd quite like to take some photographs.'

'Of the bistro?'

'Uh-huh. It's my business, remember.'

'And you have your camera with you?'

She tapped her bag. 'I never go anywhere without it.'

'OK. Well I must go. This may be a late one, so I'll see you tomorrow.'

She watched him push his way out of the swing doors, then glanced around the bistro with a professional eye. Nick had said he wanted another set of pictures within the month and at the time she hadn't thought she'd be able to come up with a single idea, let alone the goods. But the atmosphere in the bistro had fired her, making her actually want to work for the first time since she had heard the news about Greg Martin. Thank heavens for that! she thought – what a relief to be able to think about something other than the same endless questions that had chased their tails inside her head for the last few days. What a relief not to have to simply return to her room alone and brood – sleep, she knew, would be hours away, especially after her extended nap this afternoon.

She pulled out her camera and slung it around her neck. Yes, there would be some excellent shots here – the British barmaid in the back of beyond, surrounded by roughnecks and hobos, the chefs, sweating over the griddles, the Western-saloon type decor. And perhaps, given the opportunity, she could set it all in context, for Darwin and Northern Territory appeared to be totally unlike most people's conception of Australia, which was usually portrayed as blue sky, bright sunshine, wide open spaces and golden beaches. This was a whole different Australia – dripping wet and muddy, hot as Hades, with a totally untamed feel to it.

She got up, feeling excitement stir as it always did when she was on the brink of something good. As she approached the bar twenty pairs of male eyes followed her.

'Hello there, darling! All alone now?'

'Buy you a drink, sweetheart?'

A small smile lifted the corners of her mouth.

'All right – so long as you'll let me take your pictures. Not posed – nothing silly – just doing what comes naturally!'

It was after midnight when Harriet finally left the Bistro. Persuading the customers to forget the camera was pointed at them and behave naturally had been a long job – it always was, but posed pictures were no use for the kind of feature Harriet was after. Eventually, to her relief, a colourful character named Bluey had rolled in, sozzled right out of his check lumber shirt and jeans, and much too drunk to know the camera was on him, much less care.

'Bloody electric storms!' he had complained, covering his eyes with his hand when the flash bulb sparked, and the others, including Sandra, the barmaid, had been sufficiently amused by his performance to relax and forget themselves.

Harriet let herself into her room. It felt like a sauna. She threw the French windows open but there was no breath of air going.

Next door Tom O'Neill's room appeared to be in darkness. Either he was asleep or still out – still out unless he slept with the curtains fully open, she guessed, and realised she was disappointed – she must have been half-hoping to see him before going to bed and find out what he had discovered.

She closed the windows again, undressed and lay nude under one thin sheet, but still it was too hot to sleep. For a long while she tossed and turned, all the thoughts that her photo session had chased away returning to haunt her. It seemed she had been lying there for hours when she heard footsteps outside followed by the slam of Tom O'Neill's door, and realised it was what she had unconsciously been waiting for.

You're very late, Tom O'Neill. I hope you got what you wanted . . .

Her skin felt sticky and crawling somehow as if ants were creeping all over it. What the hell was wrong with the air conditioning? she wondered. It couldn't be working properly – in the morning she would complain at reception, though she didn't imagine that would get her very far. The happy-go-lucky Australian attitude would probably be: 'We'll fix it – no worries' and nothing would change.

Unable to bear it a moment longer Harriet threw back the sheet, stomped over to the window and threw it open once more. A little breeze whispered in and she breathed a sigh of relief. That window was staying open this time. Nothing would induce her to close it, not even the fear of being raped or murdered in her bed.

Harriet lay down again on top of the sheet and this time fell into a heavy exhausted sleep.

She was awakened by a knock at the door. Breakfast, probably. She had placed an order last night for it to be served to her room, ticking off the items she required on a bookmark-shaped list and hanging it out on her door-knob. She struggled fully awake and got up, pulling on the kimono. Another tap. 'All right – all right – I'm coming!' she called, wondering why they didn't just leave it outside.

She opened the door. Tom O'Neill stood there, holding a tray set with croissants, an assortment of individual portions of jam in plastic pots and coffee.

'Breakfast is served, Madam.'

He looked very fresh for someone who has had a very late night and probably a good deal to drink, wearing a white polo shirt and cream canvas slacks. Against them, dark blue toweling socks jarred.

'Take this and I'll fetch mine,' he said, thrusting the tray towards her. 'I thought we might as well have breakfast together and talk.'

She put the tray down and combed her hair with her fingers, conscious of her own unkempt appearance.

'Well, how did it go? Did your young lady know anything?'

He set his own tray down on the low table and sprawled his long frame into one of the pair of easy chairs, pouring coffee.

'I've got an address. It seems Vanessa has a property in Darwin – a very expensive exclusive property up on East Point. At least, it's in her name. Robyn – my informant – says general opinion is that it was bought for her by Rolf Michael – that's what Martin calls himself up here – and set up as a love nest. If that is so then it's as I suspected – he had a bolt hole prepared.'

'Clever.'

'He's certainly nobody's fool,' Tom agreed. 'Unfortunately this time vanity let him down. He should have kept quiet about his connections with Vanessa if he wanted to be safe there with her, but he couldn't resist parading her at Darwest Construction. A young beauty on his arm made up for what *anno domini* has taken away from him in terms of looks – the bimbo syndrome. *I can't be such a poor old man if I can pull a bird like this.* He isn't the first to fall into a trap like that and I don't suppose he'll be the last. Tongues at Darwest started wagging and the jungle telegraph did the rest.'

'It sounds as though you had a very productive evening,' Harriet said.

'Oh I did, I did.'

'Well you were certainly very late back,' she said – and immediately regretted it.

'Did you miss me then?' he asked wickedly, spreading jam on a croissant. 'I did feel I should make an evening of it. I could hardly barge in, ask the pertinent questions and leave, could I?'

'Of course not. I never suggested you could . . .' Harriet began, then broke off, slightly shocked as she recognised for the first time the emotion that was making her irritable every time she thought of Tom with his young lady informant. Jealousy. She was jealous. It was almost unbelievable – she hadn't even realised she liked him. She set down her coffee cup.

'So – what is the next move? Visit the address, presumably?'

'That's the general idea.'

'Can I come with you?'

'If Greg is there things might get nasty.'

'If I come face to face with him that's very likely.'

His eyes narrowed. 'I'm not sure it's a good idea. I've got a job to do, Harriet. I don't want you throwing spanners in the works.'

'I won't,' she promised.

'All right then. As long as you stay in the background and keep quiet. No sudden passionate outbursts. No accusations. No revealing who you are.'

The sudden uncomfortable thought occurred to her that whether she said anything or not he might possibly realise who she was simply by looking at her. From the photographs of Paula she knew she bore a striking resemblance to her mother. But she pushed the thought aside. Greg wouldn't be expecting a ghost from the past on his doorstep and if he did recognise her it was simply too bad. In any case there was always the possibility that the shock might prompt him into letting down his defences. But she did not think she would chance suggesting this to Tom. He might not agree – and it was too important to her that he should allow her to go with him to risk him changing his mind now.

'I'll leave everything to you,' she said.

'O. K. In that case I suggest the sooner we get over there the better. I'll leave you to get dressed – pretty as you look in that kimono.'

The door closed after him and Harriet realised she was trembling. Impatient with herself she drained the last of her coffee and headed for the shower.

The morning was already humid but as yet the sky was clear unbroken blue above the scarlet-leaved crotons and banana palms, filtering sunlight through the branches of the huge spreading old banyan trees. Another few hours and the heat haze would begin to seep in from the sea bringing with it the clouds that would empty rain, rain and more rain on to the steaming earth, but at present there was a sweetness in the air that smelled of frangipani and henna with the occasional whiff of bitumen.

Tom had hired a car the previous afternoon, a Renault sporting the huge cow-catcher bars on the front bumper which seemed to be obligatory in Darwin. He manoeuvered it with confident ease through the town and headed out along the East Point Road. To their left the waters of Fannie Bay were as blue as the sky, fringed with the bougainvillaea that rioted along the clifftop.

Darwin in all its tropical glory, thought Harriet, pictures to give a totally different perspective to the bar room scene. But last night's flush of enthusiasm had faded now, eclipsed by the possibility that they were very close to Greg Martin.

The address Tom had been given turned out to be a modern bungalow, very English in design, Harriet thought, set in a neat garden. Pleasant, comfortable, but hardly luxurious and certainly a far cry from the Sydney mansion where Greg had lived with Maria. Because her money had paid for that palace – or because Greg had not wanted to attract attention to himself here in Darwin? An old aborigine was working in the garden, clipping back bushes that had shot out in all directions in the greenhouse atmosphere; he looked up, grinned toothlessly and continued with his lazy chopping without a word.

'Anyone at home?' Tom called.

The aborigine shrugged his shoulders in reply, grinned, and lolloped out of sight around the spreading bush.

The windows of the bungalow were open, letting in what air there was going before the downpour started once more, and the door stood ajar. Tom rang the bell and after a few moments a thin woman in a sleeveless cotton shift appeared, brandishing a duster. The daily help, obviously.

'Good morning,' Tom greeted her. 'Is Mr Michael in?'

She looked merely puzzled. 'Who?'

'Rolf Michael. He lives here, doesn't he?'

She ran a hand through her hair which was tied up with what appeared to be an old stocking.

'I think you've got the wrong place. No one of that name here.'

'Vanessa McGuigan then?' Tom tried again.

The woman's heavily lined brow cleared. 'Oh yes. Miss McGuigan.'

'Is she in?'

'No.'

'Do you know when she will be?'

The woman fiddled with the stocking band.

'I couldn't say. She comes and goes. But this I can tell you. She won't be here much longer. The place is on the market. She was here the day before yesterday. "Make the house look good, Madge," she says to me. "I'm selling it." Damned nuisance. I've only been here three months and it's a good little job. Easy, like, with her hardly ever here. Made my day, I can tell you, knowing I'll have to look around for something else.'

'I see. Who's the house on the market with?'

'Abbott and Skerry, Smith Street. You interested in buying, then?'

'I might be,' Tom said. 'Could we have a look around?'

The woman hesitated. 'I don't know about that. You'd better see the agents.'

'It would save us driving out here again,' Tom said. 'And if we do buy, of course, we shall be looking for daily help.'

He smiled at her. Middle-aged and plain the woman might be,

she was no more impervious to his easy charm than the nineteen-year-old receptionist at Darwest had been.

'Well, I s'pose it'll be all right . . .' She stood aside, allowing them into the bungalow. 'What do you want to see?'

She bustled ahead of them, opening doors and flicking at specks of dust with her cleaning cloth.

'This is the kitchen – not a bad size, is it? The fridge and cooker are fitted – she'll have to leave those. And this is the sitting room – bathroom down the hall . . .'

The bungalow, never having been used as a home, had an impersonal feel, too neat, too tidy. It told them nothing. Only the bedroom had the touches that gave some clues about the occupant – a filmy négligé hanging on the door, perfume spray and neatly arranged cosmetic jars on the dressing table and a large framed photograph on the table beside the bed. Tom picked it up. Looking over his shoulder Harriet saw a beautiful girl in a strapless evening gown, blonde hair cascading over her bare shoulders, smiling toothily up at a man in a tuxedo and bow tie. Obviously Greg and Vanessa. Something sharp and painful twisted within her and she turned away just as the woman said reprovingly: 'Don't touch things, if you don't mind.'

Tom replaced the photograph. 'She's a lovely girl.'

'Oh, she's that all right.' The woman smiled thinly. 'She's won beauty contests, you know. Could have been Miss Australia if she'd stuck at it if you ask me.'

'And the man?' Tom asked casually. 'Who is he?'

'Her fiancé, of course. Mike, she calls him. I've only seen him a couple of times. He's a busy man, I understand. And I'm only here in the mornings. Now, if you've seen all you want . . .' She fussed in the doorway.

'Yes. Thanks for all your help, Mrs . . .?'

'Peake. Madge Peake. Look – if you do decide to buy the place you won't forget me, will you? I'm a good reliable worker and I live close enough so I can always get in if you want anything extra.'

Tom gave her the benefit of his smile.

'We won't forget, Mrs Peake. We haven't made up our minds

yet, of course, but we'll get in touch with – Abbott and Skerry, was it?'

'Abbott and Skerry, yes. It's a nice house, good neighbourhood.' She was following them now, almost sorry to let prospective employers out of her sight. 'Can I take a message in case Miss McGuigan phones? Your names?'

'We'll take your advice and deal through the agents,' Tom said smoothly.

He ushered Harriet down the path. At the gate she took a last look back at the house, where Madge Peake still stood in the doorway watching them go. She didn't suppose she'd see it again.

'That was cool,' she said as Tom opened the door of the car for her to get in. 'I begin to see why you're so good at your job.'

'I just make the most of my opportunities. It didn't get us far though, did it? Except for the picture. I now know what Martin looks like nowadays, even if I don't know for sure what he's calling himself.'

'Do you have a good memory for faces?' she asked, fastening her seat belt. 'I can picture him now, but give me a couple of days and I'll have forgotten, though I suppose I would recognise him if I met him.'

'Oh, I don't rely on memory if I can help it,' Tom said, swinging the car in a wide arc to go back towards Darwin, then fishing in the pocket of the casual jacket he had put on to go into the bungalow. 'I've got this – see?'

He dropped it into her lap – a small photograph, about an inch in diameter, in an antiqued silver frame. Unmistakably the same man as the one with Vanessa in the large photograph – Greg Martin.

'Where did you get that?' Harriet asked accusingly.

'It was on the bedside table with the other one. I made a show of looking at that – and pocketed this one. My sleight of hand almost fits me for the Magic Circle, wouldn't you say?'

'But that's stealing!' Harriet said, shocked.

'Yes,' he agreed, smiling. 'But in a very good cause.'

'If Vanessa sets the police on your tail don't think you can drag me into it! I shall deny all knowledge . . .'

'And I thought you were willing to go to any lengths to catch up with Greg Martin! Ah well!'

Harriet grinned, looking along at him. 'Oh, I am, I am. I'm only annoyed that I didn't notice the damned picture and think of stealing it myself!'

Darwin town centre was busy. Everyone, it seemed, was going about their business before the rain began again.

'Where the hell is Smith Street?' Tom asked.

Harriet, busy studying the map provided by the car hire company, traced it with her finger.

'It's here – a really long street.'

'Where's here? Where are we now?'

'Slow down – hang on – Daly Street. Keep going and we can't miss it.'

'Famous last words. I'm going to look for somewhere to park and we'll walk.' He did so, manoeuvring into a kerbside space. 'Come on.'

They got out. Already Harriet could feel her shirt sticking to her back where it had been pressed against the seat. She wriggled uncomfortably. How did anyone ever manage to work in a climate like this, so energy sapping? A big old Morris car, painted in garish colours, racketed by with a horde of grinning aborigines hanging out of the windows waving bottles and beer cans. That partly answered her question. Some people didn't work at all. They got drunk and went joy riding – and who could blame them?

As Harriet had seen from the map Smith Street was long and straight. Cranes engaged in building work towered above the buildings on the skyline, stretching long arms towards the fast-thickening sky. Darwest Developments? she wondered. Clearly there was money to be made in real estate and construction in Darwin and those responsible for rebuilding after Cyclone Tracy could only be admired. The new town was well planned with a pleasant suburban feel to it – just the kind of enterprise to attract someone with money to invest and a nose for the right place to put it. No one could accuse Greg Martin of not being shrewd.

The offices of Abbott and Skerry were situated between a fast food shop and a launderette. Large boards decorated with photographs and details of houses for sale filled the windows. Tom and Harriet scanned them briefly looking for the bungalow at East Point but could not see it. Perhaps it was too fresh on the market.

'I'll handle this one alone if you don't mind,' Tom said. 'Go and do some window shopping – buy a burger – whatever you like. I'll see you back here in ten minutes.' His tone left no room for argument.

A little annoyed at being so summarily excluded but knowing she had not the slightest grounds to object, Harriet wandered along the street and back again. Another group of aborigines were squatting against a wall, bottles between their knees, black faces grinning vacantly. What the hell do we do to the natives when we take over their country? Harriet wondered. Either they are shoved into reservations or else they are left to become the misfits in a civilisation totally foreign to them. Her hand hovered over her camera, tucked inside her bag. A couple of pictures like this might well find a place in the set and the abos would make marvellous subjects – they would never notice she was photographing them. She ducked into a doorway to fit the right lens to her camera then spent ten minutes unobtrusively clicking away.

'Hard at work, I see,' Tom's voice said in her ear. She was so engrossed she had not noticed him approaching.

'I thought I might as well make use of my time,' she said, covering the lens and packing her camera away. 'How did you get on?'

He put a hand under her elbow.

'Come on, lady, walk. I think those abos have seen you. Is it aborigines who think they'll lose their soul if they are photographed – or is that red indians? If it's abos they'll probably try to snatch your camera, if not they'll be pestering you to pay them.'

She glanced over her shoulder. There was something disturbing about the vacant grinning black faces.

'They could do with a hand-out by the look of them.'

'They'd only spend it on booze. Keep going.' His hand was still beneath her elbow, his sleeve brushing her bare arm. Suddenly she was very aware of it – and not only as yet another example of his irritating bossiness.

'You haven't answered my question,' she said to hide her discomfort. 'How did you get on?'

'So-so. It's true – Miss McGuigan has put the house on the market. They don't know a Mr Michael Trafford or a Rolf Michael. She's obviously dealing with it all herself.'

'And where is she?'

'At present – out of town. But she told them she will be back in Darwin the day after tomorrow. I don't think we can usefully do any more until then.'

Harriet pulled a face. 'Two whole days wasted . . .'

'We haven't much option. And we don't want to ask too many questions and warn them off. Better to wait and try to catch Vanessa unawares. So whilst we're waiting I suggest we keep well out of the way. How do you fancy a trip to the outback?'

'The outback!'

'Why not? It seems a shame to be in the Territory and not see some of it. Besides, you could get some marvellous shots.'

'I suppose I could.' But she was finding it difficult to think about such a trip in terms of photography and she knew she was reacting to it as a woman. Two days in the outback with a man she was finding increasingly attractive . . . a man who had a way of making her forget the only reason they were together was to discover the truth about events that had taken place more than twenty years ago.

'So? What do you say? Shall we do it?'

Was it her imagination or had his hand tightened slightly around her elbow.'

'Oh – why not?'

'Good. That's settled. And now, Miss Varna, you have another decision to make. It's about to start raining again if I'm not much mistaken. Can you summon up the energy to run, or shall we just get wet?'

The first spots, like the very beginning of a cool shower, felt refreshing to her hot skin.

'Oh, let's get wet!' she said recklessly.

Back at the hotel Tom put through a phone call to London.

'Karen? Any news?'

'Not yet boss, but I'm working on it.'

'Good girl. Now listen – I'm going walkabout as the aborigines say for a couple of days. As soon as I get fixed up at a hotel I'll let you know where I am. Don't forget – I want to know the minute you have anything.'

'I won't forget.' A slight pause. 'Is *she* still with you? Harriet Varna?'

Tom grinned, amused at the pique in her voice.

'Yes, Karen, she is. Everything is going according to plan. If you want to be the one to collect the kudos you'd better start detecting because when the lady's guard is down I might get her to tell me all I want to know.'

'You can count on me boss,' Karen replied emphatically.

Tom was still smiling as he replaced the receiver.

CHAPTER SIXTEEN

The Stuart Highway runs due south from Darwin all the way to Adelaide, more than two thousand miles of fast road through the tropical greenery and wetlands of the Top End, with its rivers, magnificent canyons and escarpments, into the red desert of the dead centre and back to the gender country of Southern Australia.

The following morning Tom and Harriet set off in a four wheel drive vehicle known locally as a 'ute' which Tom had exchanged for the Renault the previous afternoon at the offices of the rental company.

'We thought we'd go down to have a look at Alice Springs,' Tom had said to the girl, neatly uniformed in the scarlet skirt and white shirt with a neck scarf bearing the logo of the company, and she had raised a sceptical eyebrow.

'You realise you are talking about an eighteen-hour drive? And you can't travel at night. No one drives after dark in the Territory. If you do you're liable to get a buffalo through your windscreen.'

Tom and Harriet had exchanged glances. They had not yet become accustomed to the vast distances of Australia.

'Well maybe not Alice Springs,' Tom conceded. 'We've only got a couple of days. Where would you suggest?'

She pulled a face. 'This isn't the best time of year. If you want to sightsee you should come in the Dry, but I guess you could go down to Katherine. That's only two hundred miles or so. There's the Gorge and the National Park – brilliant scenery if the weather is clear. And the river will be running high, that's for sure.'

'We'll see how we get on,' Tom said.

'That's up to you – but don't forget about the buffalo. Many of the roads are unfenced and the bars won't save you if you hit one. Oh – and I'd stick to the main highway. Lesser roads are often not made up and can be impassable in the Wet.'

'What a cheerful little soul!' Harriet remarked as they left the office.

'I suppose she's only doing her job. They probably get sick to death of idiot Poms out here. We don't understand the place. If we did we'd never have dropped that clanger about going to Alice.'

Once again the early part of the day was clear and blue, though humid. Tom put his foot hard down on the accelerator and left it there and the ute skimmed along the almost deserted highway, eating up the miles. Noonamah, Adelaide River, Pine Creek, all were left behind, and with them the threat of the rain mists rolling in from the sea. By lunchtime they were in Katherine, their only worry the fact that the needle of the fuel gauge had been hovering on empty for the past twenty miles, their only discomfort slight stiffness. Speed had created a breeze so that they had scarcely noticed the sun heating down; only later did Harriet realise her forehead, nose and forearms had been scorched and a deep V stencilled at the neck of her shirt.

In the winter Katherine would overflow with tourists but at this time of year it was almost deserted. They selected a hotel, old-fashioned colonial in style, standing on stilts, with a deep verandah, and booked in with no trouble. The receptionist, plump, pretty and sporting an ugly mosquito bite on her wrist, seemed surprised to see them.

'A room? Yeah – no worries.'

'Two rooms,' Tom corrected her.

'We could have gone on further,' Harriet said as they followed the girl along the narrow passage. 'By nightfall we could have been halfway to Alice Springs.'

Tom pulled a face. 'I've had enough of driving for one day. And I don't suppose there's much to see between here and Alice. Just dust and desert.'

'I could have taken my share of the driving,' Harriet said, wondering why she hadn't thought to suggest it.

'Yes, you could have,' he agreed. 'If we go out again this afternoon you can drive if you like and give me a rest.'

They had cool drinks and a snack in the hotel bar and then spent the afternoon exploring. But Tom drove; the question of Harriet doing so was not even mentioned.

They ate that night in a little bistro, the only two customers at the check-clothed tables, and afterwards sat on the verandah of their hotel watching the moon rise, a huge orange balloon smudged around the edges by a shrouding of river mist. In the darkness around them mosquitoes hummed, crickets chirped noisily and on the banks of the river, which was running high and deep, frogs croaked.

'It must have been nights like this that started the legend of Dreamtime Tom said.

'Dreamtime?'

'When the world was young. A kind of Aboriginal Garden of Eden.'

'Oh I see. Dreamtime. I like it,' Harriet said, thinking that certainly there was a magic in the night; in the soft still-hot air, in the pink-tinted mist and the sounds of nature undisturbed. Here, with the hint of a breeze sighing in the ghost gums, reality seemed very far away. She glanced at Tom, sitting very relaxed, chair tipped back, feet propped through the bars of the verandah, and thought that it was difficult to believe this was the same man who had questioned her so searchingly about her mother.

As if he had felt her eyes on him, Tom turned and looked at her quizically and she felt awareness twist sharply again. At once her defences came up and she looked away, flustered by the tangle of emotions.

'I'm very tired. I think maybe I'll have an early night.'

In the small silence that followed she half expected him to try to persuade her to stay. There had been something in the way he had looked at her which had made her think for a moment that he was feeling much as she did. But the moment passed and she was glad. She was not sure she was ready to find out if she had read that look correctly, any more than she was sure she was ready to extend the parameters of what had so far been no more than a partnership of convenience. She found him attractive, yes, no denying it, but she really was tired – and emotions were likely to be exaggerated when one was at a low physical ebb.

'You don't mind if I go to bed then?' she said, getting up and hoping that at least she was giving the appearance of her usual contained self.

'Not at all.' His voice was light and easy. 'Don't forget your mosquito net.'

'I won't. Goodnight.'

He raised a hand, casual gesture of farewell. But as she got up and went into the hotel she knew his eyes were following her.

When she had gone Tom sat on the verandah watching the velvet night creep in, thinking about Harriet and admitting to himself for the first time just how much he wanted her.

He had found her attractive right from the start, of course – perhaps more so than he had cared to acknowledge, for hadn't he experienced something very close to jealousy every time Harriet made mention of her editor, Nick? It was obvious to everyone but a fool that theirs was far more than a business relationship and Tom had cast iron proof of it. After his first visit to her flat in London he had parked up the street for a while to keep observation, guessing that when he left her she would do some telephoning and it was quite on the cards that someone would arrive at the flat to talk things over. That someone had been Nick (Tom had established his identity by getting one of his pals in the Metropolitan police to run a PNC check – against the rules, but who was to know?) and when Tom had driven away in the grey dawn his car had still been there, parked outside her flat.

But he hadn't given much thought to her as a woman beyond the typical red-blooded male response that he would like to get her into bed – and that had been a passing thought only. Far more important was the job in hand. He was determined to get to the bottom of the Martin/Varna business and proximity to Harriet offered him a window on her world. With all his investigative instincts aroused he had been quite prepared to make use of her.

But somewhere along the line things had changed. When had it happened? He couldn't be sure. All he knew was that he had looked at her tonight and felt as if he had been kicked in the stomach by a mule. As the thought occurred to him he smiled briefly. What an expression! But it did sum up perfectly the way he felt – and for him it was something of a new experience.

Ever since he had passed the stage of uncertain adolescence Tom had realised he was attractive to the opposite sex. More often than not women threw themselves at him and without the slightest vestige of conceit Tom had come to take the ease of his conquests as a fact of life. But they had been passing fancies only. He could not remember one who had affected him the way Harriet was affecting him now. Was it the way she looked – stunning in an almost careless way? Or the undeniable self-assurance that came from being raised in a privileged background? Possibly that had something to do with it. But it was more than that. There was her determination to succeed in a demanding career when it would have been so easy to rely on inherited wealth, but also a vulnerability beneath that tough veneer. And there was the promise of warmth beneath the coolness, a capacity for passion beneath the restraint. Had Nick tapped that capacity? Tom's stomach contracted again as he thought of it and he got up abruptly.

This kind of diversion was not conducive to good investigating. But at least he had another day to kill before he could continue with his pursuit of Greg Martin; another day alone with Harriet. A half smile lifted one corner of his mouth. Tom O'Neill intended to make the most of it.

The country around Katherine is some of the most beautiful in the Northern Territory – in the whole of Australia perhaps. The Katherine River, named by the explorer Stewart for the daughter of the South Australian pastoralist James Chambers who financed three of his expeditions into the Territory, has cut its way through the sandstone cliffs to form thirteen spectacular gorges, some with walls two hundred feet high, as it winds its way past Smith's Rock and Jedda Rock, and through the lush tropical greenery of the National Park.

In the dry season when the river is quiet and slow, boat tours ply the river, enabling visitors to see the full glory of the towering walls of the Gorge, but now, with the river full and fast flowing and the tourists too few and far between to make the trips viable, Harriet and Tom had to content themselves with driving into the Park and exploring on foot. But they were not disappointed. The tropical greenery had flourished under its annual watering; it rioted now around the ancient canyons and escarpments and the tranquil lagoons, with water so clear that every shade of colour of the pebbles at the bottom was clearly visible, were adorned with water lillies the size of dinner plates.

Here in the quiet reserve the bird life abounded – bower birds rose noisily from their nests on the rainforest floor, while tiny insect-eaters fluttered and skimmed through the overhanging canopy of branches, like huge brilliant butterflies. And everywhere, of course, were the parrots – white sulphur crested cockatoos, vibrant rosellas and lorikeets, chattering flocks of noisy grey and pink galahs. Harriet's camera shutter clicked incessantly – she did not think the pictures would be any use to *Focus Now*, they were too much of a tourist indulgence and had all been done before and probably better in National Geographical Magazine, but she took them anyway, for her own pleasure.

The hotel had supplied them with a packed lunch and they sat down to eat it near a lagoon fed by a little waterfall – fresh bread rolls with cheese and ham, plump juicy tomatoes and bananas from a local market garden. The sun beat body down between the trees providing a pattern of deeply dappled light and shade as they ate, sitting on Tom's Barbour which they had spread on the ground.

'I could stay here forever,' Harriet said softly, speaking her thoughts aloud. 'It's so peaceful!'

'You can say that again. You'd soon miss your fix of the daily hurly burly, though. Peace is all very well in small doses but for the likes of you and me it would soon become tedious, I suspect.'

'I suppose so. Just at the moment I feel I could take any amount of it. I think I'll stay here and refuse to go back.'

'And what would Nick say about that?' He hadn't meant to say it but the words were out before he could stop them.

'I could take photographs for him out here as well as anywhere else,' she said, deliberately misunderstanding.

'I wasn't thinking of the photographs you might take. It was his personal reaction that I meant.'

Instantly the sharp awareness was there, itching beneath her skin like prickly rash.

'Nick wouldn't have any right to say anything,' she said. 'He doesn't own me.'

'Harriet, the man who thought he could own you would be a fool.'

'You've got it all wrong. Nick is just a friend and also my editor.' She reached out to pick a tiny delicate flower growing in the grass and then went on: 'You know an awful lot about me and I know nothing whatever about you. I don't think that's very fair.'

He shifted his long frame.

'Oh, there's nothing much to know. I live quietly in a hellishly untidy flat in Battersea – when I'm not half way around the world chasing up some job or other.'

'Do your jobs often take you around the world?'

'A few have – well, abroad, anyway. This is the farthest, I must admit. But you don't want to hear about my work.'

'No, I want to hear about you. Where you come from. That sort of thing.'

'I told you – Battersea.'

'With a name like O'Neill I'd guess it was much more interesting than that.'

'All right – I do have Irish blood in my veins if you want to know. I suppose that appeals to the American in you.'

'Anglo-American, not Irish,' she reminded him. 'Go on. Where are your roots?'

'County Kerry. But they are buried pretty deep. My great grandfather – or was it my great-great-grandfather? I always get them confused – came over in the potato famine. I'm more Liverpool than Irish – but then they call Liverpool the capital of Ireland.'

'Brothers and sisters?' Harriet persisted.

'One brother, older, clever and respectable – he's a surveyor, one sister, younger, married with two kids. Uncle Tom – that's me.'

'And you're not . . . married?'

'What makes you assume that?'

'You don't *feel* married. You're obviously free to jet off anywhere at the drop of a hat. No, I don't think there's a Mrs O'Neill at that flat in Battersea.'

He grinned. 'You're right, of course. But I think it's my undarned socks that gave me away, not my obvious freedom. I feel sure a liberated lady like you wouldn't deny a man the same privileges.'

'How did we arrive back at me? We were talking about you.'

'You are a much more interesting subject.' She looked at him sharply, caught unawares. He was sprawled back on the Barbour, propped on one elbow, can of beer at hand, but when his eyes met and held hers there was nothing lazy about them.

Her breath constricted, she was hypnotised by those eyes – nothing could have induced her to look away.

'Much more interesting,' he said again. His arm went round her and still she did not move. The prickle was back beneath her skin, warm and creeping, and her stomach felt weak. He pulled her towards him and she did not resist. For a moment she was aware of him as never before, as if she were standing back and observing him with every one of her senses, detached yet at the same time intimately involved. The smell of his sun-warmed skin was in her nostrils, the line of his chin with the faint dark shadow of beard showing through looked strangely beautiful, the touch of his lips as they brushed her forehead started dark fires within her. She sat motionless yet every nerve ending seemed to be yearning towards him, nerve endings she had never realised she possessed. Her whole body was alive and singing, there was no room for thought, no will to draw back.

As he kissed her on the mouth a shudder ran through the very core of her. Her arms were around him now, feeling the long hard lines of his back beneath her hands as he pushed her back onto the ground. She lay beneath his weight returning his kisses and feeling the attraction spark between them like electric short circuits.

After a moment he rolled away, resting on one elbow and looking down at her.

'I've been wanting to do that ever since I met you.'

She half-laughed; anything to relieve the tension she was feeling. 'Why didn't you then?'

'In your flat? In London? Oh come on now, that would have been asking to get my face slapped.'

'You could just be right.' Her voice was unsteady.

'I don't think you liked me very much,' he said ruefully.

'I don't think you liked me! Kiss me, indeed!'

'You don't have to like someone to want to kiss them.'

'Oh!' She arched her body provocatively, teasing. 'So you still don't like me?'

'I never said that.' He reached out and took a strand of her hair, twisting it between his fingers. 'You are very beautiful, with a lot of what they used to refer to as "spunk," you may be talented for all I know, and when you relax you can be quite fun.'

'Good.' She teased him with her eyes, wanting him to kiss her again.

'My pleasure.' One corner of his mouth lifted wickedly. 'You are of course also stubborn, spoiled and when upset you are likely to bite.'

'Beast!' She made to hit him and he caught her wrist, pinning it to the ground above her head. Then slowly, deliberately, he lowered himself so that his face blotted out the sky. Again she felt the surge of electricity between them.

Above them the sky was growing darker but neither noticed. He kissed her soundly, taking his time about it, keeping her arm twisted above her head with one hand while the other cupped her chin then ran down the line of her neck and shoulder. She felt the first heavy spots of rain on her outspread palm and ignored them. For long moments they continued to kiss, too engrossed in one another to care about anything but their closeness. Then as the storm became a downpour and the first lightning split the sky they could ignore it no longer.

Tom scrambled to his feet, swearing. His shirt was already soaked and clinging to his back. Harriet was less wet – his body had protected her – but long before they reached the ute she too was drenched.

'Thank goodness my camera was in the bag!' she gasped, as water dripped out of her fringe and ran down her face.

Sheet lightning illuminated the sudden darkness, almost like night, and rain lashed the windscreen of the ute.

'We'd better get out of here,' Tom said above the grumble of the thunder. 'We don't want to get bogged down.'

He started the ute and moved off along the unmade-up track which was already turning to quagmire beneath the churning wheels.

The ferocity of the storm was awesome and in spite of the cloying heat Harriet shivered. This was elemental nature in all its raw majesty.

The ute bumped over a rise and down the other side into a morass of mud. The wheels spun, fighting to get a grip. Tom put his foot down hard and the engine raced but the ute remained stationary.

'Take the wheel.' He opened the driver's door. 'I'll see if I can push it out.'

He jumped down, mud squelching over his shoes, and ploughed around to the rear of the ute. Harriet moved into the driver's seat, stretching to reach the pedals. Her sandals too were filthy, mud clinging between her toes. As Tom pushed she tried to pull away and eventually, just when she had begun to think it never would, the ute inched forward.

'Keep it going!' Tom yelled.

She drove slowly and he ran to catch her up, hauling himself into the passenger seat. 'You want to take over?' she asked.

'No – just keep going.'

She drove with intense concentration, manoeuvring the muddy track. As they hit made-up road the storm seemed to ease, the lightning sporadic, the thunder no more than an echoing rumble, the rain dying to a thick steaming mist.

She jerked to a stop, her ankles going into cramp from stretching to reach the pedals.

'Thank goodness for that! You can take over now.' She turned to look at him and burst out laughing. His hair was dripping, face and clothes spattered with mud that had flown from the churning wheels. Yet he still looked as attractive as ever.

'You can laugh!' he said ruefully.

'I'm sorry. It's just that . . .'

'I know. I'm in a bit of a mess.'

She looked down at her skin, clinging wetly to her legs, and her own filthy feet.

'I don't suppose I'm much better.'

'You,' he said, 'are still the most beautiful girl in the Northern Territory.'

He reached for her wrist, holding it fast while he kissed her again.

'Don't, Tom!' she warned. 'We'll probably stick together.'

'I can't think of anything nicer, can you?'

She couldn't.

'Move over then and let me drive,' he said some time later.

After dinner they sat once more on the verandah of their hotel with the heady perfume of the wet shrubs in their nostrils. But tonight there was a sense of anticipation keeping the atmosphere electric. It was there each time their eyes met or their hands brushed, even three feet apart the air crackled with it as it had this afternoon with the energy of the storm.

'What about a walk before bed?' Tom suggested.

The main street of Katherine, which followed the bank of the river, was almost deserted. Light spilled out from a bar but the garage had closed down for the night, its pumps standing like silent sentinels outside the sprawling workshop and office.

Tom took her hand and the attraction sparked again, sending sharp tingles up her veins.

No one had ever made her feel this way before, alive with longing. She thought of Nick and the pathetic efforts she had made to respond to his lovemaking but she found she was unable even to conjure up a vision of his face. He seemed so far away now – it was almost as if he had never existed. And perhaps he never had for her. What had unlocked her emotions? Was it the stress of the past week? Or being in a different country? Whatever the reason it was unimportant. She was in a trance now except that it seemed the trance was reality and everything else mere shadows.

They walked in silence, the tension growing between them until it was an almost tangible thing. When it became too much to bear he pulled her into the shadow of a doorway, kissing her, running his hands the length of her back, and the tension exploded to a fury of desire. Without a word they turned back towards the hotel. She stood back, waiting, while he got the keys, and her whole body was on fire with longing.

'Your room or mine?' he asked roughly.

'Mine.' She rumbled her key into his hand.

He unlocked the door and the moment it closed after them they were in each other's arms. He began unfastening her blouse and simultaneously her fingers were busy with the buttons of his shirt.

Her breasts were bare, nipples thrusting at the thin silk. He freed them, burying his face in them, sliding her skin down over her hips. Her body arched towards his, aching with wanting him. Earlier she had dumped her wet clothes unceremoniously on the bed, now he swept them to the floor and turned back the covers, lifting her bodily and laying her down on the cool cotton sheet. She lay in an ecstasy of total abandon watching him undress and loving every line of his muscular body. She held out her arms and he came to her without preamble for they were already past the point where they could sustain the waiting a moment longer. For a brief agonising moment the suspense mounted to unbearable proportions, then he was in her and nothing in the world existed beyond the united movement of their charged bodies.

Too soon it was over. They lay entwined, skin damp with perspiration, Tom's hand still cupping her breast. She ran a hand down his long hard thigh muscle, enjoying the delicious languour of passion satisfied, glowing with an inner happiness she had never before experienced in the aftermath of love making.

I believe I love him! she thought and suddenly longed to say so, to whisper it into his shoulder and shout it to the world. But something held her back, some echo of her former self. The emotion was new and so was the desire to share it and she felt shy suddenly and oddly defensive. Better to cherish this moment and hug it to herself. Later there would be plenty of time to tell him how she felt.

The languour crept up her limbs; her eyelids felt heavy. She was almost, but not quite, asleep, when the telephone rang.

Startled she reached for it and heard the receptionist's voice, energetic Darwin as opposed to laid-back Sydney, with each sentence ending on a raised note.

'Would Mr O'Neill be with you by any chance? There's a call for him from London and I've been ringing his room but there's no reply.'

'Yes, he's here.' Harriet transferred the telephone to her other hand, holding it towards him. 'Tom – it's for you.'

Instead of relieving her of the receiver he got up and reached for his slacks.

'I'll take it in my own room.'

His businesslike manner was in such contrast to the intimacy of a few minutes before that she felt ridiculously hurt at the sudden exclusion. She watched him go out the door and lifted the receiver to her ear again to check that the call had been transferred. As she did so she heard the click of his extension being picked up but instead of her own line going dead she heard a girl's voice with a broad Cockney accent say: 'Boss? It's Karen. Sorry if I interrupted something but you did say ring any time.'

'That's right, I did. And you didn't really interrupt anything.'

'Whew, thank goodness for that! When I realised you were in her room I thought I might have caught you at just the moment when she was going to spill the beans. After all, you did say you were going to try and catch her when her guard was down, didn't you? Is that what you were up to?'

'Something like that.'

'Hmm, trust you, boss, to manage to mix business with pleasure. Perhaps you don't need my info any more. Perhaps you've already found out everything you need to know from her . . .'

'Karen,' Tom said sharply. 'This is a long-distance call, very long distance, and it is charged by the minute. If you don't want your wages docked just get on and tell me what you've found out, OK?'

'OK.' She sounded disgruntled. 'I've been checking on the movements of the Varna family at the time of the accident.' Her voice was eager; instinctively he knew she had unearthed something and the sixth sense that made him a good investigator began to jangle like the trip wire of a booby trap.

'And?'

'All very much as you'd expect. Except that . . .'

'Yes?'

'A couple of months after it was all over Sally, Paula's sister, went to Italy. She'd gone haring off to the States from her home in London when the news broke, taking her son with her, and moved in with the family. Then quite suddenly she buzzed off on her own. To Italy.'

'Perhaps she wanted to see for herself the place her sister sailed from on that last fateful cruise.'

'Perhaps. But Hugo didn't go – and she didn't take her son either. And she didn't go to Positano. From my investigations it appears she went to the Aeolie Islands. They're a group of small islands off the toe of Italy, north of Sicily.'

'I know where they are,' Tom said a trifle impatiently. 'They are where Aeolus, King of the Islands, gave Odysseus the bag of wind to speed him back across the sea to Ithaca.'

'Pardon?' Karen said blankly.

'Homer's *Odyssey*. Didn't you do it at school? Anyway, never mind your classical ignorance. It's Sally Varna I'm interested in, not Odysseus. Which island did she go to?'

'I don't know,' Karen confessed. 'I haven't been able to find out.

But if she intended to have a holiday there she didn't stay long. A couple of days later she was on her way back to New York and a week or so later she was flying to London.'

'Going home?'

'Again, she didn't take her child, and again she was gone only a few days. In the six months following she went to London three times – all short visits.'

'But she didn't go back to Italy, again?'

'No, not as far as I can make out. I don't know if it means anything, boss, but I thought you ought to know.'

'Thanks, Karen. Stick with it,' Tom said. There was a click and the line went dead.

Harriet sat with the telephone still at her ear, shocked into total immobility. She should not have listened to the conversation, of course. She should have replaced the receiver the moment he'd picked his up. But she was only glad she hadn't. No wonder he hadn't wanted to take the call here, lying in bed beside her! He had been using her and she had been too stupid to realise it. How could she have allowed herself to be taken in so completely? She'd thought, she'd really thought, that he had felt the way she did and there was something special between them, when all the time . . . What was the expression that dreadful girl had used? 'Catch her with her guard down.' Well he was a convincing worker, not a doubt of it. And she had fallen for it like a naive school girl.

Suddenly Harriet was furiously angry. What a heel! She slammed down the receiver, pulled on her kimono and picked up Tom's shirt which was still lying on the floor where he had discarded it. She slammed out of her room and down the corridor to his, throwing the door open without knocking.

Tom had his back to the door, the fingers of one hand were splayed through his hair as if he were deep in thought. As she threw the door open he spun round, surprised. 'Harriet!'

'Yes, Harriet,' she grated. 'I've brought your shirt.'

'What did you do that for? I was coming back . . .'

'Oh you were, were you? To see if I could tell you where my aunt went just after the accident and why, I suppose. Well you needn't bother. I know nothing, Tom – nothing. From the start I've levelled with you. And fool that I was I thought you were levelling with me. But you weren't, were you? You were using me.'

'Did you listen in to my phone call?' he accused.

'Yes – and thank goodness I did! I never have realised that anyone could stoop so low . . .'

'Harriet, for heaven's sake, it wasn't like that!'

'No? Don't try to pretend, Tom. I'd heard what that girl said. You were trying to catch me when my guard was down. And you didn't contradict her. God, what a fool you must take me for! I'm only sorry your plan didn't work. It must have been a great disappointment to you after all the hard work you put in . . .' She broke off, trembling with fury and hurt.

'Harriet, listen to me!'

'I think I've listened enough, don't you?'

'No!' He crossed the room to take her by the forearms. 'You've got it all wrong.'

She shook herself free. 'Tell that to your assistant. It seems she's got it wrong too.' She flung the shirt at him 'I'm going to bed now. I suppose I'll see you in the morning. I still want to get to the bottom of this business whether you believe that or not. And in any case I suppose I'm still dependent on you to get back to Darwin. But don't ever – *ever* – try to make a fool of me again, Tom. Because I promise you, it won't work.'

She slammed out of the room. But it was only when her own door closed after her that the tears began – hot, angry tears that quickly became tears of hurt and regret for what might have been.

Tom swore as the door slammed shut after her, crossed to the small refrigerator equipped with miniatures of spirits and mineral water, and poured himself a whisky.

What a foul-up! Why the hell had he been careless enough to carry on a conversation with Karen without making sure he was not being listened to? An elementary mistake and one he'd made, no doubt, because his mind had not been on the job. Instead he had been thinking about Harriet and the way he felt about her.

It was a mistake he had never made before, letting personal considerations interfere with professionalism, and it was a measure of the way she had affected him that he had allowed it to happen now.

Well, thanks to his laxness she had heard the lot and understandably she was mad as hell. Not only did she know her aunt had been involved in some very suspicious comings and goings, she also believed his only motive in making love to her had been trying to trick her into revealing family secrets. He could hardly make up his mind which mattered most.

He tossed back the whisky thinking what supreme irony it was. A few short days ago he had been quite ready to exploit Harriet for the good of the job, now, with the memory of her warmth and passion fresh in his senses, the very idea that she should believe him capable of such a thing appalled him. What the hell had happened to him that he should have undergone such a complete change of heart? In love? He'd have laughed in the face of anyone who had suggested it could happen so suddenly, so unexpectedly, and most of all to *him*, and yet . . .

'Damn it to hell!' Tom exploded.

He returned to the refrigerator and took out another small bottle. He had a feeling it was going to be a long night.

CHAPTER SEVENTEEN

Next morning Harriet failed to appear for breakfast. Tom, who had made a valiant effort to be there (in spite of a thumping hangover) in order to try and make amends, drank three cups of very black coffee and went in search of her.

'Harriet, can we talk?' he asked when she opened her door to him.

'We have nothing to say, have we?' She was pale, unsmiling, with dark weals beneath her eyes that suggested she might have been crying.

'Yes – we have. You've got it all wrong. I know how it must have sounded, but . . .'

'Exactly. It could hardly have been clearer. In spite of everything you still believe that I and my family have somehow cheated your clients and you were quite prepared to seduce me to try and find out what you wanted to know – just as you seduced that poor girl at Darwest Construction, no doubt. I'm sorry I wasn't as forthcoming as she was and this time your efforts were in vain. But the simple truth is I don't know anything.'

'Listen – I believe you.'

'It's a bit late for that kind of protestation, don't you think? Now that you have made a complete fool of me? You must be feeling very pleased with yourself. Do you always manage to mix business with pleasure? A regular James Bond, aren't you, though come to think of it he usually manages to bed at least three women during the course of a mission.'

'Harriet . . .'

'And what's more he could take his drink better than you. You look absolutely dreadful.'

'For Christ's sake, Harriet, will you believe I did not make love to you in order to gain information?'

She looked at him standing there pale, dull-eyed, heavy-lidded, and almost believed him. She wanted to, for heaven's sake – oh how she wanted to! But she had heard that conversation with her own ears – it had not been something passed on and exaggerated or misrepresented in the telling. It had been perfectly obvious that Tom had already discussed her with his assistant and told her what he planned to do – boasting, probably, and maybe laughing too. Bitterness rose like gall in Harriet's throat.

'Let's just leave it, Tom, shall we?' she said tightly.

And Tom, his head thundering as if someone was tightening a steel vice around his skull, decided to do as she said for the time being. There would be another time, another place. She would be around until they located Greg Martin, at least. When he felt better he would talk to her again and somehow, one way or the other, he'd make her understand he was telling the truth. But for the moment all he longed for was peace, quiet and dark!

'When are we leaving?' Harriet asked. 'Shouldn't it be very soon if we are to be in Darwin by lunchtime?'

'Yes, I suppose so,' Tom said wretchedly.

It was quite plain he was not going to get any of them.

They drove back to Darwin in virtual silence. The rain that had begun early today on the coast came out to meet them rolling down The Track in a thick mist. Tom, whose head was still thudding, swore softly to himself. It was easy to see why the Wet was known as Suicide Season. Everything seemed that much worse when one was slowly suffocating in a steam bath and he could imagine even small everyday problems could easily assume gigantic proportions under such conditions.

He turned into Telford Top End and pulled up outside the reception office.

'Do you want to get out here?' he asked Harriet. 'There's no point in two of us getting wet.'

She nodded, grateful to him in spite of herself, and dived for the shelter of the office.

The receptionist was the same girl who had checked them in when they first arrived.

'Did you have a good time?' she asked.

'Yes. Fine,' Harriet said flatly.

'Right. You're in a different room today, let's see . . .' The girl burrowed in her paperwork, then her face changed. 'Oh, I almost forgot – there's a message for you, love. Can you ring home right away? A Mrs Sally Varna was trying to reach you. It's urgent, she said.'

'When was this?' Harriet asked.

'The day you left for your trip. I told her we didn't have an address for you but I'd pass the message on as soon as you got back.'

Harriet checked her watch, frowning. Why on earth should Sally be trying to contact her?

'It'll be a bit late to ring now, won't it? It must be the early hours in New York.'

'You may be right,' the girl said, unsmiling, 'but the message was for you to ring as soon as you returned, whatever the time.'

A nerve pulsed in Harriet's throat.

'Can you give me a line?'

'Pick up your phone when you get to your room and I'll have it for you.'

In her room Harriet reached for the receiver and stood tapping it impatiently as she waited for the international numbers to connect. Then the telephone was ringing and moments later she heard Mark's voice on the line. Immediately her anxiety increased – Mark was rarely at his mother's house and certainly not at this time of night. Even when he was in New York he usually stayed with friends.

His first words did nothing to reassure her.

'Harriet? Thank goodness! We'd almost given up trying to get hold of you.'

'What is it, Mark? What's wrong?' Her anxiety spilled over into her voice.

'Bad news, I'm afraid. It's your Dad. He's had a heart attack.' Her own heart lurched; her mouth was dry. 'Dad? Dad has had a heart attack? Oh Mark, you don't mean . . .?'

'It's all right, Skeeter, he's not dead, but I'm afraid he's not very well either. It was touch and go and at this stage there is always the risk of another one, like aftershocks with an earthquake, you know what I mean?'

'When – where – did it happen?'

'Two days ago. At the showroom. Skeeter, I really think you should come home.'

'Don't worry, I'll be there. On the first available plane.'

'Good girl.'

'Yes. And Mark . . . give him my love.'

She replaced the receiver, her head whirling. Ring the airport – book a flight – at least I'm already packed, I can just. . . go. Oh Dad, poor Dad, you will be all right, won't you? You must be all right!

'Is something wrong, Harriet?'

It was Tom, standing in the doorway. Clearly the receptionist had told him about the emergency phone call.

She looked at him, so comfortingly solid somehow, and experienced a sharp wave of longing. Oh, to have his arms around her again, as they had been last night! Oh, to lay her head against his shoulder, share her fears and take comfort from the sharing. But the hurt was still there, a barrier that could not be so easily hurdled.

'It's my father,' she said. 'He's had a heart attack.'

'Oh – I'm sorry. You'll want to get home as soon as possible.'

'Yes. I shall fly out as soon as there's a plane to take me.'

'Would you like me to ring the airport for you and check?'

'Oh Tom, would you?' Again, that wave of gratitude – and longing. But this was neither the time nor the place to try to sort out their differences, and before she could put anything of what she was feeling into words he had gone.

The jet took off from Darwin and was almost immediately over the sea. Harriet looked down as the Australian coastline was lost in the clouds and thought briefly she was little closer to solving the mystery than she had been when she arrived. But it seemed unimportant now. After all, it had happened so very long ago. What mattered now was getting home to her father. He was still alive – just. Harriet unclipped her seat belt, folded her hands in her lap and said a silent prayer that he would still be alive when she landed in America.

CHAPTER EIGHTEEN

Fergal Hillyard was almost six feet tall, with the sort of frame that had made him an ideal selection for the back row of the rugby team at college, a smoothly handsome face and a long lick of light brown hair carefully arranged across a balding crown. In his dark business suit with a flamboyantly striped tie he cut an impressive figure; as he came down the marble staircase to the lower floor of the West End restaurant where Theresa and Linda were waiting he looked every inch the successful businessman who was, in Linda's words, 'rolling in money' to the extent that he had been able to set his wife up in an exclusive boutique in order to 'give her an interest'. Waiters scurried forward solicitously but Fergal brushed them aside with a curious blend of impatience and charm, making straight for the table where the girls were sitting.

'My apologies – I was delayed. An important telephone call. Linda – lovely to see you again. And you must be Theresa. Well, my dear, you are every bit as beautiful as you are talented, if I may say so. It's a pleasure to meet you.' He took her hand, kissing it.

'It's a pleasure to meet you too,' Theresa said, but the flamboyant gesture had done nothing to make her feel any more at ease. Theresa was slightly overawed by the plushness of the restaurant and extremely anxious to make a good impression. It was so vitally important to her that this evening should be a success. The survival of her design venture – her whole future – depended on it. If she could impress Fergal Hillyard sufficiently to make him want to back her with some of his considerable fortune then she was in with a chance, buying time to establish herself and set up a decent workshop with new machines, top quality fabrics and perhaps even a showroom. If she failed then she could not see how she could keep going much longer.

She glanced at Fergal as he seated himself on her right. Since Linda had had the good fortune to meet him she had done a little checking on him. He had made his money in computer software, she had told Theresa, getting into the market at just the right time, and he was known to be shrewd, ruthless – and a voracious womaniser. He had, it was rumoured, bought the boutique for his wife in the hope she would be less likely to notice his junketings if she was busy with her own business. When Linda had told her this, Theresa had dismissed the comment as the kind of idle gossip induced by envy; now meeting him for the first time she could believe it might be the truth. As a purely instinctive reaction Theresa did not think she liked Fergal Hillyard very much. And in any case, where was his wife? If her boutique was going to be stocking Theresa Arnold designs, surely it would have made sense for her to have come along?

'Shall we order first and get down to business later?' Fergal suggested, opening the enormous leather-bound menu. 'And what will you have to drink? Champagne, perhaps?'

The girls exchanged glances. Apart from cheap Spanish bubbly Linda had never tasted champagne; but Mark had once shared a bottlewith Theresa and the memory of their happiness as they toasted one another in front of the fire in his flat before going to bed for a long, luxurious evening's lovemaking ran a thrill of sadness through her so sharp she could hardly bear it.

'I was much impressed by your designs,' Fergal said, turning to her. 'For one so young and so new to the business they show amazing perception.'

Theresa flushed with pleasure and if it crossed her mind to wonder what a man who had made his money from computers knew about fashion design she pushed the thought aside.

'Very, very saleable,' Fergal continued. 'There were one or two details of the finish that need work but ...'

Theresa's pleasure faded. 'What details?'

'I didn't feel the corners of the cuffs were as perfect as they might be and your labels could be better. When one is charging top prices without a known name as a selling point everything must be absolutely faultless.'

'I couldn't agree more,' Theresa said. 'And I certainly wasn't aware there was anything about my samples that could be criticised. If there is I'll make certain it's put right, and at risk of sounding like the poor workman blaming his tools, as the old saying goes, I'd like to explain that some of my machines are a bit past it and I think the outworkers have the same problem. It's because we're all working on a shoe-string, Mr Hillyard.'

'Fergal, please.' He smiled at her, his eyes lingering on her face.

'I appreciate your problems, my dear. I think you need assistance to help you rise above them. That's why I'm here.'

'You really think . . .' Theresa began eagerly, then broke off. She and Linda had agreed their strategy before coming; it would not be politic to appear to eager. It was important that Fergal Hillyard should see her as an up and coming designer who could make him a worthwhile return on his investment, not as a lame duck who needed rescuing. 'I need cash, Mr Hillyard – Fergal –' she continued, trying to impress with her directness. 'I won't deny that. It's the one thing I haven't got. But otherwise I have every confidence in what I'm doing and if you, or anyone, were to back me I know you wouldn't regret it.'

He raised his glass, looking at her over the top of it.

'You're very positive, Theresa. I like that. Well, I may be able to help you. I'm not making any promises yet awhile but let's explore the possibilities, shall we? What direction do you see your business moving in?'

'Terri designs for the young sophisticate,' Linda said. 'Clothes that would take the high-powered executive from the boardroom straight on to the smartest of evening engagements.'

Fergal's thick lips twisted with barely concealed amusement but he hardly so much as glanced in Linda's direction. His eyes were still firmly fixed on Theresa and there was something openly salacious in his expression.

'I'd like to hear Theresa's plans from the lady herself,' he said smoothly. 'If I'm going to be putting my money into something I prefer to cut away all the dead wood. So, Theresa, tell me in your own words how you would like to spend my investment if I decide to give it to you.'

Linda subsided, slightly put out. She was not unaware of the fact that Fergal was virtually ignoring her and since it had been she who had set up the meeting she felt a little hurt at being invited to play so little part in it. But she had the good sense to keep quiet. As long as Fergal could be persuaded to put up some money what did it matter who he talked to?

Throughout the meal Theresa outlined her hopes and plans and Fergal's questions and keen observations began to raise her hopes. Perhaps the man didn't know much about fashion – though he had certainly been astute enough to recognise good design when he had seen it in the shape of her samples – but he certainly did know about making money.

If only he could do for me what he's done for his computers all my worries would be over, Theresa thought, feeling almost light-hearted for the first time.

When the coffee was served Linda got up and excused herself, heading for the ladies' cloakroom and leaving Theresa alone with Fergal. With the coffee had come tiny delicious petit fours – and liqueurs. 'I really think I've had enough to drink,' Theresa had objected, but Fergal had been so insistent, that it had seemed rude to refuse. Theresa sipped her Cointreau allowing the syruppy liquid to slide down her throat and feeling the warmth spread through her veins.

'So,' she said, looking at Fergal over her glass. 'Have we convinced you that Theresa Arnold is a name worth backing?'

'Possibly.' His eyes narrowed in a face that was now slightly flushed. Theresa held her breath. 'There would be a few provisos, of course,' he went on. 'First, I would want to see someone with more experience running the business side. Your friend Linda is keen, she's a good saleswoman and perhaps one day she'll make a first class chief executive, but for the moment if I make a sizeable investment I should have to feel my money was in rather more capable hands than hers.'

'I couldn't throw her out,' Theresa said. 'She's part of the team and she's been with me from the beginning.

'I'm sure there would be a place for her. As I said, one of these days, with experience, she will be an asset to any company.

'What are the other conditions? Theresa asked.

'That you use a bank and an accountant of my choosing.'

'I can't see any problem with the accountant, but I do already have a bank loan for which my mother's house is collatoral.'

'I see.' A single frown line furrowed Fergal's smooth brow and Theresa felt slightly sick. He obviously had not realised she was already in considerable debt.

Oh God, she prayed, please don't let it make any difference!

'Well,' he continued, after a moment. 'I expect we could work something out on that score, providing . . .'

His voice tailed away. Theresa looked up sharply to see those speculative eyes watching her narrowly.

'Providing what?' she asked and heard the little tremor of nervousness in her own voice.

He smiled slowly. 'Oh, we don't want to discuss that now, do we? Come to my office and we'll talk about it there. Or better still, my little bachelor pad. We won't be interrupted there.'

Theresa's heart had begun to pound. It echoed hollowly at every pulse point and made her feel sick again.

'I . . . I don't know . . .'

'Now don't be a silly girl!' His voice was smooth and confident, the voice of a man practised in this sort of thing. 'I'm sure we can work very well together – an excellent team.' He took a card from his wallet and passed it to her. As he leaned close she caught a whiff of stale breath. 'The address of my little pad,' he said. 'I'm off to Brussels on business tomorrow for a few days – phone me next Monday and we'll fix up a time that suits both of us.'

Theresa's mouth was dry; she couldn't speak. She crumpled her linen napkin into a ball on the table top.

'Ah, here's your friend coming back,' Fergal said in the same smooth tone. 'She will be pleased to hear the good news, I expect.'

'Good news?'

'That you and I are on the point of coming to a very satisfactory agreement.' He smiled at her again; now that she had smelled his breath once she fancied she could smell it again, right across the table. 'I think we should drink, don't you, to the success of the hottest new label in town – Theresa Arnold!'

He raised his glass and Theresa did the same. So – it looked as though her business worries could be at an end. She would have the money she needed to help pull her out of her difficulties and ensure her mother's house was safe. And with the management Fergal would put in she would be able to leave the business to people who knew what they were doing whilst she concentrated on designing just as she had always wanted to. It was all there on offer, everything she had hoped for . . . more. But at what a price!

Theresa looked at the smooth, lascivious man beside her and shuddered. She was honestly not sure if it was a price she was prepared to pay. But what choice did she have? If it had been just her own business at stake she knew what she would have done – told him, what he could do with his offers. But it was more, much more than that.

As she so often did Theresa thought of her mother, so kind, so caring, who had risked everything she owned to give Theresa her chance, and felt sick at the thought of what she stood to lose.

I can't do it to her, Theresa thought. What would she do? Where would she go?

Slowly, sick at heart, she raised her glass and clinked it with Fergal's. The bargain was sealed. Theresa was only glad she had a week's grace before she had to deliver her part of it.

CHAPTER NINETEEN

'Dad?' Harriet said softly. 'Are you awake, Dad?'

For a moment there was no response and a nerve jumped in Harriet's throat.

He looked so frail lying there in his hospital bed with tubes attached to his arm and a monitor bleeping seismographical patterns on to a screen at the foot of his bed.

'Dad?' she whispered again and his eyes nickered and opened, staring blearily into the middle distance then focusing on her.

'Harriet?' His voice was slightly creaky, as if his lips were parched. Then, more strongly: 'Harriet! What are you doing here? I thought you were in Australia!'

She drew up a chair and sat down, taking his hand in hers.

'I came back as soon as I heard the news. Sally got a message to me.'

'Sally?' His hesitance made her realise he was drugged. 'Oh, Sally. Yes, she's a good girl.'

'How are you, Dad?'

'Oh fine, fine. Stupid thing to happen though, wasn't it?'

Harriet nodded, her throat too full to speak. From her conversation with Sally, Mark and the doctor in charge of the case she knew he was anything but fine. He was lucky to be alive. Had he been at the Ranch or one of his more far-flung homes he might not be. At least having a heart attack in the centre of New York guaranteed immediate medical attention.

'Just imagine – me having a weak heart!' Hugo murmured incredulously. 'Goddammit, I always thought I was as strong as an ox!'

'You are, but you are also human,' Harriet said gently. 'You have been under a lot of strain recently.'

He did not answer for a moment. There was a faraway look in his eyes.

'Yes, yes . . . I suppose I have.' Those eyes swivelled to her face, sharp suddenly in their dark sockets. 'How did you get on, Harriet? Did you find out anything?'

'Not now, Dad,' she cautioned. 'You mustn't worry your head about anything. Just get well.'

'But I want to know!' he persisted stubbornly. 'Did you find Greg Martin, the bastard?'

'No. Forget him, Dad, please. It's all so long ago.'

'He took your mother away from me, you know,' he said in the same dreamy voice. 'She was leaving me for him. God knows what she saw in him. Charm, I suppose. Charm – and money. He always made out he was so goddammed rich.'

'Dad . . .'

But there seemed to be no way of stopping Hugo from talking.

'I loved her so much I'd have died for her, Harriet, you know that? And instead . . . I never meant to hurt her, you know. I never wanted that. I just couldn't help myself. All that love – it seemed to go sour in me. I couldn't help myself!'

'Dad, please!' Harriet begged, distressed. 'You'll make yourself ill again.'

His fingers curled convulsively around hers. 'But I never meant to hurt her, Harri, you must believe that! I only wanted . . .'

The monitor began to bleep more urgently and Harriet felt a chill of fear. She freed her hand from her father's grasp and ran into the corridor, hailing a white-uniformed figure.

'Nurse! Come quickly, please! I think he's having another attack!'

The nurse hurried past her, moments later she was joined by a doctor. Harriet stood helplessly in the doorway, hands pressed to her mouth as she watched them working frantically. Then there was a firm but gentle hand about her waist and another nurse urged her away.

'Come on, sweetie. Let's get you a cup of good strong coffee.'

Harriet hung back. 'But my father . . .'

'There's nothing you can do there except get in the way. He's in good hands, I promise you.'

'But. . . will he be all right?'

'If Dr Clavell can't save him, no one can,' the nurse said comfortingly.

It was only when she was alone in the luxuriously appointed waiting room, pacing the floor with the untouched cup of coffee forgotten on the low glass-topped table that Harriet realised the nurse had not really answered her question. Sally had been at the hospital night and day since Hugo's first attack but had taken the opportunity afforded by Harriet's arrival to go home for a few hours' break, a shower, a change of clothes and a short sleep in her own bed. Now, Harriet had been forced to telephone and tell her the news that Hugo was once again in crisis. Sally had sounded distraught; now she would be on her way back to the hospital, her chauffeur fighting his way with all possible speed through the New York traffic.

As she waited alone, both for Sally and for news, Harriet found her mind playing and re-playing the conversation she had just had with her father like a scratched gramophone record stuck in the same groove and she paced the room wondering just what it was that had been going on in his confused brain when he had mumbled those agonised words.

Her first assumption had been that he was referring to the terrible fight he and Paula had had the night before she left to go to Italy – the fight the four-years-old Harriet had witnessed, unnoticed by either of them. She had been woken by the raised voices, got out of bed and toddled along the corridor to the door to her parents' room where she had stood in the doorway wide-eyed and frightened – more frightened than she had ever been before in her young life and probably more frightened than she ever would be again for a very long time.

She had not understood what was going on at the time of course. Only later had she been able to piece together the fragmented shards and even then she was unsure just how much was reality and how much imagination, distorted like a dream on exposure to daylight. Now, hearing her father's tortured ramblings, she thought that it must have been every bit as bad as she had feared.

Of course, it could be that he blamed himself for Paula's death. He shouldn't – she certainly didn't. Row or no row Paula had been going with Greg – wasn't that what it was all about? But grief plays unkind tricks with conscience. Perhaps Hugo felt that if he had acted differently Paula would be alive today.

'I never meant to hurt her . . .' The words echoed again, each one spilling anguish, and a terrible new thought caught Harriet unawares, making her go cold. She pushed it away, unwilling to examine it even for a moment, yet it crept back like a shadow around the corners of her mind.

'I never meant to hurt her . . . All that love seemed to go sour in me . . . I couldn't help myself . . .'

Harriet clapped her hands across her eyes, horror struck: 'No!' she whispered and a voice inside her head seemed to echo it but with a scream, not a whisper. 'No! You *didn't*, Dad. You *couldn't* have had any part in it.' Yet even as she denied it the terrible suspicion was growing like a cancer.

Sally had been to Italy shortly after the explosion, Tom's assistant had said. Why? And why had she been so upset when Harriet had made known her plans to try to solve the mystery? Was it that she knew something – something she wanted to remain hidden and that she was terrified Harriet might unearth?

Harriet paced the room, tight-coiled as a spring, while the unwelcome thoughts chased one another around her mind. With her whole heart she prayed that her father would come through this latest attack and recover, but at the same time the dread lay heavy in the pit of her stomach. If he did pull through – what then? Was it possible there would be another ordeal for him to face? And was it fear of the future, as well as anguish for the past, that had finally overtaxed his heart and brought on these totally unexpected attacks?

Harriet dug her hands deep into her pockets and the nails made half moon crescents in her palms. For the moment there was nothing to do but wait.

It seemed to Hugo that he was drifting, totally divorced from the pathetic frail body in the hospital bed. Dimly he was aware of the people in white coats, urgently ministering to him, but they seemed oddly unreal. It was the others who had substance, the wraith-like ones who had kept him company these last drug-befuddled days: Greg Martin, dark, swarthy, almost indecently handsome in his white yachting trousers and open neck shirt; his own past self, looking as he had done in the days of his youth; and Paula. Yes, most of all Paula.

Christ but she was beautiful! he thought, and the love and all-consuming desire she had always excited in him was there once more, undiminished by the years. How he had loved her! – loved her still, in spite of everything.

Paula, oh Paula, so desirable and yet so infuriating, driving him crazy with adoration, reducing him to wild corrosive jealousy. Paula, whom he had never for one moment owned, in spite of being married to her. Paula, taking everything she wanted as she moved through life with never a thought for the consequences of her actions, yet still with the power to make him her slave.

The white-coated figures had disappeared now; he was no longer aware of them at all. Only Paula was real and it seemed to Hugo that he had moved into the past with her, not just remembering but living again the events of twenty years ago.

PART FOUR

The Past

CHAPTER TWENTY

'New York, New York – I'm gonna wake up in the city that never sleeps!' sang Paula, and Hugo, emerging from the shower wrapped in an enormous monogrammed towelling robe, smiled and turned away before he could be tempted to make love to her yet again. There was no time for that now – any interruption to Paula's toilet would certainly mean they would be late for work. The length of time she spent on preparing herself to face the world was one of the tiny irritations that had begun to niggle at Hugo in four blissful months of marriage – she was quite lovely enough to go out without a scrap of paint on her face in his opinion. But it was a minor aggravation only and Hugo dismissed the thought as quickly as it arose. Paula was used to earning her living by her looks. And he was much too ecstatic at having won her to allow any hint of censure to mar the idyll.

And idyll it certainly was, for Paula adored New York. The moment she arrived she had fallen head over heels in love with the glittering, zinging city and her eyes had shone like the myriad of lights reflected in the dark waters of the East River that circled Manhattan. He had taken an almost childlike pleasure in showing her around, though the bitter February wind still blew the dust into swirls on the sidewalks beneath the skyscrapers, the seagulls rode the gusts over the river and the cabs made bright sunshiny splashes of yellow against the uniform grey. She loved the department stores, especially Bloomingdales, and the shopping malls, she loved the glittering jewels she saw at Van Cleefs, where Hugo had promised to buy her a piece for each and every anniversary, she loved the glamour of Broadway and the air of purposeful relaxation of Central Park.

The one thing she had not loved had been sharing a house with Hugo's mother, the redoubtable Martha, and Veronica, the youngest of his three sisters who was, at thirty-five, still unmarried. With the first fruits of his success Hugo had moved them all from the Bronx to a fine old town house in the East Sixties and it had quite simply never occurred to him to find a place of his own. They were a family – it had made sense for them to stay together, for although he was doing well he was not yet so flush that he could run two houses and employ two sets of servants without considering the cost. When his father had died the previous year Hugo had been glad he had been on hand to be of comfort to his mother, who was devastated by the loss of the gritty little man with whom she had fallen in love almost fifty years earlier, and she had clung fiercely to Hugo, her only son, who reminded her so poignantly of his father.

Paula, however, had been appalled by the idea of sharing a home with her in-laws, even if Hugo did have his own suite of rooms. Spacious though the duplex was it reminded her of her childhood when she, Sally and their parents had been forced to live with her grandparents. She had not the slightest intention of returning to such an arrangement, especially since she did not much like either Martha or Veronica and they did not seem to like her. Veronica did little to disguise the envy of a plain woman for a beautiful one and Martha resented the fact that she no longer had first call on her son's attention. Living in such close proximity to them made Paula edgy; she begged, pleaded and cajoled, and to please her Hugo had taken a suite at the Waldorf Towers whilst they searched for a home of their own.

At last they had found just the place – a huge house of pale grey marble on East 70th Street and the moment she had seen it Paula had forgotten what she considered to be its greatest drawback – that it was only just around the block from Hugo's old home. She had almost gasped aloud in delight as she went in through the impressive front door and saw the sweeping staircase, shipped out from England and lovingly reconstructed by the previous owner, and she had run from room to room like a child. Her London flat would have fitted into a corner of just one of the floors and there were three of those, not to mention a huge garden which would keep one man busy on a full-time basis and might require extra help at certain times of the year.

There was even an indoor swimming pool, constructed in a vast room that had once been a ballroom. Paula could scarcely believe her luck and for the hundredth time she thought how glad she was she had married Hugo – in England it might have been years before she could aspire to a home like this, for ever. Even the titled gentlemen she knew would have some difficulty finding the wherewithal to keep up such a place.

Hugo had employed one of the best interior decorators in New York and Paula revelled in poring over the fabric samples and 'pasteups' that the designer brought for her approval and spent hours leafing through catalogues and touring antique shops to find pieces for her new home – everything from a beautiful Meissen fruit bowl to an imitation Chippendale bureau-bookcase. Hugo was a little disturbed by the size of the bills that appeared on his desk but he said nothing, treating them with the same indulgence that he showed towards everything where Paula was concerned. Furnishing a new home was bound to be a costly business and he could afford it. Business was booming, orders were flooding in, and he needed a home that reflected his success. Even more important – Paula was happy. That was his first and only consideration.

Would she have married him if he had been a penniless immigrant like his father? It was a question Hugo preferred not to ask himself, for deep down he was quite sure she would not. She had told him that night in the restaurant that she could not be bought but he suspected it had been the diamonds and the promise of more where they came from that had persuaded her – just as he had intended they should. But knowing it did not make him love her any the less. If allowing her to spend his money was the price he had to pay for possessing even a part of this delectable creature then he would pay it, and gladly.

What worried him more was Paula's insistence on attending every social event to which they were invited – and there were far too many of those. Nowadays fashion designers had broken through the barrier of social acceptability – in fact it was quite a cachet to have one's charity ball or restaurant party, benefit or fund raiser graced by at least one of the big names – Bill Blass, Oscar de la Renta – or Hugo Varna. Hugo was delighted at the opportunity to show off his bride and everyone was eager to meet her – perhaps that was why the invitations were coming so thick and fast, he thought shrewdly. But he was not really one for a great deal of socialising, necessary though a certain amount was. Too many late nights, too much rich food and a constantly refilled glass did not suit him – he needed a clear head and a refreshed system in order to work properly. But again he was prepared to bear with Paula for the moment. Obviously she was eager to meet people and form a circle of friends, but he hoped she would soon tire of the endless round once they were settled in their new home.

In any case they were due to leave on a two-week 'trunk show' tour in the Mid West soon, taking samples to major department stores in several cities where potential customers who would never travel to New York to shop could see the collection in its entirety, try on any piece that took their fancy and order without the restriction imposed by a middle-man store buyer who might be overcautious about choosing some of the more revolutionary lines. Hugo disliked trunk shows almost as much as he disliked excessive socialising but knew they were an economic necessity and for maximum effect he always went along in person together with one of his most experienced sales ladies and two hand-picked house models. On this trip Paula was to be one of the models – he had not been able to bear the thought of leaving her at home and she was anxious to see as much as possible of America, though he had warned her there would be little time for sightseeing – a trunk show in one city was very like a trunk show in another – arriving, unpacking, showing, selling, packing and moving on again, all in the claustrophobic atmosphere of almost identical department stores. Hugo knew of old what an exhausting business it was – at the end of it, he thought, Paula would be only too glad to settle for a quiet life. And if not, well, he would just have to explain quietly but firmly that if she wanted to be able to continue to spend his money with the same lavish abandon then she would also have to be prepared to allow him enough early nights to be able to create with a clear brain.

Yes, all in all Hugo was more than happy with his new way of life. And judging by the way she was singing to herself as she prepared to go with him to the showroom, Paula was happy too.

The honeymoon lasted precisely six months. Hugo, employed his favourite trick of burying his head in the sand, managed to ignore the first warning rumbles of the storms ahead, but one morning in early July he was unable to ignore them any longer.

He was in his office, hard at work, when there was a knock at the door and Laddie Mitchell looked in.

Laddie was Hugo's assistant and had been from the time Hugo had moved into the big time and was no longer able to produce his collections unaided. Like so many designers, Laddie was homosexual, unlike some he did not parade the fact. In many ways he looked more like a clean-cut college boy than a gay fashion designer; in his Shetland crew neck sweaters and immaculate white yachting trousers he also looked ridiculously young. It was only at close quarters when the deep creases in his tanned face and the grey streaks in the close-cropped light brown hair were visible that one realised that he was years older than he first appeared and would certainly never see thirty again, and perhaps not thirty-five.

Laddie was everything Hugo could have wished for in an assistant. He was hard working and reliable and most important of all he had been able to adapt and channel his talent so that it mirrored Hugo's own. Hugo could leave him to work on a sketch or choose a fabric knowing full well that it would be in keeping with his own style and the finished item would be instantly recognisable to the trained eye as a Hugo Varna original. But for all his obvious talent Laddie was perfectly happy with his role as assistant. He never seemed to mind that his name did not, and never would, appear on the label, or resent the fact that his own ideas had to be subjugated to the Varna line. In truth he lacked the confidence and the drive to branch out on his own – he much preferred to let someone else take the bouquets – and the brickbats – enjoy his fat salary cheque and leave the financial worries to others.

'Could I have a word with you, Hugo?' Laddie asked.

'Of course. Come in,' Hugo said, a little disturbed by Laddie's serious expression. 'Sit down, Laddie.'

Laddie sat, then jumped up again, nervously prowling around the office and the fear that is every designer's nightmare raised its ugly head to leer at Hugo. 'Nothing has happened to the new designs, I hope. They haven't been stolen, have they?' he asked.

Laddie looked almost surprised. 'No – nothing like that.'

'What then? For goodness' sake, man, I can tell just by looking at you that something is wrong.'

'I don't quite know how to say this,' Laddie began, 'but there is a lot of unrest amongst the staff.'

'Unrest? Don't tell me they want their wages reviewed. Heaven knows I already pay them more than any other designer in New York to ensure I have only the best.'

'No, it's not wages.' Laddie shifted uncomfortably. 'It's Paula. She has been upsetting them.'

Hugo's brows came together. 'Upsetting them? Who? How?'

'It started with the models. I didn't take much notice at first. I thought it was just that their noses were put out of joint – what with Paula doing the truck show and all the big benefits . . .

'What do they expect?' Hugo interrupted. 'She's my wife, for Chrissake. Of course I took her along.'

'But it wasn't just that,' Laddie persisted unhappily. 'She has started carping at them. Now I don't have to tell you, Hugo, American models are the most professional in the world. They pride themselves on it. They resent an English girl coming in and throwing her weight around.'

'Simple girlie bitchiness!' Hugo snapped. 'They *are* professional, I agree with you, I'd never hire them otherwise. But they are also hellishly insecure. And most of them are on "uppers" to cut their appetites and stay thin – thank God Paula has no problem with her weight! That makes them edgy. They'll take offence at the smallest thing – you know that as well as I do.'

'I think in this case they have a point,' Laddie went on doggedly. 'And it's not just the models. Paula seems to be overlooking everyone in the workrooms, criticising and changing things. She's even had a go at me a couple of times. The staff don't know how to react. They are used to taking their orders from you, me and Maura Hemingway.' (Maura was the chief sales person, an immaculate blue-rinsed matron who had also been with Hugo from the early days). 'They are not used to being bossed around by one of the house models. But she is your wife, which makes it difficult to ignore her. I tell you, Hugo, if you don't do something about it you will have a mutiny on your hands.'

Hugo was trembling with anger.

'All right, Laddie, you've said enough. You are quite right, Paula is my wife and as such I expect her to be treated with respect – though I suppose a certain amount of resentment is inevitable to begin with amongst people who have been with me for a long time. What does surprise me is that you should take part in it. I would never have expected you to come crawling to me with tales about my wife.'

Laddie's jaw tightened. 'It's not something I've enjoyed doing. But I thought you should know what is going on, or one day you might turn round and find yourself minus half your staff.'

'Don't be ridiculous.'

'Including me,' Laddie said. Now that he had got over his initial nervousness he was determined to finish what he had come to say. The continued smooth-running of the Varna showrooms depended on it.

Hugo's eyes narrowed. '*You?* Good God, Laddie, you're not thinking of leaving me are you?'

'I wouldn't want to, no,' Laddie said steadily. 'I've been very happy working for you, Hugo. We make a good team. But I work for only one boss. I've made allowances for Mrs Varna so far – I realise this is all new to her and she's feeling her feet. But I won't be walked over by anybody. Not even by your wife.'

'I'm sorry you feel like that, Laddie,' Hugo said, badly shaken.

'Well I do and I thought it was best to get it off my chest,' Laddie said. 'All I'm asking is that you open your eyes to what's happening. This has always been a happy outfit. I don't want to see it degenerate into a dog's dinner.'

Hugo was still angry at the criticism of Paula but he had a great deal of respect for his assistant and he was wise enough to realise Laddie would never have sought this interview unless there was some truth in his accusations.

'Paula is just feeling her way I guess,' he said in a conciliatory tone. 'She's a long way from home and it's all very different to what she's used to. I'm sure when she settles down everything will fall into place. But I'll have a word with her, Laddie.'

For a moment his assistant looked on the point of bursting into tears of relief, then his good-looking brow cleared and he nodded.

Thanks, Hugo. I'm sure she'd be a lot happier as well as the rest of us if only you would.'

All day Hugo turned the interview with Laddie over in his mind. He was hurt and angry that anyone should dare to criticise Paula yet in his heart of hearts he knew there must be at least a nugget of truth in what Laddie had said. He had not been entirely oblivious to the change of atmosphere at the showroom, the air of resentment that had an edge of frost in spite of the searing temperatures of New York in a July heatwave, and he supposed that the traits in her character which he regarded as lovable foibles might be interpreted by others as haughty supremacy and bossiness.

Strange really, he thought, that someone with as ordinary a background as hers should be able to give such a good imitation of a princess of the Royal House – strange, but darkly exciting. As for telling the bastards their jobs, that was just the act of a small girl pretending to be grown up. But he had promised Laddie, so he had better have a word in her ear.

They had now moved into the house on East 70th Street and

this evening was one of the rare ones they spent at home. They had dined quietly on a delicious selection of cold meats prepared by their newly-employed housekeeper and now they were relaxing with the remains of a bottle of Moët et Chandon in the garden with the strains of Vivaldi wafting out to them through the open French windows.

'Honey, I want to talk to you.' Hugo moved his chair a little closer to hers, reaching for her hand and feeling his stomach contact as it always did when he touched her silky flesh. She looked so beautiful sitting there with the last rays of the dying sun turning her hair to molten gold and her long bare legs, emerging from the briefest of silk mini-shifts, elegantly crossed to expose her smooth honey-coloured tan. For a moment he was tempted to abandon the attempt at gently chastising her and make love to her instead, right here in the garden with the scent of the roses and banks of sweet-smelling stocks heavy in the air. But the sooner he set her right about her role at the showroom the better.

'I talked with Laddie today,' he began. 'Honey, you are going to have to be more careful what you say to the staff. Some of them are taking offence at you telling them how they should do their jobs.'

A quiver of indignation ran through Paula but she tossed her head.

'Oh, you mean the models being bitchy. Well, they usually are. I've put up with that all my working life. I can handle it.'

'I know you can but I can't afford a bad atmosphere,' Hugo said gently. 'But it's not just the models. Even Laddie has taken umbrage. Look, I know it's all fresh to you and I expect some of them are jealous and unpleasant because of it but can you soft-pedal a bit – for me?'

Paula stared. There was a hard little gleam in her eyes.

'So Laddie has been to you behind my back telling tales, has he?'

'It wasn't like that, honey. Laddie was simply reporting on the way the staff feel and saying you weren't always as tactful as you might be.'

'And you believe him?' Paula withdrew her hand sharply from his.

'Laddie is an excellent assistant,' Hugo said soothingly. 'I've come to trust his judgement.'

'Even when he tells tales about your wife? How dare he! Surely I am entitled to a certain amount of respect!'

'Of course you should be treated respectfully,' Hugo agreed. 'But respect in a professional capacity has to be earned. Take your time, feel your way and I'm sure you'll get it. But antagonising people is not the answer, believe me, honey.'

Paula leapt to her feet. She was furious with Laddie and even more furious with Hugo for listening to him.

'Well thank you, Hugo, for standing up for me so gallantly!' she snapped. 'If I'm such a nuisance at the showroom I won't embarrass you by coming there anymore. I can find plenty of things to do – shopping, lunch parties with the girls, charity do's – and when I get tired of that I might even find myself a modelling job with some other designer. There are plenty who'd be glad to have me – Hugo Varna's English *wife*.'

He caught at her wrist. 'You're blowing this up out of all proportion. Sit down, have another glass of champagne and stop being silly.'

Enraged by his conciliatory tone she snatched her wrist free.

'Thank you, I don't want any more champagne.

She turned and marched into the house. In the doorway she almost bumped into Doris, the live-in maid, who was wearing the smart black dress and white lace apron that Paula insisted on.

'For heaven's sake look where you are going!' Paula snapped.

'I'm sorry, Mrs Varna, I was just coming through to tell you that you have a visitor.' The girl's cheeks were slightly flushed; there was an air of over-excitement about her – as if she had just been told she could compete for one of the big prizes on a game show, Paula thought.

'A visitor? At this time of night? Who is it?'

'It's *Mr* Varna's visitor really,' the girl qualified, her excitement surfacing again in a hastily suppressed giggle. 'He says his name is Mr Martin, Mr Greg Martin, and that he's a business associate.'

Paula almost stamped her foot with annoyance. The. last thing she wanted at the moment was to be forced into a social situation.

But of course Hugo would want to see Greg Martin. He had been out of New York for the last six months so she had not met him, but from what Hugo had told her she knew the two men were good friends as well as business partners. Well, with any luck she'd be able to excuse herself as soon as the introductions were over and go to her room. Perhaps a good soak in the bath tub would make her feel better.

Doris was hovering like a huge trapped black and white butterfly.

'Very well, Doris,' Paula said. 'You'd better show Mr Martin in.'

CHAPTER TWENTY-ONE

'You must be Paula,' the stranger said, holding out his hand.

She took it, her anger forgotten. She felt exactly as she had felt when as a child she had crashed out of a tree still clutching the broken branch to land flat on her back on the ground beneath. All the breath had been knocked out of her then and as she gasped for air she had felt as if her diaphragm had glued itself to her backbone. It was the same now.

'And you are Greg. I've heard so much about you.'

'All good, I hope.' His voice had a lazy drawl to it; she tried to place it and couldn't. She wasn't yet sufficiently used to identifying the nuances of accent and placing them – Boston, East Coast, Mid West. The only ones she instantly recognised were twanging Bronx – because Hugo retained traces of it – and Deep South drawl, because she had seen *Gone with the Wind* at least six times.

'All good of course!' she said, smiling.

His hand felt firm and cool on hers; she did not want to relinquish it. But behind her she heard Hugo's exclamation: 'Greg! I didn't know you were back in town!' and she stepped aside and watched the two men embrace, clapping one another on the back and grinning like eager schoolboys.

In spite of the Italian ancestry on his father's side, Greg towered over the slightly-built Hugo and in every other way, Paula thought, his Mediterranean heritage was clearly stamped on him. His shoulders were broad, his hips slim, his complexion deep-tanned and swarthy. Jet black hair sprung from a classically patrician face, dark eyes smouldered like some sleeping volcano. There was a slight hook to his nose and his teeth gleamed very white.

'I see you have met my wife,' Hugo said. 'Paula, this is the guy I owe all my success to. If it hadn't been for him I'd still be running a couple of sewing machines on Mom's kitchen table.'

Greg laughed. 'That's nonsense and you know it. If I hadn't spotted your potential someone else would have.' But he looked pleased all the same.

'We're in the garden, Greg. It's too good an evening to be indoors. Let's crack another bottle of champagne. This is an occasion – the return of the prodigal!'

He steered Greg towards the French doors and Paula followed, feeling a little left out. She was used to the almost entirely undivided attention of any man she met – this one scarcely seemed to have noticed her. And oh, she wanted him to notice her! It mattered more than it had ever mattered before – and not simply because her ego required it. She was quivering from head to toe with barely suppressed excitement – no wonder Doris had looked so flustered! There was something about Greg Martin that had reduced her to a veritable jelly of desire. She knew she would do anything – *anything* to have him look at her with those fiery dark eyes boring into her very soul.

'Ask Doris to bring out another bottle of Moët, would you, honey?' Hugo said over his shoulder and her irritation flickered again. First he chided her as if she were a naughty schoolgirl, then he ordered her about like a servant – how dare he?

As she joined the men in the garden she was annoyed to find they were talking business. Boring! Dollars – and millions of them – only became interesting when she could spend them. She settled herself in the garden chair opposite Greg, crossing her legs provocatively and watching him from behind her long lashes. To her disappointment he still seemed quite oblivious to her.

'So you had a profitable trip then?' Hugo was saying.

'Uh-huh.' For the first time since she had sat down the jet-dark eyes swivelled to look at her. 'So, by the seem of it, did you!'

Hugo smiled. 'I went to see a fashion show and came back with a wife. I wish you could have been at the wedding, pal, but it all happened so fast. Just wait, Greg, one day the same thing will happen to you!'

Greg laughed, waving his hands in protest.

'No way. I enjoy being an eligible bachelor too much for that.'

'So did I. But marriage is an institution I can thoroughly recommend.'

Hugo beamed at her. Oh yes! she thought. Less than an hour ago you were carping at me, passing on sneaky complaints from your twopenny-halfpenny staff. Marriage is an institution – that's rich!

But the moment she looked at Greg her annoyance died again. Impossible to remain in a bad temper looking at that handsome face and beautiful body. Look at me, Greg, please *look at me*!

Darkness fell, Hugo turned on the soft floodlighting and still they sat talking. Paula watched them, feeling the small quivers of desire tickling her inner thighs, scarcely listening to their interchange.

At last Greg rose. 'I'd better be going, Hugo. I'll look in at the showroom one day next week. I can't say exactly when – I've got several important deals to sort out. But you'll be there, I guess?'

'Why don't you have dinner with us one evening?' Paula suggested.

He swung round, giving her the full benefit of those dark eyes. She thought there was just the slightest hint of amusement in them.

'That would be nice. Would it be all right if I brought someone with me? I'd hate to play gooseberry on the newly-weds.'

Her stomach lurched uncomfortably. He knew! He knew what she was thinking and he was rejecting her!

'Of course,' she said smoothly.

'Who will it be?' Hugo asked, apparently unaware of the tension hanging in the air. 'Which one is in favour at present?'

Greg shrugged. 'I'm not sure. I've been away for rather a long time and I only got back today, remember. But I'm sure I can find somebody to make up the party.'

'You bet you can!' Hugo laughed, and added, to Paula: 'Greg is never short of a partner. His little black book reads like a directory of who's who in the world of glamour.'

'I'm sure,' Paula said icily.

'Goodnight, Paula, it's been a pleasure to meet you.' He took her hand again and bent to kiss her cheek. Her pulses raced.

When he had gone Hugo put his arm around her, drawing her close.

'Shall I tell you something, honey? Greg's little black book might be full of glamour girls but not one of them is as lovely as you. And stud that he is, he doesn't know what he's missing. Come to bed, huh?'

Paula, too weak with longing to protest, let him lead her up to the elegantly decorated master bedroom and undress her. But as she lay in the huge four-poster bed with its silk drapes, submitting to Hugo's fevered embraces, it was Greg's face she seemed to see in the darkness and when she reached her shuddering climax it was as a result of imagining Greg's lips tugging and teasing her, Greg's arms around her, Greg's body upon and within her, not Hugo's at all.

For three whole days Paula could neither eat nor sleep. That first night while Hugo snored gently beside her she lay rigid, quite unrelaxed by their lovemaking, her whole body aching and quivering as she thought of Greg. Eventually she got up and wandered around the house, picking up the beautiful pieces she had bought to adorn it and putting them down again, afraid they would fall from her trembling fingers and be broken.

At breakfast, toying with a piece of toast while Hugo ate a huge, pile of sunnyside eggs and ham, she asked him about Greg. 'What exactly does he do?'

Hugo smiled good-humouredly. 'Good question. He calls himself a financier but that covers a multitude of sins. He started, in real estate, I believe, and used that as a basis from which to branch out into mortgage securities and investment consultancy. He's got a finger in more pies than you could name – and to be honest the only thing that has ever concerned me is that he was rich enough and interested enough to put up the money that set me on the road to success. When I needed a backer, Greg was there. I'll never stop being grateful to him for that.'

'As he said, if he hadn't been someone else probably would have.'

'Perhaps, but it so happens that Greg was the one,' Hugo said, washing down his ham and eggs with scalding coffee. 'He's a character, though, make no mistake of it and I think he sometimes sails closer to the wind that he should. But that's how he's made his fortune – by taking chances – and I'm sure when you get to know him you'll like him as much as I do. In fact, I don't know anyone who doesn't like Greg. He's a charmer.'

'Yes,' Paula said, pressing her knees tightly together and thinking how shocked Hugo would be if he guessed just how well she hoped she would get to know Greg Martin.

So obsessed with him was she that she went to the showroom that day and the next with Hugo, barely giving a thought to the conversation they had been having when Greg had arrived. Pettifogging jealousy and bitchiness seemed supremely unimportant set against the possibility of seeing him again. But though she almost jumped in anticipation each time she heard the elevator purr to a stop on their floor he did not come. Always it was someone else – a buyer or a press attaché, a house model or a pattern cutter, or simply one of the porters wheeling a rail of samples, carefully concealed beneath the plastic sample bags, on their way back from the Puerto Rican workshops just around the block in the sidestreets between 8th and 9th Avenues.

'Have you made a definite date for our dinner party with Greg Martin?' she asked Hugo on the third day, unable to contain herself any longer.

'Oh honey, I forgot to tell you,' Hugo said. 'I'm afraid that's had to be postponed.'

Paula's heart missed a beat. 'Why?' she asked, trembling and hating herself for it.

'He's out of town again – off to Texas, of all places. He swears it's business but personally I think the very lovely daughter of a certain oil magnate is behind it. He's been seeing her lately, I know, and it could be that Daddy is giving him the once-over.'

Paula could have wept with disappointment and rage. She had so been looking forward to seeing him again and it was bruising to think he had chosen to rush off to Texas with some woman, no matter how rich her daddy might be, when she was horribly sure that he had suspected her motives in inviting him to dinner might be rather more than friendly.

Dammit, he's probably laughing at me! she thought, remembering the way he had looked at her when she had issued the invitation – eyes very dark, very knowing, lips curving away from very white teeth in a way that was almost vulpine. But in spite of the feeling of humiliation and the sudden wave of something close to fleeting hatred for the man who had inspired it, the attraction was as strong as ever, perhaps stronger: Paula was not used to rejection. It added a new dimension to her desire and made her more determined than ever – one of these days she would possess Greg Martin just as she had possessed every other man she had ever wanted.

Whilst Greg was away from New York and she could do nothing to advance her plans to capture him, Paula turned her thoughts to another matter. Ever since she had learned that Laddie had talked to Hugo about her she had been determined to find a way to get back at him and now, in her spare moments (which were many since Hugo was very busy with the new season's collection) she considered various methods of revenge before rejecting them all. It would be too easy – and too crude – to sabotage his sketches or his samples, and to simply get him fired would not hold any long-term satisfaction. No, Paula thought, what she would really like would be some hold over him, for to her power was still the greatest thrill she could imagine.

Sex, she realised now, was only the beginning of it, for when the boys had flocked around begging for her favours it had been the sense of power which had been the aphrodisiac. But it had not been long before she had realised there were other ways to be in control. There was emotional blackmail – very powerful, that, and best used on those closest to one, and there was the game of making others indebted and then calling in favours – or constantly threatening to, as she had done with Gary. Now, in her position as Hugo's wife, there was straightforward supremacy, the power that position could bring. But none of these had worked on Laddie. He was Hugo's friend as well as his assistant, he had Hugo's ear – and she knew that he did not like her. There has to be a way, thought Paula. He has to have a weakness. And I am going to find out what it is.

Her determination kept her going to the showroom though she had begun to hate the atmosphere there. Now that it had been pointed out to her how unpopular she was with the work force the sudden silence that descended the moment she entered a room became more obvious to her than ever and she could feel the eyes that followed her with dislike when she left. Worse, she had to bite her tongue and refrain from telling the workers what to do, or risk another lecture from Hugo and knowing they must know, every last one of them, why she had changed her ways made her feel angry and humiliated and fuelled her determination to find a way to get even with Laddie.

It was one stiflingly hot afternoon in July when her opportunity came and when it did it happened by the sheerest chance. Paula was in the showroom when she saw Laddie come hurrying out of his office and she thought there was something oddly furtive about the way he looked around to see if he had been observed. Paula experienced a small thrill of anticipation which owed more to some sixth sense than to anything she had yet seen. As Laddie started down the stairs (he suffered from claustrophobia and had a terror of elevators) she slipped into the lift, then waited until he appeared, panting a little, at the bottom of the stairs and followed him outside into the street. There was a car drawn up at the kerb and at the wheel was a boy, very clean cut, very good looking – and with a face that was familiar to Paula because of the circles she moved in. As she watched unseen from the doorway Laddie hurried around to the passenger side and climbed into the car. The boy turned eagerly toward him, Laddie leaned over, put an arm around the slim shoulders and kissed him on the cheek. After a moment when they appeared to simply sit looking at one another the boy put the car into drive and it took off into the honking hustling traffic.

Paula stood in the doorway, a smile playing around her mouth, as she savoured the implications of what she had just seen.

She had known, of course, from the moment she had met him that Laddie was homosexual and she had scarcely given it a second thought. The fashion world was riddled with gays and Gary, perhaps the best friend she had ever had, had been one. But what she had just witnessed was something else again, for the boy in the car had been Chris Connelly, son of the senator Jimmy Connelly who might, it was rumoured, run for President next time around.

Tingling with excitement Paula watched the car disappear in the heavy afternoon traffic. So – Chris Connelly was Laddie's lover – no wonder he had been so discreet! A whisper of scandal like that would do the Senator no good at all – he was always portrayed as a regular family man with a regular wholesome family. If it ever got out that his son was gay the news media would have a field day.

Chris must have phoned Laddie and asked him to meet him urgently or the designer would never have left his office in the middle of the day and perhaps they had thought one moment of carelessness would not matter. How wrong they had been!

Paula returned to the showroom, her mind busy with plans to make the best use of her knowledge. Laddie was out for over an hour and when she heard sounds of movement in his office Paula decided to act.

'Is everything all right, Laddie?' she asked in mock solicitude, knocking on his door and looking in.

'Yes, of course – why shouldn't it be?' he replied, but she could tell he was not being entirely truthful.

'I was concerned when I saw you rushing out like that,' Paula said. 'And then when I realised it was Chris who had called, wanting to see you urgently, I thought there might be something dreadfully wrong in your private life ...' Her tone was ingenuous, her expression concerned, but her eyes were sharp and eager. She was guessing, of course, that it had been a phone call that had sent

Laddie scurrying out of his office and down to the street but the moment she said it she knew she was absolutely right. Laddie's boyish face had turned pale and he was quite unable to hide his expression of utter horror.

'Oh Laddie – I'm sorry – is it a secret?' she asked in mock concern. 'Of course – I can see that whatever it is it must be terribly sensitive with Chris being who he is. It could be so embarrassing for everyone concerned, couldn't it, if word got out. But you need not worry. I won't breathe a word. Your secret is quite safe with me.'

She saw high spots of colour begin to stain Laddie's ashen cheeks and the feeling of power she so enjoyed began to surge through her. How he must be cursing himself for his carelessness! Well, she had him now. He would never dare to talk about her to Hugo – or anyone else – again.

Paula smiled to herself. He wasn't to know she meant it when she said his secret was safe with her. She wouldn't tell it because once she did she would no longer have any hold over him and it was that that was making her feel so good, as if she had just had the biggest orgasm of her life.

'If there is anything I can do to help just let me know, won't you Laddie?' she said sweetly.

He was still staring after her in horror as she left the room.

The discovery that she was pregnant came as an even bigger shock to Paula than had the news from England that her young sister Sally had given birth to an illegitimate son whom she intended to keep and bring up alone. Paula had been surprised but not dumbfounded when the letter had arrived – wasn't it always the quiet ones who ended up in what her mother would refer to as 'trouble'? The fast ones were too streetwise to find themselves in such a predicament and if they did they would get out of it, fast. But it was quite in keeping with Sally's nature that she should have refused both an abortion and adoption. 'Silly idiot, she's ruined things for herself now', Paula thought, and promptly forgot all about her sister.

When her own pregnancy was confirmed however she was shocked beyond belief. She had had no intention of starting a family yet – if at all! – and had been meticulous in the use of her diaphragm. Except . . . yes, there had been one occasion, a lazy Sunday morning when she had felt too languorous to get out of bed and visit the bathroom. And just that once had been enough seemingly.

Her first thought was dismay at how drastically her social life would be curtailed for the best part of a year, her second was anxiety for her looks. What would having a baby do to her body? Her breasts weren't big enough to sag much but if they lost their firmness they'd turn into a couple of fried eggs and slim as she was any thickening of her waist would destroy the balance of her figure so she would end up looking like a plank, straight up and down. Lax tummy muscles and varicose veins were just two more horrors to be feared and the fact that millions of women cope with such problems and emerge virtually unscathed was of little comfort. It wasn't enough for her that she would still be a very attractive woman no matter how many children she bore; Paula could not be satisfied with less than perfection. She knew she would look in the mirror and hate every inch of bulge and she dreaded the discomforts of early morning sickness, indigestion, the clumsiness, the indignity of it all.

Hugo, on the other hand, was as excited as a child on Christmas Eve when she told him the news.

'Don't kid me, Paula,' he said, gazing at her with an expression of wonder that said he half-believed her already.

'I'm not kidding. Would I, about something like that? People do have babies you know, especially when they make love as often as we do.'

'I guess they do!' he said, still sounding amazed. Unable to contain his delight a moment longer he picked her up and whirled her round, then just as suddenly set her down again, terrified he might hurt her. 'I'm sorry, honey, but it's such wonderful news.'

'It's all right, I won't break,' Paula said, laughing because his happiness was infectious.

'This calls for a drink!' He turned to her anxiously. 'Is it all right for you have a drink?'

'I don't suppose a glass of champagne will hurt me.'

'I'm going to make sure you're completely spoiled,' he said when he had opened a bottle and filled two flutes. 'Good food, plenty of rest . . . you'll stop working immediately, of course.'

'I suppose so,' Paula said, sipping her champagne and feeling pleased for the first time since the doctor had confirmed her condition.

Her only real pleasure in going to the showroom these days was knowing the discomfort her presence caused Laddie; it would really be very nice to have a cast iron excuse not to have to go in again except to swan in occasionally in the wardrobe of beautiful maternity clothes she felt sure Hugo would design for her. It was a pity that mini skirts were in – they were not very flattering with a bulge. But Hugo would come up with something that was both fashionable and attractive, she was sure, and she would be the most glamorous mother-to-be in New York.

Perhaps being pregnant was not so bad after all.

By the time Harriet was born Paula had changed her mind yet again. She had been right first time – being pregnant was awful! As the months had passed she had viewed her increasingly ungainly body with distaste. Ugly – so ugly! Would it ever return to its former shape? And her poor skin, stretched like a child's balloon over that enormous bulge, would it ever be smooth and taut again? Twice a day she massaged almond oil into it, but still she worried, and the lovely nutty perfume of the almonds which she normally loved made her feel nauseous. In fact almost any kind of smell, pleasant or otherwise, did the same.

'Cheer up, honey, a bad pregnancy means an easy confinement', Melanie Shriver, her greatest friend amongst the lunch set, comforted her, but Paula was soon to discover that that was just another old wives' tale.

The birth was long and difficult. When Harriet Bristow Varna finally came screaming into the world Paula was too exhausted to want to look at her, let alone hold her. She lay back on the delivery bed, hair damp and straggling about a waxy face, vaguely aware that a great deal of fussing was going on around her lower half which felt strangely wet, hot and sticky. She heard the word 'haemorrhage' mentioned, but registered more annoyance than alarm.

'Lie quite still now, Mrs Varna, don't try to move,' a nurse said in a worried voice and Paula merely thought: Silly cow! As if I would!

More fuss, more voices. 'I'm going to give you an injection, Mrs Varna, to stop the bleeding.' The needle sinking deep into the vein. Anxious faces. The stickiness had spread; she could feel it around her shoulders and in her hair. But she really was much too tired to care.

Everything was muzzy now, the faces floating, the voices seeming to come from a long way off.

Never again, thought Paula as she slipped into the soft blanketing mists. Never, never again!

'Honey, are you awake? There's someone to see you.'

Paula, lying back against the pillows, sighed inwardly. Since she had been allowed home from hospital a week ago it seemed there had been an endless stream of visitors and she was sick to death of them.

The ladies she met at charity lunches and fund raisers had come, mostly under the pretext of bringing a gift for Harriet, though Paula suspected half of them had come because they were curious to see the new house and the other half wanted to evaluate how well her looks had stood up to her ordeal. Then there had been a delegation from the showroom, headed by Maura Hemingway bearing a huge bouquet of flowers and a card signed by each and every employee – 'Hypocrites!' thought Paula bitterly.

But most of all she resented Hugo's mother and sisters. They had never liked her but now they took a proprietorial interest that was both irritating and cloyingly claustrophobic. They hung over the lace-bedecked crib, cooing at the baby, straightening the covers and discussing how this feature was exactly like Grandmother Docherty and that one the image of Aunt Sophia.

'That's the Docherty nose for sure!' Hugo's mother said triumphantly and Paula had to bite back the urge to scream – It's not! It's *my* nose! I'm her mother, for goodness sake, surely you'll allow she can be just a little like me?

Besides hanging over the cot Martha insisted on sitting beside Paula's bed like a sentinel, as if being the baby's grandmother also gave her the right to watch over Paula, and she refused to be budged even by the nurse whom Hugo had employed to take care of 'his girls' as he called them and who was seriously concerned about the strain on Paula of the constant stream of visitors.

'New mothers need their rest,' she had said politely, but Martha had bridled.

'You think I don't know that? I've been a mother myself four times. How many times have you been a mother, young lady?'

Ellie, the nurse, had kept her patience with difficulty.

'You must know then how tiring visitors can be. I don't want Mrs Varna's temperature to go soaring up again. She has been very poorly.'

Martha had sniffed loudly. A lot of fuss about nothing, that sniff seemed to say.

'We're not visitors, we are family,' she said aloud.

'I'm sorry. The doctor's orders are that Mrs Varna must be kept quiet otherwise he will take her back to hospital again. I'm afraid I must insist you leave now.'

So eventually she had enforced her authority and Martha, looking indignant, had left. Paula had smiled to herself. It was good to have someone else to fight her battles, especially when she felt so dreadfully weak and tired.

This afternoon, however, Ellie was having a few hours off and there was no one to object when Hugo looked in to announce that Paula had a visitor.

'Oh Hugo, I'm not feeling too good. Can't you send them away?' she begged.

'It's Greg, honey,' Hugo said gently.

Greg. Her heart leapt and suddenly she was not tired any more.

Since that July evening in the garden she had not seen him. Business had taken him to Europe direct from Texas – and Paula had been glad, for by then she had been pregnant and she had not wanted Greg to see her looking anything less than her best. As the months had passed she had all but forgotten the effect he had had on her. Now, as Hugo told her he was here to see her, it all came flooding back and with it something close to panic.

She couldn't see him looking like this – make-up minimal, hair mussed up by the pillows! But oh how she wanted to just the same! A pulse was beating in her throat and she felt her hands trembling.

'Paula. Congratulations. How are you?'

He was in the doorway, every bit as handsome as she remembered him, carrying a huge bouquet of flowers and a basket of fruit.

'Oh I'm quite well.' Her voice was slightly breathless; she hoped he would not notice.

'You certainly look it! Well, Hugo, you old son of a bitch, I can't leave you alone for five minutes can I? First time you're out of my sight you get yourself married, the second you become a father.'

'Hardly in five minutes,' Hugo remarked drily. 'You have been gone more than six months.'

'Yes, I suppose I have. Anyway, I'm quite sure that left alone with Paula I would be every bit as bad as you.' His eyes met hers, teasing, and she felt her cheeks growing hot. 'For you, Paula, the most beautiful mother in New York,' he said, holding out the flowers for her to take.

'Thank you, they're beautiful . . .' She thought, oh God how stupid I am! I've never been like this with a man before – any man! 'Let me take them, shall I?' Hugo suggested. 'I'll get Doris to put them in water. And what about something to drink? We should open a bottle of champagne to wet the baby's head, don't you think?'

'What a good idea,' Greg said. 'Still the same old Hugo, drinking champagne at the least excuse.'

'Our first child is hardly a flimsy excuse,' Paula said lightly as Hugo left the room. 'Wouldn't you like to have a look at her? She's asleep, but . . .' She reached over to draw aside the lace drapery around the crib but Greg made no attempt to move and when she glanced up questioning she met his eyes, still on her – and still very disconcerting.

'I'd much rather look at her mother,' he said almost insolently and the words make something tight and sharp spiral within her.

'Mr Martin . . .'

'Greg,' he corrected. 'Oh yes, mothers are much more interesting.'

His eyes were moving over her lazily, mentally undressing her, removing the nightgown of virginal white silk and gazing at her breasts, fuller and more voluptuous now than they had ever been. She had had injections to stop the milk coming in but they did not seem to have been entirely successful – she still felt uncomfortably full and occasionally a spot of liquid squeezed from her nipples and moistened the white silk. Now, beneath his gaze, she felt herself colouring once more, but this time the blush seemed to spread all over her body.

'Get well soon, Paula,' he said in the same tone, light and teasing but with hidden meaning. 'It will be good to see you back on the social circuit. We've never really had a chance to get to know each other, you and I, have we? I hope it won't be long before that can be remedied.'

She couldn't reply, her breath had constricted in her throat. How dare he talk like this, with Hugo practically in the next room? And yet what had he said? Nothing out of place, really. No, it was the way he looked at her as he said it that gave his words a deeper meaning.

'Here we are then!' Hugo appeared, bearing a bottle of Moët et Chandon in a silver bucket. 'I've been keeping the stuff permanently on ice! So – what do you think of my little Tumbleweed, Greg? Isn't she the most beautiful baby you ever saw?'

'I haven't actually seen her yet,' Greg admitted.

Paula drew the lace drapery aside again hoping she was managing to conceal her excitement and confusion and this time Greg peeked inside.

There was no doubt Harriet was a beautiful baby. Paula did not think she could have borne it if she had been ugly – red, wrinkled and bald. But she was not. She had a smooth cherubic face with wide blue eyes and a button nose and her well-shaped head was covered with corn coloured strands of silk.

'Thank God she doesn't look like you, pal,' Greg said to Hugo. 'She's just like her mother – a little beauty.'

'I'm glad you like her,' Hugo said seriously, 'because I have been thinking – 'I'd like you to be her godfather.' He heard Paula's quick indrawn breath and glanced at her, 'I know we haven't discussed it, honey, but I figured we wouldn't have had much to offer this little tumbleweed if it weren't for Greg and there's no one I'd rather trust my daughter to if anything happened to me.'

'Christ, Hugo, I'm honoured, but I certainly wouldn't trust me!' Greg ran a hand through his thick dark hair. 'Hey, you think about it, pal. Talk it over with Paula.'

Hugo has embarrassed him! Paula thought, enjoying the experience of seeing Greg fazed in spite of her annoyance that Hugo should ask him to be Harriet's godfather without consulting her.

'Well, you think too,' Hugo said, pouring the champagne. 'Here's to my daughter! To Harriet!'

'To Harriet.' Greg raised his glass, then turned. 'And also to Paula.'

His eyes met hers. The challenge in them was unmistakeable. Her heart began to pound again, her stomach fell away. With a lurch of lust she found herself wondering what it would be like to be held against that hard muscular body, have those sensuous lips taking hers and those lean brown hands on her swollen breasts. Oh how she wanted him! Her whole body ached for him. Yet at the same time she felt ashamed, diminished by the emotions over which she seemed to have no control.

'Yes, and to Paula, my beautiful wife,' Hugo said proudly, totally unaware of her wayward thoughts.

'You know, honey, I thought I had lost you,' Hugo said. He was lying beside Paula, holding her tenderly.

It was the first time he had put into words the terror that had filled him when he had seen her after Harriet's birth, lying pale and exhausted with the dried blood from her haemorrhage caked in her dull gold hair and beneath her nails. The sight of her had affected him too deeply, submerging even his pride in his child in the nightmarish realisation that she could so easily have died – would have done, probably, just a few short decades ago before the means to cause blood to clot had been discovered. Her life could have literally drained away from her then and she would have been just another pathetic statistic – a woman who had died in childbirth.

The thought was such a dreadful one he had decided there and then – he couldn't tempt fate again, could not put her through another such ordeal for his own gratification. If anything happened to Paula he would never forgive himself. And without her his own life might as well be at an end.

'I don't think we should have any more children,' he said now.

Paula was aware of a huge spasm of relief. But the actress in her made her ask solicitously: 'Don't you want any more?'

'Not particularly,' Hugo answered truthfully. 'My little Tumblewood is everything a father could wish for. It's you I'm concerned about now, honey. You mean everything to me, you know that.'

'Yes,' Paula murmured, sliding her hands up his silk pyjama-covered back, secure in the knowledge that he would make no attempt to make love to her for some weeks yet. 'You are very good to me, Hugo, much better than I deserve.'

'Nonsense. You've made me the happiest man alive,' Hugo said into her hair. 'I never thought it was possible to love as much as I love you. And if I should lose you I couldn't bear it.'

Paula lay very still.

Hugo had meant if she should die. But there are more ways of losing a woman than to death. In the soft dark Paula's arms were around her husband but she was thinking of Greg Martin.

CHAPTER TWENTY-TWO

Harriet grew from a beautiful baby to a beautiful toddler. Hugo spent every spare moment he could with her, taking her for outings to Central Park, reading to her from books with colourful illustrations and sometimes bathing her and melting her up in bed himself. Two nannies came and went, their noses put out of joint by what they termed his interference and Paula became quiet jealous of the attention he lavished on his little 'Tumbleweed'.

Had she but known it Hugo was in fact compensating for their own deteriorating relationship and lavishing on Harriet all the love he had to give but which Paula no longer seemed to want to accept from him.

Since Harriet had been born they hardly ever made love any more. When the baby was six weeks old he had made the first gentle but eager attempt but she had gone cold and stiff in his arms.

'What's the matter, honey, are you still sore?' he had asked, his voice husky with suppressed passion.

'A little,' Paula had said, wriggling away. 'And anyway, you'd better not, in case . . .' Her voice tailed away meaningfully.

'I'll be real careful, honey.'

'I know, but . . . Hugo, I'm scared. I don't want to get pregnant again. I couldn't stand it. And you feel the same. You know what you said . . .'

'Yes,' he said a little guiltily, feeling the desire go out of him like the air from a punctured balloon.

'I'm just afraid to trust any method of birth control now,' Paula went on, her voice soft but insistent. 'Look what happened with my diaphragm. Nothing is a hundred per cent safe.'

'I thought you got pregnant that time you didn't use it,' Hugo said. 'And anyway, I'm sure we can find a method that is 99.9 per cent.'

'How can you bear to take even the smallest chance?' she persisted. 'Hugo – couldn't you have a vasectomy? That way we'd be quite certain.'

In spite of himself Hugo was a little shocked. He had thought of a vasectomy himself but he hadn't expected Paula to suggest it.

'Honey, that is something that needs a lot of thinking about. We'd need to really talk it through, be absolutely certain, before I did that. It's not reversible, you know – at least not at present. They couldn't guarantee a thing.'

'So you *have* looked into it?'

'I've talked with Buster Hertz, yes.' Buster Hertz was their doctor, a jolly, beer-drinking father of six who had shown no sympathy for the idea.

'Good God man, whatever would you want to do that for after just one child?' had been his reaction. 'Now if you had six like me it might be a different matter.'

'What did he say?' Paula asked now eagerly.

Hugo hesitated. He didn't feel the time was quite right to pass on Buster's next comment – that though she might have had a bad time Paula was a young, fit woman who would quickly forget what she had been through.

'He wasn't in favour,' Hugo told her. 'He doesn't think at our stage it's an option we ought to consider.'

'Why not? We agreed – no more children.'

'I know but it's conceivable we might change our minds. And Buster said it's highly unlikely you'd have so much trouble a second time.'

'*Buster* said! What does he know? It wasn't him lying there hour after hour in agony. If it had been . . . well, he wouldn't have put his own wife through it six bloody times.'

'Paula, I'm not saying we should have another baby, just that we should keep our options open. Suppose something should happen to Harriet – God forbid, but . . .'

'Nothing is going to happen to Harriet,' Paula snapped. 'She is a perfectly healthy baby. How can you even think of such a thing?'

'I know it's too dreadful even to contemplate,' Hugo agreed. 'But suppose something *did* happen and I'd had the chop? We've got to think it through, honey – be absolutely sure about what we are doing.'

'I am sure!' Paula said determinedly. 'I thought you were too. But it seems you care more about your manhood than my well-being. Well, I'm not prepared to take any chances even if you are. And I think until we come to some decision we ought to have separate rooms.'

'That's a bit drastic, isn't it?' Hugo said, shocked.

'I don't see why. It's quite sensible really. Lots of married people have their own suites and we've got plenty of room here.' Paula was warming to the theme. 'Actually I'd quite like a suite of my own. Somewhere that would be just mine. I'm sure you would too. Think how nice it would be to have some privacy when you're working. If you got an idea in the middle of the night you could jump up and sketch it before it slipped away without having to worry about disturbing me.'

Hugo refrained from saying that the only ideas he got in the middle of the night since their marriage were all concerned with making love to Paula.

'I think we should see about it,' she continued firmly. 'It would be more more civilised.'

'We'll talk about it some other time,' Hugo suggested thinking that when Paula recovered her strength she would forget such peculiar notions. Buster Hertz had said as much and warned Hugo to watch out for what he called 'baby blues'. 'It's all in the hormones,' he had said cheerfully. 'They can play havoc with a woman – make her behave totally out of character. But she'll get over it, never fear.'

Lying beside her, the warmth of her body reaching out to his own, Hugo fervently hoped Buster was right and Paula would drop the absurd idea of separate rooms. But she had not. He had returned from the showroom one evening to find her deep in conversation with the interior designer – discussing how to turn part of the upper storey into a second self-contained suite. He was angry that she should have gone ahead without consulting him but he decided nothing was to be gained from making a scene in front of the woman. He would look foolish and Paula ... well, perhaps he should humour her as Buster had suggested. That way she might return to normal the sooner.

But she had not returned to normal. The suite was prepared and she moved into it without the slightest sign of regret. And to be honest his own initial distaste for the idea had mellowed somewhat for Paula these days was not a great deal of fun to be with.

Just how she had changed he could not be quite sure but changed she had. She had always been the ice-maiden, of course, always cool and contained, keeping her true feelings hidden beneath that glacially regal manner. But now he sensed it was more than that. There were times when she was almost withdrawn. She would seem to go right inside herself to a place he could not reach, her eyes glazed and faraway as if she was seeing things that no-one else could see. At other times she seemed depressed – once he found her crying and she could not – or would not – tell him what was wrong. And then again there were the times when she made mountains out of ant hills, as his mother would have said, imagining slights where none were intended and becoming quite agitated by them.

The first time he noticed it was when she had brought Harriet to the showroom one day. He had been busy and had to leave her alone in his office for a while. When he returned she had gone.

'What happened to you, honey?' he asked when he got home.

Paula shrugged. 'I didn't want to stay. The staff have never liked me, as well you know, but today it was worse than usual. They were all talking about me – looking and whispering. I felt very uncomfortable.'

'I expect they were remarking on what a beautiful baby Harriet is,' Hugo said, but he was surprised. Paula had always seemed impervious to what others thought of her.

The next thing he noticed was that she had begun to complain about the time he spent away from her.

'You're always working. Why do you have to work so late?' she asked, sounding peeved.

'Honey, you're well acquainted with the fashion business. You know there are busy times.'

'And when you do come home early more often than not you go off to see your mother.'

'She's getting older and she hasn't been well lately. I like to see her when I can – and it's not that often for God's sake! You could always come with me.'

Paula pulled a face. 'And have her telling me how to bring up Harriet? No thanks. Your mother hates me. She's always criticising and I know she talks about me.'

'Talks about you? Whatever do you mean?'

'I've heard her say things. I can't imagine why you don't hear her. She's a vicious old woman.'

'Nevertheless she is my mother and I intend to spend a few hours a week with her while I can,' Hugo said, his voice hardening.

Paula pouted. 'I don't think you love me any more.'

'Now you are being ridiculous,' he said, exasperated.

'You see? You just get cross with me.' Tears were glittering in Paula's eyes.

'Because I just don't know what's got into you. You say you want me here more but when I am it's a different story. You have everything a woman could wish for and I honestly don't know what else I can do to make you happy. To be truthful I don't think you know what you want yourself.'

'I want them to stop talking about me.'

'Who?'

'Oh – everybody.'

He could see she was lapsing into one of her black silences and pulled her into his arms.

'Honey, you have to snap out of this. Do you want me to arrange for you to see a shrink? Maybe if you talked things through . . .'

'No! I don't want to see a shrink. There's nothing wrong with me.' But she sounded very lost, very frightened. Hugo made a mental note to speak to Buster again about her.

He kissed her tenderly and she stayed unresisting in his embrace, but when he glanced at her she was staring vacantly at a point somewhere over his shoulder, her eyes blank and pained.

'Oh Paula!' He kissed her again, undressing her, trying to lift her mood with a show of physical affection. She did not protest but it was a very long time before he felt her beginning to respond. Desperate that she should not slip back into the blackness he ran kisses down her stomach until he reached her most secret places. This was something she always enjoyed, presumably secure in the knowledge that he could not make her pregnant with his mouth! As he worked with his tongue between the soft folds he felt her body begin to rotate in rhythm and her fingers clutched convulsively at his hair. He blew gently and felt her stomach and thighs tighten in rigid spasm: His own desire was subjugated now, he wanted nothing but to please her, make her know how much she was loved. As her excitement mounted he thrust his tongue in deeply and felt her tense into a tight-strung climax.

As the quivers and aftershocks subsided in her deepest, most secret muscles a sense of warmth and well-being flooded him. He slipped up the bed towards her, aching now to take his own pleasure, only to feel her hands on his shoulders, pushing him away.

'Hugo – no! I haven't got my diaphragm . . .'

You do it for me then as I did for you, he wanted to say, but somehow he could not. It was not in his nature to plead for her to do the thing she never had, anymore than he could force himself on her when she did not want it, no matter that he was aching and throbbing with need of her. In that moment he could have died to have her take him in her mouth but he knew she would not – cool, fastidious Paula who would accept cunnilingus for her own pleasure but never give fellatio. In the days when he had been free to make love to her fully it had not mattered. Tonight it did.

He could have wept with frustration and a sudden loneliness but even now his concern for her outweighed his own needs. He wrenched his body away from hers, but when he could trust himself to look at her he was dismayed to see she was staring vacantly into space again.

For the first time he felt a stirring of anger towards her, his frustration turning to sharp impatience. What the hell is wrong with you? he wanted to say, but he did not. He got up abruptly, desire gone. As he slammed out of the room she was still lying motionless and wide-eyed like someone in a hypnotic trance.

Puzzled, wretched, his patience tried beyond endurance, Hugo spent more and more time with Harriet, lavishing on her the love that Paula now rejected. He adored her, his little Tumbleweed, and could scarcely believe he could have fathered such a perfect child. He loved to play with her, tossing her into the air to make her chuckle, loved to take her to Central Park in the long warm evenings though Nanny complained he was upsetting the child's routine, loved to point out the landmarks to her though she was far too young to understand. It was Hugo who was there when she took her first faltering steps, holding out his arms to her as a safe haven, sweeping her off her plump little feet and swinging her high in the air when she finally triumphantly reached him. It was Hugo who coaxed her for the best part of an hour to repeat her first word – 'dog-dog', the name of the huge fluffy toy husky who was her favourite bedtime companion, after Nanny reported hearing her say it quite clearly when she had been putting her down for her afternoon nap. And it was Hugo who read to her every night when he was not delayed too late at the showroom. He hated those nights when he came in to find her already tucked up in bed with the curtains drawn and only the little nightlight – an elf in a glimmering toadstool – giving just enough light for him to pick his way over to her cot. What did please him was that she was seldom asleep but the minute he bent over to kiss her and smooth the covers up around her silky fair hair her thumb would go into her mouth, her eyelids would droop and within moments she would be breathing evenly. It was as if she had been waiting for him to come home.

Love would fill him then, swelling with all the power of the North Atlantic rollers and the sweetness of an orchestral crescendo and he would sit in the semi-dark wondering that such a tiny scrap could arouse such intensity of emotion.

Sometimes he longed for Paula to sit here with him sharing the precious moments, but he told himself he could not have everything his own way. Paula simply was not a maternal person and it was not reasonable to expect her to change simply to fit in with his specifications. Already he had far more than many other men – and certainly a great deal more than he deserved on a basis of fair shares for all.

Hugo felt that to be ungrateful would be to tempt fate. Thanking his stars for what he had he tried not to mind that Paula was not the wife and mother he might have wished her to be.

Had Hugo known just what was going on inside Paula's head he might have been less inclined to be patient. For Paula was a woman with an obsession – one that was taking her over body and soul – and that obsession was Greg Martin.

What was it about him, she asked herself repeatedly, that affected her this way? He was handsome, yes, but she had known handsome men before without ever experiencing the potent chemistry that worked within her every time she was in the same room as him. When he looked at her with that deep tantalising gaze of his her stomach would contract, when he touched her, greeting her with a kiss that lasted just a fraction too long for a casual greeting, or leading her onto the dance floor at some function, she could feel her flesh rising towards him as if he were a powerful magnet and she was the smallest of steel pins. 'You fascinate me, Paula Varna', he had whispered once into her hair, and a shudder ran through her, but later that same evening he was all but ignoring her, turning all his attention to the Texas beauty who was still his regular date, so that it was difficult to believe that his interest in her was anything but a product of her own fevered imagination.

There were times too when she felt he was laughing at her, perhaps at both of them, mocking, teasing, leading her on to make a fool of herself and enjoying every moment of it. The switchback ride of emotion was stressful, veering between elation and frustration, desire and despair, so that she never knew from one day to the next exactly how she would find him – or herself – and it only made her want him more – more than she had wanted any man, more than she had wanted anything ever before.

When the longing was upon her she withdrew into herself, not wanting to talk to anyone, even Hugo or Harriet, because conversation was an intrusion into her thoughts, and though she knew the world was still there, outside her head, she seemed strangely detached from it.

At other times the world seemed all too uncomfortably close and the people around her oddly threatening. She had never been popular, she knew, but in the past she had never cared. If someone did not like her or what she did that had been – in her words – their problem. Now the disapproval of others seemed to creep up on her unawares and occasionally she fancied she could hear them whispering about her. The voices were disconcerting, she longed to tell them to be quiet, but instead she would, retreat into that strange private place and remain there for hours at a time. Sometimes it was a good place to be, a wonderland where everything could be as she chose it, sometimes it was chaotic, sometimes it was bleak and lonely. And sometimes it seemed the walls would begin to close in, trapping her. She would fight her way out then, and for days at a time she was almost herself – except that she could not forget Greg. He was always there, and everything she did was with him in mind – When would she see him again? – How would he be?

Truly, Paula was a woman obsessed.

Gary was coming to New York for a few days' visit and for the first time in months Paula was able to think of someone other than Greg.

It would be wonderful to see Gary again – she had so missed his undemanding friendship and his adulation – and she found herself longing to catch up on all the gossip from 'back home'.

'We must have a party for him!' she said to Hugo – and realised there was yet another advantage to Gary's visit – Greg would certainly have to be included in the guest list.

'By all means – go ahead and arrange it,' Hugo agreed, pleased to see Paula taking an interest in something. 'Only let's not make it too swell an affair – maybe twenty guests? I honestly don't want to bother with more, it gets so tiring and you never actually get the chance to speak to any of them for more than five minutes.'

'Well, we'll see . . .' Paula bubbled. 'I thought we would invite people from the design world – Oscar and Bill Blass and John Fairchild . . .'

'And Greg of course.'

'Of course! No party would be complete without Greg.'

'And Laddie. Don't forget Laddie.'

Paula's lips tightened. 'Laddie. Do we have to?'

'He is my assistant, Paula, and I think Gary would like to meet him.'

Paula sniffed. She didn't want him in her house but she didn't see how she could avoid it. And in any case with the prospect of both Greg and Gary at the party it was impossible to stay in a bad mood for long.

Paula throw herself into the arrangements and Hugo was delighted at the change in her. He hadn't seen her so happy for months.

On the day of the party Gary managed to arrange his schedule so as to have lunch with Paula and the two of them lingered as long as possible, swapping gossip and catching up on one another's news. The House of Oliver was doing well, he told her, the clientele now included several famous society names, not to mention a minor Royal.

'That's wonderful. I feel very proud to think I can take at least some of the credit,' Paula said archly and Gary nodded, generous and naive as ever.

'Oh yes, you certainly helped me get off to a good start, Paula.

I just wish you were still with me . . . But you are happy, aren't you? You don't have any regrets about marrying Hugo and coming to the States?'

'Oh none!' Paula said – and for the moment she meant it. 'And now I suppose I had better get back and make sure everything is going well for the party and you had better get off to your appointment.'

Paula took her new happy mood home with her. She hummed to herself as she supervised the flower arrangers and checked the seating plan – Gary on her right, where she could talk to him, Greg almost opposite so that she could catch his eye. It was going to be a wonderful party, she thought, even if the numbers had crept up well beyond Hugo's limit of twenty. But her excitement was short-lived.

'I'm afraid Greg won't be coming,' Hugo said when he arrived home from the showroom.

Paula felt sick with disappointment. 'Oh no – why not?'

'Business, he says. But knowing Greg there's a lady involved as likely as not. I don't know how he manages it . . .' He shook his head, chuckling.

For an hour or so as she bathed and dressed Paula hovered on the brink of her dark secret place. Bad enough that Greg would not be at the party tonight – worse that he would be with another woman. The thought tormented her and she wished desperately she could cancel and simply be alone. But it was too late for that and besides she owed it to Gary to make an effort. By the time her guests began to arrive none of them could have guessed at the black depression beneath the familiar sparkle that was Paula at her best. Over a delicious meal she laughed and joked, bright and brittle as the frozen surface of a pond caught by the cold gleam of a January sun. Only Hugo, who knew her moods only too well, and Gary, who was almost frighteningly perceptive, realised everything was not as it seemed.

'What has happened, Paula?' he asked, drawing her to one side as she moved between her guests, to all appearances the perfect hostess. 'When we had lunch you were really happy. Now . . .'

'Now I'm still happy.'

'No. You *appear* happy but it's all a big act. You can't fool me, Paula. I know you too well.'

'Then you will also know there are times when it is better not to ask questions,' Paula said tardy. 'Please, Gary – some time I'll tell you but not now. Right?'

'Right. But tomorrow – if it's something you want to talk about you know were to find me.'

She squeezed his arm gratefully. What a good friend he was! And how she missed him! Perhaps if he was in New York more often things would not get on top of her so.

It was some time later that Paula began to be aware that Gary was paying a great deal of attention to Laddie. At first she told herself she was imagining it, but as the evening wore on it became increasingly obvious that she was not. Something was developing between the two of them.

As she circulated Paula watched them covertly, her agitation growing, and when she saw them disappear together through the French windows the fragile control she had been exercising all evening snapped. How dare Laddie come to her party and seduce her best friend! He was a nasty sneaky little man who was secretly involved with a boy half his age and not content with that he had set his cap at Gary. The sense of betrayal was enormous; it seemed to Paula he had done it on purpose to spite her and suddenly she was trembling with anger.

For a while she imagined herself marching up to Laddie the moment he reappeared and telling him, in front of all her guests, exactly what she thought of him and his behaviour but tempting though the prospect was her sense of self-preservation was too strong to allow her to do it. She would be finished socially if she did such a thing. Not even Hugo's status would be able to save her. No, she would have to be more subtle than that if she was to get her revenge on Laddie for using her party to seduce her dearest friend. And she knew exactly how she was going to do it.

Unnoticed by any of her guests Paula slipped away. In the privacy of her own suite she got out her little address book and thumbed through it. Yes, that was the number she wanted – Zachary Rhodes was an investigative reporter with a taste for a juicy story. The few times she had met him she had disliked him although he had gone out of his way to flatter her, yet for some reason she had put his number in her little book. It was, she thought, as if she had known it would come in useful one day.

Paula settled herself in her cane and velvet boudoir chair, took another sip of her drink and lifted the receiver.

'Zachary?' she said when he answered. 'I have a story you might find it worth your while to investigate. A homosexual affaire between a man well-known in the fashion world and a young boy whose father is in a very sensitive position.'

There was a silence.

'Who is this?' Zachary asked.

'Oh no,' Paula said silkily. 'I don't think you need to know that, do you? The only names of interest to you are the names of the two individuals concerned. And those are . . .'

When she had finished talking she replaced the receiver and her eyes were very bright. Even without taking another drink she felt quite intoxicated.

Maybe the secret was no longer hers, but what power – what power! Oh Laddie, you'll wish you'd never crossed me or gone after my friends, she thought with a son of crazed glee.

And it seemed to her in that moment that she had taken her revenge not only against Laddie but against everyone who had ever hurt her – and most especially against Greg.

There was nothing in the newspaper the next day about Laddie and the senator's son, nor the next, and although common sense told Paula that Zachary would have to check the story thoroughly before using it, she was still disappointed. It was an anticlimax to tear the paper open eagerly each day and find nothing or to wait for Hugo to come home from the office with news of the scandal only to be disappointed, and after a week of waiting Paula began to sink back into her depression, much to Hugo's concern.

'She's not getting over those "baby blues" as you called them, at all, Buster,' Hugo confided one day when the two men met.

Buster looked surprised. 'I thought how well she was looking at your party last week.'

'I know. But it's all a big act. Buster I'm worried.'

'I still think she'll snap out of it,' Buster said. 'But if you like I could arrange for her to see a shrink.'

'She won't do that. She became quite upset when I suggested it.'

'The English don't trust them – I know. Well, you'll just have to sit tight and let her work through it by herself,' Buster said. 'Quit worrying! You're just not used to women, that's all.'

But Hugo could not help worrying. It was all very well for Buster to take Paula's depression lightly – he didn't see her when she was down.

Hugo sat at his desk, rolling his pencil round and round between his fingers and thinking about Paula when he should have been planning his new season's range. And at last, like the inspiration for a truly innovative design, the idea came to him.

He would ask Sally to come over for a holiday. Paula had been delighted to see Gary, after all. Perhaps having her sister around was just the tonic she needed.

CHAPTER TWENTY-THREE

The moment Sally confirmed that she would fly to the States for a month's holiday Hugo rented a summer house on Long Island. July in New York would be hot and sultry – much better for the girls to be able to relax on the lovely sandy beaches and little islands of the southern shore where the tamer reaches of the Atlantic washed into the bays and lapped the sandbars and dunes. The house he found for them was on Shinnecock Bay, a shingled mansion with its own rose gardens and croquet lawn, well within reach of the tennis club and with plenty of room to comfortably accommodate them, the children and the staff who would go with them.

It also had the advantage of being close enough for him to be able to drive out to join them at weekends and sometimes, work permitting, for evening dinner as well. This was an important consideration; he could not bear to think he might miss a whole month of Harriet's development – at this age, just over a year, she seemed to be doing something new every single day. For this reason alone he had turned down Greg's offer for the girls to spend the month on his newly acquired yacht which he had based at Palermo, Italy. Busy as he was there would have been no way Hugo could join them there. But he had not told Paula of Greg's offer. He had a feeling she might have sunk into one of her moods to think she had missed the opportunity – and there would be others. Perhaps later when she was well the three of them could go together. The idea pleased Hugo, for his father's seafaring blood ran in his veins.

When Sally arrived she, Paula and the children motored down to Shinnecock Bay. Hugo had offered to take a day off to go with them and see them settled but when he suggested it to Sally after meeting her at Kennedy Airport she told him there was absolutely no need.

'Your time is much too precious, Hugo. We shall be perfectly all right', she assured him.

'But Paula is not at all herself,' he said. 'I'm worried about her, Sally. That's why I persuaded her not to come with me to meet you – I wanted a chance to speak to you alone. She gets these very peculiar moods when she refuses to communicate. You'll see for yourself, of course, but I wanted to warn you. Buster Hertz, our doctor, seems to think it's just some kind of delayed reaction to Harriet's birth, but surely she should be getting over that by now?'

Sally, who had fought her own way through moments of black depression after Mark had been born and she was struggling to establish some kind of life for them alone, looked thoughtful.

'I'd have thought so – but who knows? I'm sure a month of total relaxation and sisterly chat will do her the world of good. Don't worry, Hugo, I'll look after her.'

Hugo nodded, glad to be able to share his concern. Sally was, after all, Paula's sister. He glanced at her, sitting beside him in the stretch limo and liked what he saw. Two years ago in London he had been too obsessed with Paula to notice her much but he remembered her as being very young and gauche, a little like an overgrown puppy. Now she was older and thinner, with a few little worry lines on her face and a new found self-sufficiency that was very attractive. In her simple pink linen dress she looked cool and unruffled in spite of the long flight and he felt sure she was quite capable of coping with Paula. It was a comforting thought.

Paula was almost as delighted to see Sally as she had been to see Gary. Somehow Sally always made her feel good – perhaps because she had always been there to witness Paula's moments of triumph – and Paula with an audience was a happy Paula. The two girls embraced, then Sally rescued Mark, who was hanging back shyly behind her legs.

'This is your nephew – Mark, say hello to your Auntie Paula.'

'Lo,' Mark said obediently.

He was a chunky little fellow with bright curls and a face almost too pretty for a boy. Later, perhaps, his hair would grow straighter and darker, and the baby roundness disappear from his cheeks, for the moment he looked for all the world like a Botticelli cherub standing there in his pale blue shorts and stripey jersey, white ankle socks and sensible buttoned sandals.

'Oh Sally, he's so big!' Paula gasped. 'It makes me realise just how long it's been. Why haven't you been to visit us before?'

Sally smiled ruefully. So far she hadn't seen much evidence of change in Paula. She was still exactly the same as she had always been – totally self-centred.

'I haven't had much money to spare for trans-Atlantic flights. I know this is probably difficult for you to believe, living in the lap of luxury, but actually I've had quite a struggle to make ends meet.'

'Well why didn't you say so?' Paula looked amazed. 'I'd have sent you the money.'

'I'm not in the business of begging,' Sally said tardy. 'In any case – you could have come to London. Planes do fly in both directions, you know, and Mum and Dad would have been so pleased to see you as well.'

Paula's eyes shadowed and for a moment the darkness was there, just out of sight. Then she smiled again.

'There just doesn't seem to have been a moment – time has flown! What with work, and then Harriet, and . . . oh, you have no idea of the pace of life out here, Sally. Hectic!'

'Where is Harriet?' Sally asked.

'In the nursery. Shall we go up and see her?'

The nursery! This is a whole different world, Sally thought, amused, thinking of her own cramped flat in London, with Mark's little bed squashed into a corner opposite her own and of the baby minder she had to take him to each day to enable her to go to work.

'I suppose you have a nanny, too,' she said wryly.

'Well of course!' Paula was leading the way up the broad staircase. Sally paused to scoop up Mark, whose chubby legs were buckling with the effort, tired as he was after the long journey.

In the nursery Harriet was having her tea, sitting at her own little table. She looked up, wide-eyed, as they all trooped in. Jam had spread across her mouth and cheek. She looked cute and adorable.

'Paula, she is beautiful!' Sally said, setting Mark down.

Instantly the little boy seemed to forget his tiredness. He trotted straight over to Harriet, gazing longing at the fingers of bread and butter. Harriet's small jammy mouth curved into a smile and she thrust the piece she was holding towards him. He took it, cramming it into his mouth. The instant rapport between them was obvious. Sally and Paula both burst out laughing and Hugo, watching from the doorway, smiled in relief.

His idea had been a good one. Sally and Mark would be good for Paula and Harriet. Perhaps everything would be all right after all.

Paula wriggled her bare toes in the warm sand, watching it trickle over her scarlet-painted toenails. At the edge of the beach the sun sparkled on blue sea; just beyond the reach of the breakers Mark and Harriet sat digging happily and beside her Hugo was dozing, oblivious to the fact that his back was turning dark red from sunburn.

It was their first weekend at Shinnecock Bay. Hugo had packed up early at the showroom, leaving Laddie in charge, and motored down to join them. But the hard work he had put in all week to enable him to leave early on Friday was catching up with him somewhat. Paula stretched lazily and turned her attention to her sister, who was watching the children intently.

A week's sunshine had turned Sally's skin pale gold and bleached her hair to a tawny mane. As a precaution she had slipped a shirt on over her bikini but her curves were still obvious – more curves than I will ever have, Paula observed wryly – and her legs, with the slight sheen of Ambre Solaire, were long and shapely.

I shall have to watch out, Paula thought, with a faint stirring of jealousy. The ugly duckling has turned into a swan. And she is younger than I am.

The thought was enough to make her pull her floppy sun hat lower over her face. Too much sunshine was ageing – everyone knew that. And lately the spectre of ageing had hung over Paula like a persistent storm cloud. It had first appeared when she was swollen and ugly with pregnancy and she had felt vulnerable as she realised how transitory beauty could be. She had regained her figure now – diet, massage and a strong exercise regime had soon tightened flabby muscles and loose skin, but the stretch marks had remained, though faded now to little silvery flecks, a constant reminder of the grossness she had been forced to endure. Then she had begun to notice the tiny lines that had begun to appear between nose and mouth and at the corners of her eyes. Almost imperceptible to anyone else, perhaps, but clear enough in her magnifying mirror – the first signs of ageing. Peering at them Paula had felt a great well of panic opening up inside her. The rot had begun to set in. From now on it would be an endless battle, one that she would ultimately lose. No woman likes the thought of losing her looks, of catching a glimpse unprepared in a mirror one day and thinking: 'That middle aged woman can't be me!' But to Paula the prospect was purgatory. Usually she managed to allay the chill fear by telling herself she still had years and years of youth left; today, looking at Sally, it stalked her from the depths of her subconscious and she felt a sharp dislike for her sister. It was almost as if Sally's new found beauty detracted in some way from her own, as if Sally had stolen something that was rightfully hers.

Her mouth hardened and her mind turned in on itself, searching for the one weapon that would punish and hurt and deflate.

'I'm surprised you haven't found yourself a husband by now,' she said silkily. 'Isn't there anyone even remotely interested whom you could persuade to marry you and make Mark legit?'

'I'd have written and told you if there was.' Sally turned over, reaching for the Ambre Solaire. 'And I don't have time for husband-hunting even if I wanted to, which I don't.'

'But you must have a man of your own,' Paula insisted, feigning sisterly concern.

'What for? I've had enough of men to last me a very long time.

Anyway, who would want to take me on with a child to support? It's quite an undertaking. Stuart didn't want to – and Mark was his son. So what chance have I with anyone else?'

'That's true,' Paula said solicitously. She was feeling better with every passing moment. 'But there must be *someone*. An elderly widower, perhaps, with children of his own. Or a lonely divorcee, pining for family life. Perhaps you should join a singles club, or even sign on with a marriage bureau . . .'

Thanks, Paula, but I'm quite all right as I am.'

'I can't believe that, darling. Oh, I wish I could think of someone. Then you'd be able to stay out here and we could spend lots of time together, just like in the old days. And every summer we could come down here for a couple of months. Did I tell you, Hugo says he is thinking of buying a place on the coast for us? He does spoil me so.' She paused to allow the comparison to sink in, then continued: 'The trouble is everyone I can think of is already attached, one way or another.' Except Greg, she added mentally, but I'm certain not pointing *him* in your direction.

'Can't we drop it?' Sally said. 'Look, Mark is having terrible trouble. He's trying to build a sandcastle and Harriet keeps knocking it down again. I'm going to help him.'

She stoppered the bottle of sun oil and pulled herself up. The movement disturbed Hugo; he shifted slightly, lifting his head and treating Sally to a lazy wink.

A flush that had nothing to do with the sun crept up her cheeks. She'd thought he was asleep. How much of the conversation had he overheard? Not that they had really said anything but it was embarrassing all the same.

She walked down the beach to the children recalling what Paula had said and her own vehement denial that she needed a man. Now if it was *Hugo* on offer then it would be a different matter, she thought wryly. There really was something rather gorgeous about him. . . . But Hugo belonged to Paula. It was not Sally's way to steal other people's husbands, especially her sister's, even if she could – which she doubted.

Near the breakers Harriet was waving her spade threateningly above Mark's latest effort.

'Castle – gone!' she shouted triumphantly, suiting actions to words with a hearty thwack of her spade.

'Harriet!' Mark admonished, but he did not seem too upset.

Let's hope he can take the destruction of his private castles with such fortitude when he's grown up, Sally thought. Goodness knows, if life hands him only the knocks determined by the lowest common denominator he'll need to be able to!

Paula had long since given up scouring the newspapers for Zachery Rhodes' exposé of the scandal she had whispered to him, She was disappointed that her attempt at revenge had come to nothing and puzzled by the non-appearance of the story but she assumed Zachary must have his reasons. Perhaps he had not believed her, or had checked the story out and not found anything substantial enough to take into print – a little surprising in view of the fact that she was sure the affair was still going on, albeit very discreetly. Or perhaps Zachary was a supporter of the senator and did not want to cause him embarrassment – a fairly unlikely explanation since reporters of Zachery's ilk were totally without scruples and made their living at the expense of those people in the public eye who had skeletons rattling in their cupboards. No, Paula could not imagine either Zachary or his editor had kept the story quiet out of squeamishness – though they might have been influenced by the threat of a lawsuit which might cost them thousands of dollars. But whatever the reason the story had not appeared and Paula, who did not bother with newspapers at all down here in Shinnecock Bay, had almost forgotten about it.

One Friday afternoon, returning from the beach, she was greeted by the maid with a message – Hugo had telephoned and wanted her to call him back urgently. Paula was surprised but not unduly concerned. Hugo had been planning to join them for the weekend; perhaps something had happened to delay him. As she sat waiting for the call to connect she was relaxed and happy, more relaxed and happy than she had been for months.

I believe this holiday has done me good, she thought. I've hardly thought of Greg at all and there has been no one to whisper about me. I shall have to make sure Hugo keeps his promise to get us a summer place down here on Long Island.

'Paula – honey?' Hugo's voice was on the line but the moment she heard it she knew something was dreadfully wrong.

'Hugo – what is it?' she asked, her nerves overreacting as they always did these days to make her skin prickle uncomfortably.

'Honey – I'm sorry but I'm not going to be able to join you as planned. All hell has broken loose here.'

'All hell? What do you mean?'

'I don't suppose you've seen a newspaper today?' he said – and the tingling beneath her skin grew stronger so that it was as if electric currents were passing through her.

'A newspaper? No. Why? What's in it? But already she knew.

'It's Laddie,' Hugo said heavily. 'Some son of a bitch reporter has done a filthy exposé on him. How they got on to it I haven't a clue and why anyone should be interested in such trash is an even bigger mystery to me but there it is. Whatever the reason they've done it.'

'Oh dear – I suppose Laddie is upset,' Paula said feigning sympathy though she was secretly elated.

'Well of course he is – what would you expect?' Hugo said tersely. 'But there's worse. The boy Laddie has been involved with is Jimmy Connelly's son – *Senator* Jimmy Connelly. You can imagine the scandal – and the fuss Connelly would kick up. As far as the press and the public is concerned he's Mr Nice Guy – and he plays hell with all those closest to him to make sure that image is maintained.'

'Dear, dear. The fur is really going to be flying then,' Paula said.

'It's flown. Chris Connelly was a sensitive lad – he couldn't face up to the consequences. He's killed himself – took his car out on the freeway and drove it straight into a ten-ton truck.'

'Oh my God!' Paula said, horrified.

'Yes – awful isn't it? That poor kid . . .'

'Couldn't it have been an accident?' Paula asked.

'Because he was in such a state, you mean? Well, it could have been, I suppose, but they don't think so. The truck driver said he came straight for him and there was nothing he could do. But whichever it was – accident or suicide – you can say that bastard Zachary Rhodes killed him. It just wouldn't have happened if it hadn't been for the garbage he wrote and I only wish I could lay hands on the bastard!'

A nerve jumped in Paula's throat as a terrible thought occurred to her. 'You don't know where the reporter got his story from, I suppose?' she asked. 'Did someone tip him off?'

'I haven't heard but I should think it's quite likely. And whoever did such a thing deserves to be horsewhipped!' Hugo declared.

As she replaced the receiver Paula was trembling. Why the hell had the stupid boy had to go and kill himself! She had never expected anything like that to happen, and now because of what she had done a young man was dead.

She thought of it again, repeating the conclusion in her mind, and as she did so the horror of it, and the feeling of awesome responsibility took on a slightly different hue and gave birth to a spiral of something like excitement. She had been right to feel in control when she had discovered Laddie's secret. In her hands she held the power of life and death!

Suddenly Paula was not afraid of being found out any more. Intoxicated by the sense of her own omnipotence she began to laugh. She was still laughing when Sally found her.

Sally had thoroughly enjoyed her holiday at Shinnecock Bay. After the somewhat austere life she led in London it was a little like being granted a passport to heaven and with the sun on her skin and the sand between her toes all her everyday problems seemed very far away. She swam each day and played tennis whenever she could persuade Paula to join her and she was delighted to see Mark being spoiled with all the little luxuries she was normally not able to give him.

Only her increasing irritation with Paula marred the idyll. The two girls had always sparred, of course, as sisters do, but now

Sally found herself becoming furious with Paula's total self-absorption and the condescending manner she used to everyone around her. Had she used to be as bad as this, Sally wondered, or had easy living made her worse? Possible, of course, especially since Hugo spoiled her so. But it could just be that now Sally was older and less mesmerised by her sister's glamour, she simply noticed her faults more and was less inclined to make excuses for her. As for what Hugo had said about her suffering post-natal depression, Sally had noticed no evidence of it at all during the holiday. In fact if anything she seemed to be on something of a high. Why, she had even reacted with something close to hysterical laughter when Hugo had telephoned with the sad news about the death of the senator's son, yet since that day she had given no sign at all of having been upset by the tragedy. If such a terrible thing had happened to someone I knew I'm sure it would have cast a cloud over the holiday for me, Sally thought, but Paula seems totally indifferent to it.

Hugo, on the other hand, had clearly been put under some strain by the tragedy. When he eventually came down to Shinnecock Bay again he looked tired and sad, as if some of the grief and guilt of his friend and assistant had rubbed off onto him. Yet his primary concern was still Paula, and when he and Sally were alone he brought up the subject immediately.

'I've been really worried about her, Sally. She's been acting so strangely. But you think there is an improvement?'

'She seems very much herself to me. She's a bit hyper, that's all.' Sally paused, mustering her thoughts and trying to analyse Paula's manner. 'She's not pregnant again by any chance, is she?'

Hugo looked startled. 'Good heavens I don't think so! Why should you think that?'

Sally considered. 'It's just something about her . . . I don't know, some kind of secret excitement. Oh, it's probably my imagination.'

Hugo smiled. 'I'd be delighted if she were pregnant, but I don't think excitement would be the way Paula would react if it were that. She's very definite about not wanting any more children – more's the pity.'

'And you're willing to go along with that?' Sally asked before she could stop herself.

'I love her, Sally,' Hugo said simply. 'All I want is for her to be happy.'

'I know that, Hugo,' Sally said, and thought, not for the first time, that her sister was a very fortunate lady.

By the time the holiday was over the nine-days' wonder over the scandal of Chris Connelly's suicide had died down and Laddie had returned to work in an effort to bury his sorrow.

Paula bid Sally a theatrically tearful farewell but in fact she was not sorry to see her sister go – four weeks was quite long enough to spend cooped up with any one person, especially one who knew her so well and was liable to see through her little charades. Besides this Sally was a constant reminder of the past and the perfectly ordinary council-house girl she had once been. Paula had no fond memories of her humble origins; she had long since put them behind her, wanting only to be known as the successful former model and wife of an acclaimed fashion designer.

New York was still a little empty – many of the socialites of the Shiny Set had gone on from their summer vacations at the beach to villas in France, Switzerland or Tuscany, or sailing on the luxury yachts they referred to as 'boats', but there was still a pile of invitations to lunches and private parties awaiting Paula's attention – and an enormous bouquet of flowers from Greg with a card inscribed 'Welcome Home'.

Paula was elated at the gesture, especially when Hugo told her that Greg's long-time girlfriend, the Texas beauty, had finally tired of trying to tie him down and gone to France for an extended holiday with friends of her father's family. With the coast clear perhaps she would be able to make some impression on him at last, she thought delightedly, and turned her attention to the invitations.

In view of her own lack of popularity it never failed to surprise Paula how much in demand she and Hugo were. Such a short time ago fashion designers had had no more social standing than tradesmen – now it seemed everyone felt that their party would be more significant if it were graced by the presence of Hugo Varna. The fact that she was English helped of course – there was a certain snobbery among those with new money but no history where the 'old world' was concerned. But their enthusiasm stemmed in the main, she knew, from the hope that their photograph would appear in *Womens Wear Daily* with the telling caption: 'The hostess, who elected to wear Varna, pictured sharing a joke with the designer himself.'

The invitations had been even more numerous in the days before he had married her, she imagined. So many of these society ladies were grass widows whose husbands sweated long hours at their banks or oil fields to make the fortunes they so loved to spend and spare men were invaluable. But even now that he was no longer a free agent the invitations still rolled in and Paula knew it was only sensible to accept at least some of them. Those same pictures that pleased the publicity hunting 'poor little rich girls' were also beloved of the presidents of the Fifth Avenue stores that stocked Hugo's ready-to-wear collections for as advertising they were worth a great deal more than any picture posed by a model. Where the Shiny Set led, American womanhood would follow, hoping to emulate their glamour.

Paula sorted through the invitations, a little annoyed that Hugo had simply left them all for her to deal with. A few were already out of date and she thought glumly of the apologetic letters she would have to compose. They were sure to blame her – didn't they always? Even now she seemed to hear their voices whispering at her from the corners of the room: 'How rude! I can't imagine what Hugo Varna ever saw in her!' She closed her ears to the whisperings and ploughed on through the invitations.

Almost at the bottom of the pile was one that pleased her. Robert Dudley, a prominent attorney, was giving a party for his fiancée, Cassidy Wells. Now that one certainly looked interesting!

Cassidy was an actress with a string of box-office successes to her credit. She had even been nominated for an Oscar this year. Besides being a wonderful actress she was stunningly beautiful, with flaming red-gold hair and eyes green as a cat's. She looked good in everything she wore – as a heroine of pre-historic times she had even looked good enough in mud-coloured sackcloth to have the entire world-weary crew fall in love with her – but when she wore Varna she looked marvellous and Hugo, on learning she had a particular liking for his clothes, had decided to cash in on the fact, allowing her enormous discounts on couture garments and even loaning her special gowns so that she was a constant living advertisement. Paula had met Cassidy several times and liked her – in spite of her success she was unspoiled with a wicked sense of fun and unlike so many actresses she was not conceited or self-centred. Even wearing Hugo's clothes was a game to her – she chose them with all the excitement of a small girl let loose in her mother's wardrobe.

When she had become engaged to the attorney a few eyebrows had been raised, but Cassidy's past seemed to be as free of blemish as her lovely face and soon the gossip columnists had given up trying to dish the dirt and accepted that she was set to become the wife of a very influential man.

Oh yes, this was one invitation well worth accepting, Paula decided, for the combination of Hollywood glamour and the law was irresistible. She entered the date in her diary and set the invitation on one side. Busy as Hugo might be, she was going to make quite sure he was free to take her to Cassidy and Robert's party.

'Honey, we can't possibly go,' Hugo said. 'Surely you must know it's on my mother's birthday.'

'Your mother's birthday,' Paula repeated flatly. 'The very same day as Cassidy's party.'

'There's no need to sound so disbelieving. I'm not inventing it to be awkward,' Hugo said patiently. 'Surely you knew it was Mom's birthday?'

'I suppose so, but I forgot. Why should I remember for goodness' sake? It's nothing to me.'

'I realise that, Paula.' Hugo's voice had become a little starchy. He had never really reconciled himself to the fact that his wife and his mother had so little love for one another. 'But nevertheless I should have thought you would have known. Just as you should know I always have dinner with Mom on her birthday. A family dinner. Honey, this is just another party. We go to plenty of them.'

'It's not just any old party – it's Cassidy's. Anyway, I've accepted now. We'll have to go.'

Hugo's mouth tightened. 'I'm sorry, but this is one occasion when I intend to stand fast.'

'Choosing your mother instead of me.'

'Don't be ridiculous. But I am not going to upset her for the sake of some black-tie bash. She's not well, Paula. This could be her last birthday. I intend to make it a happy one for her.'

Paula snorted impatiently. 'She's a creaking gate if ever I saw one. She'll still be manipulating you ten years from now.'

Hugo's eyes turned cold. Like any good son he deplored criticism of his mother.

'I assume you won't be joining us for dinner.'

'Too true I won't.' But his icy glare was making her nervous. Disapproval did that to her these days. Pleadingly she wound her arm through his. 'Well, if you must go to dinner, couldn't you leave a little early? Your mother isn't a late bird. By the time she's ready for bed the party will only just be starting.'

He looked down into her ingenuous face and weakened. How he loved her! It didn't matter how outrageously she behaved, he only had to look into her lovely blue eyes and he was all too ready to make excuses for her. He'd do anything in the world for her – except disappoint his mother on her birthday. But Paula was quite right. Dinner would be at seven and his mother would be ready for bed by eleven at the latest. He could always wear his tuxedo – his mother would probably be flattered. Then he would simply drive round the block, pick up Paula, and they could go on to the Senator's home where the party was to be held.

He put a hand on Paula's arm, resisting the urge to crush her to him and cover her with kisses.

'All right, honey, I'll meet you on that one. If you don't mind being a little late . . .'

Paula beamed. The sun always seemed to come out when she got her own way.

'It's called making an entrance, Hugo,' she teased.

CHAPTER TWENTY-FOUR

When she was dressed and ready for the party Paula went to the nursery to say goodnight to Harriet.

The child was tucked up in bed, her hair still damp and her face rosy from her bath, but she was not yet asleep and Paula sat down on the edge of her bed, drawing her close so that her head rested against the green silk that draped toga-style over Paula's small breasts leaving one shoulder bare.

'Nice smell,' Harriet murmured, wrinkling her nose contentedly.

Paula smiled. The closeness of the firm little body made her feel quite maternal, though she knew it was not an emotion that would survive long if she had not been able to leave Harriet in the care of her nanny the moment the fancy left her.

'Mummy is going to a party. Do you like my dress?'

'Pretty!' Harriet approved, snuggling closer.

Paula was suddenly overcome with fear that Harriet might dribble on the green silk or make fingermarks.

'It's time you were asleep, Harriet,' she said, easing herself away. 'Mummy has to go now'. She always used the English 'mummy' rather than the Americanised 'mom.'

For a moment Harriet clung to her then Nanny moved briskly forward.

'Come along now, Harriet, be a good girl and let your mother go.'

'No!' Harriet wailed.

'Yes,' Nanny said firmly.

Paula fought back a nightmarish fear that she might be trapped for ever by chubby arms and sticky, pouting lips. She hurried out of the nursery.

'It isn't really a very good idea to over-excite her at this hour,' Nanny said disapprovingly, following her. 'She should be asleep. Most children her age are.'

'She is not most children though, is she?' Paula said.

She had half-closed the door when she thought she heard Nanny retort: 'You're not much of a mother, are you, Mrs Varna? Only coming here to disturb her when you want to show off.'

Paula froze. She hadn't heard people talking about her lately and she had thought perhaps they had given it up. Now Nanny was at it. She pushed the door open quickly, expecting to discover Nanny lurking on the other side and whispering maliciously, but to her surprise she saw that the woman was moving around Harriet's bed, tucking her in.

She's a crafty one, Paula thought. She must have moved away from the door like greased lightning. She guessed I'd overheard her, I suppose.

Feeling uncomfortable she went downstairs to wait for Hugo. Then as she entered the garden room she stopped short, her pulses racing, as she saw a tall tuxedo-clad figure silhouetted against the French windows.

'Greg!' she said, excitement and sudden fear making her voice sharp. 'What are you doing here?'

He turned towards her, smiling lazily.

'I'm sorry if I startled you, Paula. The maid let me in. I stopped by to see if we could go to the party together.'

She was at a loss for words suddenly. How could he do this to her – turn her from an assured woman to a gauche girl simply by his presence?

'You're on your own, I suppose, now that your girlfriend has gone off to Paris,' she said foolishly, and instantly regretted it.

'I'm never alone unless I choose to be,' he said, eyeing her with amusement. 'I though you might be pleased to see me.'

'Yes – yes, of course. But we're not going to the party yet. Hugo is having dinner with his mother – it's her birthday.'

'Yes, I know. I talked to Hugo at the showroom this afternoon.' His smile was disconcerting.

'Oh! Then why . . .?' She broke off, her cheeks growing hot. She already knew the reason he was here.

'It was you I came to see, Paula. I hardly ever see you on your own.'

Her knees felt weak. She was trembling. Oh, he'd played these games before many times. But they had never before been alone together in a house with only a maid, a nanny and a tiny child. Greg had known Hugo would not be here – he had just admitted it. Could it be that this time . . .?

'Would you like a drink?' she asked. Her voice was brittle; she hoped he would not notice how nervous she was and how fearfully, tremblingly excited.

'A drink? Yes, why not. That would be nice.'

She crossed to the cabinet and his eyes followed her. Suddenly she thought she could not trust herself to pour the drinks without spilling them.

'You get it,' she said. 'And you can make a G and T for me while you're at it.'

She watched him pour the drinks, thinking how wonderful he looked in his tuxedo. Beneath its perfect cut she could see the ripple of his muscles and she went weak again. When he passed her the glass she took it and sipped quickly, holding the glass tightly as if she was afraid she would drop it.

'You are looking very lovely tonight, Paula,' he said, his eyes appraising her, deep and teasing. 'But then you always do! As I believe I've told you before, you really are the most fascinating woman.'

'Greg . . .' She didn't know what to say; she was utterly tongue-tied.

'Fascinating,' he repeated. He set his glass down on the broad mantelpiece and smiled at her, a slow, tantalising smile. 'Come here, Paula,' he said.

For a moment she gazed at him, scarcely able to believe she had not misunderstood him. Breath caught in her throat; she felt faint with fear.

So many times in imagination she had lived this moment and gone beyond it; so many times she had dreamed what it would be like to have his lips on hers, not briefly as they had been in the past but with passion and possessiveness; to feel every part of him with her hands and her body; to belong to him utterly and completely. In that private place within herself she had lived with the dream, now, faced with the reality she was suddenly afraid that he might not. Could the dream ever translate – did she even really want it to?

As she hesitated, frozen to paralysis, his smile widened, those deep eyes of his issuing even more irresistible a command that his words. 'Come here, I said.'

And as if he were working her like a marionette, pulling the strings that controlled her legs, she felt herself going towards him.

He did not move until she was standing close beside him, simply watched her with those hypnotic eyes seeming to look right inside her. Then he put out a hand to clasp her about the waist. Where his fingers touched they felt like dry ice through the thin silk, burning her skin and sending out small electric shock waves.

His mouth was hard on hers, brutal almost. No one had ever kissed her like this before, with such careless mastery. Her cool beauty had always affected her lovers – Hugo included – so that they treated her with something like reverence even at the height of their passion. There was nothing reverent about the way Greg was kissing her. He had played her for too long and knew that his games had driven her wild with desire. Now his hand moved possessively the length of her spine, tucking in beneath her buttocks and crushing her against him. She felt his hardness against her and went weak again so that she thought if he released her her legs would buckle and she would sink to the ground. But all the while the very core of her was yearning towards him.

With one hand he caught the green silk where it rippled over her shoulder, pulling it down. She heard the fabric tear and did not care. She was naked now to the waist; his greedy hands took her small breasts, squeezing until a scream gurgled in her throat. When she thought she could bear it no longer he released her, finding the zipper at the back of the dress and deftly sliding it down. The green silk slithered down her legs. Beneath it she wore only a wispy G-string – anything more would have shown ridges beneath the clinging dress – and her legs were still sufficiently tanned not to need tights. He took the fragment of silk and tore it off, then held her away, looking at her.

Paula felt her head roll back on her neck in a gesture of abandon and she sobbed softly, her whole body on fire with longing.

Slowly, deliberately, he lifted her up and lay her down on the rug. She writhed in an agony of desire as he towered over her, fully dressed. Then he knelt over her, unzipped his trousers, and with one quick thrust was inside her.

She arched towards him, oblivious of everything but her own need. Never before had she been so totally possessed. Too soon it was over. He rolled away from her, casually almost as if what he had done to her was no more important than stubbing out a cigarette he had just smoked. He stood up, zipping up his trousers, and after a moment, embarrassed now by her nakedness yet still experiencing a tumult of conflicting emotions, she scrambled up too, reaching for her dress and holding it in front of her.

'Greg.' She held out a hand to him, pleadingly. She honestly did not know what it was she was seeking – gentling, reassurance, or simply to have him do it all again – but he made no attempt to touch her. His expression now was almost contemptuous.

'You'd better get dressed, Mrs Varna, if you don't want your husband to come home and find you like that.'

'But . . .'

'We have a party to go to, remember.'

'Oh . . . yes . . .' She had forgotten it completely.

His hand shot out, imprisoning her wrist and pulling her towards him again. 'Just remember – you're mine now,' he said softly. His face, inches from hers, was smiling, but it was not a nice smile.

'When will I see you again?' she whispered.

'I'll let you know.' He kissed her again as if to imprint the brand of his ownership on her. There was no warmth in it, no tenderness, but even as she realised it her own body betrayed her and she clung to him as a child being abandoned at the school gates clings to its mother. 'Now for God's sake get dressed,' he said harshly, disentangling himself.

There was nothing for it but to do as she was told. The torn seam of her gown gaped from armpit to waist.

'I can't wear this . . .'

'Go and change then.'

She scooped up her G-string and ran upstairs. Fortunately she did not meet any of the staff and the door to the nursery was closed.

In her dressing room she stuffed the ruined gown into a drawer out of sight and pulled out another one, in silver lamé. Then in the bathroom, she straddled the bidet on shaking legs. She was beginning to realise the chance she had taken, making love with Greg here in her own house, with an unlocked door. Anyone could have come in – the thought made her go cold. Yet even now she could not regret it. 'You're mine now', Greg had said. Her knees went weak again as she remembered it. The lack of tenderness and concern she preferred to forget. She had waited too long for this moment – and she knew that whenever and wherever he wanted her she would always be ready and eager for him.

As she went back downstairs she heard Hugo come in. Her heart hammered. Wouldn't he know . . . just by looking at her? But he smiled up at her from the hall, quite unaware.

'You're ready then?'

'Yes – just. I got held up. Greg's here . . .' To her own ears her voiced sounded a trifle breathless but Hugo seemed not to notice.

'Greg? Oh good. We can all go together then.'

'How was your mother?' she asked, delaying the moment when she had to face Greg again.

Hugo looked surprised. It was unlike Paula to ask.

'She's getting frail. It's heartbreaking to see. She was always such a strong woman. But I think she enjoyed her birthday. Honey, I'm sorry it clashed with your party . . .'

'It's all right,' she said, sliding past him, not wanting him to touch the flesh Greg had so recently possessed. 'You're here now.'

Greg was standing on the hearth where she had left him, glass in hand. Not by a single flicker did he betray what had taken place. Only when Hugo's back was turned did his eyes meet hers, amused eyes, full of secret meaning.

How she got through the party, Paula would never know. She was on auto-pilot, she supposed, a pre-set pattern of social behaviour she had rehearsed over and over again so that now she could follow it even though her mind was whirling and she still felt like a jelly. Exchanging small talk, laughing, dancing, picking at the pressed caviare and smoked salmon canapes, sipping champagne, a little too fast, her eyes kept searching for Greg and whenever she caught sight of him she felt as if she were on the verge of having an orgasm. He was circulating, chatting with this society woman, dancing with that Hollywood actress, and jealousy burned in her fiercely. Was he going to ignore her all evening? Then, just when she thought that he was, there he was beside her, taking the glass from her hand and smiling at Hugo.

'I can steal a dance with your beautiful wife, can't I?'

'Of course,' Hugo replied with all the ease of an unsuspecting old friend.

Greg led her on to the floor and as their bodies moved in unison it was like a parody of their love making.

'Come to my apartment tomorrow. I'll be home at three,' he said, his head and upper body a respectable distance from hers while his hips touched and pressed insistently.

She nodded imperceptibly. There was no way she could have refused. She knew she would move heaven and earth to be there.

At the end of the dance he returned her to Hugo.

'You don't take your wife out often enough,' he chided.

'Work, friend, has to come first.'

'And your mother – and the rest of it – I know.' Greg was smiling easily. 'But Paula needs some fun. You'll have to employ me as her walker.'

'A second Jerry Zipkin, you mean?' Hugo grinned, looking over the heads of the dancers to where the rotund little man who was New York society's favourite one-man escort service was entertaining the lady he had partnered tonight. 'I didn't know you had ambitions in that direction, Greg.'

'I haven't – as far as most of these overdressed ladies are concerned.'

'Overdressed? That's my creations you are maligning!'

'Sorry – slip of the tongue. No, the gowns are fine, I guess. It's the faces I can't stand – skin as taut as a . . .' His eyes flicked to Paula, wicked, teasing eyes, before he finished, 'as taut as a pair of surgeon's gloves.'

Hugo laughed, totally unaware of the meaning behind the innuendo.

'I haven't seen much evidence of you being landed with only the glamourous grannies. You've numbered a nubile beauty or two amongst your conquests tonight if I'm not much mistaken, so don't expect my sympathy!'

Paula could not look at him. She felt as if she were blushing all over. But her heart was beating with excitement and her pulses were echoing it. Tomorrow . . . tomorrow . . . She did not know how she could bear to wait.

Over the next months their affaire continued, as erratic and disturbing as his persual of her had been.

Why now? she asked herself when she paused to draw breath. Why after waiting so long had he moved in so suddenly and possessed her? Because his relationship with the Texas Rose had come to an end, presumably. But she preferred not to think about it too deeply, simply revel in what they were sharing, this crazy intense tempestuous affaire. Since that first time, which Paula was convinced Greg had planned as carefully as he planned everything he did, they made love whenever and wherever they found themselves alone together – in his apartment, in the bathroom of some house when they were at the same party, in her own suite. The danger seemed to act as an aphrodisiac to Greg, and Paula was almost past caring if they were caught or not. At least if Hugo found out then she and Greg could be together openly; it would be an end to those other times, the ones she found unbearable when he left for days on end with no explanation, not contacting her. For in spite of the fact that she was so totally obsessed with him that she could think of nothing beyond when they would be together again yet still she could not be sure of him, He wanted her – there was no doubt in her mind about that – he possessed her and made her his in ways she would never have dreamed possible – yet he was also master of himself as well as her, sometimes withholding himself with total self-control, sometimes ignoring her just as he always had so that she felt she would scream with need of him, frantic for a smile, a gesture, never mind more, that would tell her he was aware of her very existence.

She was living on a knife edge. He had her exactly where he wanted her – she, who had always made the men around her dance to her tune. And though it was torture the very uncertainty kept her interest. In the rare moments when she was able to think rationally she knew it was true, even as she longed for reassurance. But she could think of nothing beyond when he would take her again, bring her again to the sharp sweet ecstacy that only he could induce, and which left her always trembling and wanting more. Even the fear that had haunted her since Chris Connelly's suicide was pushed to the back of her mind – if Zachary had been going to point the finger at her he would have done so by now – and why should he? She had not identified herself and even if he had recognised her voice and guessed at who his informant might be he would never dare say so without proof. As for the possibility of someone else putting two and two together, it was not as if she was the only one privy to a State secret. If she had known about it so must others. No, Hugo was unlikely now ever to discover that she had sneaked on his assistant and friend. But there was always the danger he might discover her adventures in another quarter.

In the bitter New York winter Hugo's mother's health deteriorated fast. In vain Hugo tried to persuade her to move to warmer climes – she had never lived anywhere but New York, she said, and she intended to die there. As a worried Hugo spent more and more time with her Paula could only rejoice that she was free to be with Greg whenever he called her. Sometimes Hugo played right into their hands, allowing Greg to escort her to the parties he could not attend, and Paula could summon only the slightest feelings of guilt. If Hugo could be so blind, then he had only himself to blame.

In January Martha Varna died and for Paula her funeral was memorable because Greg followed her to the bathroom where he took her with breath taking speed and the wry explanation that: 'I never saw you look more fuckable than you do in mourning.' After that he left for a business trip and she did not see or hear from him for almost six weeks.

The turbulent affaire was still continuing in the same way when summer came.

'You two have got to spend some time on my boat this year,' Greg said. 'I won't take no for an answer.' To her delight Hugo agreed and the three of them flew to Italy where they spent three weeks together, sunbathing on the white scrubbed decks by day, sipping champagne and talking into the balmy nights. The holiday was torment for Paula; to be so close to Greg and not be able to have him was hell on earth. The yacht, though luxurious, was small enough for Greg to be able to sail alone, without a crew, island hopping rather than sea going, and this meant there was nowhere where they could be alone together. But Greg seemed almost to enjoy the irony of it, enjoy his own enforced celibacy, enjoy watching her squirm with desire. Eventually Paula could stand it no longer. She pleaded with Hugo that she was missing Harriet and they cut the holiday short by a few days and flew home.

'One day I'll buy a big boat,' Greg promised, double-talking as usual. 'Perhaps then you'll stay with me, Paula.'

'The way your business is going you'll soon to able to buy and sell us all three times over,' Hugo said.

Greg did not come home with them, claiming that he wanted

to do some business whilst he was here in Italy. There were fabric manufacturers he wanted to see – people with plans for setting up fashion cartels. With his own Italian origins the idea appealed to him.

'I might be able to do you some good, Hugo,' he explained.

Hugo smiled. 'It sounds a little like a fashion Mafia to me, but I'm happy to leave the business side to you, Greg. It leaves me free to get on with what *I* am good at – designing.'

Paula said nothing. She could have commented that there were a few other areas where Greg excelled besides business deals. But they were not the sort of things one talked about.

CHAPTER TWENTY-FIVE

Hugo was not quite as oblivious to Paula's obsession with Greg as she believed. He was far too deeply in love with her to be unaware of the extra sparkle that radiated from her when his partner was around. But it did not occur to him that there was anything sinister about it. Hugo knew women and liked them – wasn't that the basic reason why his designs were so successful, because he wanted to make them look good and could empathise with what they could also wear comfortably? He knew that women had their dreams – it was another piece of instinctive knowledge that he used in his work – and he did not hold it against them. If Greg fulfilled some part of Paula that he could not and brought a little colour and romance into staid married life then where was the harm? And here Hugo committed his fatal mistake, for he trusted Greg implicitly in the real old American buddy fashion. Greg was his partner and his friend – he wouldn't cheat on him. Womaniser he might be – they had often laughed over Greg's conquests whilst sharing a drink – but he would never shit on his own doorstep as the rather inelegant saying went. Hugo was confident of that – and it made him indulgent towards Paula and her fancies. Besides – Greg never gave the slightest indication of any interest in Paula beyond the fact that she was a beautiful woman and the wife of his friend. For a very long time that was the end of the story as far as Hugo was concerned and when he did begin to entertain his first doubts they were concerned not with Paula but with the financial wizardry of the man he had trusted to manage his affairs. Rumours, as yet mere whispers, had begun to circulate that some of Greg's dealings were not as lily-white as they might have been and Hugo was shocked when they reached his ears. At first he discounted them, loyal as ever to his friend. He had long suspected that Greg sometimes sailed close to the wind but then didn't most men who called themselves financiers? It was by taking chances that their money was made and he could not believe Greg could be responsible for something downright dishonest. But the whispers continued to grow louder and for the first time Hugo experienced doubts as to Greg's sincerity. For what they were saying was that Greg was sinking a great deal of money into launching a young Italian fashion designer.

Though Hugo was now well established and though he had the sense to know he did not have a monopoly on talent he was still hurt and puzzled that Greg had not mentioned the venture to him.

'What's this about you dabbling in Italian fashion now?' he asked one day when they were lunching together. 'Isn't the US big enough for you any more?'

Greg smiled, showing his very white teeth.

'I make money where I can, pal – and I have a feeling in my bones there is a lot of money to be made in Italy if I play my cards right. Besides, I am part Italian, remember.'

'So who's the designer – and what's the deal?'

'You wouldn't know the name yet. Though I guarantee you will. The deal is simple – I persuade a big fabric firm and manufacturer to bankroll my protégé. They will bear the cost of the first few collections and keep most of the profits until the designer has earned back his share.'

'So what's in it for you?' Hugo asked, trying to quash the ridiculous feeling that Greg had switched allegiance.

Greg laughed and tapped the side of his nose.

'I shall do all right, never fear. Fixers always do.'

'Yes,' Hugo said wryly, thinking that for all his success Greg was far better off than he.

He mentioned as much to Laddie next day and was surprised when his assistant looked grim.

'I've heard things lately about Greg that have me a mite worried,' he confided.

'It's galling, I admit,' Hugo agreed. 'But I can't see that a new Italian designer will hurt us much. Our market is mainly here, in the States.'

'That wasn't what I meant.' Laddie ran a hand through his close-cropped hair which had turned snow white overnight with shock when Chris had killed himself. 'What I heard is much closer to home. I haven't mentioned it because I know Greg is a friend of yours and anyway the chat was confidential.' His voice tailed away and Hugo guessed that it had been with one of his other homosexual friends, perhaps high placed and still in the closet. 'It's to do with his financial dealings,' he continued after a moment. 'I hope to God I'm wrong but there was a suggestion he might be investigated.'

'Christ!' Hugo sat very still but inwardly he had gone cold. What the hell had Greg been up to? And what implications might there be for him and the business if there was any truth in it?

It was soon after this conversation that Hugo noticed that Paula was changing for the worse, slipping back into bouts of silence, moody and tense, interspersed with almost hysterical outbursts. Once he woke in the night thinking he had heard an intruder and went downstairs to find her wandering about like a sleep walker.

'Honey – what's wrong?' he asked anxiously.

She stared at him wide-eyed as if she had seen a ghost.

'What is it?' he pressed her, and she flew at him.

'Nothing – nothing! Why can't you leave me alone? Why does everyone have to go on at me?'

'No one is going on at you', he soothed. 'But it's four in the morning. Can't you sleep?'

'No, I can't. And is it any wonder?' She burst into floods of tears, beating at him with her hands when he tried to put his arms around her.

'Sweetheart, I don't know what's wrong with you and I can't help you if you won't tell me what it is,' he said, exasperated and anxious. 'For goodness' sake go back to bed. Nothing will seem so bad in the morning.'

He persuaded her back up the stairs though she was sobbing so loudly he was afraid she would wake Harriet, if not Nanny and the other staff. She was shaking like a leaf, cold and apparently frightened, but he got her into bed, fetched her a glass of brandy and sat on the bed beside her, making her sip it.

'Was it a bad dream?' he asked her gently, as one would ask a child, when she was calmer. She shook her head but still seemed incapable of telling him what had upset her so. He gave her a couple of sleeping tablets and stayed with her until they took effect. He was tempted to slip into bed beside her and hold her close but he was afraid this might make things worse instead of better. With Paula one could never be sure, and she seemed to have such an aversion to love-making.

He would speak to Buster in the morning, he decided – ask him to have a look at her. But he shrank too from doing that. Paula was so adamant there was nothing wrong with her – and how could he explain the situation? It had been bad enough when he had been able to offer Harriet's birth as a cause of Paula's strange behaviour but Harriet was now almost four years old. It struck at the very roots of Hugo's masculine pride to have to admit that his wife simply could not bear to have him near her. His body ached with need of her and his heart ached with love. He had had such hopes when he had brought her to New York and he had been so determined to make her happy. Everything that was his he had offered her yet somehow none of it could satisfy her. He adored her, worshipped her almost, so that he had been prepared to overlook all her short-comings as a wife and mother simply to have her there. But it was still not enough. She was slipping away from *him*, body and soul.

Shivering in his thin silk pyjamas in the cold grey dawn Hugo sat on the edge of her bed, watching her sleep. Her face, in repose now, was as beautiful as it had ever been, her hair fanned out on the pillow. Hugo touched it and ran a finger down the line of her jaw to her throat.

How easy it would be to kill her as she slept – to take a pillow and press it down on her face, or to wind one of her own stockings around that delicate throat and pull it tight!

If I killed her now I would only lose her to death, he thought, not to someone else who can perhaps make her happier than I can . . .

It was the first time the thought of losing her to someone else had consciously occurred to him though from the ease with which it slipped up into his mind he somehow knew that deep down he must have been aware of the possibility for a very long time.

She has never loved me as I loved her, he thought. Perhaps there is someone who could awaken and fulfil her . . . but I'll be damned if I'll ever let her go to find out. Yes, if it came to that, I *would* kill her first . . .

He began to shake, partly from cold, partly from the strength of his own emotions and because he could no longer trust himself he got up from the bed, crept out and went back to his own room. But he could not sleep. Dawn broke fully and became day and still he lay there, tormented like Pandora by the sight of the horrors within the box of tricks he had unwittingly opened.

What a fool I have been, he thought, a fool and a dreamer, believing I could keep my ice-maiden in her ivory tower for ever. So much for the romantic. So much for a love so strong that it blinds one to sweet reason – and makes one turn away from unpalatable facts.

Now, with a shocking and almost inexplicable suddenness the blinds had been torn from his eyes. Forced at last to face what he had until now refused to acknowledge Hugo knew with sick certainty that nothing would ever be the same again.

Paula was in torment. It was weeks – months now – since she and Greg had been together and in her darkest moments she was horribly afraid they would never be together again.

The prospect was unbearable. It hung over her like a huge dark cloud invading every waking thought and creeping into her dreams to instil a sense of nightmare. She didn't want to eat – food tasted sour and her stomach revolted against it; she couldn't hold a proper conversation because half her mind was constantly occupied with her own private dread. Greg couldn't have left her forever – could he? Heaven knew, he'd given her hard times before and had always come back. But the facts were inescapable. Even when he had been in New York he had not called and when he had come to the house to see Hugo he had not given her one single sign of his interest. Throughout the spring and early summer she waited in a ferment of anxiety and frustration. Hugo suspected there was something wrong, she knew, and had done ever since the night he had found her wandering sleepless and beside herself, but she could not summon up the energy to care.

Nothing mattered, nothing was the least bit important, except seeing Greg again, being with him, making love – if that was what such a frenzied, yet detached, act could be called.

It was June now, six whole months without him. Was there someone else? Was that it? In New York he was the same, social grasshopper he had always been but he was abroad a lot. Besides, there was always the possibility that his new amour was as secret as their liaison had been. But she would know, Paula thought, if that were the case. If Greg was behaving with someone else as he had behaved with her she would be the first to spot it. She would recognise that casual cruelty anywhere.

The summer heatwave hit the city early. In the house on East 70th the air conditioning kept the rooms from becoming unbearable but outside dust settled on the leaves of the trees, and a heat haze shimmered just above the grey ashphalt of the roads and sidewalks.

In boardrooms and offices the temperature was rising too, though this owed little to the weather. Greg Martin's name was being bandied about and coupled with such descriptions as charlatan, con-man and crook and the investors who had placed money with his investment service began to become restive.

Eventually Hugo, beside himself with worry, called a hasty meeting with Greg. But far from allaying his fears his backer's breezy, unconcerned attitude only made him more sickeningly certain that something was terribly amiss.

'Christ knows what he's playing at,' he said to Paula over dinner. He had not meant to talk to her about his business worries – she would not want to hear about it, he thought, and it might drive her into another of her withdrawn moods – but somehow, overwhelmed with concern as he was, there was no way he could keep from talking about it, and to his surprise Paula responded as if she was actually interested.

'Greg? Why should he be playing at anything?'

Hugo shook his head. 'I don't know. But if there is any substance to the rumours that are flying around we could be in big trouble, Paula. Very big trouble. Everything I've worked for could be on the skids.'

'Why?'

'Oh honey – because Greg put up the money to get me going. And now I'm beginning to wonder just where that money came from. The business is mine – thank God Greg and I never became partners officially – so I think it should be safe. But if the money he put in belonged to his investors then I may have to find a good few thousand dollars in one hell of a hurry. We could be ruined, Paula.'

'What about Greg?' Her eyes were bright and hard.

'I don't know, honey, I honestly don't know. But the bloody incredible part is that he is taking off on holiday tomorrow. Would you believe such a thing? He says it's been planned for weeks and he's not going to cancel just because of some stupid panic on Wall Street.'

Suddenly Paula was very aware. 'Where is he going?' she asked tautly.

'Italy, of course – where he always goes. Can you believe it – that he'd just swan off as if nothing was wrong?'

Paula said nothing but a pulse had begun to beat in her throat for suddenly she was remembering a conversation she had once had with Greg. A well-known New York businessman had just gone bankrupt, and lying in bed with Greg in his sumptuously decorated apartment, Paula had asked: 'What would *you* do, Greg, if you were to lose all this?'

He had laughed, trailing a finger across her small breast. 'Don't worry, I won't.'

'How can you be so sure?' she pressed him. 'Even the most unlikely people are going bust all the time.'

'True. But I have every eventuality covered. Believe me, I wouldn't be a poor man.'

'But how can you insure against something like that?'

He trickled the finger up her breastbone, neck and chin to tap her nose. 'That's for you to ask and me to know, *cara mia*. But I will tell you something. I wouldn't stay around here to be humiliated. Oh no, I'd hightail it away to where I'd be well off again.'

At that point she had made a small snapping bite at his finger which was by now hovering over her lips and as the love-play started again Paula had completely forgotten the conversation. Now, however, it came back to her with startling clarity and she found herself trembling with a certain unwelcome knowledge.

Greg was in trouble and Greg was going away – she was certain of it. The holiday was just a blind to get him out of the country and then he would pick up the money she was certain he had stashed away somewhere and disappear for a few years. He had always known something like this might happen and he had prepared for it. She might almost have laughed at his cleverness if she had not been so terrified that it all meant she would certainly never see him again.

'Look, honey, I'm afraid I have to go out,' Hugo said when they had finished dinner.

'To see Greg again?' she asked.

'Not this time, no, though it is about Greg. I'm sorry, honey, I know you don't like spending the evening alone . . .'

'Oh I don't mind,' she said, trying to hide her delight. For Hugo to be out was just what she wanted, for all through dinner she had been formulating a plan . . .

The moment Hugo had gone she picked up the telephone and called Greg's number. Let him be in! she prayed. Oh, let him be in!

At last he answered. He sounded, she thought, slightly edgy, and she smiled to herself. For the first time in months she felt powerful again. It was a good feeling.

'Greg – hi. It's me – Paula.'

'Paula!' He sounded surprised.

'Aren't you pleased to hear from me?' she asked almost playfully. 'It's been so long! And now I hear you're planning to take a little holiday.'

'That's right,' he said tersely.

'So – darling, since we haven't seen one another in simply ages, why don't you take me along?'

There was a small cold silence. Then Greg asked: 'Are you mad?'

'No. Just tired of being ignored. I miss you so much, darling and I'm sure you must miss me. So why not take me with you?'

'I'm sorry, Paula, but I can't possibly do that.'

She smiled, the sense of power beginning to grow.

'Oh Greg, I'm quite sure you can! That is, of course, unless you want me to tell what I know.'

She heard the swift intake of his breath, but his voice when he spoke was still tautly controlled.

'And what is that?'

'Well, darling, that you don't plan to come back, of course. From what I hear there are quite a few people who would be distraught to hear that – they might even want to prevent you from going. And then of course there is your secret cache . . .'

'What secret cache?'

'The money you have hidden away for a rainy day . . .'

'How do you . . .' He broke off, but she knew what he had been going to say – How do you know about that? Did you go snooping at my flat whilst I was in the shower or whatever? She hadn't, of course. She had nothing to go on but that one conversation and her own sharp assessment of what it had meant, but his reaction now told her she was absolutely on the right track.

'Oh yes, it would be a pity if you lost that, wouldn't it?' she said silkily.

For a moment there was complete silence, then he said: 'Perhaps you're right, Paula. I would miss you.'

'Oh, you would. You would.'

'All right then – be here first thing in the morning. But we are just going on holiday remember. Don't tell anyone anything more than that or you'll ruin everything. Do you understand?'

'Oh yes, Greg – yes!' She was elated now; she had won!

'If you breathe a word about anything else I won't take you with me. Can I trust you?'

'Of course you can, Greg!' she said. 'I wouldn't be so stupid, would I? After all, it's not just your future that is at stake, darling, it's mine too.'

She replaced the receiver and sat hugging herself, so excited she could barely keep still. She was going with Greg. Not just for a holiday but for the rest of her life. He would never be able to treat her with casual indifference again – not now. For the first time she had him in her power just as she had always wanted. They would be together and they would have the money he had stashed away in South America or a Swiss bank account or wherever and it would be wonderful – wonderful!

Paula threw back her head and laughed with almost manic delight.

When she was calm again Paula asked Doris to pack her suitcases, explaining that she was taking a holiday. When she detailed the things she wanted Doris raised her eyebrows but said nothing – she was used to her employer's excesses. But all these things for just a few weeks! Ah well, better just do it, Doris thought philosophically. It didn't do to argue with Mrs Varna.

Paula prowled the house too tight strung with excitement to settle in any one room. When it was Harriet's bedtime she went to the nursery to kiss her goodnight and the child clung to her, sensing something was amiss. Paula hugged her, put her away, then dragged her into her arms again, burying her face in the soft fair hair, overcome for just a moment by a rush of maternal love. Could she take Harriet with her? No, it simply was not practical. It would spoil everything to have a child along. But perhaps one day when she was older Paula would send for her.

'Goodnight, baby,' she murmured, tears that sprung more from a theatrical display of emotion than from real feeling welling in her eyes, and suddenly the voices were whispering at her from the

corners of the room: *She hasn't been much of a mother, has she?*
Bloody rotten, really. But what else would you expect?

Paula raised her head, glowering into the shadows.

'Be quiet, can't you? Be quiet and leave me alone!'

The whisperings subsided so she could no longer hear what they were saying, only an indistinct accusing buzz.

She kissed Harriet again, tucked her up, and went downstairs. It was almost eight-thirty when Hugo's limo brought him home. It had been one hell of a day and he was very tired.

He had lunched with John Fairchild, the larger-than-life supremo of Fairchild Publications who had turned *Womens Wear Daily* from a boring trade newspaper into compulsive reading for anyone with an interest in fashion and because he was enjoying himself he had allowed the lunch to go on too long and drunk a little more than he usually did in the middle of the day. John was such good company – although like everyone else in the fashion industry Hugo had a healthy respect for the man whose cutting one-liners and 'In' and 'Out' lists could make or break a designer, a garment manufacturer or a member of the Shiny Set, he never failed to enjoy the publisher's often outrageous behaviour and impeccable good taste. When he had returned to the office, however, it was to find Jason Hearst, his lawyer, waiting to see him, full of gloom and despondency about the Greg Martin rumours, and when the meeting was over there were still a hundred and one things to be done before he could pack up and go home.

Paula was in the garden room and one look at her told him she was in a strange mood – 'hyper' as Sally had described it. Her face was flushed, her eyes very bright, and she had obviously been drinking. Determined to treat her normally he poured himself a whisky and threw himself down in a chair to drink it, but Paula remained standing, flittering about the room as if she were a trapped butterfly, desperate for escape. Suddenly she laughed, a high little giggle that made him look at her sharply.

'Paula? What's up, honey?'

She lifted her chin, fiddling with one earring and looking at him with a strange smile that was halfway between excitement and triumph.

'I've something to tell you, Hugo. I'm going away with Greg tomorrow.'

For a moment his mind went utterly blank. 'What?'

'I'm going to Italy, with Greg. I thought you ought to know.'

He stared at her, uncomprehending. 'What are you talking about?'

She laughed again, a high-pitched trill of tension.

'I'm going to Italy with Greg. What could be clearer than that? Oh Hugo, don't look so shocked! You must know about us. Even you couldn't be quite that blind. It's been going on for long enough.'

'What's been going on?'

'Greg and me. We're in love. We have been for years. And now I'm going away with him. Tomorrow. It's all arranged.'

He felt sick suddenly, all the wine he had drunk at lunch time turning sour in his stomach.

'Paula – for Christ's sake . . .' He took a step towards her. She retreated as if afraid of his touch.

'Don't, Hugo. Don't try to stop me.'

'I don't believe this,' he said, still sounding stunned. 'Nothing has been going on between you. I'd have known about it. It's all in your imagination, Paula. You haven't been well. You're not well.'

'You would say that. You're like *them*. You're against me – all of you. Except Greg.'

'Don't be so bloody ridiculous! Nobody is against you. You've got to see someone, Paula. I believe you're really sick. I'll talk to Buster in the morning. He'll arrange for you to go to a really good shrink.'

'No!'

'Honey, you need help.'

'No. I need Greg.' Her eyes were wild now, her mouth twitched as if she was about to laugh again and her voice rose hysterically. 'You don't believe me, do you? You still don't believe me. You think I'm making it up. But it's true, Hugo. We are lovers and we have been for ages. The first time he took me in this very room. The night of your mother's birthday dinner.'

'My mother's . . .'

'Don't you remember, you went alone. We were going on to a party. Greg called for us. And he made love to me. Here –' the giggle escaped, 'on that rug. Just where you're standing.'

Hugo froze. Something in her tone, something in her face, told him that unlikely as it sounded, insane as Paula might be, she was only speaking the truth. Yet he could not, would not, believe it. It was too monstrous.

'Don't lie to me!' he yelled.

'I'm not lying, Hugo.'

'Greg wouldn't . . . I know he's a womaniser, but he wouldn't Not here, not in my home.'

Her mouth hardened. It was as if his denial was a denial of Greg's love for her.

'If you won't believe me, I'll show you proof!'

She flung out of the room and he heard her running upstairs. He stood motionless, running his fingers through his thinning hair. Sweat was streaming down his face. His stomach was churning.

After a few minutes when Paula had not returned he began to panic. In her state who knew what she would do? He took the stairs two at a time. A light was showing from her suite. He pushed open the door.

Paula had taken off the dress she had been wearing and was struggling into a green silk evening gown. She looked up at him defiantly, shrugging into one shoulder and reaching behind her to fasten the zip.

'See – d'you see?' she demanded. And he saw.

The dress was creased from lying all the while where she had thrown it that night but it was the ripped seam that demanded attention. Paula giggled again triumphantly.

'I was going to wear this to the party. Didn't it cross your mind to wonder why I changed? You knew it was my favourite. But you never asked me why I didn't wear it. Well – now you know. It was because Greg did this in his eagerness. He couldn't wait for me to take it off. And neither could I!'

A bombshell seemed to explode behind Hugo's eyes, sending a

searing pain through his temples. He rarely lost his temper, but he lost it now, all control erased by that blinding flash.

'You bitch!' he spat and saw a moment's fear come into her eyes. 'You bloody little bitch! I worshipped you, Paula, I put you on a pedestal. I'd have died for you. But you . . . God, I ought to kill you!'

She took a step backwards, the fear crystallising. The torn dress slipped from her shoulder. She jerked it up, holding it around her.

'I ought to kill you,' he said again. 'I was so darned patient with you, Miss Ice Maiden. I stayed out of your bed because I thought you were afraid of having another baby and all the time . . .'

Paula stood frozen with terror, believing for a moment that he really might be going to kill her. As he reached for her she screamed, twisting away, but his grip on her arm was unrelenting.

'Bitch! Whore! Fucking with him while I . . . well, I am going to fuck you now. I am your husband for Christ's sake and I am going to fuck you so darned hard you won't be able to walk for a week.'

His eyes had gone small and hard but his lips were engorged. He ripped the dress from her, exposing her small breasts, her slender body, her long tanned legs. She shrank away but he picked her up bodily, fury lending him a strength he had not known he possessed and threw her onto the bed so hard that she bounced. She sobbed, trying to crawl away, but he grabbed her arm again, twisting it above her head so that her shoulder wrenched in its socket.

'Hugo – please, please! You're hurting me . . .'

He ignored her. She was no longer his cherished wife but a chattel and his driving need now was not to express his love but to dominate, to humiliate, to punish. He drove into her roughly while she writhed, sobbing, against the searing pain in her shoulder and the fire between her legs.

In moments it was over though it seemed to Paula it had gone on for ever. She curled herself into a small protective ball, trying to cover herself with her hands.

'I hate you . . . I hate you . . . how could you?'

He looked down at her and briefly the shadow of his

overwhelming love for her was there, tinged with the foretaste of terrible remorse. But the hurt was too great, the betrayal too complete. Not even the loveless act of domination could expunge it.

'Go with him,' he said, his voice low and terrible. 'Go, if that's what you want, Paula, and I wish him joy of you. For you are the most selfish woman I have ever met.'

She did not reply, simply lay sobbing.

'I would have given you the world if I could,' he said. 'Anything you wanted. But it wasn't enough. Well, I'm through trying. Go to him – now, tonight. I don't want to spend another night under the same roof with you. Go to him, and I hope to God you find some peace at last.'

Neither of them had noticed the small figure peeping around the door. Harriet, woken by the shouting, had crept along the corridor from her room, not understanding, yet aware that something terrible was taking place, she had stood there, frozen with fear. Now as Hugo turned to the door warning bells rang inside her childish head. Would he hurt her as he had hurt Mummy? Shaking with fear Harriet turned and scampered for the safety of the nursery. By the time Hugo reached the door she was nowhere to be seen.

Paula left without saying goodbye.

Hugo never saw her alive again.

PART FIVE

The Present

CHAPTER TWENTY-SIX

When he had driven Harriet to the airport Tom O'Neill turned the car on to the East Point Road. Had things been progressing well between him and Harriet he would have left the visit to Vanessa McGuigan until the following day, stealing a few extra hours with the woman who fascinated him as no other had done for longer than he could remember. But things had not progressed well. He had managed to foul them up and before he had had a chance to make amends she had received word of her father's heart attack and gone rushing back to the States.

'Take care,' he had said when he dropped her outside the Departures Lounge. 'I'll be in touch.'

But she had looked at him as if she was almost unaware of his existence, anxiety for her father making her oblivious to anything or anyone else and he had thought she might have been a stranger, cool, polite, faintly hostile, and certainly bearing no resemblance to the warm and exciting woman who had lain in his arms.

It was understandable, of course. Last night she had been hurt and angry, convinced he had used her to further his investigations, and he knew he had only himself to blame. Today fate had taken a hand. Perhaps if she had not had such devastating news he might have been able to convince her it wasn't true but the opportunity to try had been denied him and he was amazed at how much it mattered to him.

Damn it to hell, she's only a woman! he told himself, and the world is full of them. But the weight around his heart was a denial of the casual dismissal. There was only one Harriet – and he wanted her.

It's as well she's gone, he told himself, trying a new tack. You have a job to do and she might interfere with it. Romantic involvement always interfered with work – the fact that he had none had been one of the reasons why he was such a good investigator. No heavy dates that couldn't be broken, no little woman waiting at home and complaining about lonely evenings and spoiled meals. Most important of all no emotional distractions to interrupt the processes of deduction. He had been free to concentrate on the job in hand, give it his full attention and go wherever was demanded of him, able to fall asleep at night turning the problem – and the clues – over in his mind and wake refreshed, sometimes with the answer right there staring at him from his subconscious. When sleeping with a woman who was more than just a casual liaison that wasn't possible. Continuity was lost. And with Harriet it was even worse. She was heavily involved in the case – one which he was certain was not all plain sailing. There were hidden intrigues here, facts that had not yet come out, he knew it in his bones. It could be that they would incriminate people she loved and the learning of them would hurt her. If that were the case might he not be tempted to hold back for her sake? If he did he would be short-changing the people who were paying him, if he did not there would be bitterness and recriminations between him and Harriet – last night's episode had been just a feather in the wind compared to how she would blame him if he brought her face to face with skeletons in her family cupboard, or, worse, was the instrument of their disgrace or ruin. No, far better that she had gone back to the States leaving him to pursue the investigation without personal considerations to cloud the issue.

Rain was falling in a thick grey mist as he drove along the East Point Road, obscuring the waters of Fannie Bay, so that the bougainvillaeas on the cliff tops might have marked the edge of the world. The heat was cloying – he could feel his shirt sticking to his back. No wonder Vanessa McGuigan had put the house on the market – to a girl used to the balmy climate of the south this place at this time of year must seem like an outpost of hell.

He parked outside the bungalow and looked down the drive.

No aborigine handyman working in the garden today – the priming would have to wait until the rain stopped. But there was a white Mercedes sports car drawn up on the hard standing. His spirits rose. He thrust all thought of Harriet to the back of his mind and ran for the shelter of the porch.

Almost immediately the door was thrown open. The girl who stood there was as tall as he, slender and elegant in a cool pink sarong dress. A cascade of blonde hair had been caught with a matching scarf at the nape of her neck, cornflower-blue eyes widened slightly behind artificially darkened lashes, then narrowed again, giving the beautiful face a faintly provocative look.

'Miss McGuigan, I presume,' Tom said lazily.

'Yes.' She tilted her head to one side and the long bunch of hair fell over her shoulder. 'You must have come to view the house. Did Abbot and Skerry send you? They should have phoned to let me know you were on your way. Well, you'd better come in.'

Tom followed her inside. Only when he was safely over the threshold did he disillusion her.

'I'm not here about the house, Miss McGuigan. I'm looking for Rolf Michael.'

For a second she froze and he saw something like alarm flicker in the cornflower eyes.

'My fiancé? I'm sorry, he's not here, Mr . . .?'

'O'Neill. Tom O'Neill.' He produced one of his cards and handed it to her, watching her face closely. She studied it.

'An insurance investigator! Why on earth should you want to talk to Mike?'

He made a mental note. She had called him Mike. Because it was a shortened form of his surname – or because she also knew him as Michael Trafford?

'I think that's something I should discuss with him,' he said smoothly. 'Could you tell me where I could find him?'

'I'm sorry, no. He's out of town. Mike is a very busy man.'

'I'm sure he is,' Tom said and thought wryly: He would be! Quite apart from his business dealings, juggling three identities must be pretty time-consuming. 'However, you must have some idea where he can be reached.'

Her face seemed to go shut. 'I'm sorry, I don't. And even if I did, why the hell should I tell you, Mr O'Neill?'

She moved towards the door as if to see him out. Tom stood his ground.

'In view of all the circumstances I thought you might prefer to talk to me rather than to the police,' he said easily.

Her hand froze on the door-catch. He felt, rather than saw, her panic, and experienced a stab of satisfaction. He was on the right track, not a doubt of it. A moment later his suspicions were confirmed when she swung round, chin tilting defensively, eyes meeting his with something like defiance.

'I don't know if I can help you, Mr O'Neill, but perhaps you had better come in and talk about this.'

She led the way to the living room, took a cigarette from a packet that was lying on an occasional table, and lit it. He saw that her fingers were trembling slightly.

'I'll ask you again, Mr O'Neill, what this is all about,' she said after a moment.

'You don't know?' he asked, watching her closely.

'Would I be asking if I did?' Not by so much as a single flicker did her expression give the lie to her apparent innocence. Either she was some actress or she really did not know, Tom thought.

'As you saw from my card I am an insurance investigator,' he said. 'I am checking out a claim involving a great deal of money. I believe your fiancé can help me with my enquiries. When do you expect him back?'

For the first time he caught a hesitation in her manner. Then she recovered herself.

'He'll probably telephone me some time. I'll tell him you want to see him.'

'There's no need of that,' Tom said swiftly. The last thing he wanted was his quarry frightened off. 'Just tell me where I can find him and I need not bother you any further.'

'I don't know, I tell you. Look – I really think you owe me some kind of explanation. What kind of insurance claim are you investigating?'

'A death. Two deaths, as a matter of fact.'

The colour drained from her cheeks. 'In Sydney?' she asked before she could stop herself.

Tom's antennae began flashing messages. Maria Vincenti, he thought. She believes something has happened to Maria Vincenti and Martin is responsible. So there was some truth in her allegations that Martin was trying to have her killed.

'Not in Sydney, no,' he said. 'In an explosion on a yacht off the coast of Italy. It happened more than twenty years ago.'

The unguarded expressions that flashed across her face as he said it spoke volumes. First relief, then surprise – and consternation. Then, as quickly, the shutters were up again. She laughed, a high, brittle sound.

'Twenty years ago! Good heavens, that's history, isn't it?'

'Not to me,' he said grimly. 'Nor to the company that paid out on the life of Greg Martin.'

'Greg Martin? I don't know anyone of that name.'

'I think you do. Just as you know Michael Trafford.' She ground out her cigarette, rounding on him angrily. Her guard was down now and it was plain to him she was not the innocent bimbo she had at first appeared to be.

'This is all because of that woman, isn't it?' she said harshly. 'Her and her stupid lies and imaginings! She'd say anything to get her own back on him, the jealous cow. She couldn't stand to think he'd left her for a younger woman. But is it any wonder? God – you should see her! Gone to seed, drunk most of the time, what does she know about keeping a man like Mike?'

'So you admit your fiancé, Rolf Michael, and Michael Trafford are one and the same?'

'What's the point in denying it? You've obviously done your homework. Changing his name was the only way he could get away from her and her malicious mischief. But this Greg Martin business – the whole thing is a figment of her overworked imagination. God knows where she dug it up from. Some old newspaper lining her drawers, maybe.'

'I don't think Maria Vincenti is the sort of woman who lines drawers with newspaper,' Tom said drily. 'Well, you do seem to know quite a bit of the story, Miss McGuigan.'

She fit another cigarette.

'How could I avoid it? It's been big news. But I can assure you, Mr O'Neill, Mike is not some long lost part-Italian financial wizard. Surely you don't think he could have lived a high-profile life here for the past twenty years if he was?'

'Stranger things have happened.'

'Oh well – if you don't believe me . . .'

'I'd be more likely to believe it if Mike, as you call him, were to tell me himself.' As she glared at him, he resorted to blackmail again. 'Otherwise I'm afraid I shall have to take my suspicions to the Darwin police. I can call in at the station on my way back through town.'

'Oh damn you!' she flashed. Her face had assumed a vixenish look, her features becoming sharp and pinched. He thought that at this moment she did not look beautiful at all. 'All right – he'll be home the day after tomorrow.'

'What time?'

'Some time during the afternoon. He's taking me out to dinner. He should be here by four or five.'

'Right,' he said, thinking that he did not trust Vanessa McGuigan one inch and would have to spend the next day and a half staking out the house, watching the comings and goings and following her if necessary to see where she went and who she met. She might be telling the truth and then again she might not. Either way he would have succeeded in flushing Greg Martin out.

'And there's no need to bring the police in on this?' she pressed him.

'None – if you are being straight with me.' He smiled, bringing his considerable charm to bear.

'You really are a very ruthless man, Mr O'Neill,' she said. The telephone shrilled suddenly and the wariness returned to her eyes. 'Excuse me, I must answer that.'

As she went out of the room he followed her to the door, listening. If it was Martin on the phone now and she warned him, he wanted to know about it. But the drift of the conversation was quickly obvious – it was Abbot and Skerry, the estate agents, calling to arrange an appointment for a prospective buyer to view the house.

Tom eased the door closed, taking the opportunity to have a look around the room. There was nothing to suggest that a man had been here today – everything was more or less exactly as it had been when he and Harriet had last been there. But on the occasional table beside her cigarettes was an airline folder. Swiftly he flipped it open, then his lips tightened. Two reservations on a Quantas flight to the States – dated tomorrow! So she had been giving him a line! In telling him Greg would be home the following day she had been buying time – or so she thought. If he had been stupid enough to believe her by the time he returned for his appointment with Martin the pair of them would be out of the country. Oh he was a slippery customer, all right – and seemingly never without a beautiful woman to help him cover his tracks!

He heard the sharp 'ting' as the phone went down and swiftly closed the airline folder. By the time Vanessa re-entered the room he was standing where she had left him, examining an entry in his note book.

'Well, I don't think we can usefully do any more today, Miss McGuigan,' he said lightly. 'I'll be back the day after tomorrow, when I hope your fiancé will be able to help me clear up the case satisfactorily.'

She nodded. He thought he caught a gleam of triumph in the cornflower eyes. 'I'm sure he will, Mr O'Neill.'

Back at the Telford Top End Tom placed a call to Robert Gascoyne in Sydney. It went against the grain, handing over hard won information like this, but he could not see that he had any alternative. If Martin and Vanessa intended to leave the country they had to

349

be stopped and the policeman was the one to organise that – if he had something he could charge Martin with.

To his relief Gascoyne sounded more interested than he had done during their previous encounter.

'Well done, O'Neill,' he drawled. 'You've just saved me a great deal of work. It seems the FBI have picked up the reports and we've been asked to set an investigation in motion. Martin is wanted in the States on various fraud charges – if he's alive.'

'Oh I think you'll find he most certainly is,' Tom said. 'And just about to step back into the lion's den.'

'It's tempting to let him go – and leave them to clear up their own mess,' Gascoyne remarked. 'But I suppose I had better act on your information and have him picked up at the airport. Well, I suppose this means your job is over – you've got your man and saved your clients a great deal of money.'

'Oh, I haven't finished yet,' Tom said. 'In fact in some ways you could say I was only just beginning.'

'How come?'

Tom set his jaw. In that moment he looked more ruthless than ever.

'My job will not be complete until I discover just what happened to Paula Varna.'

CHAPTER TWENTY-SEVEN

Sally arrived at the hospital just half an hour after taking Harriet's frantic phone call. She came into the waiting room still holding her fur coat around her as if she were cold in spite of the almost overpowering heat inside the building.

'Harriet – how is he?'

'Holding his own as far as I can gather. But it's touch and go.' Harriet's face felt stiff; it was an effort to talk but she was glad not to be alone any longer.

'What happened?' Sally asked.

'Well. . . he had another attack. I was with him. It was . . .' her voice tailed away and she steeled herself to continue, 'it was horrible. He looked so *ill*, Sally – and that damn machine wailing away like a banshee . . .'

Sally covered her eyes with her hand. She looked pale and tired and Harriet guessed she had not had time to catch up on much lost sleep before the telephone call had summoned her back. But for all that her make-up was intact and her hair as carefully coiffured as ever. Whenever did Sally look less than well-groomed, Harriet wondered? She'd probably turn up at her own funeral looking immaculate.

The door opened and they both jumped. A white-uniformed nurse came in and they stood waiting like coiled springs, half-expecting some news. But she merely shook her head with an almost imperceptible movement and offered them coffee. Harriet sipped it gratefully, glad of the liquid to moisten her parched throat, but Sally set hers down untouched on a small white painted table alongside a pile of glossy magazines.

'I can't understand it. . . he seemed so much better when I left. Perhaps it was the excitement of seeing you again.'

'Perhaps . . . But he was talking so strangely, rambling really. He's very upset . . .' Harriet broke off. There were so many questions rattling round inside her head and she felt instinctively that Sally might be able to answer some of them. But this was not the time or place. Later, perhaps, when they knew if he was going to pull through again.

Sally was pacing the room, window to door and back again, like a caged lioness. All her usual composure was gone. Harriet crossed to her, putting her arms around the aunt who had been more like a mother to her.

'Come and sit down, Sally. You'll be making yourself ill next and that isn't going to help anyone.'

Sally pressed her hands to her mouth. Her scarlet nails made vivid patches against her pale skin.

'He's got to be all right, Harriet! I couldn't bear it if he wasn't. Oh God – I love him so much!'

Harriet squeezed her gently. 'I know you do.'

Sally shook her head, obsessively, like an animal in pain.

'No, no, you don't understand. All these years I've lived with it and now . . . it's like a judgement. I was so wrong . . . so wicked . . . but I loved him so. I couldn't bear to lose him then and I can't bear to lose him now.'

'You're not going to lose him,' Harriet soothed with more conviction than she was feeling. 'Dad has a tremendous will to live and he's getting the very best of medical attention.'

But half her mind was churning – what the hell did Sally mean? First her father making cryptic remarks – now Sally tormenting herself about . . . what? There is something here I don't know about, Harriet thought, something that has been hidden from me all these years and sooner or later I am going to find out what it is. Dad might simply have been talking about what he did to Mum that last night, but that is not what Sally is referring to. She had nothing to do with that – she wasn't even in the country. No, she is talking about something quite different, something that has haunted her through the years, something *she* did that was 'so wrong, so wicked'.

'I was so afraid of him finding out the truth,' Sally was moaning. 'Just last week I was thinking I'd give anything – anything – so long as he never knew. And now this . . . If he's taken of course he never will know. But that's not important any more. Nothing is important except that he should get well.'

'And he will. He will!' Harriet said fiercely.

'Will he? I don't know. He's never been mine in all these years. Not really. I stole him, Harriet. I stole him from her and now she's taking him back . . .' Her voice cracked.

'For goodness' sake stop this, Sally!' Harriet exploded. 'You're hysterical. I don't know what you are going on about but you couldn't have stolen him from Mom. She was dead. I didn't want to believe it, but now I do. She was dead. She has been dead, Sally, for more than twenty years.'

Sally's shoulders were shaking; her slim frame in the enormous fur looked almost emaciated. 'No – no! Not for twenty years . . .'

Harriet turned cold. Prickles of ice ran up and down her spine. She stared at her aunt, her eyes hard and blank.

'What are you saying?'

The door opened. They both spun round. It was Dr Clavell. He looked grave and Harriet's heart lurched again.

'Doctor – is he . . .?' she tried to say but no words would come.

'No, I'm not bringing bad news.' He smiled thinly. 'The crisis seems to have passed – for the moment.'

'You mean he's going to be all right?' Sally was motionless now, hugging herself.

'It's a little early to say for certain. Prognoses in cases such as this can be difficult and I don't want to raise too many false hopes. The human heart can take just so much and no more. But for the moment the situation seems to be under control. Would you like to go in and see him now?'

'Can we?' Harriet asked.

'As long as he's not upset or over-excited again.' Dr Clavell turned his mournful gaze on her. 'I can't stress too much he is a very sick man.'

'I think we realise that,' Harriet said.

She turned to Sally. Her aunt's eyes were still wild in her pale face but her lips were parted in an expression half way to hope.

Harriet put her arm around her. Whatever dark secrets lay between them this was not the time to dwell on them. As Sally had said, nothing mattered but that Hugo should pull through.

'Come on, Sally,' she said softly.

Together they followed the doctor along the corridor to Hugo's room.

By the time Danny, the chauffeur, returned Harriet and Sally to the triplex on Central Park South it was late evening. Jane the cook had prepared them a cold supper and a pan of home-made watercress soup which only had to be heated the moment they arrived and whilst Harriet knew it would be delicious as it always was, she also knew she was past eating and she guessed Sally would have no appetite either.

'What I need is a drink.' She crossed to the cabinet, poured herself a large vodka and tossed it back in one. 'What will you have, Sally?'

Sally gave a small shake of her head and Harriet poured her a brandy.

'Drink it for goodness' sake. You look as if you need it.'

As Sally sipped her drink a little colour returned to her pale cheeks. She had gone into herself now, so silent and withdrawn that Harriet found herself half wondering if she had imagined the outburst at the hospital. Lack of sleep was making her feel light-headed and unreal, but she had gone past being sleepy. Her whole body felt tight-strung, her mind was racing. She had to know what Sally had meant by the things she had said. But how could she ask her now, when she was in such a state of distress?

Suddenly Sally drained her glass, coming out of her reverie with a snap.

'What was your father saying to you when he was taken ill again?' she asked, her voice low and steady.

Harriet avoided her eyes. She did not want to repeat the tortured self-accusations.

'Just ramblings. I couldn't make head or tail of them. But I think he blames himself for Mum's death.'

'Yes, I think he does,' Sally agreed. 'He shouldn't, of course. He was a wonderful husband, generous, loving. He gave her everything she wanted and he would have been prepared to forgive her anything ... well, almost anything.' She broke off, her eyes going far away, and after a moment, when she continued, her voice was so soft Harriet had to strain to catch her words. 'That was the trouble, really. I thought ... yes, I thought he'd still take her back. Even after what she'd done – how she'd hurt him. Even, God help us all, as she was ... I thought he'd take her back and I couldn't bear it. Not for me – I loved him so much – and not for him either. What sort of a life would it have been for him? For any of us?'

Harriet leaned forward, clutching her glass between hands that had begun to tremble.

She hadn't known how to raise the subject with Sally again but now Sally had brought it up all by herself. It was as if Hugo's brush with death had unlocked the flood gates on twenty years of silence and now there was no way to stop it all pouring out. But still it made no sense, these tortured, disjointed fragments.

'Sally – are you saying what I think you are saying?' Harriet asked. 'That Mum didn't die, any more than Greg Martin did?'

Sally's face contorted slightly. Then she gave an almost imperceptible nod. Harriet's heart was pounding so hard she could scarcely breathe.

'You mean – she is alive?'

'No – no. She's dead now.'

'But she didn't die in the explosion?'

'No.'

'And you knew it – you've known all these years? My God, did Dad know too?'

'No.' Sally shook her head vehemently; she appeared close to tears. 'He doesn't know, Harriet, and he mustn't. That's what I've been so afraid he'd find out, ever since Greg Martin turned up and the investigators started probing. It's all going to come out now isn't it? Oh God, he is going to hate me so much . . .'

'Why, Sally?' Harriet pressed her, though the pieces of the jigsaw were beginning to fit together to form a picture she was not at all sure she wanted to see. 'Why will he hate you?'

'Because I knew she was alive and I didn't tell him. I let him think she was dead . . . I kept it from him, Harriet. I kept it all to myself. Oh, I kidded myself it was for the best. That I was saving him – and you – a lot of pain. But it was pure selfishness really. I always thought Paula was the selfish one but in the end I was just as bad – worse. She was at least up front, honest, selfish, while I . . . I was sneaky and underhanded. I cheated you all, Harriet, may God forgive me!'

She raised her glass to drink, found it empty, and tossed her head back with a small strangled sob. Harriet crossed to the drinks cabinet, fetched the bottle and refilled both Sally's glass and her own. She needed it – and would need more yet by the time this was over, if she was not much mistaken.

Sally was sitting on the very edge of one of the antique Sheraton chairs; Harriet fetched a pouffe and brought it over. She felt shaky yet oddly calm, like the eye of a storm.

'I think you had better tell me the truth, Sally, don't you?'

Sally's face was almost in repose now as if she had faced the worst and survived. After all these years the ice was broken – from here on in all she could do was explain and hope Harriet would understand. But whether she did or not, it was almost a relief to share the secret she had borne alone for so long. No more lies, no more deception – Harriet, at least, would know her for what she was.

'Where do you want me to begin?' she asked.

Harriet sipped her drink, eyeing her steadily.

'At the beginning.'

'Very well,' Sally acquiesced.

It was going to be a long night.

'I came over to New York as soon as the news broke,' Sally began. 'Hugo – your father – telephoned me. He was in a dreadful state. At first he simply said that Paula had been on holiday with Greg when the accident happened but I could tell he was beside himself. I threw a few things for Mark and myself in a suitcase and booked us on the first available flight. I was in a state of shock myself as you can imagine and all I could think of was getting to Hugo – and to you. Family solidarity was the most important thing – we needed to be together, giving one another support. Then when I arrived Hugo told me the whole story. Paula had been having an affaire with Greg – she told him about it the night before she left. Naturally, he went crazy. He threw her out there and then and told her he never wanted to see her again. She flew to Italy with Greg and the very next day they sailed from the marina in his yacht. Other people with boats there saw them go – alone. I already knew that much, of course. It had been in all the newspapers, along with reports of the explosion and as far as I was concerned at the time that was the whole story. Hugo was dreadfully upset, blaming himself, though that was quite ridiculous, and I agreed to stay in New York for a while at least to comfort him and to look after you.' She paused, looking at Harriet. 'At first that was honestly all it was. But then things began to get complicated. Because I fell in love.'

'With Dad', Harriet said softly.

Sally nodded. 'Yes. I'd always thought him attractive, of course, and Paula a fool not to appreciate him. But in the aftermath of our grief we grew very close. He is a wonderful man, Harriet – but then I don't need to tell you that – and he was grief-stricken. Whether he turned to me because I reminded him a little of Paula, whether it was simply because I was there, or whether even then it was something more, I don't know. Things developed between us – too quickly, perhaps, but develop they did, and suddenly for the first time in my life I was not only deliriously happy with a man, but comfortable too.'

She paused, remembering the wonder she had felt when she had first realised Hugo returned her love. All her life she had felt inadequate, unworthy of love. Now, suddenly, here was a wonderful man who needed her. How long had it taken to reach this watershed? She did not know. But when the realisation came it had come suddenly, bowling her over with its intensity.

It had been late one night, she remembered. Hugo and she had been sitting in the garden together after the children were in bed when Hugo had suddenly buried his face in his hands, overcome by despair.

'Where did I go wrong?' he had asked, and she had gone to him, putting her arms around him.

'You didn't, Hugo. Believe me, it wasn't your fault,' she had comforted him. 'Paula couldn't help herself. She was always the same – it was just the way she was.'

'But she was a sick woman, Sally. I knew it and I should have got help for her.'

'Hugo, don't torture yourself. I'm sure you did all you could.'

'I did what I thought was best.' She could feel his agony; it was almost tangible, running in waves through his body. 'I thought I could make her love me but I couldn't. That was my greatest failure.'

'Paula wasn't capable of loving anyone,' Sally had said, stroking his hair. 'She was beautiful and vivacious, but she couldn't love.'

'She loved Greg.'

'I don't think so.' Sally had felt she was drawing on some deep truth. 'She was obsessed with him because she couldn't have him. Paula always wanted what she couldn't have.'

He had been silent for a moment, then he had turned his head into her breast like a child.

'Oh, why couldn't she have been more like you, Sally?' It was a cry from the heart.

Sally had felt something sharp and sweet twist within her. For a long time they had remained motionless, she the comforter, he the soul in torment. Then, almost imperceptibly, the tiny shudders of awareness had begun. At first she had tried to suppress them, telling herself it was wrong to lust after her bereaved brother-in-law.

But then as his head moved against her breast and his hand moved tentatively across her back she realised with something like wonder that she was not alone in these new stirrings. She pressed closer, all else forgotten in the sudden exultant joy in his nearness. He lifted his head from her breast and she slid down so that they were looking at one another, looking, just looking, their very souls naked in their eyes.

Even now, across the years, she remembered that moment so clearly – the scent of the roses hanging in the still-hot air, the muted sounds of the city, and Hugo, looking at her as no one had ever looked at her before.

'Oh Sally.' He sighed, a deep shuddering sigh and then his arms were around her, his lips on hers. 'Oh Sally, Sally, Sally . . .'

Their need was born of deep unsatisfied longings, they drew together like children of the storm and found a completeness neither had known existed. There in the garden, isolated on their island of grief and despair, a new love was born, and the heights and depths were all there at once so that it was potent and totally overwhelming. Without a word spoken they staggered into the house and up the stairs.

There was nothing of Paula in the bedroom. How could there have been? It had been Hugo's alone for so long. But even if there had been Sally did not believe it would have made any difference. She loved him too desperately. Since Stuart there had been no one – she had not wanted anyone. Now there was Hugo and it was so wonderful that momentarily it blotted out all else from her mind.

Later, when she lay in his arms, she had begun to be afraid. Would he despise her? Had she provided him with simple release? But no. She was amazed and delighted to find that instead he treated her in the same courtly way he had treated Paula and which she had so envied. The total adoration was missing, of course. It was too early yet for that and perhaps that had been a blind, once-in-a-lifetime thing. There were still the times when she saw him staring into space with pain in his eyes but now there was no despair – that seemed to have gone – and she took pride and joy in feeling that it was she who had exorcised it.

As the weeks passed they had grown ever closer. Across the years the glow she had felt then warmed her and she wrapped her hands around her knees, remembering. Oh, it had been so wonderful – love and happiness and security all rolled into one. And she had basked in the security of love that transcended anything she had ever known before – the love of a man who would never let her down.

'Sally?' Harriet's voice broke into her reverie and she looked up, a little bemused, as if coming back from a long way off.

'Yes?'

'You haven't told me what happened. I'm sorry, but I must know.'

'Yes. Yes, I suppose you must. Well, as I say, I fell in love with your father and I thought he had fallen in love with me. We had to be discreet, of course, people would have said it was too soon, indecent, but it really wasn't like that. He didn't love Paula any the less, I knew that, nothing we shared detracted from his love for her. But she was dead and I was alive – and he needed me. The summer came to an end and it was time for me to come back to England – Mark had to start a new term at infant school. I was dreading it! But Hugo asked me to stay. "I lost Paula, I couldn't bear to lose you too," he said. So of course I stayed. Well, why shouldn't I? Hugo wanted me to, and you wanted me to. You were very unsettled by Paula's disappearance though she had never paid that much attention to you; perhaps it was everyone else's distress that communicated itself to you. Anyway, I could calm you when no-one else could and I didn't want to leave you in the care of a succession of nannies, especially if your father sank into the depths of depression again. And Mark – well, it was good for Mark too. It hadn't been easy bringing him up all alone with precious little money – there had been baby minders and day nurseries and later on he would either become a latch-key kid or have to go without all the little luxuries my wages could buy – and heaven knows, they were few enough! Here in the States he could enjoy all the benefits of an affluent home. And me? Well, as I already said, I was happier than I'd ever been in my life. Everything in the garden was rosy, you might say. And then came the bombshell.'

'What?' Harriet asked. Her chest felt tight, she could scarcely breathe.

'A letter came – from Italy. It was addressed to your father but he was away, doing a trunk show, so I opened it. To this day I don't know why I did it – I'm not in the habit of opening other people's mail. But some sixth sense told me it was important. Do you know I felt physically sick as I opened that letter – as if I knew the bottom was about to drop out of my world.'

'Was it from Mum?' Harriet asked.

'No – oh no. I'd have known her writing. No, it was from a Sister Maria Theresa. Strange, isn't it? That name is imprinted on my heart. I'll never forget it. Sister Maria Theresa.'

'Who was Sister Maria Theresa?'

'A nun. She belonged to an order who ran a small hospital on a tiny island off Sicily. A very special sort of hospital, as a matter of fact.'

'And . . .?'

'The letter said that Paula was there. Not dead at all. Alive.' She broke off. Her eyes had gone far away again, as if she were seeing it again for the very first time, that letter that had spelled the end of her new-found happiness.

It hadn't been that simple, of course. There had been the first flood of joy that her sister was alive, together with something close to disbelief. But then realisation had dawned and with it a sinking feeling inside that she was ashamed of but could not stifle. If Paula was alive then Hugo was not free at all. Not legally and not emotionally either. Sally knew with a sick heart that whatever they had become to each other she could never compete with Paula. All the experiences of her youth had taught her she had never been anything but second best. No one had ever favoured her. Hugo, adoring Paula as he did, most certainly would not. She shivered now as she had shivered then, seeing her dreams crumbling to ashes, hating herself for the selfishness of her emotions and not being able to do a thing about it.

'Sally?' Harriet's voice recalled her again. 'What are you saying? That Mum had been injured in the explosion and was being cared for by nuns?'

'Not injured, no. There was no mention of anything like that.'

'Then what was she doing in hospital? And why didn't anyone know she was there? This was – how long after the accident? A couple of months? Surely these nuns would have reported it to the authorities?'

'It seems not. They didn't know who she was.'

'But the reports of the explosion must have been in all the newspapers.'

'They didn't have newspapers. It's a very tiny island, remote and primitive, and they lived a totally isolated life.' Harriet shook her head in disbelief.

'If Mum was alive and not injured why didn't she tell them who she was? Why didn't *she* get in touch herself?'

Sally was silent for a moment. A shadow flickered across her face and she twisted her hands together in her lap. Then she looked up directly at Harriet.

'She wasn't injured, and she wasn't ill in the accepted sense. I'm afraid the truth of the matter is that your mother was quite insane.'

Harriet froze, numbed with shock.

'What did you say?'

Sally swallowed. Her eyes were full of compassion now as well as shame and torment.

'I'm sorry, but it's true. She had been showing signs of it for some time only none of us realised how serious it was. She'd been withdrawn, paranoid, often slipping into a world of her own – I'd seen a little of it when I'd come to visit a couple of years earlier – and Hugo had been worried about her for some time. But you know how it is – you keep hoping you're wrong. Looking back now I can see it – I believe she was suffering from the early stages of schizophrenia. If she had been helped then – who knows? Things might have turned out differently. But when she left your father and went off to Italy with Greg something happened to push her over the edge. By the time the nuns wrote she was desperately ill, beyond help, though what treatment was available had been tried on her. She had gone totally into a world of her own – she didn't even know who she was.'

'I don't understand.' The first almost cataleptic trance of shock had passed and Harriet was shaking now. 'If she didn't know who she was how did they come to contact Dad? And what was she doing on this island anyway? She sailed with Greg Martin – there were plenty of witnesses to that.'

'Perhaps no one will ever know the whole truth,' Sally said. 'Only Greg could tell us that – if *he* knows it. All I can tell you is what Sister Maria Theresa told me. Some fishermen had found Paula drifting in a dinghy, half-drowned and out of her mind with terror. They didn't know who she was – as I said, the island was very isolated, and even if they had seen the newspapers I doubt if they could read. They did the only thing they could think of – they took her to the hospital. And the nuns took care of her.'

'I can't believe no one reported it or tried to find out who she was! It's crazy! Surely someone would have made enquiries?'

'People who live in communities like that are a law unto themselves. Perhaps they thought it was in her best interests to keep her there for a time at least rather than return her to the world that had induced her madness. I don't know. I can only tell you, Harriet, what happened.'

'You still haven't explained how they came to write to Dad in the end. If she didn't know who she was and no one had bothered to find out.'

'Apparently one day she was more lucid than usual and she gave them your father's name and address and they decided it was their duty to write to him. Only I opened the letter instead.'

'Dear God!' Harriet whispered. She picked up the bottle, refilled her glass, and drank deeply. 'So – what did you do?' she asked after a moment.

'I went to Italy, of course,' Sally said. 'I went to see her.'

'Without telling Dad.'

Sally's face worked, her eyes closed, then opened again.

'Yes. It was wrong of me, I know, but at the time I rationalised it to myself by saying I needed to know exactly what the situation was before worrying him. I knew he would be distraught and I wanted to spare him. But if I'm honest I knew it was more than that. I didn't want him to know she was alive, Harriet. God forgive me, I wanted to keep *him* to myself as long as I could. Oh, if there had been a chance of her getting well I'd have told him, of course. I couldn't have lived with myself if that had been the case. But when I saw her I knew there was no chance of that. She wasn't the Paula we knew and loved any more. That girl had gone forever and in her place was a mute wild beast who whimpered and stared. Nothing else. Just whimpered and stared. So what good would it have done for me to tell him? It would have been torment for him to see her as she was.'

'But surely he had the right to know,' Harriet said in a low voice. 'How could you keep it from him, Sally? She was his wife for God's sake – and my mother!'

For a moment Sally did not reply and when she did the words were torn from the very heart of her.

'Do you think I don't know that, Harriet? Do you think I haven't lived with it every minute of every day since? I've no excuse to offer really. It would be easy for me to try to say I did it all for him, although God knows, that's true too. Think what it would have been like for him – tied to a woman who had completely lost her reason. He would never have left her – Hugo just isn't like that. He would have devoted himself to caring for her for the rest of her life – and for what? She wouldn't have appreciated it or known any different. She was as happy there as she could be anywhere. And then there was you to think of. You'd suffered enough, Harriet – I wanted to spare you the nightmare of knowing your mother was in an institution, and later worrying that you, or your children, might inherit her madness.'

Harriet shook her head helplessly. The implication of Sally's last statement was lost on her. All she could think of was her mother confused, frightened, sick, and surrounded by strangers on some remote island.

'How could you do it, Sally?' she demanded. 'I just can't believe you could leave her there like that!'

'Harriet don't, please!' Sally had begun to cry. 'She was well cared for and it was a beautiful place. At least she could feel the sun on her face. You know she always loved the sun – when she wasn't worrying it would give her wrinkles! Oh, don't be like this, Harriet, please – I can't bear it. It's bad enough blaming myself, but if you blame me as well . . . We've been so close, Harriet. I've always looked on you as my own child . . .'

She stretched out a hand to Harriet, desperately seeking reassurance, but Harriet shrank away, unable, for the moment, to give it. The Sally before her now was not the woman she had known and loved but a stranger, secretive and ruthless. If her story was true – and Harriet was certain it was – she had cold-bloodedly condemned her sister to a living death amongst strangers whilst allowing those nearest and dearest to her to believe her dead. It was awful – unbelievable. Harriet felt as if the earth had collapsed beneath her feet.

'What the hell is this going to do to Dad?' she asked harshly.

'Oh I don't want him to know, Harriet,' Sally wept. 'He's a sick man as it is. Something like that would kill him!'

Harriet bowed her head into her hands for a moment as the enormity of what Sally had told her overwhelmed her. It was true – her father couldn't take a shock like this in his condition. She herself was cold and shaking – and she was in perfect health. No wonder Sally had been so upset that the whole business was being raked up again, no wonder she had begged Harriet to leave well alone. Yet in the end it had been her own guilty conscience that had brought an end to the years of secrecy and deceit.

'I honestly don't understand how you could do it,' she said again. 'Keeping quiet about something like that – how could you live with yourself?'

'I didn't abandon her, Harriet.' Sally's words were tumbling out now, a desperate plea for forgiveness. 'I sent money as long as she was alive to help support the hospital.'

'And when did she die?'

'She lived for about five years after it happened.'

Five years. Harriet closed her eyes again. *When I was eight years old my mother was still alive and I didn't know. When I started at nursery school, when I had my first pony, when I fell out of the tree in the garden and broke my arm – what were you doing, Mum? Not much, if Sally is to be believed. But you were alive and I thought you were dead.*

'Christ, Sally!' She brought her head up with a jerk. 'How did you hope to get away with it? Didn't you know it was bound to come out one day?'

Sally nodded, hugging herself with her arms. 'I guess I did. But when you start something like that there's no right time to finish it. Yes, you're right, I've been afraid, but the lies trap you, there's no way out. I couldn't bring myself to tell Hugo I'd deceived him; I couldn't bear to see the way he'd look at me. After she died I thought at least I could begin to put it all behind me but I never could. Not quite. She's been there, all the time, a shadow. I've never really been able to lay her ghost.'

For a few minutes they sat in silence, then Harriet asked: 'What was it called – the island where she was?'

'Savarelli. It's one of the Aeolie Islands.'

The Aeolie Islands. Of course. That was what Tom's side-kick had said on the telephone – that Sally had gone there a couple of months after the accident. Harriet tried to picture them, those windswept rocks where her mother had lived out her last years, and failed. But Tom's assistant had said something else – that Sally had also been to London on a brief visit. Going home? Maybe. But she had not taken Mark with her. Oh, there was probably no connection, and yet . . .

'Sally, you have told me everything, haven't you?' Harriet asked, unsure why she had asked the question, except some sixth sense that was prodding her to do so and to her dismay she saw a strangely furtive expression cross her aunt's face briefly.

'Of course I have! Why shouldn't I? I've told you more than I've ever told anyone.' Her voice had a slightly aggressive tone and Harriet thought, No, there is something else, Sally, something you are not telling me and I want to know what it is. Well, there is one way to find out the whole truth and that is what I am going to do.

'I'm going to go to Savarelli,' Harriet said.

'No! What good will that do? It's all so long ago . . .'

But Harriet had seen the quick gleam of fear in Sally's eyes and it confirmed her decision.

'The least I can do is pay a homage visit to the place where my mother spent the last years of her life. I'll go tomorrow.'

'But Harriet, you can't! Not while your father is so ill . . .'

'I'll check with the hospital in the morning that his condition is still stable and I shall only be a few days. Better that I should go now whilst he is still in hospital and can't ask awkward questions. Don't you agree?'

'No – oh, Harriet, I don't want you to go there at all!'

For the first time since the revelations Harriet reached out and squeezed her aunt's thin cold hand.

'I'm sorry, Sally. I don't want to upset you any more. But I think you know what I have to do.'

Harriet heard the telephone begin to ring as she came down the sweeping staircase carrying her suitcase in one hand and her grip in the other. For a second she froze. Could it be the hospital? She had telephoned earlier and they had assured her Hugo had had a comfortable night and his condition was stable, but there was always the possibility of a relapse, she knew, and she had tortured herself with wondering whether perhaps she should postpone this self-imposed odyssey. Suppose Hugo suffered another attack whilst she was away? She would never forgive herself. But it was too late to turn back now. Her flight was booked and her mind made up.

By the time she reached the foot of the stairs Jane was waiting for her. 'Telephone for you.'

'For me?'

'Yes.'

Harriet snatched up the receiver to hear Tom O'Neill's voice. 'Harriet – hi. How are things with you? How is your father?'

'Poorly, but stable. He had another attack yesterday but he seems to have pulled through it again.'

'Right.' He hesitated. 'I'm really ringing because I thought you'd like to be kept up to date with developments. Something has happened that you should know about.'

I already know a great deal more than is comfortable, she thought. 'What?'

'I think I have run Greg Martin to ground. I've seen Vanessa and she was less than helpful. But there were airline tickets for the States in her living room – two tickets. I think she and Greg plan to make a run for it and I've alerted the police. With any luck they'll be picked up at the airport when they try to leave Darwin.'

'Oh.'

'You don't sound very pleased,' he said. 'I thought you would be glad.'

She bit her lip. Yesterday she would have been. Today she was less sure. If Greg Martin was caught the whole story would come out. Heaven only knew what it would do to her father.

'Yes, thanks for letting me know,' she said, and suddenly he was grasping at straws; he didn't want her to hang up. It was too good to hear her voice.

'What are you doing? You'll be staying in New York, I suppose, until you know your father is on the mend?'

'Yes, I expect so,' she lied, looking at her suitcase and grip, packed and ready to go, and wishing she could share the truth with him. But why should she? All very well for him to telephone her today, pretending to be up front; in Australia he had persuaded her to trust him too and all the time he had been keeping things from her – and using her. Perhaps that was why he was dribbling information to her now – for no better reason than to keep tabs on her.

'Take care then, Harriet,' he said. 'I'll be in touch.'

When she put the telephone down she felt bereft for a moment. All very well to tell herself she hated him, useless to pretend she did not care about the way he had treated her. Tom had stirred her in a way no man had ever done before. More than that, she had felt somehow she could rely on him. It had been an illusion, of course, she knew that now, but the loss was just as real.

With an abrupt movement Harriet picked up her bags once more. The hell with all of it! She was going to Italy – and when she'd learned the truth maybe she could find some peace.

CHAPTER TWENTY-EIGHT

The tiny island of Savarelli rose like a small green tump from the blue waters of the Mediterranean. Seeing it for the first time from the decks of the hydrofoil that had brought her from Reggio Calabria on the mainland Harriet had experienced a great choking wave of emotion. Was this really the place where her mother had lived her last years, and, if Sally was to be believed, died? It looked so isolated, so lonely, windswept and buffeted by the rough seas those same winds could whip up at a moment's notice. About a hundred and fifty people lived on Savarelli, she had been told, not counting the nuns, but from here it was impossible to imagine it. The island looked virtually uninhabited, a haven for sea birds and no more, certainly not for a civilised woman like Paula.

As the boat drew closer to land Harriet was able to make out the rocky cliffs beneath the mushroom of green and the terraces corrugating the gentler slopes above. She had never seen anything quite like those cliffs, she thought, fashioned into bizarre shapes by the volcanic activity that had thrown up this island like a toy for a giant's child, an outpost of land amongst the underwater fumaroles which made the sea around it seem to boil.

Off the island the hydrofoil bumped to a stop; there was no pier on Savarelli where it could land and the only way in was for Harriet to transfer to rowing boat. As she stepped down into the tiny wildly rocking craft she wondered how she would have fared had the wind been blowing at its fiercest – the crew of the hydrofoil had described the sea as calm today. As the boat took her towards the island the hydrofoil bumped away making for its next port of call and Harriet knew that for the moment at least there was no going back.

The beach was a narrow rocky strip, the stones turned to a kaleidoscope of varying colours by the fumaroles. In one place steam still rose from the ground and wafted like drifting smoke on the wind. A swarthy peasant lad with a couple of mules was waiting for her, sitting on one of the boulders and swinging his legs; there was only one way from the beach to the island's one and only hotel – a hairpin path up the rocky cliffs. Was this the beach where the fishermen had landed with her mother? Harriet wondered. And had they then taken her this same way – up the narrow rocky mule track?

The hotel, white like the icing on a wedding cake, was clearly the focal point of the village, for the scattering of humble pink and white houses spread away from it along the green terraces like fingers from an outstretched hand. Here was the only telephone on the island, here the bar where the villagers gathered to drink wine from the local vineyards. But there was no electricity – civilisation had not extended that far.

Harriet's room was small and basic but scrupulously clean. The walls were rough stone, the floor polished stone tiles arranged in a pattern that reminded her of Crete and the influence of the Minoan civilisation there. A meal was waiting for her – tomatoes, capsicum and olives in a delicious dressing followed by locally caught aragosta – lobster – and to her surprise Harriet found her appetite had returned. So much for the sea air! But it had also had the effect of making her very sleepy. Her investigations would have to wait until tomorrow, she decided.

She closed the wooden shutters, lay down on the rather hard bed with its brightly coloured patchwork bedspread, and before she could even begin to think about her plans or allow her imagination to wander again, she was fast asleep.

Tom O'Neill supposed he had no business going to Darwin Airport. It was out of his hands now. When Greg and Vanessa attempted to board their flight to the States Robert Gascoyne's Darwin colleagues would be there to pick them up and all the might and majesty of the law would be brought into play. He hoped they would grant him the facility to interview Martin at some stage though in an international case like this with such wide-reaching implications he could not be sure that they would. However, the wheels had been set in motion and at least half his brief had been completed – he knew for certain that Greg Martin was still alive. As to Paula Varna, that was another matter. The truth of what had happened to her might be more difficult to come by. Martin was not likely to admit to being responsible for her death – he would hardly want a charge of murder added to his already awesome list of crimes so he was more than likely to suggest she was still alive, leaving Tom with the near impossible task of finding her.

Or was it so impossible? Tom's mouth hardened as he thought of the telephone call he had made the previous evening. After speaking to Harriet he had had a few drinks and buoyed up with Dutch courage he had decided to ring her again. There was so much misunderstanding between them; stupid to pussyfoot around the issue – how much better it would be to come straight out and tell her that however it looked he really was interested in her on a personal level, not simply as a means of getting information for his investigation. Knowing it would be mid-morning in New York he had placed the call. But to his amazement he had been told that Harriet had left – for Italy. At first he had disputed it – there must be some mistake! But the maid was polite, firm, and completely believable. Miss Varna had left an hour ago. She did not know when she was expected back, but yes, she thought the trip had something to do with the Greg Martin business. The information had sobered Tom completely and utterly. He had been speaking to her not more than a couple of hours earlier and she had told him she was staying in the States for the time being, while all the time she had been on the point of leaving for Italy! Why? There was still a hell of a lot that he did not know – and Harriet was a part of it. The fact that she had gone off to Italy whilst her father was still certainly ill – and deliberately hidden her intention from him – proved it. Had she been pulling the wool over his eyes all along?

He didn't like to think so. It made a complete fool of him on so many levels. But he was beginning to think that perhaps for the first time in his career he had indeed been a complete fool.

Tom O'Neill, hardened insurance investigator, one of the best in the business, taken in by a pretty face. It hurt – oh yes, it hurt. Tom's jaw set. Well there was not a damned thing now he could do about it except learn a lesson from the experience that he should already have known by heart – don't mix business with pleasure. Tom had thought long and hard about it, and now, wondering how to set about tracing Paula Varna, if she was still alive, he realised that his personal loss was a professional gain. If Harriet did indeed know Paula's whereabouts she could lead him to her and he need suffer no more pangs of conscience, no more squeamishness about 'using' her. If it were so *she* had made use of *him* trapped him by the oldest trick in the book – for some purpose he could not yet begin to fathom. Now she could begin paying off some of her dues, he thought, and she would find out just how dangerous a game she had been playing. In the meantime . . .

In the meantime he was going to Darwin Airport to see Greg Martin picked up. For one thing he was curious to see the fellow in the flesh. For another he would enjoy watching the bastard get his come-uppance.

Tom had ordered an early breakfast – coffee, rolls and jam, taken in his room – and he set out in good time to allow for Greg Martin and Vanessa's checking-in time at the airport. He parked and wandered into the terminus. Even at this early hour it was quite busy, but since it was a good deal smaller than most termini he was afraid he might be conspicuous. Martin wouldn't know him, of course; Vanessa certainly would. He bought a coffee and a newspaper, stationed himself discreetly in a corner from which he could see without being seen, and settled down to wait. The grey dawn crept in through the windows, travellers yawned, drank coffee and trundled suitcases about, and Tom occupied himself with planning his next move. Should he try to contact Harriet again, or go direct to Italy? Karen Spooner, his assistant, had done some pretty meticulous research to discover that Sally had been there over twenty years ago, but after all this time it would be a near impossibility to ascertain just where her destination had been. Tracing Harriet's movements after just a couple of days should be a great deal easier. Of course, what he really needed was a photograph of her. He cursed himself for not having somehow wheedled one out of her – it would have been easy enough when they were in Katherine. He could even have taken one himself if he'd had a camera with him. But in Katherine photographs had been the last thing on his mind.

Two men came through the airport door and Tom's mouth quirked slightly in wry amusement. Although they were casually dressed in lightweight bomber jackets and light coloured slacks he thought they might as well have had 'policeman' written all over them. They spoke to the girl at the check out desk, who shook her head, then moved to a corner opposite Tom, smoking and watching the door furtively.

Tom began to feel uncomfortable. He thought that if he were Greg Martin he'd spot the three of them – himself and the two policemen – immediately. To him they stuck out like sore thumbs. But to leave now would only call more attention to himself. He might run slap bang into them in the doorway . . .

A moment later he was blessing his intuition for Vanessa McGuigan came into the terminus. Tom raised his newspaper to cover his face, watching her over the top of it, but she did not so much as glance in his direction. She was dressed with the same understated elegance – loose pyjama-style trousers and a lightweight Burberry style raincoat. She was pulling a large suitcase on wheels and she was alone.

He saw the two policemen stiffen, their watchful eyes following her to the check-in desk.

Hold it, hold it! he warned them mentally. Don't go off at half-cock! She's not the one you want. She is just the window dressing.

Vanessa checked in, her suitcase disappeared from the scales and even from where he was sitting Tom saw the look that passed between the stewardess and the two policemen. For goodness sake!

he thought irritated, write it on a banner that she's under surveillance, why don't you? But Vanessa seemed oblivious of the drama being played out around her. She walked coolly to one of the plastic seats and settled herself in it. She looked oddly out of place – as if she should be in the First Class Lounge – and Tom found himself wondering suddenly why she was not. The flamboyant Greg Martin and the beauty queen bimbo travelling tourist? Oh well, he supposed they must have figured they would draw less attention to themselves that way.

Where the hell was Martin anyway? Even if they had not travelled to the airport together surely he should be here by now? But the minutes ticked by and no-one joined the elegant blonde. What was even more disconcerting, she did not appear to be in the least disturbed. Usually someone awaiting the arrival of a fellow traveller shows signs of agitation – even when there is plenty of time they tend to check their watch and look anxiously towards the door every so often but Vanessa did none of these things. She simply sat glancing through a glossy magazine, cool and poised, waiting for the call to go through for departure.

Something is wrong here, Tom said to himself. Somehow something has gone wrong – the plans have been changed. Although there was still twenty minutes to go to departure he knew it in his bones. Greg Martin was not coming.

He shifted, trapped in his corner for fear she would spot him, and sick at heart. You are losing your grip, he thought. The bloody man has slipped through your fingers again. He could see the policemen too were getting restless. Any minute they were going to barge up to Vanessa McGuigan and the whole thing would be blown. Although it would hardly matter. It was blown already.

The message clicked up on the display unit a second before a disembodied voice announced it. The flight to New York was boarding. Vanessa rose, cool, unhurried, not looking around her even once. One of the policemen followed her, the other went outside – going to see if any late arrivals were hurrying towards the terminus, presumably. As she reached the door the policeman approached her, touched her arm, and spoke. Tom could not hear what he said but he could imagine. 'Miss McGuigan, I wonder if you would accompany me . . .'

He saw her startled response; for just a brief second her whole demeanour registered something like fear. Then her chin was up, her expression haughty, as she demanded, no doubt, to know what they wanted with her, why she was being prevented from taking the seat she had reserved. More conversation, this time with gesticulations that spoke louder than words. 'My luggage is on its way to the United States!' he could imagine her protesting.

The policeman was polite but firm. Moments later he and Vanessa left the terminus, his hand still lightly resting on her elbow.

Tom stood up; passengers for the New York flight had all gone through now, the next lot of bored travellers were congregating.

Outside it was raining, a thick, warm mist. Across the tarmac he could see Vanessa being helped into a waiting car; closer at hand the second policeman was still looking round, the collar of his jacket turned up against the rain, his eyes narrowed in a sort of watchful resignation. Of Greg Martin, or anyone who might have been Greg Martin, there was no sign.

Tom swore, quietly but vehemently, and made for his own car before he was spotted and blamed for this whole fiasco.

The Convent of Our Blessed Lady straddled the hillside on the steepest side of the island of Savarelli, a gaunt old building reached by a stairway of stone steps cut into the sloping ground.

In its time it had provided a haven for the sick, particularly those suffering from mental or psychological disorders, as well as a retreat, but nowadays it was no longer used for this purpose, Harriet had been told when she had enquired at the hotel. Modern medicine and treatments in specialist institutions on the mainland had rendered it unnecessary and the few members of the order who still lived there occupied their days with their devotions and with working together to eke out a communal existence.

It was a pity, Harriet thought, for there was an atmosphere of peace here which was very soothing and the very stones exuded that feeling of goodness that comes to a place that has been hallowed ground for many centuries.

She paused for a moment on the stairway looking down at the sea, grey and windswept today, far below, and wondering if her mother had once stood here. Had she been aware of her surroundings? Or had she gone too far into the nightmare world of the schizophrenic to know or care?

A sister came towards her down the steps carrying a large basket – going to the village for fresh fish for lunch, perhaps. She would have a long walk along the mule tracks – those same tracks that Harriet had just followed, winding around the hillside. She looked questioningly at Harriet, who was all too aware of her scant knowledge of Italian.

'I would like to speak to someone who was here when the convent was a hospital,' she said.

The nun's expression was puzzled, her eyes piercing blue in her ageless unmade-up face.

'Mi dispiacio, non capisco . . .'

Harriet struggled with her phrase-book Italian.

'Parla qualcuno qui inglese?' (Does someone here speak English?)

She knew her pronunciation was suspect and the nun continued to look perplexed.

'Non lo so . . .' Suddenly her unlined face lit up with a sweet, almost childlike smile. 'Si! Si!' She turned back into the building, indicating that Harriet should follow, and then leading the way along a stone-flagged passage, through a cloister topped with what might have been a Norman gallery, and into the part of the building which Harriet guessed had once housed the hospital. The floors here were polished stone tiles, the walls white-painted. The nun tapped on a door, a solid chunk of some dark gnarled wood, and opened it when bidden.

The room was sparsely furnished with heavy old furniture that looked as if it might have been fashioned from the same wood as the door but on a pedestal in a corner a statue of Our Lady smiled serenely at the Holy Child in her arms and on the wall immediately facing the door an ancient and probably priceless triptych glowed with the rich colours that had survived down the centuries. At a huge cluttered desk a nun was working. She looked up, pushing her little round spectacles up her nose and straightening her veil as they came into the room and Harriet saw that although her face too was curiously unlined she was much older. The nun who had met her on the steps addressed the other in rapid Italian and Harriet waited. Then, to her utter amazement, the older nun spoke with an American accent.

'You are looking for somebody who can speak English, I believe.' Her eyes twinkled mischievously behind her spectacles at Harriet's surprise. 'I'm Sister Anne. How can I help you?'

Harriet held out her hand.

'Harriet Varna. I was hoping to speak to someone who was here when the convent was a hospital – about twenty years ago. I'm led to believe my mother was a patient here. Were you . . .?'

Sister Anne shook her head. 'I'm afraid I have only been here the last five years. In fact it is less than ten since I took my vows. I was a late convert, you might say – though I sometimes think God called me in order to make use of what few talents I had in the outside world – I was a book keeper with a firm of solicitors in Boston.'

'Then perhaps you have heard of my mother,' Harriet said eagerly. 'Paula Varna. And my father is Hugo Varna, the fashion designer.'

'Varna, yes. I don't have much interest in fashion, of course . . .' another wicked twinkle, '. . . but I believe I have heard the name. And your mother was a patient here, you say?'

'Twenty years ago, yes. She was suffering some kind of mental breakdown, I believe.'

'Yes.' The nun's face saddened. 'She would have been. All the patients here came into that category. Some came looking for peace . . . I hope God was merciful and they found it. Some were brought here by their families – brushed under the carpet so to speak when they became a nuisance or an embarrassment. Very sad, but I believe we did a good job, providing them with every comfort and love and the peace of God. However, the authorities didn't think we were capable of running what amounted to an institution, even though we had been doing it very successfully for many years. They closed us down – I say "us" but of course it all happened before my time.'

Harriet nodded. The nun's reference to relatives 'sweeping sufferers under the carpet' had upset her again. Wasn't that exactly what Sally had done?

'How is your mother now?' Sister Anne asked.

Harriet pressed her fingertips on to the surface of the huge old desk, staring down at them.

'My mother is dead.'

'Oh, I am so sorry . . .'

'At least, I think she is. That is really what I've come here to try and find out.'

The nun tilted her head quizzically, waiting. Behind her spectacles her eyes were bright and sharp. Harriet pushed her hair behind her ear with a quick defensive movement.

'It sounds silly, I know. And it's rather a long story.'

Sister Anne glanced at the first nun, spoke in rapid Italian, and smiled gently at Harriet.

'I've asked her to rustle us up some coffee. I guess you'd like a cup. Won't you sit down, Miss Varna?'

Harriet sat, relieved.

'Now, perhaps you'd like to tell me what all this is about and I'll see what I can do to help you.'

It was very peaceful in the room. Soft grey fight filtered in through the window and only the distant sound of a bell broke the stillness. It might have been a confessional, Harriet thought, and wished, for the first time in her life, that she had been brought up to a strong religious faith.

'I was told when I was four years old that my mother was dead,' she began and the simple statement opened the way. It was easy, suddenly, to talk about Paula, a relief to be able to express her doubts and fears to this calm kindly woman. The other nun brought coffee in enormous breakfast-sized cups of plain white pottery but Harriet's remained untouched on the dark wood desk until she had finished.

She raised her eyes to see Sister Anne looking at her with compassion and sadness.

'You poor child.'

Ridiculously Harriet felt like crying. It was years since anyone had spoken to her in such gentle tones and she could not remember anyone ever calling her 'a poor child'.

'Can you help me?' she asked. 'I have to find out the truth, Sister, whatever it might be.'

The nun nodded thoughtfully.

'All the old records will be filed away and I expect we could turn them up for you. But I've a notion I can do better than that. Most of the nursing sisters moved on when the hospital closed to carry out their duties elsewhere. But one or two were too old.' She smiled gently. 'A nun never retires from being a nun, but the time comes when she can no longer be a nurse. They remained here.'

A nerve jumped in Harriet's throat.

'Sister Maria Theresa?'

The small bright eyes sharpened.

'Now how do you know that?'

'It was she who wrote to my father. Is she still here?'

'Yes, she is. I don't know how much help she will be to you. She tends to be a little forgetful – she is over eighty years old now. But there are times when her mind is as sharp and clear as yours and mine – and old people often remember events that occurred many years ago more clearly than what happened yesterday.'

A pulse was throbbing in Harriet's temple. She pressed on it with her fingers to still it.

'Could I talk to he?'

'Wait here, my dear. I'll see what I can do.'

Their return was heralded by the tapping of a stick on the stone-tiled passageway. Harriet turned as the door opened.

'This is Sister Maria Theresa,' Sister Anne said.

Sister Maria Theresa was small and birdlike with a wizened face that reminded Harriet of a little brown monkey. Although she leaned heavily on her stick her movements were quick and jerky and her eyes were bright and alive. Sister Anne pulled up a chair for her but for a moment she stood staring at Harriet in almost disbelieving wonder.

'So you are the daughter of Paula. Si, I can see it.' Her English was broken, spoken with a strong regional accent in a sharp querulous voice but totally comprehensible. 'You are like her.'

'Harriet wants to know about her mother,' Sister Anne said, quite loudly as if she knew the older woman's hearing was somewhat impaired. 'You do remember Paula, then?'

'Si ... si. . . of course I remember. It was I, Maria Theresa, who cared for her, was it not? I speak a little English so she became my special charge. Though she would say little enough, and often I do not know if she hear what I say to her.'

'Tell me about her, per favore,' Harriet said.

'Hmm?' The old nun cocked her head questioningly and Sister Anne repeated more loudly: 'Can you tell her?'

'Inglese? My English is not good now. I am too old . . .'

'Your English is as good as it has ever been. But speak in Italian if you prefer. I will translate', Sister Anne offered, adding quietly to Harriet: 'It will be easier for her if she doesn't have to think of the words.'

'When did you first meet my mother?' Harriet asked when Sister Anne had settled the old nun in her chair.

'Quando? Oh, I don't remember the year but it was in the summer – June? July? I forget which. Some local fishermen brought her to us. She was in a bad way. Ah, what she had been through, the poor child! She was soaked through, hungry, thirsty, burned by the sun and the wind. We did what we could for her, made her comfortable and nursed her body back to health. But she would not speak – could not, or would not, tell us who she was. I do not think she wanted us to know. Sometimes when she was alone I could hear her talking, just as if she was having a conversation with someone she could hear and we could not, but she would not answer our questions. We thought it was best not to press her, for such questions only seemed to cause her distress and she was oh, so sick in her mind. Sometimes she tried to harm herself. We had to watch her night and day. I worried about her very much and prayed for her every night. Then one day it seemed my prayer had been answered. She seemed to come out of her dream world. "Why doesn't Hugo come to see me?" she said, as clear as anything. "Who is Hugo?" I asked her. "He is my husband, of course. Don't you know that?" "I don't know anything", I said, "unless you tell me." And she gave me an address in New York. I asked the Reverend Mother what I should do and she gave me permission to write to this Hugo, even though Paula seemed to have slipped back into that strange world she inhabited which none of us could see. I hoped when she saw her husband it would help her, though looking back now I don't think it would have made any difference. Anyway, he did not come. Instead a lady came – a very beautiful lady. She cried when she saw Paula. She said she was her sister. Paula just sat and stared. She wouldn't even speak to her. I asked the lady – what should be done? She said we should keep Paula here with us, where she was safe. She would send us money. This she did – every month, faithfully, until Paula died. Then she sent a generous donation to help us with our work. Since then we have heard nothing from her. That is all I can tell you.'

Harriet had sat motionless, her hands knotted in her lap, listening whilst Sister Anne translated. So, it was just as Sally had said. But still there were so many questions unanswered.

'How did she die?' she asked,

'It was pneumonia – though in her state it could have been anything. She wandered off one day, the wind was blowing as it does here so often, and it was cold and raining. By the time we found her she was soaked to the skin and chilled. She died a week later and we counted her lucky for at least her immortal soul had been saved.'

'What do you mean?' Harriet's mouth was dry.

'She had tried so many times to harm herself, poor lamb. If she had succeeded . . . ah, it is a mortal sin to take one's own life. Yes, I think the Good Lord in his mercy sent her out that day into the rain. He saw she had suffered enough and he put an end to her misery.'

There was an almost plaintive note to her voice as she said it, as if she too was waiting for the Good Lord to beckon her.

'Is that all?' Sister Anne asked briskly. 'There is nothing else you can tell Harriet?'

The old woman shook her head, her wizened face wistful. 'Well, well,' she said softly. 'I never thought I'd live to see it. Dear Paula's little baby – here.'

'Not such a baby,' Sister Anne said robustly. 'Paula's daughter was four years old when her mother disappeared.'

'Four years old?' The old woman looked puzzled, her mouth working as her mind clicked over almost visibly. 'Then you're not . . .?'

'Not who?' Sister Anne pressed her.

'The baby. Our little baby.'

She is rambling, Harriet thought, wandering in a world of her own. But Sister Anne persisted genially: 'What baby? What are you talking about, Maria?'

'The baby!' Maria Theresa insisted querulously. 'The baby who was born here, in our hospital. Didn't I say? When Paula came to us she was with child. We didn't know at first – it was early days. But when her belly began to swell we knew all right. And she knew, I'm sure she did, though she pretended not to. She seemed to hate it. Whenever she saw herself in a mirror it made her worse. She would scream and cry, trying to tear at her stomach. I was very frightened for her. I thought maybe when the poor wee bambino was born she might be better. But she wasn't. She was never any better. Not for long.'

Harriet's nails were digging deep crescents in her palms and she could hear the blood thundering in her ears. It couldn't be true! Yet why should this woman be mistaken? She had remembered everything else just as it had happened, as Sister Anne had said, probably more dearly than she remembered the events of just yesterday. But a *baby* . . .?

'What happened to the baby?' she asked. Her voice sounded high and tense to her own ears.

'It was a little girl. That's why I thought "But what became of her?"'

'Sally, Paula's sister, took her away. She arranged for her to be adopted. We never saw her again . . .'

'And didn't Paula mind?'

'Oh no. She would have nothing to do with the baby. I tried once to put her in her arms. She said: "Take it away. I hate it! I don't want to see it – ever!" It was one of the times when she was quite lucid. Oh yes, she could make herself clear when she wanted to. "You mustn't do this," I said to her. "Your baby needs you." But: "No!" she said. "It's not mine. I didn't want it. He knew I didn't want it and he made me. I hate him – and I hate the baby. Take it away or I'll kill it." So you see, there was nothing to be done.'

'Did she say who "he" was?'

'No – no names. I supposed it was Hugo, who never came. Perhaps it was because of him she was – as she was. If so, then I can never forgive him. Oh, I know I should be generous, and I should love all God's creatures, no matter, what, but I am old and weak and there are some things I cannot forgive. That beautiful girl, turned to madness by some man . . .'

'All right, Maria, don't distress yourself.' Sister Anne placed a comforting hand on the old woman's skinny shoulder. 'It was all a very long time ago.'

'Was it? It seems like yesterday. The past is with me, you know. She is with me.' She looked at Harriet. 'I thought you were Paula, made whole and well. But you aren't.'

'No,' Harriet said, 'I'm not. But you are right – the past is still alive. Her baby is alive. Somewhere . . .'

'Yes, she is, isn't she?' The old woman's face brightened. 'God bless and keep her, the poor little mite.'

'Do you want me to check our records to confirm all this?' Sister Anne asked Harriet. 'I don't suppose we can tell you who adopted the baby, but there may be something.'

'Would she have been adopted here, in Italy?' Harriet asked.

'No – no!' Sister Maria Theresa interrupted sharply. 'The sister took her, I tell you. She said she was going to take her to England.'

'Thank you,' Harriet said. 'I've taken up enough of your time. I'll pursue my own line of investigation now. But believe me, I am most grateful.'

She crossed to the old nun, kissing her lightly on the wrinkled cheek. 'And thank you especially Sister, for your kindness to my mother, and for loving her. I'm not sure anyone else did. But even when she was . . . as she was, you cared for her. God bless you.'

'Ah, luie, he has,' she said in Italian. 'More than you will ever know.'

The wind was blowing hard from the sea as Harriet emerged from the convent but she was scarcely aware of it. She had come to Italy to learn the truth and now she had it what was she going to do with it? For the moment Harriet did not know. Only one thing was at the forefront of her mind, beating a tattoo with the dull ache that had begun in her temples.

Paula was indeed dead but somewhere in this wide world was a child she had given birth to in confusion, pain and madness.

I have a sister, Harriet thought, and I never knew it.

Even confused and shocked as she was the knowledge was like a shout of joy.

CHAPTER TWENTY-NINE

The triplex on Central Park South appeared empty when Harriet let herself in. She dumped her bags in the entrance hall and headed for the kitchen.

As she passed the den, however, a voice called: 'Mum, is that you?' The door was thrown open and Mark poked his head round. 'Harriet! I thought you were in Italy?'

'I was. Quite the jet-setter these days, aren't I?' she said lightly, but her voice was tired. The strain of the last days was really beginning to tell on her now. 'I'm dying for a cup of tea. Come and help me make one, Mark.'

'You must be in a bad way!' he teased, but he followed her anyway.

The kitchen was deserted; it was Jane's afternoon off. Mark perched on a stool, Harriet put on the kettle and sank onto the bench that ran the length of the huge refectory table.

'How's Dad?'

'Making steady progress, as far as I can make out. Sally is visiting him now. She'll be with him all afternoon, I imagine.'

'Oh yes – Sally', Harriet said, the bitterness spilling out into her voice.

Mark looked at her quizzically. 'Hey, what's wrong?'

Harriet shrugged, chewing on her thumbnail. She wasn't sure if she was ready to talk about it yet.

'Come on, Skeet, what's Mum done to warrant a black look like that?'

She nicked her eyes up, opened her mouth to tell him, then changed her mind. She loved Mark dearly, he was a friend and brother, but Sally was his mother. She was reluctant to make trouble between them.

'What are you doing here anyway?' she asked instead.

'Oh, I thought I'd give myself a few days off and stay around until we're sure Hugo is going to be all right. Things are reasonably quiet on the business front, it's a long time since I took a holiday, and Mum has been in such a state about everything that I felt I should be around to support her in case of emergency.'

She nodded. It was typical of Mark. No one could call him a mother's boy – he lived his own life too successfully for that – but he could be relied on to be there if he was needed.

The kettle boiled and she made the tea – Earl Grey, just the way she liked it.

'Do you want a cup?' she asked Mark.

'That scenty muck? No thanks. I'll have a beer.'

He took a can from the refrigerator, snapped it open and drank straight from the can. Sally would have a fit if she could see him, Harriet thought wryly.

The tea was refreshing her – but not enough.

'You look tired, Skeeter,' Mark said.

'I am. Very. Wouldn't you be?'

'I guess I would. Oh, by the way, there was a call for you. A Tom O'Neill.'

'Oh no! What did he want?'

'I don't know. He didn't say. It was you he wanted to speak to. I told him you were in Italy and he said he had phoned before and Jane had told him that but he had thought she must be mistaken. I said no, you were definitely in Italy, and after a sort of deathly silence he asked what you were doing there.'

'None of his business.' Not that that was true. It was too much his damned business!

'What *were* you doing in Italy?'

'None of your business either.'

'Skeeter,' Mark fixed her with a long hard look, 'what the hell is the matter with you?'

'Nothing.'

'Don't give me that. Something is. And it's not just that you are worried about Hugo, either. You are on to something, aren't you?'

'Am I?'

'You know damned well you are. And whatever it is it's worrying you. There's more to this whole business than meets the eye, isn't there?'

What could she say? She was too tired to deny it and besides he would have to know sooner or later. She nodded.

'Yes.'

'What is it? Paula's not still alive, is she? She hasn't been in Australia with Greg Martin all this time, has she?'

'No, she's dead, I'm afraid. But she didn't die in the explosion any more than he did. She died in a sort of asylum on the island of Savarelli.'

'*What?*'

'She went mad, Mark. My mother died a madwoman.' And suddenly it was all pouring out. Tears ran down her face as she told him. He put his arm around her and she let her head rest against his shoulder, her body shuddering with silent sobs. At last he held her away, fishing in his pocket for a handkerchief and handing it to her.

'Poor Paula. But how the hell did she come to be drifting in a dinghy?'

'I don't know. But I wouldn't mind betting Greg Martin does. I've been thinking and thinking about it and I can only think he was behind it. I suppose she threatened all his carefully laid plans turning up when she did and he tried to get rid of her. Anyway, whatever happened it was enough to send her completely over the edge. She never recovered, either mentally or physically. And there's something else, Mark.' She blew her nose, wiped her eyes again and brushed her cheeks with her fingers. 'When all this happened Mum was pregnant.'

'With Greg Martin's child?'

'I don't think so. The baby was born almost exactly nine months after the explosion. From what Sally told me Paula hadn't seen Greg for some time until they left for Italy. He'd been out of town.

But there's every chance the baby is Dad's. I don't know how to tell you this, Mark, but something happened between her and Dad the night before she left. He raped her and I saw it. I saw it all.'

She broke off. She was shivering again, reliving that night when she had stood and watched from the doorway of his bedroom, shaking with fear. She had thought then, because of the raised voices, that he was hurting her mother, and of course in a way he had been. But there had been more to it than that. As an adult she had realised the implications of what she had witnessed. But it had never occurred to her that she might have seen her sister conceived.

'Oh Skeeter, For Christ's sake ...' Mark was nonplussed now, totally lost for words and oddly embarrassed as if it had been him, not her, who had watched the forbidden through the eyes of a child.

Her nose was running again though she was no longer crying. It was as if the tears had lost their way.

'I know. It's awful, isn't it? It stayed with me for years, like a nightmare that wouldn't go away. But I never knew ...' She broke off, crumpling his handkerchief fiercely between her fingers. 'I feel now as if I never want to see any of them again.'

For a moment they sat in silence, awkward, not companionable. Then he said suddenly: 'What happened to the baby?'

'She was adopted – in England, the nun, Sister Maria Theresa, said. Sally took her away and had her adopted. I don't know what became of her but she'd be almost twenty-three now.'

She glanced at Mark. He was motionless, his expression one of total blank shock.

'Mark?' she said.

The emotions began to chase one another across his face, each more fleeting that the last. Every working of his mind was there in minute detail and yet she could not read them, could not understand.

'Mark – what is it?' she cried, frightened. 'What have I said?'

He looked at her unseeingly, looking away again. Then he buried his head in his hands.

'Theresa,' he said. It was little more than a sob.

PART SIX

The Past

CHAPTER THIRTY

They had told her, as soon as she was old enough to understand, that she was adopted. Perhaps they had told her even before that, because it came as no shock.

'You are very special, Theresa,' her mother had said, cuddling her, along with her huge-fluffy teddy bear. 'Most mummies and daddies have to take the baby they get. It wasn't like that with us. We chose you. That's what makes you so special.'

Theresa had smiled, sucking on her thumb. Chosen – special – yes, she *felt* special. Special for Daddy, who called her 'dumpling' and played with her every night before bed, special for Mummy who kissed and cuddled her a lot, let her have a spoon to clean out the mixing bowl when she made cakes and didn't mind her hiding in the laundry basket when she was doing the washing. Her room was special, with stars stuck on the ceiling that glowed when the curtains were drawn and there was only the tiny pink nightlight by her bed because she was a little afraid of the dark. They both read to her a lot and that was special too, sitting curled up on a comfortable lap, looking at the bright pictures and listening to the familiar loved voices. She didn't have any brothers or sisters but she didn't mind that. It just made her feel all the more special.

As she grew older Theresa sometimes wondered who she really was. Perhaps her real mummy was a princess or a pop star. Or perhaps she wasn't an ordinary person at all but a visitor from another world. It was exciting to daydream about it. But never for one moment did Theresa wish to exchange the mummy who was here all the time, who picked her up and dried her tears when she fell down, and sat beside her bed feeding her ice-cream on a spoon when she was recovering from tonsillitis. That mummy was real. The other one ... well, she was no more than a character from a fairy story.

When she was fourteen she asked a few questions and they told her all they knew – which was not a great deal. When she was eighteen she applied to Somerset House for a full birth certificate, partly because she was curious and partly because she thought it would be nicer to have the 'proper thing' rather than the short form that dated from her adoption. But she had no real intention of following up the information contained in it. Her feelings on the subject had not changed since she was a child – Les and Doreen Arnold were the substance, the woman named in the birth certificate was just a shadow. Theresa did not think she wanted to meet her. That way would surely he disappointment and disillusion. Besides it would hurt Les and Doreen. Theresa cared for them too much to want to do anything that would cause them pain.

She read the details on the birth certificate, wondered a little about them – and the glaring omission – and put it away in her dressing table drawer along with her National Insurance card, premium bonds and a photograph of Sadie, her Jack Russell cross dog. It was a very long time before she looked at it again.

From the time she was a little girl Theresa had been interested in fashion. She loved to dress up herself, parading in her mother's shoes and various assorted garments that Doreen had put in a 'play box' and her favourite doll was Cindy, with her extensive wardrobe. Theresa never cared much for playing 'mummy' to the baby dolls; they lay neglected whilst she dressed and undressed Cindy and her pocket money was always saved towards buying new outfits from the breathtaking selection at the local toy shop.

Besides her interest in clothes Theresa was a talented artist and sewing came naturally to her. By the time she was twelve she was far more proficient on her mother's sewing machine than was Doreen herself, and Doreen, who usually managed to get the bobbin in a tangle or jammed the needle and broke the thread, gave the machine over to her lock, stock and barrel.

'I'll do that, Mummy,' Theresa would say with condescending amusement when she saw Doreen struggling to sew on a button or turn up a hem. 'For goodness sake – like *this* – look! It's so easy!'

'It might be easy for you,' Doreen would retort, gratefully relinquishing the task and thinking that one of the fascinating things about having an adopted daughter was that you never knew what they were going to be good at because you hadn't a clue who it was they were going to take after.

Good as she was, however, it still sounded like pie-in-the-sky when Theresa announced she wanted to be a fashion designer. It really wasn't the sort of thing ordinary girls from ordinary homes, educated at the local comprehensive, did – was it?

'Shouldn't you think about *a proper* job?' Doreen urged her. 'You can always sew for pleasure, but there's not much money in it. People aren't prepared to pay for all the time it takes.'

'I'm not going to sew – not myself,' Theresa explained patiently. 'Other people can do that. I want to design!'

Doreen shook her head indulgently. Sometime, she supposed, Theresa would come down to earth. But as time went by she never wavered in her ambition and to Doreen's surprise Theresa's teachers did nothing to discourage her. At sixteen she counted 'A' grades in both art and needlework amongst her O-level successes and even before the A-level results were announced she had gained an unconditional place on a foundation course at the nearby College of Art.

'Just be careful who you mix with,' Doreen warned her, for what she had seen of art students made her think they were a weird lot and the whole place was probably rife with drugs.

Theresa only laughed.

'I shall be working far too hard to have time for that sort of stuff,' she said confidently and after a while Doreen ceased to worry. Theresa was indeed working very hard – anyone who considered art an easy option was quite wrong, Doreen thought as she went to bed night after night leaving Theresa hard at work on some project or thesis.

The year would have been a happy one for Theresa but that it was marred by Les's sudden death. What he had long imagined to be indigestion proved in fact to have been the warning signs of heart problems. One night when Doreen had gone to London on a Christmas shopping trip Theresa arrived home from college to find him collapsed on the kitchen floor. As long as she lived she would never forget the horror of it – coming in as usual laden with her portfolio and a bag containing all she would need to make a nursery-rhyme mobile – the current project – calling 'Hi, anyone home?' into the warm but oddly quiet kitchen – and then seeing his legs protruding from behind the big wing chair.

'Oh my God – Dad!' she screamed, going down on her knees beside the inert form in a state of utter shock and panic. First she tried mouth to mouth resuscitation – she had learned the rudiments in First Aid at school – then she dialled 999 for an ambulance, then she tried mouth to mouth again. But even as she worked, trembling so much she could scarcely manage to count between breaths, she knew it was no use and when the ambulance men arrived minutes – though it seemed like hours – later she could tell from their faces that there was nothing to be done. She learned later that he must have been dead for at least an hour and although it was a relief to know that not even the most experienced medico could have saved him by the time she had found him it somehow added to the horror and made her wretched with guilt too. *If* she hadn't stayed so late at college, *if* she had caught an earlier bus, *if* she had decided to work at home that day instead of going in to be part of all the Christmas preparations, then she would have been there when he collapsed and maybe, just maybe, she could have saved him.

That Christmas was the most miserable Theresa could remember. They went through the motions, she and Doreen, because Doreen said he would have wanted them to, but the sad decorations mocked them, the unlit tree lights reminded them he was no longer there to get them working as he had had to every year since Theresa could remember, and though they worked together in the kitchen cooking turkey and bread sauce, Brussels sprouts and chestnuts for Christmas dinner as they did every year, neither of them had the heart to eat it. At last, unable to bear the pretence any longer, they drowned then sorrows with a bottle of apricot brandy, switched off the television which was blaring enforced jollity, and went to bed early, a horrible depressed end to a long sad day. Christmas, Theresa had thought, lying numb and sleepless, her head aching from too much Apricot Brandy, would never be the same again.

Life however had had to go on even if it was emptier than before and a good deal more of a struggle financially. Theresa was all too aware of the sacrifices Doreen was making to enable her to stay on at college and she promised herself that one day she would more than make up for them. The desire to be successful enough to be able to afford to buy Doreen all the little luxuries she so richly deserved gave an extra biting edge to her ambition. She threw herself into her work heart and soul, even winning a national competition organised by an important fabric manufacturer with her designs for a day-into-evening ensemble, and the lecturers at college were all agreed – Theresa Arnold was a talent to be reckoned with.

In the spring before she was due to graduate Theresa began hunting for a job. Many of her fellow students intended to travel before settling down to their careers – one was going to Paris, another to Italy, a third wanted to travel in the USA. All very well if you could afford it, Theresa thought, envious but not jealous. She was too anxious to drive on towards her goal to be lured off the path by the prospect of glamorous adventures. The trouble was, lulled into a sense of false security by their casual attitude, she had left it a little late. Many of the big companies, such as Marks and Spencer, insisted on applications before Christmas, and already had more than enough hopefuls to meet their requirements. Theresa spent a long weekend laboriously writing letters and CVs (how was it practically everyone else on her course seemed to have access to a word processor?) and posted them off, but the replies were not encouraging. Some came back a simple refusal, others promised to 'put her name on file' – not much good since she would need a job in less than three months. As a last resort she stretched her allowance to allow her to subscribe to the *Drapers' Record* and scanned the advertisements there. But they were not very promising either. The majority wanted someone with experience.

How can I gain experience if I can't get started? Theresa wondered.

She was just beginning to think the search would have to wait until, she had the time to set out and leg it around to see individual designers when she saw an advertisement that interested her. A world-famous design manufacturer in the West Country was looking for an Assistant Buyer – no experience necessary, training would be given. Buying was not really what Theresa wanted to do but at least it would be a start.

She wrote away immediately, was interviewed first by an employment consultant and then invited by the company to their head office for a second interview.

She set out, dressed in an outfit of her own design – a jacket and skirt in burnt orange wool, smart enough for an interview but sufficiently innovative to show her flair, worn with a brown silk camisole top. The manufacturer's headquarters was way out in the country and Theresa took a taxi to ensure she would arrive looking fresh and respectable. But she did not think her finances would run to a taxi back to Bristol, where she had to catch her train. She would hitch-hike, she decided.

It was late afternoon when she left the smart new office block, the early summer sunshine turning the straight, tree-lined road into a ribbon of silver. In the hedges birds swooped and fluttered busily and the may made great white splashes against the fresh green leaf, beyond them, in the fields, cows grazed. Beautiful and peaceful, but Theresa felt tense and depressed. She was not at all confident about the impression she had made on the woman who had interviewed her but she felt in her heart she had not got the job.

The woman, the chief buyer, had made too much of the fact that Theresa was primarily a designer – even wearing her own suit had been a mistake.

'You made what you are wearing?' the woman herself

immaculately dressed, had asked, and when Theresa confirmed it she had said: "Are you sure buying is what you want?'

'Oh yes, I'd like to get some experience on the business side,' Theresa had said eagerly and immediately realised her mistake. They would think she was applying for the job as a stepping-stone and truth to tell they would be right.

A few cars passed her on the road but none stopped though she looked at them hopefully. Perfect! she thought. All she needed now was a fifteen-mile walk and already the high-heeled shoes she had worn to set off her suit were raising a blister on her heel. When she heard another car approaching she raised her thumb without much hope but to her relief it braked to a halt just past her – an old, but immaculately maintained royal blue TR6 with the hood up. The door opened and Theresa found herself looking into a pair of the bluest eyes she had ever seen.

'Where are you headed?' he asked. He had a nice voice, light, with just a touch of humour.

'Bristol. Well, actually, I'm going back to London but I get my train in Bristol.'

'Hop in,' he said. 'You are in luck. It so happens I am going back to London.'

She felt a moment's trepidation. It was too pat, too coincidental. Suppose he should be some kind of sex fiend, enveigling her into his car? They didn't have to look like monsters. Some appeared perfectly ordinary, perfectly respectable, until you looked into their eyes.

Theresa looked into those blue eyes, fringed with long lashes like a girl's, clear, honest, *merry* eyes – and made up her mind. No way was this young man a sex fiend. In fact he was gorgeous. She got into the low bucket seat as gracefully as the tight little skirt would allow.

'This is incredible,' she said. 'You are really going all the way to London?'

'Yep, but I shan't even touch Bristol. My favourite route is cross country, then hit the M4 at Chippenham. Should take about three hours, depending on the traffic. Where in London do you want to go?'

'Well, it's Beckenham actually, but anywhere will suit me fine. Once I'm back in civilisation transport will be no problem.'

'Back in civilisation! I take it that means you are not going on holiday. Anyway, you don't have any luggage.'

'I've just been for an interview for a job.' It was incredible how easy it was to talk to him. 'I'm a student,' she explained.

He raised an eyebrow. 'You don't look like one.'

'Because I'm all dressed up to impress! I don't usually look like this.'

'What are you studying?'

'Fashion design.'

'Ah,' he said drily, 'that explains *it*. So how did your interview go?'

'Not too well. I don't think I'm what they are looking for.'

His glance indicated that he thought anyone turning down Theresa must want their heads reading but he was far too intelligent to say anything so clichéd.

The country through which they were driving was beautiful, small towns and villages strewn along the road like beads on a necklace. Beyond burgeoning hedgerows the patchwork of fields undulated away, green, darker green, and yellow where the first crop of rape was beginning to ripen.

By the time they reached the M4 they were like old friends. She had learned his name was Mark Bristow and he was in advertising. But he didn't say what he had been doing so far from London and she did not ask. She was too busy thinking what an amazing coincidence it was that his name was the same as her real mother's.

The Friday evening traffic was heavy but Mark drove fast and well, speeding up the outside lane to overtake then tucking back in again, and the TR, though a little cramped, was a joy to ride in with the throaty roar of the engine so close and the road contact sending little quivers and tremors up her spine. She glanced at him out of the corner of her eye – good-looking, clean-cut profile, thick fair hair, casual polo shirt worn beneath a well-cut tweed jacket, and the new set of quivers owed nothing to the TR engine.

Theresa had had plenty of boyfriends. She was a friendly, outgoing girl who managed to simultaneously present just the slightest suggestion of mystery, though no-one who knew her could have explained exactly why. Perhaps, they thought, it was her unusual face – high cheekbones and slightly flattened features – which almost suggested foreign blood in her veins, perhaps it was the way she could suddenly change from effervescence to stillness, as if she was drawing on some inner strength to replenish the power and energy that drove her. But for the most part her friends did not try to fathom her – it was not their way. They were artists, not psychologists, they looked at form and line, not the innermost workings of the mind. And in the same way the friendships were superficial – fun relationships, never more than skin deep. She had been in love, she supposed – at least she had called it that – but she had never truly given of herself and never wanted more than was on offer. Now she looked at a stranger and felt something new and exciting stir within her.

'I feel as if I know you,' she said – and then thought: What a stupid thing to say!

For a moment he did not reply. He was concentrating on overtaking a juggernaut. Then, as he returned to the central lane, he said:

'Funny you should say that. I was thinking the same thing.'

She was surprised. 'As if you know me too, you mean? We haven't met, have we?'

He laughed. 'I don't think so.' As if I'd ever forget! he added mentally.

The exchange made them awkward for a few minutes; it had contained too much unspoken intimacy for comfort. Then he said: 'What do you do for fun, Theresa?'

'Fun? I don't have much time for fun. Fashion is a very demanding course. We don't even get to do much student roistering. Sometimes I think I should have chosen something simple for my degree, like engineering or classics.'

'Hmm.' He wondered if he should tell her about Hugo and decided against it. It might sound like boasting.

'It's infuriating,' she went on. 'Everyone seems to think an art degree is an easy option. It's not, believe me. For one thing, it's continuous assessment – project marks count towards your final grade. There's a thesis to write – I did mine last summer, so that's out of the way, thank goodness, and they are so fussy about the way each project is presented. I spend a fortune on letraset and binding and so on for source sheets and that's even before I begin to make anything up. Now I'm doing my final collection – and that is a hellish expense, I can tell you. If you don't use nice fabrics you can't show off your designs to their best advantage – and nice fabric for fourteen or so pieces doesn't come cheap.'

'I guess not,' he said, and the nonchalance of his tone embarrassed her again.

'I'm sorry, I'm boring you,' she said. 'It's just that sometimes I get very despondent. I'm determined to succeed and I work my socks off and still end up getting lower grades than some of those who do next to nothing because I just can't afford to present it as they do.'

'That's tough.' Mark, who had started out with every advantage in life, had seen something of the other side since he had been in business on his own account.

'Never mind,' she said, determinedly cheerful, 'I'll get there in the end. Practically no one fails a fashion degree anyway, so that's a comfort, even if it means they don't get any sleep for a fortnight before the final collection show.'

Again Mark was tempted to remark that at the top end of the business things were much the same, again he refrained, saying instead: 'You wouldn't be able to take time off for a drink one evening then?'

Theresa's heart lifted; her pulses had begun to hammer. – 'Is that an invitation?'

'Well – yes.'

'In that case I don't suppose one evening would make much difference,' Theresa said, and thought that if it meant staying up all night for three weeks before her final collection show it would still be well worth it.

She was in love, crazily, madly, head over heels in love and it was wonderful. As she had warned him there was little time in those last months before graduation for anything but work and in any case Mark, too, led a busy life, chasing accounts, working overtime on brilliant new ideas and jet-setting between London and New York, but what time they could spend together they made the most of. Sometimes he took her out, grand style, to a show or a restaurant, sometimes they shared a drink with friends in an unpretentious bar or watched a video, curled up with cans of lager and a Chinese take away. Occasionally Mark cooked for her, suprisingly good spaghetti bolognese or chicken curry, and the last night before her final projects had to be handed in for marking he supported her with his presence while she napped: 'Oh shit, I'll never get it all done in time!' handing her the spray mount as she arranged last minute source sheets for her portfolio and clearing up the heap of cuttings that littered the floor. He made coffee for her as she sewed on buttons, neatened hems and pressed seams, he had a handkerchief ready when she burst into tears over a revere that refused to sit properly no matter how she fiddled with it, and again when she told him she had been awarded a 2.1 degree.

'That's wonderful. You are a clever girl', he congratulated her.

'No I'm not – I wanted a first. And I've worked so hard for it!' she wept, over-emotional through sheer exhaustion.

'Doesn't meant a thing. Who cares what degree you've got as long as you've got it? Your work is what counts – and it's good,' he comforted her.

'The examiners obviously didn't think it was that wonderful.'

'The examiners are blockheads. If they'd seen it on the catwalk instead of hanging on rails they'd know how good it is. It's a very commercial collection, babe, and you'll have no trouble selling it.'

'I hope so. I've got to recoup some of what I've spent on it – or rather what poor Mum has spent on it!'

'You will. You'll see.'

And of course he had been proved right. After the final collection showing Theresa was approached by several people who were interested in buying individual items and by the boutique chain who wanted to take the complete collection, lock stock and barrel, with orders for repeats and a proviso that she would also be designing a spring collection.

'You see – what did I tell you?' Mark swung her round jubilantly. 'You've got to go into business now. Forget about all these other pissy little jobs and go for the big one. Your own label!'

'But I wouldn't know where to start . . .'

'You get yourself a little work room somewhere, hire some outworkers and let your talent do the rest.'

'You make it sound so easy but I don't know a thing about running a business . . .'

'What about your friend Linda George? She's just finished at commercial school, hasn't she? She'd be just the one to help you with that side of things. You worry about designing and let her worry about the business details.'

'And where on earth would I get the capital to set up something like that?'

'Go and talk to your bank manager – that's what banks are for.'

'Oh Mark – I'm scared . . .'

'I thought you planned to be a famous designer.'

'I do.'

'Then have the courage of your convictions – go for it!'

She took a deep breath and her eyes had begun to shine with determination.

'Perhaps you're right. If I don't take chances I'll never get anywhere, will I?'

He kissed her. 'I am very proud of you, lady. Very proud indeed.'

Although they were in love both Mark and Theresa had held back certain facts about themselves, each for their own reasons.

Mark had omitted to mention the fact that his mother was married to Hugo Varna, merely saying his family lived in the States where his step-father was 'in business', for he was something of an inverted snob who was embarrassed by the wealth and success that had given him so many advantages in life. Besides this he still felt, foolishly perhaps, that to admit to connections with such high echelons of fashion when Theresa was still on the bottom rung of the ladder might be interpreted as 'swank'.

As for Theresa, even in their most intimate moments she had never admitted to Mark that she had been adopted. This was partly because she seldom thought about it herself and partly out of a sense of loyalty to Doreen. When she talked about her past it was always in terms of life as it had been, not as it might have been. She was Theresa Arnold, her mother was Doreen Arnold, her father was dead and she had been brought up in Beckenham – end of story.

But when she came to try to set up her own business she discovered for the first time in her life that it did matter to her that she was adopted – though not for any of the usual reasons. And as she and Mark discussed it, the truth came out.

As Mark had suggested, Theresa had paid a visit to the bank manager. He had been interested in her proposals and not unhelpful, but he had pointed out the necessity for collateral on a loan of the size she required. When she heard of the conditions Doreen had not hesitated. Inordinately proud of Theresa and anxious to give her the best possible start in her chosen career she had immediately offered to put up her house as security and though grateful and filled with love for her mother, Theresa was overcome by a sense of terrible responsibility and fear of failure.

'I don't think I can let her do it,' she said to Mark. 'It's too much to ask.'

'You haven't asked – she has offered,' Mark pointed out.

They were sharing a curry at Mark's flat, but Theresa's was almost untouched as she pushed the rice around her plate with her fork.

'I know she's offered, that's not the point. Supposing I should fail?'

'You won't fail. Eat up your curry.'

'I might. And if I did she'd stand to lose everything. It's not even as though Dad were alive. He didn't leave her much – the house is all she's got. If she lost it she'd have nothing. What the hell would she do? I can't let her risk it.'

'Look.' He finished his curry and pushed his plate back across the low table. 'A – you're not going to fail. B – if the bank want collatoral you don't really have much choice – I'd help you if I could but I'm mortgaged up to my ears myself. C – she *wants* to help you. Mothers are like that.'

'But she's done so much for me already. I can't tell you the sacrifices she's made for me. It's time I was paying her back, not taking her for every penny she's got.'

'If this comes off you will be paying her back,' he argued. 'You will be able to afford to keep her in luxury for the rest of her days . . .' He broke off, thinking of how Hugo had been able to spoil Martha, not only with material things but with the reason for pride in her offspring that warms a mother's heart. 'Believe me, you've got to let her do it. Nothing worth having comes without taking a few risks. You know the old maxim – you have to speculate to accumulate.'

'I know, I know, but . . .' She hesitated. 'She's done so much for me already, and . . . well, there's something I've never told you. She isn't actually my real mother. I was adopted as a baby.'

'So?' He was surprised but not shocked.

'Well – I feel doubly responsible.'

'Why?'

'Because I don't want to disappoint her or let her down. God knows what son of a life I'd have had if they hadn't adopted me. They gave me everything – all their love, a wonderful home, everything. I don't want to repay all that by ruining her.'

He reached for her hands. Although his flat was centrally heated they felt cold as they so often did and a little stiff. He massaged them gently.

'I keep telling you, honey, you have to have confidence in yourself. You can do it – you can! And as for disappointing her, that is the biggest load of rubbish I ever heard in my life. She is proud of you already and she'll be prouder yet.'

He pulled her towards him, kissing her hair, her eyes and finally her mouth. Because of her pre-occupation it was a little while before she began to respond, then his nearness worked its old magic and she temporarily forgot all her worries as her body became sensitised with longing.

Mark was a generous and considerate lover, waiting for her at every stage and drawing her to heights she had never achieved with those boys who rushed in eager for their own gratification. When at last it was over and she lay in his arms, relaxed and replete, the problems of everyday survival seemed a long way away.

Sometimes after lovemaking Mark smoked a cigarette and he did so now, propped against the pillows with her head resting against his shoulder. She nuzzled his skin with her nose, enjoying the faint smell of fresh perspiration mingled with soap on his skin and the wafting smoke of the cigarette. She felt drowsy and happy, glad she had gone down to the west country that day four months ago even though she had not got the job, for if she had not she would never have met him – unthinkable! After such a short time she felt she had known him all her life and when he said: 'So, you are adopted. You never told me', she was glad there were no more secrets between them.

'It didn't seem important,' she said. 'Most of the time I don't even think about it,'

'Do you know anything about your real parents?' he asked casually.

It was natural curiosity, there was no hint, no suggestion that what she was about to say would change both their fives.

'Next to nothing. I applied for my birth certificate when I was eighteen but I never did anything about it. I didn't feel I wanted to follow it up. As I said, I look on Doreen and Les as my real parents. They are the ones who were always there for me.' She hesitated, running one finger down the feathering of fair hairs that clustered down the line of his breastbone. 'One funny thing, though, my real mother's name was the same as yours – Bristow.'

'Really? How odd. I've never thought it was that common a name.'

'It's not, is it? She was called Sally, Sally Margaret Bristow and her address was given as somewhere in Kensington. My father wasn't named though. The space for that simply said "Father unknown".'

Almost intuitively she felt him stiffen.

'What's wrong?'

'Nothing. Nothing at all.' But he withdrew his arm and got up, pulling on his jeans. 'Shall we go back in the other room? There's a good film on TV I'd like to see.'

'All right.' But she had sensed him going away from her and she was hurt and puzzled. She didn't know what was wrong but she could tell from his attitude that he was not going to explain. Somehow, some time during the last minutes a barrier had gone up between them that had never been there before. Suddenly Theresa was cold with misgiving, her whole body feeling heavy and numb the way her hands so often did.

'Mark, I love you,' she wanted to say, in the hope that somehow miraculously everything would be all right again just as it had been before . . . what? But she did not say it. Instead she levered herself up off the bed, reached for her clothes and followed him into the living room.

Mark Bristow poured himself another scotch – his third since Theresa had left – and stood swirling the liquid around in the glass. The small carriage clock on the mantlepiece said twenty to two but he made no attempt to get ready for bed. He wouldn't sleep, he knew, and there was nothing worse than tossing and turning for hours. Besides, his skin crawled at the prospect of lying in the bed where he had so lately made love to her.

Christ Almighty what a mess! he thought and swigged angrily at his whisky. Christ Almighty, I don't believe this! But unless I am very much mistaken I have just made love to my sister.

At the thought his stomach turned again and he felt the sweat beading on his forehead and running in rivulets down his neck. He hadn't known, of course – had had no idea such a thing was even remotely possible, but that made no difference to the terrible, deep seated revulsion. Nothing could alter that, no explanations, no excuses. He had made love to his sister. Worse – he had fallen in love with her, and she with him. No wonder they had had that affinity from the very beginning! he thought, the taste of the whisky rising like bile in his throat. No bloody wonder. It was sick – too sick for words.

But how could he possibly have known? He couldn't. He hadn't even known she was adopted and he had certainly not had the slightest idea that his mother had borne – and given away – a second baby.

What the hell was the matter with her? he wondered, irrationally angry suddenly and ready to vent his feelings on her. He had known, of course, that he was illegitimate. She had never made any secret of it, even though after she had married Hugo the designer had treated him like a son. In any case there would have been no point in trying to conceal it. He had been old enough to remember living in London with his mother – in Kensington. He had already started at nursery school before he was uprooted and whisked off to the States. But she must have been already pregnant. He did a quick calculation guessing at Theresa's age. Strange. There seemed to be some sort of discrepancy. He didn't quite understand it but then she might be older than he thought she was. Yes, it must be that. There was no other explanation. Sally Margaret Bristow of Kensington was his mother, for sure. The chances of there being two girls of the same name living in the same couple of square miles must be a thousand to one against.

He refilled his glass yet again, running over the likely scenario. Sally had been pregnant again when Paula had disappeared. God alone knew how she had managed to get herself into the same fix twice – one would have imagined going through what she had done to have and keep him she would have been more careful a second time, especially by the end of the Swinging Sixties. But somehow she had and she hadn't been able to face going through with it a second time. Besides that would have totally blown her chance with Hugo, he imagined. So this time Sally had decided to give the baby up for adoption. And that baby was Theresa.

Who had been her father? The same as his? Or Hugo even? Her birth certificate bore the same embarrassing blank as did his – 'father unknown'. He did not understand it. There were still plenty of unanswered questions, but it almost fitted. Mark thought with a sinking heart that he was not far off the truth.

Well, there was only one way to be sure. He did a quick calculation of time zones and placed a call to Sally in the States. When she came on the line her voice was light, surprised, and he experienced a moment's hope.

'Hi, Mum.'

'Mark! What a lovely surprise! How are you?'

He did not answer her question, instead asked one of his own.

'Mum – did you have a baby adopted in London? Late sixties – early seventies?'

There was a silence. Even allowing for the time lapse as the words hummed along the lines across the vast distance it was too long. Then she said, a trifle breathless, a trifle startled: 'How did you find out?'

So that was it. No more room for doubt. No more room for hope. He couldn't bring himself to answer, much less to talk about it. Without another word he replaced the receiver and stood looking at it.

It was true then. Theresa was his sister. God help them both. It was revolting, disgusting. Even worse, even now knowing what he now knew, his heart still ached for her.

He couldn't see her again, of course. But he didn't want her to learn the truth. At least he could spare her that.

When dawn broke he showered, shaved and went in to the office.

'I've been thinking,' he said to Toby Rogers, his partner. 'About the Hemingway account. I think it ought to be handled from the New York end.'

Toby had looked at him in surprise. He'd said as much himself several times during the last few weeks, but prising Mark away from London since he had been seeing his latest girl had not been easy.

'I'll book myself on a flight sometime later today,' Mark went on. 'If you think you can run this end without me, that is.'

'Of course but . . .'

'I don't know when I'll be back. Depends on how it goes.'

'What if Theresa rings?' Toby asked astutely. 'Should I give her your number?'

He knew he had hit the nail on the head when Mark's face went closed in. God but he looked dreadful this morning – pasty pale like old parchment with red rimmed bloodshot eyes!

'No. Tell her . . . oh tell her what you like. But keep her out of my hair.'

'Fair enough, old son,' Toby said equably – and like the old friend he was knew better than to ask any more questions.

In New York Mark stayed with another friend in an apartment on the East Side. He couldn't bring himself to stay under the same roof as his mother. It was no longer his home, anyway – she and Hugo had moved the previous year to a new apartment on Central Park South which she had had done up entirely to her specifications, finally leaving behind the last echoes of Paula.

He had wondered how he would feel when he saw her again and as he had anticipated, at first it was awkward and he felt heavy with resentment. He had expected her to raise the subject of the baby, ask him how he had learned about it and perhaps try to explain, but to his immense relief she did not and he found that cold hard core of anger softening.

Judge not that ye be not judged. He loved Sally with the total love that most young men feel for their mothers and perhaps because of those early years when they had been alone together their relationship was even more special than most. Who knew what had driven Sally in those grim days? It was not her fault that he had met Theresa and fallen in love with her; she was not to have known.

Besides, to ask questions would be to have to explain himself and he did not want to do that. The knowledge of what he had done was a dark secret he wanted to keep to himself. Only that way might he one day be able to put it behind him. So the subject of the mysterious baby was never raised between them and gradually he found it in himself to forgive Sally whatever she had done for the pain she had caused him and resume their relationship as before. If anything he found he was even more protective of her.

But he had not been able to forget Theresa. Even knowing what he did she was still there in his heart and her presence was a constant shame to him. He did not see her, did not return any of her calls, and told himself it was the best way. A clean break meant she would have nothing to reproach herself with.

Mark threw himself into his work, spent as much time as possible away from England and never spoke of his innermost thoughts and feelings with a soul. One day perhaps he would no longer experience this sharp pain, this sick ache when he thought of her. One day perhaps there would be someone who would help him to forget her. But it hadn't happened yet.

And now here was Harriet, telling him a story almost beyond belief, and suddenly pieces of the jigsaw that he had not even known were missing were falling into place.

A baby born secretly, not to Sally but to her sister Paula, whom the world had thought was dead. Not his sister. Not even a half sister. A cousin, perhaps, but that was permissible, wasn't it?

He looked at Harriet, who was turning to him for comfort as she always had, and could only think that he had lost his love and all for nothing.

A baby – Paula and Hugo's baby – who had inherited her father's talent along with some of his looks (Mark knew now why she had seemed strangely familiar to him). A baby who had grown up into the most wonderful girl he had ever met.

Emotion overcame him. He buried his head in his hands.

'Theresa,' he said.

PART SEVEN

The Present

CHAPTER THIRTY-ONE

Sally returned from visiting Hugo in hospital just after seven.

When they heard her come in Harriet and Mark looked at one another, slightly apprehensive. Neither was looking forward to the inevitable scene. They had spent the afternoon fitting together the pieces of the jigsaw and trying to decide what should be done. Now, faced with telling Sally they knew the secret she had kept from them for the whole of their lives, both quaked inwardly.

In the hall Sally hesitated when she saw Harriet's things, still waiting to be taken upstairs, but when she came into the room she was her usual poised self. Only her eyes, shadowed and wary, showed the trepidation she was feeling. Harriet and Mark here together. What had she told him? What was she going to tell him?

'Harriet – you're back!' she said breezily – brazening it out, Harriet thought grimly. 'Did you have a good trip?'

Harriet ignored the question, asking one of her own instead.

'How is Dad?'

'Doing well. He really does look much better today, thank God. He was asking for you, though.'

'I'll go and see him tomorrow.'

'Yes, he'll be so pleased to see you. Look, darlings, I must go and have a bath before dinner.'

'Never mind about dinner,' Mark said, levering himself up out of the chair where he had been sitting. 'We have to talk, Mum.'

She knew from his face what it was he wanted to talk about but still she could not bring herself to admit it.

'Won't it wait? I can't bear it if I don't have a bath this minute and get rid of the smell of hospital. What is it about that smell? It clings to everything and seems to get right inside you and . . .'

'Mum!' Mark said threateningly. 'Shut up.'

Sally held his gaze but she had turned pale beneath her make-up. 'What is this? What has happened?'

'I think you know very well,' Mark said sternly. 'It's no use pretending any longer. Harriet has told me everything.'

'You mean . . . about . . .?' Sally could not bring herself to speak her sister's name. She looked as if she were about to cry now, her control hanging on a knife edge.

'Yes. Mum – how could you do it?'

Sally's face began to work and her fingers plucked restlessly at one another.

'I told Harriet. I explained. She needed peace and quiet. It was all that was left to her . . .'

'But it shouldn't have been your decision. Hugo was her husband. He had a right to know, for God's sake. Especially in the circumstances.'

'The . . . circumstances . . .?'

'Leaving Paula there in the care of the nuns wasn't the worst of it, was it?'

'I don't know . . . what you mean . . .'

'I found out about the baby,' Harriet said quietly.

Sally swayed. Mark was at her side in a moment, steadying her.

'Sit down. I know this is a shock – it has been for all of us – but now we know it's no use trying to cover it up any longer. Paula gave birth to a baby – Hugo's baby. She was Hugo's, wasn't she?'

Sally shook her head, words almost eluding her.

'I don't know. I never asked. I assumed she was *his* – Greg Martin's. I didn't see any point in hurting Hugo any more. She'd hurt him so much! I just wanted him to forget all about her and the way she had treated him. I wanted him to be happy. I knew I could make him happy. I *have* made him happy.'

'Yes, you have,' Mark agreed. 'But don't you see – it was terribly wrong, taking it upon yourself like that? And quite apart from deceiving Hugo, what about the baby? You deprived her of her birthright.'

'No, I made certain she went to a good home. She was adopted by nice people. They are very fussy, you know, adoption societies . . .' She looked up at Harriet, her eyes wild and puzzled. 'How did you find out after so long?'

'You know I went to Italy, Sally,' Harriet said with more patience than she was feeling. 'I spoke to one of the nuns who was there when my mother gave birth – Sister Maria Theresa. I assume you named the baby after her.'

'Yes, I did. I had to call her something. As soon as she was born I took her to London and registered the birth there.'

'As your child.'

'I could hardly register her as Paula's could I, when Paula was supposed to be dead? It was surprisingly easy. The registrar was just a bored looking girl. She accepted what I told her without question.' Her eyes narrowed. 'But how did you know what I called her? Sister Maria Theresa couldn't have told you that. No one knows – except me.'

'I knew,' Mark said.

Sally looked up at him with a flash of fear and total bewilderment. This was not her Mark, so laid back and charming and humorous. This was an angry young man with an edge of steel.

'You?' she asked helplessly.

'Yes, me. I am going to tell you a story, Sally, about a guy who met a beautiful young woman named Theresa Arnold. He was crazy about her – he had even entertained thoughts of marriage.' His mouth hardened, his eyes never leaving her face. 'He'd already slept with her. And then one day she told him she had been adopted as a baby and her real name was the same as his – Bristow. She didn't know who her father was but her mother's name was Sally Margaret Bristow who had given her address as Kensington. Am I ringing bells, Mum?'

Sally was totally white now, every vestige of colour drained from her face so that her rouged cheeks and painted lips stood out in sharp relief. She bent her head, covering that blanched face with her hands. She could not speak.

'I don't have to tell you who that young man was, do I? It was me. I went through hell when Theresa told me the name on her birth certificate. I recognised it at once, of course, and jumped to the obvious conclusion – that Theresa was your child – my sister. God what a situation!' Perspiration stood out in beads on is forehead now just remembering it. 'I broke with her at once, of course.'

Sally drew a long, shuddering breath.

'You didn't tell her – what you suspected?'

'Bloody hell no! How could I have told her something like that? I was going crazy myself thinking I'd committed incest. But I hadn't, had I? She wasn't your child at all, but Paula's.'

'Yes,' Sally whispered. She was silent for a moment then she seemed to gather herself together. 'How on earth did you come to meet her? Of all the girls in England . . .

'I met her in Somerset, not five miles from where you and Paula were born and raised. I'd been to visit Granny Bristow, Theresa had been down there after a job. On my way back to London I picked up a hitch hiker on the road and that hitch hiker was Theresa.'

'What is she like?' Sally asked after a moment, curiosity getting the better of her. 'Has she made something of herself?'

'It's a little late in the day to show concern now, isn't it?' Mark said harshly. 'Yes, as a matter of fact she is a lovely girl, in spite of everything. She had a happy childhood with parents who adored her and she was so secure and loved that even though she applied for her birth certificate when she was eighteen she didn't feel the need to try to trace her natural mother – luckily for you. When I knew her she had just graduated with a degree in fashion design and now she is struggling to manufacture and sell under her own label. She's Hugo's daughter all right. She has his looks – and his talent. And I think it's about time she knew the truth.'

'Oh Mark, Mark . . .' Sally rocked herself from side to side. 'You can't tell her! You mustn't!'

'Why not?' Mark asked grimly.

'Because of all the trouble it would cause! Oh, I'm really sorry you had to find out this way – I can understand you are shocked. But think how much worse it would be for Hugo.'

'You should have thought of that twenty years ago,' Mark said. 'Surely you must have known it would come out sooner or later?'

'I don't know ... I hoped it wouldn't. I convinced myself it wouldn't.' She hesitated, not wanting to admit to the shadow of fear that had haunted her through the years. 'I did it for the best,' she said stubbornly.

'Best for who? Best for you?'

'No – not just for me. For all of us. I wanted us to be a happy family and we have been. I bore the secret alone. I saved the rest of you from the consequences of what Paula did.' She was looking at him directly now, with defiance, and Harriet thought suddenly how terrifying self-righteousness could be, distorting perception, excusing any course of action, however misguided.

'What about Theresa?' Mark asked. 'Were you thinking of her best interests when you gave her up for adoption?'

'Yes, I was!' Sally retorted fiercely. 'What sort of a life would she have had here, with us? If Greg Martin was her father, as I suspected, Hugo would have resented her – just seeing her every day would have reminded him of how Paula had deceived him and he'd have been bound to treat her accordingly. And she would have had to grow up knowing her mother had died insane – that's a heavy cross for any child to bear. She'd be bound to wonder if the same thing might happen to her ...'

'Thanks a million!' Harriet interposed drily.

Scarcely noticing the interruption Sally rushed on, justifying herself.

'And as it turned out I was right, wasn't I? She had a happy childhood – she is a successful well-adjusted young woman. Why spoil it all now?'

'Because,' Mark said, 'I am in love with her. You don't seem to realise I left her because of all this.'

'But you don't have to tell her the truth!' Sally cried wildly. 'Start seeing her again if you like. *You* know now she's not your sister.

But surely there's no need to tell her all this? She never knew what it was you suspected, did she?'

'Christ no. I didn't want to hurt her more than I had to.'

'So why does she have to know now?' Sally wheedled. 'What good would it do? Don't tell her, Mark – you've no need to.'

Mark's mouth hardened.

'Unlike you, Mum, I couldn't live a lie.'

She recoiled as if he had struck her and he went on more gently: 'Look, I don't know if she'll have me back. She may have found someone else by now for all I know. But if by some miracle she does still feel the same way about me as I feel about her I am going to marry her. Now, I can hardly introduce her to my family without telling her the truth, can I? For starters, when she meets you she is going to realise you were once Sally Bristow, who lived in Kensington. She is not stupid, she is going to come to exactly the same conclusion as I did. And where would that lead us? Besides as I said I couldn't live with that son of deceit. You may look at it how you like, Mum, but as far as I am concerned it is an insult to your partner to keep secrets from them – important secrets, anyway – particularly if other people are in on them.'

'I always knew you were chivalrous, Mark,' Sally flashed. 'I didn't know you were also self-destructive.'

He did not answer. Clearly with Sally's philosophy of life there was no way she could understand his deeply-held views on the matter.

Sally appealed to Harriet.

'You haven't said anything, Harri. You understand, don't you? Talk to him, please, make him see the harm he'll do.'

'I can't do that,' Harriet said quietly.

'Why not? Why are you ganging up on me like this?' Sally asked, her voice rising a trifle hysterically.

'Because there is something you seem to have forgotten, Sally.' Harriet's voice was gentler than Mark's had been. In spite of everything she had a certain sympathy with Sally. She was not a bad woman, just misguided. Perhaps she had convinced herself that what she was doing was for the best – knowing her Harriet could not truly believe that Sally would have had it in her to hurt anyone, much less those she loved. Harriet looked at her now with compassion, seeing a woman who had given of herself freely over the years, a woman exhausted now from hours of keeping vigil at her sick husband's bedside, a woman who could see her house of cards suddenly tumbling around her. But despite it all . . .

'There is something you have forgotten,' Harriet said again, even more gently.

'And what is that?'

'That Theresa is my sister.'

The silence stretched on and on. Sally looked startled now, as if the fact had somehow escaped her all these years. She had only seen Theresa as a tiny baby, for a few hours only – the duration of the flight from Italy to London – and had never thought of her as a person at all, only as a problem that had to be overcome. Now, with a sense of shock she realised for the first time it was true. Harriet and Theresa were sisters, just as she and Paula had been. Separated by upbringing, maybe, on different sides of the Atlantic, one with all the privileges that wealth could bestow, the other having to struggle for everything – but still sisters, not even half-sisters as she had suspected but, if Mark was to be believed (and Mark's truthfulness was not something she had ever had cause to doubt) full flesh and blood.

'Mark is right, Sally,' Harriet was saying gently. 'We can't keep this hidden any longer. Don't you see – lies and deceit grow and grow. The whole bloody edifice gets bigger and more unwieldy until in the end it has to come tumbling down.'

Sally stared at her hands, still twisted together in her lap. 'Oh what a tangled web we weave,' her mother had used to say, long ago, in another life, 'when first we practise to deceive'. Yes, it was true. As Harriet had said the web had grown more and more tangled. In some ways it would be a relief not to have to sustain any more. But there were other things to be considered. All very well to indulge in an orgy of truth. All very well to dream about how nice it would be to leave pretence behind. There were still problems to be faced and the revelations would tear her world apart. What her friends in the Shiny Set would think of her when they learned the truth, she did not know. She would be ostracised, probably, pointed out as a wicked scheming woman by those who would not even try to understand. But that was not the worst of it. The worst was thinking of the man she loved – the man for whom she had done it all – and going cold at the thought of what the truth would do to him. Bad enough if he had been fit and strong, but as he was . . .

'What about your father?' she asked. Harriet was silent, and gaining courage Sally went on: 'This would kill him. You must know that.'

'It is a big problem,' Harriet agreed. 'Mark and I have been talking about it most of the afternoon. Of course he can't be told just now. It would upset him too much – he couldn't take it. But when he's well enough we are going to have to find a way.'

'No! No!' Sally raised her knotted fingers to her mouth, pressing hard as if to stop the sobs, but they escaped anyway. 'He mustn't know – he mustn't!'

'Harriet and I both think it's the right thing but clearly it is going to have to wait until he is strong enough,' Mark said firmly. 'In the meantime I am going back to London to see Theresa.'

'Oh Mark – think carefully about that!' Sally wailed. 'You don't know how she would react. Suppose she makes a splash – tells the newspapers? She could blow the whole thing wide open. It will kill him – it will!'

'Theresa wouldn't do that,' Mark said confidently.

'How do you know? She's a designer, you say. It would be wonderful publicity for her to tell the world she is Hugo Varna's daughter. You can't be sure she won't do it, Mark.'

'I can. I know her.' Her broke off, thinking that until this afternoon he had also thought he knew his mother. A lifetime's knowledge set against a matter of months. But what hope was there if in spite of everything one could not trust? 'If I'm wrong then I'm sorry. But I don't think I am wrong. Anyway,' he added bitterly, 'she may not even want to see me after the way I walked out on her without explanation. Just think, Mum, there's hope yet!'

Sally's eyes flicked up, full of pain.

'Do you hate me so much, Mark?'

He shook his head wearily. 'I don't hate you. I just don't understand how you could have done it.'

No more do I, Harriet thought, but I can guess.

'I don't think there's any more we can usefully discuss now,' she said. 'We'll end up going round in circles. If you still want that bath we'll hold dinner for a while.'

'Yes,' Sally said shakily. 'I do want that bath – and I have more than the smell of hospital to wash away now, don't I? To listen to you two I could be like Pontius Pilate, forever washing my hands, but the stains would still be there.'

She rose and crossed to the door. She felt unreal, as if she were playing out a dream. All these years she had kept her secret, lived with her conscience and with fear of discovery. Well, it was over now. All over.

She paused, looking back into the room, at Mark, her own dear son, at Harriet, whom she had loved as a daughter, and at the portrait of Hugo, hanging over the fireplace.

I have had twenty wonderful years, she thought. Twenty years of love and happiness such as I never dreamed could be mine. Whatever happens now nothing can take them away from me. And if I had my time over again and knew the stakes and the rewards, why, I do believe I'd do the same again.

CHAPTER THIRTY-TWO

Maria Vincenti was alone in the house at Darling Point. As usual she had been drinking most of the day but she was not drunk. Strange how her tolerance had increased – she could soak up vodka like blotting paper, and now she found it increasingly impossible to drink enough to bring her the oblivion that had once been her only comfort.

She got up from the low cane chair where she had been sitting and moved restlessly about the room, changing the disc on the CD player to fill the oppressive quiet with Pavarotti's rich tenor voice and drawing the curtains against the darkness which had fallen. At least the reporters had gone away now. Although they had been there at her instigation it had been unbearable when they had been camped out on the pavement maintaining their twenty-four hour vigil.

Leaches, she thought. Nasty blood-sucking leaches. How she hated them! Almost as much as she hated Greg Martin and Paula Varna and the rest of them who had made her life a misery. In fact Maria could not think of one person in the whole world she did not despise.

A solitary tear rolled down Maria's nose and dripped into her vodka. What the hell had happened to her? Once she had been happy, a happy child in a well-to-do Italian family, spoiled and feted. How long ago it seemed now! As if it had been a dream she recalled the huge happy family parties, the summers at Lake Como, the winters when she had skiied in the Alps. Poppa had seldom been there, of course, he was always so busy with the family business – manufacturing fabrics – but there had been so many others she had scarcely missed him. What wonderful times they had had – what wonderful times she might still be having, with her own children and perhaps grandchildren too, their cousins and all her other multitudinous relations. But she had renounced it all for love – for that worthless bastard Greg Martin. She would willingly have died for him, so much had she loved him. But he had betrayed her and now she was alone – all alone with nobody to care if she lived or died. Worse, she was convinced he had tried to have her killed, just so as to get her out of the way and prevent her from thwarting his plans. It was an easy conclusion to reach. She had known for many years what he was capable of. Hadn't she lived all that time with the suspicion that he had been responsible for Paula Varna's death? But Paula had been a stupid bitch; she had only got what she deserved. Maria had deluded herself that Greg had only done what he had done for her sake, so as to be with her because he loved her as she loved him. Now she knew differently. When it suited him Greg had treated her with the same callous disregard. Now she was old and no longer beautiful he had wanted to get rid of her – trade her in for a newer model just as he did his fast cars – but he had also wanted her money, which had allowed him the freedom to do just as he liked all these years.

Maria poured herself another drink. God rot him! God rot all of them! Her hot Italian blood bubbled in her veins, eager for the revenge that the Italians call vendetta. If she ever saw him again she'd kill him – for what he had already done to her, never mind what he might yet do.

My life is over, she thought – what sweet pleasure it would be to take him with me!

The bottle was empty now. With a grunt Maria threw it into the wastepaper basket, kicked off her shoes and sprawled herself on the low sofa. Around her the room shifted a little, going out of focus and back in again, and when she closed her eyes her stomach lurched in an imitation of the sensation of vertigo. But she kept her eyes closed anyway and after a little while she dozed.

Maria never heard the sound that awakened her but she knew

there must have been one for suddenly she was alert, her heavy limbs tingling. The rich tones of Pavarotti still filled the room. She lay without moving, listening. Nothing. Then just as she was about to doze off again she heard it – the creak of a floorboard almost immediately above her head.

Instantly she was wide awake and sober. Someone was in the house. She was certain of it. Oh, every place has its creaks and groans but she had spent enough time alone here to know every one of them. She swung her legs down from the sofa and levered herself up. Her heart was pumping furiously. She crossed to the telephone and lifted the receiver to dial for police assistance, then hesitated. They wouldn't believe her. That shit Robert Gascoyne would think it was another of her stories – or simply an overworked imagination. And perhaps it was. The house was quite quiet again now, even Pavarotti had sung his last song. When the squad car arrived at the front door, sirens blaring, they would find nothing and she would look a fool yet again.

Maria replaced the receiver and went instead to her writing bureau, unlocking the small secret drawer. Inside lay her protection, a tiny but deadly pistol with a jewelled handle. She had brought it with her from Italy all those years ago, hidden in her underwear. No one knew of its existence, not even Greg, but she felt safer just for knowing it was there. Now her plump trembling hand closed over the little handle and her beringed finger hovered over the trigger. If there was an intruder in the house he'd better watch out. In her present mood she was ready for anything.

She crossed the room stealthily and opened the door. Nothing. The hall was empty, the front door still firmly closed. She started up the stairs, her bare feet making no sound on the thick carpet.

At the head of the stairs she stopped, breathing heavily. A crack of light was showing around one of the doors – the door of Greg's old room. Her fingers tightened on the pistol. She went towards the light and threw open the door. Then all her breath came out in a gasp.

'Greg.'

He was bending over his bureau, rifling through the drawers.

He looked up, startled, as she spoke, a lick of hair falling over his forehead. Then a slow smile spread across his dissipated, yet still handsome, features.

'Well, well,' he said, almost mockingly. 'I thought you'd be three sheets in the wind by this time of night, my dear.'

'What are you doing here?' she asked harshly.

He extracted a document from the sheaf in the drawer, folded it and placed it in his pocket with a gesture that was almost insolent.

'There were a few things I needed. I left in a bit of a hurry, if you remember. Don't worry, I'm just going again. I've got what I came for.'

He took a step towards her and she raised the pistol threateningly.

'Stay where you are!'

His look of surprise was total; for a moment she experienced a heady sense of power. Then he laughed. 'What the hell have you got there?'

'A gun,' she said. 'And it's not a toy either. Stay where you are, Greg, or I warn you, I'll use it.'

He laughed again, a trifle nervously.

'You wouldn't know how. You are drunk, Maria.'

'I am not drunk. Not too drunk to shoot you if you try to touch me.'

'I don't want to touch you. Why the hell should I want to touch you?'

'You tried to have me killed before,' she said defiantly. 'Don't deny it.'

'Well I am not going to kill you now. For one thing all the money I need is now tucked safely away in a South American bank account, for another, I'm not into doing my own dirty work. Let me pass for God's sake. You can't keep me here all night.'

He moved towards her again, again she brought the pistol up, pointing it directly at his chest. He could see how her hands were trembling; in this state she might do anything.

'All right, all right,' he said in a soothing tone, 'what do you want me to do?'

She glowered at him, breathing heavily. What did she want? She wasn't sure. She didn't want *him* any more, that much she was certain of, though the sight of him still stirred her oddly. Oh Greg, Greg, we could have been so happy, you and I . . .

'Where have you been?' she asked.

A muscle moved in his cheek. She thought he was laughing at her.

'Oh, around. Darwin, if you must know. I flew in this afternoon. I told you – there were some papers I needed.'

'Is *she* here?' Maria asked heavily.

'Who?'

Maria hesitated. Paula, she had been going to say. But of course it wasn't Paula. No one had heard of Paula for more than twenty years. But the police had been here asking about her and so had that good-looking insurance man and the girl who said she was . . . who? Paula's daughter? Maria's brain felt thick and fuddled. She wasn't making any sense any more.

'What did you do to her?' she asked.

'Who?' He looked genuinely puzzled but she interpreted it as shiftiness. 'Paula. Paula Varna.'

'*Paula?*'

'Yes. They all want to know, Greg, and so do I. *I* want to know!'

'Christ, Maria, that was more than twenty years ago.'

'I don't care. I still want to know. You owe it to me.' She waved the pistol at him threateningly. 'I was involved, remember? I was the one who picked you up and got you away after you blew up your boat or have you forgotten? And now I want to know the answers to the questions I was always afraid to ask you. Paula Varna was with you – the bitch – when you sailed. Everyone said so. But she wasn't with you when I picked you up – God help her if she had been! – and you never mentioned her to me. Did you think I was too stupid to read it in the newspapers? Well I wasn't. And now I want to know from your own lips – was I an accessory to murder?'

There was a long pause. All these years and she never asked me before, Greg was thinking. Why is she asking me now? He looked from her face, blowsy and tormented, to the little gun wavering in her hand. Christ, he'd taken a chance coming here. But he'd needed those papers – couldn't leave for the States without them. And he'd thought he could get in and out of the house with his key without her knowing. He had expected her to be asleep by now in a drunken stupor. Well, there was nothing for it now. He had talked his way out of tight situations before and he could do it again. Maria wouldn't harm him. He still exerted power over her. Hadn't she always been crazy over him? That wouldn't have changed. But he didn't care much for the way she was looking at him, all the same.

'Well?' she said now. 'Was I an accessory to murder, Greg?'

He shrugged, deliberately casual.

'How the hell should I know?'

'She sailed with you. What became of her? Did you kill her?'

He hesitated. Well, there could be no harm in telling her now. Who would believe her – a lush? Besides, he would soon be in the States, starting yet another new life with Vanessa. She would have left already and he planned to join her. He would have gone with her – had even had his ticket – but for the fact that there were certain documents he had left behind in his haste to leave Sydney, and he had decided, confident as ever in his own ability to outwit just about anyone who dared cross his path, to come back and fetch them.

Greg Martin was a vain man – and all too proud of his own cleverness. Twenty years ago he had been on the verge of disgrace and ruin but he had managed to snatch victory from the jaws of defeat. Paula Varna had come close to thwarting all his carefully laid plans with her silly threats but he had been astute enough to think on his feet and dispose of her. In all those years he had never been able to tell anyone what he had done; now he was overcome with an irrepressible urge to boast about it.

What harm was there in it? he asked himself again. None. It was all past history.

'Put that gun away and I'll tell you,' he said. 'I'm not talking to the nose of a pistol, however pretty.'

Her bleary eyes flicked over him, looking for evidence of a trick.

Then she lowered the pistol and put it in her pocket, her fingers still curled around the butt.

'Go on then,' she challenged him. 'Tell me.'

He moved away from the bureau, deliberately casual.

'I didn't kill Paula. I told you, Maria, I don't like doing my own dirty work.'

'So what happened to her?'

'The last time I saw her she was in a dinghy, drifting in the Mediterranean. I shouldn't think she lived long after that. The seas get pretty rough round the Aeolie Islands and it was a very small dinghy. But of course you never know . . .' He smiled. It was not a nice smile, containing as it did the elements of sadism and self-satisfaction.

'How did she come to be in a dinghy?' Maria asked – although she could guess.

'I put her there of course – told her something was wrong and we had to abandon ship. I said I'd follow her. Instead I started the engines and headed full pelt for the mainland where I went ashore, rigged the explosives, and sent the yacht back out to sea on automatic. Neat, don't you think? If anyone had picked Paula up she would have confirmed that there had been a problem and I'd warned of a possible explosion before putting her in the dinghy. If they didn't – well, everyone would assume that we had both perished when the yacht blew up.'

'You bastard!' Maria said softly.

He shrugged. 'She brought it on herself. She tried to blackmail me – threatened to have me stopped from leaving the country unless I took her along. And she knew things, too, about my financial arrangements. She must have been snooping at my flat. Oh, she might have been bluffing of course, but I couldn't risk that. So I decided the simplest way was to take her with me and then get rid of her. And that is what I did.'

'Supposing she had been picked up and she had said you sailed off and left her?'

'No one would have believed her,' he said with supreme self-confidence in his own unassailability. 'They would have thought she'd gone off her head as a result of what had happened. They would have assumed I'd put her in the dinghy to save her life and stayed aboard myself trying to sort out the problem, whatever it was, until it was too late. I made sure the yacht would be in more or less the right waters when it exploded, you see. The timing of the device was very carefully worked out and I took drift into account when I set the direction. In any case it didn't matter, did it? Paula wasn't picked up. I can only assume she was lost at sea, but since I wasn't there I really wouldn't know.'

'You callous pig,' Maria said. 'What you did was worse than killing her. At least that would have been quick.'

He shrugged again.

'You didn't have the guts, did you? You didn't have the guts to do it quickly and cleanly. No, you abandoned her in a tiny boat in a rough sea.' She brought the pistol out of her pocket with a rapid movement, her hand suddenly quite steady. 'Well I'm not so squeamish, Greg. You deserve to die – and I am going to be your executioner.'

Something in her expression told him she meant it. He paled, his face turning to putty beneath the tan.

'Don't be foolish, Maria.'

She regarded him steadily.

'I should have done it long ago.'

'Do you want to spend the rest of your life in gaol? Give me that gun!' He made a move towards her and she took a step away, keeping the pistol levelled at him.

'I don't care about that. I don't care any more, Greg. My life is over. You ruined it. You killed Paula whatever you may say – and you tried to have me killed too. Well, I am going to make sure you never kill anyone again.'

'Maria!' He lunged towards her and in the same instant her finger tightened on the trigger and squeezed. He arrested, a look of surprise and terror contorting his features, and she fired again and again. He stumbled and fell and she backed away, still clutching the now-empty pistol. There was blood everywhere, staining his shin front scarlet, bubbling out of his mouth. He writhed on the floor, gasping, and making small coughing sounds.

She stood over him, watching him die, and felt nothing but triumph and something like a sense of peace.

God alone knew he had deserved this and she, Maria, had carried out the sentence. For the first time in her worthless wasted life she felt in control. For the first time she had done a service to the world at large.

When at last he was still she went back downstairs and reached for the telephone. Her fingers on the dial were splattered with his blood.

'This is Maria Vincenti of Darling Point,' she said when the emergency services operator answered. 'I think someone had better come quickly. I have just shot Greg Martin.'

CHAPTER THIRTY-THREE

'What the hell are we going to do, Skeet?' Mark asked.

'I don't know,' she replied truthfully. 'I honestly don't know.'

It was late, very late, but neither of them felt like going to bed though Sally had retired, pale and visibly shaken, as soon as dinner was over. They had always been close, Harriet and Mark; now they had drawn closer than ever so that they formed a team, more united than many blood relations.

'Do you think Hugo will ever be strong enough to face the truth?' he asked.

She shook her head helplessly.

'Who can say? It's bound to be a terrible shock to him to discover that all this time Sally has kept something so important from him. It would be bad enough if he was in full health – something like that undermines everything they have ever shared – but as he is . . .'

She broke off, thinking of her father as she had last seen him, so frail and ill. 'Sally's probably right,' she went on. 'It would kill him. But living a lie is so dreadful too. For all of us to know something he doesn't . . . it's an insult to him in a way, isn't it?'

Mark nodded. 'That's just how I feel.' He brought his hand down with a thud on the arm of the chair. 'How the hell could she do it, Skeet? I just don't understand.'

'I think I do,' Harriet said. 'I think it was just as she said – she honestly kidded herself it was for the best. And she was terribly afraid of losing everything. She had always been in Paula's shadow, from the time they were children. She just couldn't imagine Dad would still want her if he knew Paula was alive and she couldn't

433

bear the thought of losing him. In a way she was right, I suppose. If Dad had found out he would have had Paula brought home. She would probably have been confined to an asylum here but he would never have been free. Maybe she'd have lived for years and years, a sort of vegetable. And all the while he would have felt obliged to be faithful to her, because that is his way – and because he loved her so much.'

'All the same . . .' As yet Mark found it impossible to be so forgiving.

'I don't suppose it's made Sally very happy,' Harriet said. 'She's not a bad person, not hard at all really, just a bit weak perhaps. It must have played on her mind dreadfully. But the longer something like that goes on the more impossible it becomes to come clean and tell the truth. The original guilt is compounded by all the years of silence.'

'What a mess! What a horrible, unbelievable mess! Which brings me back to my original question – what are we going to do?'

'About Dad? Nothing – at the moment. There's nothing we can do. We'll just have to play it by ear. But what about Theresa?'

He shook his head. 'I don't know. In some ways, though it goes against the grain, I almost think Sally is right. Theresa is not looking to find out who she really is. She's too well adjusted to care. So why rock the boat?'

'But you said . . .'

'I know. If it weren't for the fact that I'm in love with her it might be for the best to leave her in blissful ignorance. But I am in love with her, and as I said to Sally, I am not prepared to live a lie. Besides which . . .' He got up, taking a cigarette from a box on a side table and lighting it. 'Besides which she could do with some help financially – and that much I reckon we owe her. She's a talented designer, Skeet – a talent she obviously inherited from Dad – and she's struggling. She needs backing desperately. A little of what is no more than her birthright would mean an end to her financial worries and she could concentrate on what she's good at. Dad had backing, first Greg Martin – God help us all – and then Kurt Eklund. If he hadn't he would never have got where he is today. Theresa deserves something similar and she hasn't a clue how to go about getting it.'

'Perhaps Sally . . .?' Harried suggested.

'I'm sure she would,' Mark said with a trace of bitterness. 'I expect she would quite happily come up with the readies as conscience money if for no other reason – if we were prepared to keep quiet about what we know. But I can't imagine Theresa taking money from an unknown benefactor unless she knew the reason – and perhaps not even if she *did* know. She's not that sort of girl. She's proud. She would want to know she was being backed for her talent, not for any other reason.'

'I can understand that,' Harriet said. 'I know how important it was to me to make my own way on the basis of my talent for photography . . .' She broke off. 'Oh shit!'

'What's wrong?'

'I'm supposed to be doing another assignment for Nick. I wonder he hasn't been on to me about it before now – except that he probably hasn't a clue where to find me! With all that's been going on I forgot all about it.'

'What sort of assignment?' Mark asked, quite glad to give himself a rest from their seemingly insoluble problems.

'Photo stories. I haven't had a chance to do anything special, but I did shoot off a lot of unusual stuff in Australia – aborigines, wild types in a Darwin bar, that sort of thing, that he might be able to use. In fact,' she said reflectively, 'if I'd had time to sift it and put it together properly it might be quite good. It's certainly the "other Australia" – quite different from what's pictured in the glossy travel brochures. It was the sort of place I'd like to go back to some time, though I don't suppose I ever will.'

'Why not?'

She smiled sadly, remembering the aura of magic she had experienced in the wild Northern Territory. Even now, knowing how Tom had used her, the memory of those days they had shared was imbued with a rosy glow, a happiness she had never experienced before. Not even the sense of betrayal could take that away. But if she were to go back ... no, without Tom it could never be the same.

'I'd better mail the stuff to Nick,' she said. 'Help me to remember to do it tomorrow, will you?'

Mark ground out his cigarette.

'I'll go one better than that. I'll take it with me.'

'You're going to London?'

He nodded.

'Yes. Heaven alone knows what I'm going to say to her. But I think I owe it to myself – and to her – to see Theresa.'

After being up until the small hours both Harriet and Mark slept late. From her room at the top of the triplex it was impossible to hear the doorbell but afterwards Harriet wondered if some sixth sense had disturbed her when it rang, for she was already awake, going over and over the events of the previous day in her mind, when Jane tapped on the door.

'Miss Varna – are you awake? You have a visitor.'

'A visitor? At this hour?'

'It is ten o'clock. Miss Varna.'

'It's not! I don't believe it!' Harriet shot up in bed. Her head was thumping dully and she felt unbelievably wooden. 'Ten o'clock! Good grief.'

'It is I'm afraid. I wouldn't have disturbed you, but he said it was important ...'

'He?' Harried queried, pushing back the duvet.

'A Mr O'Neill. He says he's an insurance investigator.'

Tom – here. Her heart pumped madly and the blood pounded painfully at her already aching temples. What did he want? For a delicious heady moment she imagined he had come to sweep her off her feet. Just supposing he should say: 'Harriet, I'm here because I am in love with you – I am not going to let any stupid misunderstanding come between us.' How would she react? Without even thinking about it her racing pulses gave her the answer. Oh Tom, Tom, is that why you are here – because you couldn't stay away ...?

436

She pulled on her jeans with hands that trembled, and jerked a comb through her hair, wishing she had the time to improve on her appearance. She didn't think Tom had ever seen her at her best – and he wasn't about to this morning. She sprayed her face with Evian water, patted it dry with a tissue, and applied just a touch of mascara. Her eyes still looked heavy but the mascara had the effect of opening them a little more, and because to apply blusher to her bare, still moist, face would probably have looked ridiculous she pinched her cheeks, like some latter-day Scarlett O'Hara, to bring them a little colour. Then she went downstairs.

Jane had shown him into the room Sally referred to as 'the den'. Probably the smallest room in the triplex, it was cluttered with soft leather furniture, a television and a full-size pool table. Tom was standing with his back to the door, reading the tides of some of the books on the shelves that lined the walls. He looked even taller than she remembered him, as if he had been shoe-horned into the cluttered room. Her heart came into her mouth and she hesitated in the doorway, made suddenly shy by her fantasies of a few moments ago.

Tom!' she said, and it did not come out at all as she intended it, but clipped somehow and slightly strained.

He turned. 'Harriet.' No rush towards her, no eager sweeping her off her feet.

'Why are you here?' That didn't sound the way she meant it to either, but she was so screwed up with tension she seemed to have no control over her voice.

She fancied she saw his mouth tighten a shade.

'I have some news for you.'

'Oh . . . yes?' It was all wrong. She was going to be disappointed. Stupid naive idiot for dunking it might be any different. 'What is that?'

'Greg Martin is dead.'

The words fell like stones in a pond, flat and heavy in the overheated atmosphere of the small room. She stared at him, all dreams forgotten.

'What?' she said. And then: 'When?'

'Yesterday. Last night, Australian time. I thought you would like to know.'

'Yes. But . . .' Her mind was racing in circles. 'But how?'

'Maria Vincenti shot him, quite deliberately according to the police chief in Sydney. He had gone back to the house for some documents and she found him in his room upstairs late at night. She could have claimed she thought he was an intruder or even that she shot him in self-defence. But she didn't. She made a statement saying she did it in cold blood because he deserved it.'

'And so he did!' Harriet said vehemently. 'I think I could have done it myself.' She was silent for a moment, then added thoughtfully: 'But now we'll never know exactly what happened to my mother.'

'We know more than we did,' Tom said. 'Apparently Greg told Maria he tricked Paula into a dinghy and then sailed away and left her. His intention was that she should be drowned – and when no more was heard of her he presumed that was what had happened. But I don't believe that was the end of the story, do you Harriet?'

Her heart had begun to pound again but this time for a quite different reason.

'What do you mean?'

'Look, Harriet, the last thing I want to do is upset you. You must believe that. But I have a job to do.'

'Oh yes, no doubt about that!' Would it ever stop hurting, knowing that he had used her?

'. . . and I have to say the Aeolie Islands keep figuring in my investigations. Sally went there just after the explosion, didn't she? And you have just been there – at least you've been to Italy and I wouldn't mind betting the Aeolies were where you were headed. Why, Harriet? You might as well tell me so that we can get this whole thing sorted out and put behind us.'

She had begun to shake. That was it then. He was on to it, just as she should have known he would be. The whole thing was going to come out and God alone knew what it would do to her father.

'Tom – can't you leave it . . . please?' she begged.

'You know I can't.'

'Please! For me? We had something, didn't we? I thought we did, anyway.'

'We did.'

'Then I beg you, Tom, close your files. My mother is dead. I swear to you – she is dead. Only don't probe any more. Just – don't probe any more!'

His eyes were narrowed. Behind his almost expressionless face Tom the investigator was tussling with Tom the man. But Harriet was not to know that.

'Look – I'm sorry, but I *have* to get at the truth. I have a job to do,' he said and she saw only that all the strength she had longed to cling to had turned against her.

'You bastard,' she whispered. 'Well, I'm not telling you anything. You'll have to find it out for yourself, as I did. And I only hope you can live with yourself, hurting people, deceiving them, turning their lives upside down . . .'

'Now hang on a minute!' he said sternly. 'I don't mean to do any of those things.'

'Well tough – you do!'

The only people I hurt are the ones who deserve it – the ones who try to cheat the insurance companies – no, dammit, not the companies but everyone who wants to take out a policy. They're the ones who pay in the end if their premiums are raised to cover the frauds.'

'Perhaps. But innocent people do get hurt all the same. Don't you care about them?'

'Harriet – you must believe I wasn't using you. However it looked . . .'

'I'm not talking about me. I'm talking about my father and all the others like him. He's a good man. He's never done a thing to hurt anyone else in his whole life. And he's certainly never tried to steal money that didn't belong to him.'

'Then he has nothing to worry about.'

'Oh!' she exploded. 'It's all black and white to you, isn't it, no shades of grey at all. You've no imagination, that's your trouble. You just can't see beyond your objective. That's all that matters to you. Facts, facts, facts, find the damned truth and never mind who gets hurt in the process.'

'Now listen . . .'

'Skeet? Is everything ah right?' It was Mark, alerted by the sound of raised voices.

'No, it's not all right. Mark, will you please talk to this man for me? Tell him . . .'

At that moment the telephone began to shrill and they all stopped, turning towards the sound as if each of them individually had had a premonition about the importance of the call. After a few moments the maid appeared in the doorway, her eyes flicking nervously from Harriet to Mark and back again, her distressed expression filling them with dread.

'It's the hospital. I think perhaps it might be best if *you* took the call, Mr Bristow . . .'

'Yes, of course.' Mark moved towards the door but Harriet was quicker. Her face was ashen. She already knew without being told that it was bad news – perhaps the worst.

'It's all right, Mark, I'll take it.'

The two men waited in awkward silence. A few minutes later Harriet was back. She looked shell-shocked, and she stood very upright in the doorway as if she was carefully holding onto erself, consciously controlling every muscle.

'It's Dad,' she said in a small tight voice. 'The hospital called to give us the news. He died ten minutes ago.'

CHAPTER THIRTY-FOUR

Theresa Arnold knelt on the floor in her workroom pouring boiling water from her temperamental old electric kettle onto a spoonful of instant coffee in a mug. The mug was bright blue and bore the legend 'You're the Tops' above a cartoon of a pleased-looking ginger cat with one ear and a striped bow around its neck. Theresa had bought it – from a market stall – because it amused her and the cat's smug grin had the power to cheer her up when she was feeling low. Today however she scarcely glanced at it, merely clasped it tightly between hands that felt colder than ever although the weather had taken a turn for the better.

Tonight she was due to pay her visit to Fergal Hillyard's apartment – and she was dreading it.

Oh God, I'm little better than a prostitute! Theresa thought wretchedly, for she had no illusions about the strings that were to be attached to any money he put up to back her. He had made it clear enough and for that at least she was grateful to him. At least he hadn't pretended to be interested only as an entrepreneur and then swung the conditions on her later. No, he had laid it on the line – be nice to me and I'll be nice to you – and sick though she felt every time she thought of it Theresa didn't see that she had any option if she wanted to save her business – and her mother's investment in it of everything she owned.

I can't allow her to lose her house, Theresa thought, sipping the coffee so hot that it scalded her throat. If there was any other way I'd tell him what he could do with his money, but there isn't.

In the last week since Fergal had made his qualified offer she had urged Linda to redouble her efforts to find new markets but

Linda, who thought she had already done rather well in arranging the meeting with Fergal, was less cooperative than usual and Theresa was ashamed to tell her of the boutique owner's proposition and the fact that she had, for even a moment, considered doing as he asked. But in any case, no matter how hard Linda worked for her, Theresa didn't expect she would have had much luck. Everywhere, it seemed, stores and boutiques were pulling their horns in and 'sales', as in discounted merchandise, not profits, were the order of the day – not just end-of-season sales but mid-season too, anything to move the garments off the racks. With falling profits no one was in to taking chances of any kind – and certainly not on some unknown designer. And besides Theresa was fast losing confidence in Linda and herself as a team. Once, she thought, she had been prepared to work all the hours that God sent, in whatever conditions she had to, to make a success of the business. Now all her determination seemed to have gone, sapped away by one blow after another, eroded by worries about how the bills were to be paid and repayments on the loan met, where the next lot of materials were coming from and what the hell would her mother do if she lost everything.

All week Theresa had found work almost impossible. She tore up page after page of sketches until her wastepaper basket was overflowing. And eventually, unable to think about anything else but the impossibility of the situation, she had succumbed and telephoned the number Fergal had given her. Just hearing his voice made her stomach quake, imagining that smooth smile and remembering the stale smell of his breath had made her want to vomit. But she had held on to herself tightly and tried not to give him any indication of the revulsion she was feeling. It was done now. She had arranged to go to his flat this evening. But the fact that the decision was made did not make her feel any better, any more than it helped to tell herself she was not the first, and would certainly not be the last, who had sold herself for reasons other than love or even desire.

A door banging at street level made her glance up and she heard footsteps on the stairs. Linda – with some good news just in time to save her? But the steps were heavy and too slow – Linda, bursting with energy, always ran up the stairs. Weasel, then, or one of the others. In her present state Theresa hoped not. She did not feel like being sociable.

She watched, semi-mesmerised, expecting to see the door handle turn. Instead there was a tap. Theresa was surprised. None of her friends ever bothered to knock.

'Come in,' she called.

The door opened and Theresa stared, unable to believe her own eyes.

'Hi,' he said.

And with a small gasp that was part pleasure, part astonishment, she whispered: 'Mark!' He came into the workroom, tall, fair and handsome in sneakers and jeans and a black leather jacket. Her pulses were racing; she felt slightly sick. So often she had day-dreamed about him walking in exactly like this, unannounced, but she hadn't really believed he ever would. Men didn't. They came and went – mostly went, especially if you cared deeply for them. Unexpected reunions only happened in romantic novels . . . didn't they?

'Well!' she said, setting down her mug and wondering if he would be able to see she was trembling. This is a surprise!'

'I know. I should have let you know I was coming, I suppose, but I was afraid you might say you didn't want to see me.'

'Now why should I do that?'

'Well, it has been rather a long time . . . How have you been, Theresa?' He was the only one, apart from her mother, who called her Theresa rather than Terri. She had always rather liked it, now it made her heart miss a beat.

'Surviving – just. And you?'

'Yes.' Now he was here he scarcely knew what to say. 'I wondered if I might buy you lunch – or have you already eaten?' She laughed ruefully.

'I don't eat at midday. I can't afford to. I've just had a coffee.'

'Then how about it?'

'Now wait a minute,' she said. Her heart might be beating a

little too fast, there might be a bubble of excitement sending shivers and quivers to every nerve ending, but she was not about to be made a fool of again. 'You walked out on me, Mark, without a word of explanation and no goodbye. What makes you think I'd have lunch with you now just because you see fit to breeze up those stairs and ask me?'

His face fell.

'I know it must have seemed to you I behaved very badly,' he said apologetically, 'but I did have a very good reason.'

'Such as?'

He hesitated. This would have been difficult enough if he had been in full control of his emotions. As it was, looking at her and wanting to kiss her, it was impossible.

'Theresa, if I hurt you I'm truly sorry. You must believe it was the last thing I wanted to do. In fact I left when I did to try to avoid you being hurt more.'

'Don't they all say that?' she enquired archly. 'I did it for your own good? I loved you, Mark, and you buzzed off – just like that.' She tried to snap her fingers together, but cold as they always were, and trembling as they were now, she couldn't quite manage it.

He looked at her warily. 'Loved,' she had said – past tense. Did it mean she no longer loved him?

'Is there someone else?' he asked.

'No,' she said, 'but if there was it would be none of your business.' He winced. There was going to be no easy way to do this. 'Theresa, please have lunch with me. I have to talk to you.' Her mouth set in a stubborn line.

'If you want to talk to me, talk here. Then when I've heard what you have to say I'll decide if I want to have lunch with you.' A corner of his mouth lifted in a shadow of his old carefree grin.

'It doesn't seem I have much choice.'

'You don't, Buster, you don't.'

'The trouble is I don't know where the hell to start.'

'At the beginning?'

'I'm not certain where that is. And I'm sure as hell I don't know the end. I only know what I hope it will be.'

His eyes met and held hers for a moment before she tore them away.

'Go on then.'

'Are you sure we won't be interrupted?'

'No, I can't even promise that. But for the moment, Mark, you have my undivided attention.'

'So,' he said when he had finished. 'Now you know.'

She was sitting, head bent, turning a pencil over and over between those mittened fingers. She had remained silent while he talked, stunned into silence by the revelations. Now she looked up at him and her eyes were moist.

'My God,' she said. 'Are you sure about all this?'

'As sure as I can be. Hugo Varna was your father.'

'Was?'

'He died last week. Didn't you read about it in the papers?'

She shook her head. She had been too busy to so much as glance at a paper or catch a news bulletin all week.

'He died of a heart attack, possibly brought on by all this, though no one can say that for sure. He certainly worked very hard, pushing himself to the limits.' He paused. 'I'd have liked to have been able to come over and tell you all this in time for you to come to the funeral – if you wanted to, that is. But my mother has been in a terrible state. I didn't feel I could leave her.'

'I can imagine.'

'She blames herself, of course. And so did I at first but I am beginning to come to terms with it and understand why she did . . . what she did.'

Theresa nodded.

'Poor Sally. She must have been through hell.'

'Yes.' Love for Theresa warmed him; after all this she could still find it in her to feel compassion for Sally.

'I wish you could have been there,' he said. 'You were, after all, his daughter.'

She stared down at her hands again.

'Yes. It explains so much. Where my talent comes from for one

445

thing. It just goes to show – heredity *is* important. I never saw him, never even knew, and yet. . . I never wanted to do anything but design fashion. But my mother . . . oh God', she shivered. 'My poor mother! I only hope I haven't inherited *her* traits.'

'You are not to worry about that,' Mark said swiftly. 'I'm sure it was a combination of circumstances that sent her on the path to . . . what she became. And Harriet is fine, you know. She's your sister, full blood, and you couldn't wish to meet anyone saner than Harriet.'

'Harriet Varna,' she said wonderingly. 'I've heard of her, you know. She's a photographer, isn't she?'

'Yes. A very good one. And she can't wait to meet you.'

'Oh . . .' Theresa bit her lip, afraid suddenly. 'I'm not sure I'm ready for any of this, Mark.'

'I hope you are,' he said, 'because I have a suggestion to make, Theresa. You are a very talented designer and with Hugo dead that is exactly what the House of Varna needs – new blood. Especially his blood. Come to the States. Work for Varna.'

'What?' Her eyes widened. 'Mark – I couldn't! I'm just a novice. Besides, they wouldn't want me.'

'They do want you.'

'I couldn't!' she repeated, appalled.

'Theresa, I've seen your work and I know – it's Hugo all over again. A new Hugo, of course, young and fresh, but with that indefinable something that makes clothes work. Oh, it would have to be taken steadily, of course. You'd be part of a team to begin with and Laddie would help you make the adjustment. Laddie is Hugo's assistant – he's been with him for years and years.'

'So why can't he take over?'

'Laddie is not an original designer and never will be. He lacks the spark of new ideas. But technically he is as sound as a bell. He would work with you, guide you, nurse you along.'

'How do you know he would be prepared to do that?'

'We have talked to him about it. Oh, it's quite all right. Laddie is totally loyal. He won't breathe a word about who you really are unless or until we authorise such a move.'

She laughed, a shrill, tight sound.

'It sounds as though you have everything worked out.'

'We have talked it through, yes. But of course in the final analysis it is down to you, Theresa. Maybe you want your own label. Of course, if you come to Varna you'd have recognition in time, but if you are already building up your name here and doing well, we shall understand. I know Hugo would – and he would approve.'

For a long moment Theresa was silent, twisting the pencil back and forth between her fingers. Then she raised her eyes to his.

'The truth is I'm not doing very well. It's all gone wrong. I don't even have confidence in myself any more. God knows, I'd be crazy to turn down an opportunity like this. But I'm honestly not sure I could do it. Six months ago – less than that – I was full of confidence. But now ... I'm scared I'm just a big fraud and I'll mess everything up.'

'Theresa!' He reached for her hand, touching her for the first time since he had walked through the door. 'I don't like to hear you talk like that. But it won't last – it's a temporary loss of faith in yourself, that's all and it happens to everyone from time to time. You could do it, I know you could. You owe it to yourself to take your courage in both hands and give it a try.'

She sat silent for a moment. This was more than a wonderful opportunity – it was the answer to a prayer. No more worries about survival in the fashion jungle, no more fears that her mother would lose her home, no more Fergal Hillyard. It was the chance of a lifetime – if only she dared to take it.

'Well?' Mark pressed her. 'What do you say?'

She smiled, a little wanly. 'It looks as if you've talked me into it,' she said quietly. 'I don't suppose I have anything to lose.'

'Nothing to lose – and everything to gain.'

'And us?' she said. It was spoken as a whisper, the most important question of all. 'What about us?'

'We can start all over again, if you are prepared to do that.

'Oh Mark,' she said. 'You know I am.'

He pulled her into his arms. It was quite a long time before he spoke again.

'I suppose it's a little late now for lunch,' he said. 'So how about an early supper? With champagne? I think, my love, that we have something to celebrate.'

She raised her face from the leather of his jacket. It was all too much, she had scarcely taken it in yet, but she knew she was happier already than she had ever been before.

'Oh yes, Mark,' she said. 'I do believe we have!'

CHAPTER THIRTY-FIVE

Sally Varna replaced the telephone and turned to Harriet.

'Well,' she said. 'So Paula's daughter is coming to work in New York.'

Her voice was taut, brittle, her face a beautiful mask. In the past Harriet had sometimes wondered what lay behind it when Sally wore that particular expression – now she knew. A lifetime of guilt, perhaps of regrets. It was a frightening thought.

'She accepted the offer then,' Harriet said. 'I'm glad.'

'Yes.' If Sally was nervous of meeting the girl she had had adopted as a baby she did not say so, but then the time for confidences had come and gone. Her vulnerability was hidden once more, as was her grief, behind that cool manner that she had cultivated over the years. But in a way Harriet could understand that. Everyone needs a facade, she thought. Perhaps Sally needs it more than most.

It had been a nightmarish week. Harriet could still scarcely believe her father was dead. In spite of the fact that she had been there to see his coffin lowered into the ground and had tossed a single red rose down to lie like an exotic butterfly on the shining brass plate that bore his name, it still seemed unreal somehow. When the end had come she had been curiously unprepared and the suddenness of it had numbed her senses so that she had to repeat it over and over to herself before she could even begin to take it in. Dead, that powerful personality, dead, all that talent and that capacity for loving. Her heart ached with sorrow, yet at the same time she felt almost glad that he had been spared the trauma of learning the truth. There would have been no way they could keep it from him; now they would not need to.

'When is Theresa coming?' she asked.

'Mark is arranging to bring her over next week.' Sally hesitated, twisting the rings on her fingers. 'I think he is in love with her, Harriet.'

'Yes,' Harriet said. 'I think he is.'

'I'm not sure it's right,' Sally said vaguely. 'After all she is his cousin . . .'

'But not his sister. Poor Mark, what he must have gone through!' For an instant she saw the flash of pain on Sally's face, then it was gone again.

'I suppose the only thing that matters is that he should be happy. That is all I have ever wanted for any of you.'

Harriet reached out and squeezed her arm.

'I know, Sally – and so does Mark. I don't agree with what you did but I think I understand, and so will he, when he's had a little more time. It takes men longer, you know, to come to terms with things.'

'Yes.' Sally pulled herself upright, standing there slim and beautiful in her designer black. 'And what about you? What will you do now? Go back to London?'

'I suppose so. It's time I got back to work.'

'There's no need for that, you know. Not that there ever has been. But now you have money in your own right. Your father's will has left you a rich young woman.'

'*I* need to – I need it for me,' Harriet said fiercely.

What would she have done without work this last week? Though she had been unable to do any actual photography she had been able to make plans for future features and the planning had kept her going. She had airmailed her films to Nick once she realised there would be a delay in Mark's return to London and Nick had phoned her immediately he received them, full of enthusiasm.

'Harriet, they are wonderful! Without a doubt you've found your niche. I know this is a bad time for you, love, and I don't want to put you under any pressure but the sooner you can get a follow-up story to me the better. Once we've established you it won't matter so much. You can afford to take a few breaks and people will be looking for you rather than forgetting you.'

'I know, I know – I've pretty well blown my chances.'

'No, as it happens you haven't. This Australian stuff is sensational. I'm using it immediately. But I shall need something else – soon. Just keep your camera by you and snap whatever takes your fancy. You have such a good eye for those unusual angles.'

'I'll do what I can. This week it will be out of the question, of course. You and I both know my camera is a therapy for me – it helps to keep me sane – but other people wouldn't see it like that. They'd say I was being callous and unfeeling, I dare say – a trait which seems to run in my mother's side of the family, along with madness, of course.'

'Harriet!' he admonished. 'Oh love, this has hit you hard, hasn't it? You sound very low.'

'I'll survive.'

'Come back to London soon. Let me spoil you a bit. After all you've been through in the last couple of weeks you need some spoiling.'

'You're very sweet, Nick.' She couldn't tell him how hollow the suggestion made her feel, any more than she could tell him that grief for her father and the stress of investigations into the past were only a part of it, and there was yet another reason for her depression, something else she wanted to obliterate with work – but certainly not by a replacement shoulder to cry on.

Why couldn't I have fallen for Nick? she had asked herself, replacing the receiver. Why instead did I have to lose my heart – and my senses! – to a man like Tom O'Neill?

She had not seen him since the day of her father's death and she did not want to see him. Irrationally her first reaction had been to blame him for what had happened to Hugo, as if Tom personally had been the one to open the can of worms. It wasn't true, of course. He had only appeared on the scene doing his job after Maria had blown the whistle on Greg Martin. But that didn't alter the way she felt, so that her resentment at the way he had used her rolled along like a sticky ball collecting more and more garbage as it went.

Yet ridiculously none of this had the slightest effect on the way she felt about him. This was what obsession was, she presumed, an emotional reaction that reason could not quell. Her body remembered his touch and shrank from the prospect of intimacy with anyone but him. Sharp sweet sadness ached in her constantly and when she stopped to identify its cause the answer was always the same. Tom.

'Is there anything I can do?' he had asked that day when she had returned from taking the telephone call telling of her father's death. And somehow the pain and the hurt and the resentment had all come bubbling up and she had flared: 'Don't you think you've done enough?'

He had left then – at least he had had the decency to respect their need to be alone – but he had written a note of condolence which had arrived next day. The hypocrisy of it! Harriet had stormed – and thrown the letter in the wastepaper basket.

'Don't you think you are being a bit hard on the fellow?' Mark had asked, and she had shaken her head vehemently.

'How would you feel if you'd been used the way he used me?'

'You don't know he used you, Skeet.'

'Don't tell me what I do and don't know. He was only here this morning to ask more questions about my movements.'

'He's probably only doing his job.'

'Exactly! But what a lousy stinking way to do it . . .' She broke off, remembering their love-making and knowing that no matter how used she felt nothing on earth would make her explain to Mark. Quite apart from the hurt she was idiotic enough to feel it was so downright *humiliating*!

'Well, I dare say you have your reasons,' Mark had said to her. 'But he didn't seem that bad a bloke to me.'

He wouldn't, Harriet thought wryly. Nothing and nobody appears that bad when you are viewing the world through rose-coloured glasses. Lucky, lucky Mark. For him things had turned out well. She was glad for him, of course. No one deserved to be happy more than Mark did. But she wished just a little of his good fortune could rub off on her all the same.

Well, if wishes were horses, beggars would ride.

The crux of the matter is, thought Harriet, that I am not in the least attracted to men who make themselves available, and the ones I find exciting are incapable of any kind of real commitment. A vicious circle – an insoluble problem. So, face it. Take yourself in hand and forget Tom O'Neill or you will end up like your mother.

It was a sobering thought.

In his hotel room across town Tom O'Neill was packing his suitcase.

For him the case was over. He had set out to discover the truth about what had happened to Greg Martin and Paula Varna and now he knew. Greg Martin was dead – albeit twenty years late – and Paula Varna . . .

Mark Bristow had telephoned him the day after Hugo had died.

'I don't want Harriet worried any more than she has to be. She is very upset about her father's death – they were very close. So to save her as far as possible I'd appreciate it if you would talk to me. I think I can answer any questions you may want to ask.'

'That's very decent of you,' Tom had said, feeling distinctly hollow.

Of course he wanted the case tied up, but once it was he would have no further legitimate excuse to see Harriet.

Mark had been extremely helpful. He had filled Tom in on the details of Paula's fate and Harriet's recent Italian trip and Tom had begun to understand just why Harriet had been so touchy about it. What a hell of a story to uncover! He wished he could do something to comfort her but he felt sure she would reject any overture. She had not forgiven him for what had happened in Australia and in his heart he could hardly blame her. Hadn't he started out with the intention of using close contact with her to help him discover the truth? That made him technically guilty – even if the game had changed along the way. No, for the moment Tom did not think there was anything he could do. Harriet had made herself only too clear. She did not want him around.

He had resigned himself to it. He had stayed on for the funeral and watched from a discreet distance as the mourners walked from their limousines to the graveside in the bitter wind and the occasional flurry of rain. There was enough money there around the graveside to pay off the entire national debt, he thought wryly, and some of the most beautiful and fashionable women in New York to boot – but none of them could hold a candle to Harriet.

If Paula had been a mesmeric figure, then Harriet was without doubt her daughter, for amongst all those wealthy well-dressed women she shone out like a candle on a dark night, incandescent even in grief, her face pale and creamy, half-hidden behind a short black veil, her hair bright against the severely sculpted collar of her suit. As he watched her toss a single rose down on the coffin he felt he was intruding on her grief and he turned away, sick at heart.

He spent a couple of days liaising with the FBI to tie up the last loose ends in the Greg Martin affair and filed his report. He didn't know whether British and Cosmopolitan would ever recover the money they had been cheated out of and guessed it would be some time and probably a long legal wrangle before the financial tangles were satisfactorily sorted out, but that was not his problem. His job was done. Now there was no longer anything to keep him in the States. It was time to head for home – and the next job.

Tom wished he could feel enthusiasm for it, but he could not. Dammit, Harriet was still under his skin as no other woman had ever been. If circumstances had been different perhaps it could have been goodbye to his footloose bachelor existence, hello to a whole new way of life. He had never given a single serious thought to settling down – the very suggestion of it had always turned him cold – but now, coupled with a vision of Harriet, it was a very different matter, for he knew if he had her now he would be determined never to let her go again.

Pure hypothesis, he thought grimly, for the whole thing had been well and truly blown. Of course there was always the chance that he could look her up in London when enough time had elapsed for her to realise he couldn't possibly still be delving into her family history, but it would probably be too late. Prejudices and resentment would be too deeply entrenched – and there was always that damned Nick Holmes. Back in London she'd probably team up with him again. At the thought of it Tom felt his stomach physically turn. He remembered the night he had spent keeping watch outside her hat and the parked car that had signified that Nick Holmes was staying with her. At the time it had meant nothing to him, now, in retrospect, it clawed at his guts and in the fury of fevered emotion, which was quite new to him, he made up his mind.

Bloody hell, he couldn't give her up without a fight! Fool that he was, he had to try again. She would probably send him packing but that was a chance he had to take.

He lifted the telephone receiver and hesitated, wondering what he was going to say to her. Where was the incisive private eye now? For one of the few times in his life, Tom O'Neill was scared to death.

One more try. Just one. If she refused to speak to you, you will just have to accept it. But don't give up without a fight. Not now – when the stakes are so high.

He called the number and the maid answered.

'I'd like to speak to Harriet Varna. It's Tom O'Neill.'

There – done – probably blown before he'd even begun. He waited, sweating. Then he heard her voice cool but revealing just a hint, just an echo, of his own turmoil.

'Hello?'

'Harriet, I'm just about to leave for London. But I can't go without seeing you again. I know we've had one hell of a bad start but I'd like the chance to explain. Shit – I'm not very good at this sort of thing . . .'

There was just the smallest hesitation though it seemed to him like a very long time. Then: 'When shall I see you?' she asked.

He thought furiously, cursing himself for not having it all worked out.

'Can I buy you lunch?'

'Yes, all right. I'm going down to my father's showroom to take some pictures. I'll meet you underneath the statue of the Garment Worker at twelve forty-five.'

'I'll be there.'

'Only Tom,' she said. 'No more questions – right?'

'Not a single one.'

Liar, he thought, even as he said it. There is one very big question you intend to ask her. But not today – not today.

As he replaced the receiver Tom O'Neill, confirmed agnostic, sent up a heartfelt prayer of thanks.

He'd wanted one more chance and he had it. So far so good. But tread carefully. Tread very carefully. Blow this and you'll never get another.'

She saw him the moment she emerged from the doorway, standing there at the foot of the plinth, the collar of his coat turned up against the biting wind, and her heart missed a beat.

Foolish, foolish Harriet! Ready to put yourself on the line to be hurt again . . . for what? But just looking at him, bulky in his dark overcoat, his face as craggy as if it had been carved out of the same stone as the statue, she knew the reason.

'Hi,' she said.

He turned and in spite of everything it was still there, that crazy powerful chemistry they had experienced in the outback. This might be New York, with bustling crowds and hooting taxis, the skies heavy lowering grey, the wind making them shiver, but it made no difference.

'I'm sorry if I hurt you,' he said. 'I had a job to do.'

Not the most exciting words, but they scarcely mattered.

'I expect I was a bit touchy,' she said.

'But that's all over now. If I ask you to meet me you'll know it's because I want to see *you*, not probe into your past. Harriet, I know this sounds exceptionally corny, but could we begin all over again?'

'No,' she said.

His eyes narrowed. 'No? But I thought . . .'

Her mouth curved. 'I don't want to begin again because there are some things I'd hate to erase. Really, Tom, I'd rather say "let's continue where we left off".'

He nodded, smiling. 'I'll settle for that.'

'So, where are we going for lunch?'

'Do you know, I haven't given it a thought I was so sure you wouldn't turn up.'

'Why should you have thought that?'

'Because,' he said truthfully, 'it mattered so damned much to me that you should. So, where do you suggest for lunch? You are the one who knows New York.'

'I suggest somewhere very quiet where we can have that talk.'

'I second that.'

In the end it had been so very easy, so very right. If none of this dreadful business had happened she would never have met Tom, she thought suddenly. It was an almost insupportable thought.

She smiled up at him and put her hand on his arm. In a city of eight million people there was an intimacy in the touch that tore down the last barriers.

'I know the very place,' she said. 'Shall we go?'

Together they walked along Fashion Avenue and the tall shadow of The Garment Worker seemed to follow them.

Lightning Source UK Ltd.
Milton Keynes UK
UKOW03n2243200514

231994UK00002B/3/P